WITH THE COLLABORATION OF THE ARCHAEOLOGICAL SUPERINTENDENCY OF POMPEII
AND THE SUPERINTENDENCY FOR ARCHAEOLOGICAL HERITAGE OF NAPLES AND CASERTA

POMPEII

THE HISTORY, LIFE AND ART OF THE BURIED CITY

EDITED BY
Marisa Ranieri Panetta

PROJECT EDITORS
Valeria Manferto De Fabianis
Laura Accomazzo

PHOTOGRAPHS
Araldo De Luca

COLLABORATING EDITORS
Novella Monti

GRAPHIC DESIGN
Patrizia Balocco Lovisetti
Paola Piacco

vmb
Published in the USA by
VMB Publishers®
An imprint of White Star, Italy

© 2004 White Star S.r.l.
Via Candido Sassone, 22/24
13100 Vercelli, Italy
www.whitestar.it

ISBN 88-540-0106-6

REPRINTS:
1 2 3 4 5 6   08 07 06 05 04

Printed in China
Color separation by Fotomec, Turin

TRANSLATION
Catherine Bolton

P R E F A C E

STEFANO DE CARO
*Regional Director for the Cultural
Heritage and Activities of Campania*

PIETRO GIOVANNI GUZZO
*Archaeological Superintendent
of Pompeii*

VALERIA SAMPAOLO
*Archaeological Superintendent
of Naples and Caserta*

The book project for *POMPEII: The History, Life and Art of the Buried City*, coordinated by Marisa Ranieri Panetta on behalf of White Star Publishers, was conducted by the Archaeological Superintendencies of Pompeii and Naples, in concert with the Regional Directorate of Culture of Campania.

What inspired these institutions to participate in the project was certainly not the need to offer the market yet another overview of the city's extant monuments and the artifacts, which are the pride of the National Archaeological Museum of Naples, but the comprehensive scope of the contents of this publication. Indeed, the numerous activities that have been conducted by the Superintendencies to study and protect this heritage converge with the development and refinement of the research done by the faculty of the Frederick II University of Naples to create a high-quality publishing project. As a result, the book is composed of texts based on different areas of knowledge and activities – reflecting the authors' varied professional experiences – to offer the reader specific and original views about the complex reality of Pompeii. As a result, the problems involved in the study of antiquity, which necessarily has lacunae due to the destruction wrought by time and man alike, are laid so that, like the authors, readers can apply their own insights and opinions.

Ultimately, only the success or failure of this book, which also features a rich array of photographs taken specifically for this publication, can tell us if we have achieved this objective. The extensive collection of images will indubitably enhance our readers' awareness regardless of whether they are preparing to visit Pompeii and Oplontis or simply want to refresh their memory, they can verify what the authors have written and compare the text against the impressions and considerations they have formed independently.

Over the past decade, the ancient city of Pompeii has no longer been studied and researched by Italian archaeologists alone, but also by scholars from every corner of the planet. Moreover, the influx of visitors to the city has essentially remained the same, despite current international upheaval. Regardless of these results, however, we hope that critical appreciation of this milestone in human history will not remain the closed province of the first group – the specialists – and that it will also be shared latter group, i.e. the visitors.

If the city's hasty one-day visitors would just pause to look beyond the picturesque or dramatic aspects of the excavations at Pompeii and consider its full historic significance, they would become the staunchest defenders – also by dint of sheer numbers – of antiquity and ancient monuments.

It is to these potential allies in our work – our readers – that we dedicate this book.

1
*The mosaic portrays doves drinking from a fountain
(Naples, Museo Archeologico Nazionale - MAN).*

2-3
*In this mosaic from the House of the Faun
a cat captures a bird (Naples, MAN).*

4
*This detail from a fresco in the Second Style is from
the* triclinium *of Poppaea's Villa at Oplontis.*

5
*The fresco shown in this picture is from
the House of Pinarius Cerialis.*

THE AUTHORS

MARISA RANIERI PANETTA

An archaeologist, she writes scientific news for the Italian weekly *L'Espresso* as well as specialized journals. The author of historical and archival studies, she has also been responsible for organizing conventions. Her news reports have won international awards, namely "Media Save Art" (Iccrom, Unesco, 1997), and the "Theodor Mommsen" Prize (2002). Her most recent publication is a historical essay, entitle *Nerone. Il principe rosso*,1999.

STEFANO DE CARO

An archaeologist with the Superintendencies of Molise, Naples, Caserta and Pompeii, he is also the Regional Superintendent for Campania. He has taught archaeological disciplines at several universities in the Campania region. His publications about Pompeii include works about city planning, the Temple of Apollo and the country residence of Villa Regina a Boscoreale.

PIETRO GIOVANNI GUZZO

Superintendent and Chairman of the Board of Administration of the Archaeological Superintendency of Pompeii, he has also been Archaeological Superintendent for the regions of Puglia and Emilia Romagna, and has taught at several universities. He has published reports on the excavations at Sibari, which he directed in the Seventies, and is also the author of numerous monographs on ancient Southern Italy.

VALERIA SAMPAOLO

She is currently the Archaeological Superintendent of the provinces of Naples and Caserta. She curated the new layout of the fresco collection at the Museum of Archaeology in Naples and has helped organize various exhibitions, including "Romana Pictura. La pittura romana dalle origini all'età bizantina", held in Rimini in 1998.

STEFANIA ADAMO MUSCETTOLA

She was Associate Professor of the Antiquities of Pompeii and Herculaneum at the Frederick II University of Naples. She has participated in conventions on the cults of ancient Campania and on the history of the excavations at Pompeii and Herculaneum. She also collaborated on the exhibit layout of the rooms on Pompeii and Herculaneum at the Museum of Archaeology in Naples. One of her most recent publications is *La Villa dei Papiri a Ercolano* (2000).

ANNAMARIA CIARALLO

She graduated with a degree in Biological Science, specializing in environmental studies with a thesis in botany. In 1988 she won a competition for the position of Biology Expert with the Ministry of Culture, after which she was assigned to the Archaeological Superintendency of Pompeii, where she currently heads the Applied Research Laboratory.

ANTONIO D'AMBROSIO

A graduate in Classical Literature, he specialized in Classical Archaeology at the University of Rome. He was Director Archaeologist of the Excavation Office of Oplontis, and since 1991 he has been Archaeological Director of the Excavation Office of Pompeii. He has conducted numerous excavations and has organized many archaeological exhibitions. He is the author of numerous scientific publications.

ERNESTO DE CAROLIS

Director of the Restoration Laboratories of Pompeii, he graduated with a degree in Classical Literature, specializing in Archaeology. He has conducted excavation campaigns in Herculaneum and Pompeii. He is the author of numerous publications, particularly on the lighting systems, jewelry and paintings of the area around Mount Vesuvius.

ELIO LO CASCIO

He is Professor of Roman History at the Frederick II University of Naples. His publications include *Il princeps e il suo impero* (2000), and he is also the editor of *Roma Imperiale. Una metropoli antica* (2000), *Mercati permanenti e mercati periodici nel mondo romano* (2000), *Production and Public Powers in Classical Antiquity* (2000) and *Credito e moneta nel mondo romano* (2003).

ELIODORO SAVINO

He holds the post of Researcher of Roman History at the "Ettore Lepore" Department of Historical Disciplines at the Frederick II University of Naples. The author of *Città di frontiera nell'impero romano* (1998) and *Campania tardoantica* (2004), he has also written articles about the population and economy of Pompeii during the age of Sulla, the history of Capri in the Roman era, and the demographic development of Campania in the Republican Age.

ALFREDINA STORCHI MARINO

She is Associate Professor of Roman History and Antiquities at the University of Naples. She has studied the historical problem of the formation of traditions, particularly that of Numa and its effect on Roman political and cultural life, and has researched aspects of social and economic history (slavery, debt laws, *indices nundinarii* and market circuits).

MARINA TALIERCIO MENSITIERI

She is Professor of Numismatics at the Frederick II University of Naples. Her scientific activity has followed two lines of research regarding the problems of several coinages of ancient Italy from the Archaic Period to the late Hellenistic Period, as well as the problems of monetary circulation. She coordinates the "Rinvenimenti monetali a Pompei" research program examining the currency discovered in Pompeii.

ANTONIO VARONE

He is Archaeological Director-Coordinator with the Italian Ministry of Culture, and he directs the scientific and cultural service of the Archaeological Superintendency of Pompeii. Since 1987, he has overseen excavation of the *insula* of the Chaste Lovers in Pompeii, as well as studies of the wall inscriptions in the area around Mount Vesuvius. One of his most recent publications is *Pompei. I misteri di una città sepolta* (2000).

ARALDO DE LUCA

One of the world's leading art photographers, he has published numerous works in books, catalogs and magazines. White Star has published his photographs in the following books: *Tutankhamun: The Eternal Splendors of the Boy Pharaoh* (2000), *Illustrated Guide to the Egyptian Museum in Cairo* (2001), *Egyptian Treasures: The Valley of the Kings* (2001), *Ramesses II* (2002), *The Treasures of the Pyramids* (2003).

6

This splendid painting portraying Terentius Neo and his wife is in the tablinum of the house named after its owner.

8-9

The garden painted in an oecus of the House of the Golden Bracelet portrays various species of plants and birds (Archaeological Superintendency of Pompeii).

C O N T E N T S

10-15

Scenes from the megalography in the triclinium of the Villa of the Mysteries.

INTRODUCTION

by Marisa Ranieri Panetta

N o natural catastrophe has remained so deeply impressed in our minds as the eruption of Mount Vesuvius in AD 79. Indeed, it is linked to the discovery of entire towns and their outskirts, places whose last moments of life were frozen in time by volcanic debris. As opposed to other archaeological sites, Pompeii, Herculaneum, Stabiae and Oplontis were not obliterated by decline or gradual abandonment, nor were they prey to many centuries of plunder. Buried beneath many feet of earth, as the years passed they were slowly forgotten, and until 1738 no one could even pinpoint their location. It was sheer happenstance that the theater of Herculaneum was found, and it was a Latin inscription that indicated the city of Pompeii to the first excavators. As the daily life of the 1st century AD slowly began to unfold in all its different aspects, new discoveries shaped the interest and "Neoclassic" taste that laid the foundations for the antiquarian culture and, later, for the field of archaeology as a science. Houses, gardens, artwork, utensils, household items, sacred and public buildings: all these things that could no longer be found in Rome, Naples and the other leading cities of the ancient empire were being uncovered in secondary towns, filling Europe with awe. Even today, the observation made by Johann Wolfgang von Goethe on March 13, 1787 in his *Italian Journey*, though a bit cynical, has an element of truth to it: "Of the many misfortunes that have occurred in this world, no others have given posterity such joy."

The uniqueness of these findings has made the individual sites famous around the world, first and foremost Pompeii. Given that Pompeii was easier to excavate (Herculaneum was buried by boiling mud that became as hard as concrete once it cooled), two-thirds of the entire city has been unearthed. The scope of this discovery also allowed the early directors of the excavations to undertake experiments – though not always successfully – in the organization, classification and study methods that were used. In the early 20 century, this led to the current subdivision in *insulae* (see the glossary for this and other technical terms), as well as early restoration and increasingly detailed knowledge. Every year, millions of visitors wander through the ancient streets of Pompeii, and they come here so they can personally experience the civilization the city expresses. Pompeii's supposedly "obscene" findings also contributed enormously to its fame. Initially segregated in a private collection away from the eyes of women, children, the clergy and – in the final analysis – people who were not educated enough, they are now exhibited in the National Archaeological Museum of Naples, although out of their original context. After the solemn ruins of Rome – the Colosseum, the Baths, the Pantheon, the Forums – Pompeii gave tourists a glimpse of an amusing, colorful and uninhibited ambience, and it thus came to be considered a "City of Venus" where the inhabitants' main pastime involved their sexual performance. Nothing could be farther from the truth: if other cities had come down to our own day and age in their entirety, we would have found frescoes and statues with similar subjects there as well. This kind of appeal, which is un-

This bronze ephebe from the House of Gavius Rufus reflects proud beauty
(Naples, MAN).

18

The half-naked figures from the House of the Chaste Lovers seem to flutter in midair.

19

A painted cupid from the House of the Vettii drives two fish as if they were horses.

deniable, leads us to the heart of one of the problems involved in visiting the city – a problem rarely sensed as such – that the authors of *Ancient Pompeii* would like to overcome. It involves the ability to separate our concepts of politics, marriage and leisure – and thus the various aspects of life associated with them – from the ones of the past, or rather of a specific culture of the past. In terms of artistic taste, ideal aspirations and day-to-day difficulties, all eras share common ground, and yet in other aspects that we take for granted, the way of experiencing things is completely different. For example, if we read some of the satires by the poet Horace, we smile – just as his original readers did – over the situations sketched out for the sake of amusement. However, the ensuing influence of shared moral attitudes, schools of thought and religious beliefs makes us react differently toward the sufferings and physical defects of our fellow man, which were instead a source of mirth in the ancient world.

One of the hallmarks of the tours that come to Pompeii (and this holds true for those at the Parthenon in Athens and the Pyramids of Giza) is haste: not even the best-informed tour guide can explain and illustrate lifestyles and unique architectural features in a one- or two-hour visit. Thus, we hustle about, trying to take in as many images as we can and remember as much as possible. The last gasps of life, captured eternally by the plaster casts, do indeed move us, but for just a second.

Our attention is then immediately riveted by other things: the bedrooms, *gee, they were cramped!*, the frescoes that are still on the walls, *we certainly haven't come up with anything new*, the lack of furniture, *where did they put their things?*, a stroll down Via dell'Abbondanza as if it were Via Condotti or Fifth Avenue, a keepsake photo and then on to the next stop on the tour.

We can learn about Roman civilization through Pompeii, and at least get a glimpse at provincial life and everyday habits, but only as long as our tour finally proceeds to the National Archaeological Museum of Naples. There movable artifacts and frescoes complete the range of findings and illustrate their characteristics, their artistic value and historic merit. This book, prepared with the participation of the Archaeological Superintendency of Pompeii and Naples, and with the contribution of the Frederick II University of Naples, has been written to help readers rediscover the ancient city. It thus follows the results of the latest research and focuses on the attractions of these sites, in a close relationship with the recently renovated museum exhibits. It is a special itinerary that can be undertaken in different stages or all at once, as a way of learning more about what we have already seen or to inspire a visit.

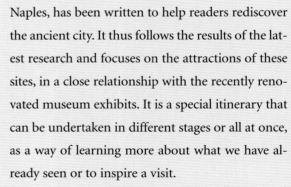

What is told and illustrated here is the outcome of decades of systematic research covering the various phases of city planning, technology and cultural contexts. This is an area of study that is seem-

This panel, made of vitreous paste, captures a scene from a bacchanal (Naples, MAN).

ingly endless, and it adds to the intrigue of the Vesuvian area. And this is because Pompeii also involves anthropologists, chemists and paleopathologists who, day after day, rediscover the city's last inhabitants and tell us about diseases, habits, trade relations and technologies. Laboratories have yielded mixtures for glue and perfumes made from natural essences, plants and vines have been cultivated in gardens where even seeds were preserved, abandoned amphorae have yielded traces of shellfish and condiments, and the faraway origins of precious stones have been discovered. Excavation continues in order to discover the oldest settlement phases, houses and public buildings are being restored, the traces of the first explorations are being examined, and the history of Pompeii is enriched by new information. Even the eruption has been studied in detail, confirming or dismissing the information handed down to us. In these pages, we can watch the terrifying sequence of events as they unfolded in the eleven hours that devastated an enchanting strip of land, and these hours have been examined with scientific precision. Thanks to the contribution of countless scholars, there are many keys to interpreting Pompeii. We can examine art, architecture, science, politics, religion, the economy and – why not? – a virtual reconstruction. In the end, however, each informative structure leads to the others, because people, objects and the natural environment have always been interrelated and only an overall understanding of their value and func-

tion will allow us to communicate with that reality.

An important part of *Ancient Pompeii* is devoted to Oplontis, modern-day Torre Annunziata, which provides an opportunity to add to the archaeological and historical knowledge of a territory that, from Cape Misenum to Sorrento, was dotted with cities, luxury vacation *villae* and farming estates. Villa A in Oplontis, in particular, represents the least-known tourist destination of Pompeii – it can now be visited with audio-guides – but it is an utterly fascinating one. When Mount Vesuvius erupted, it was one of the prestigious residences where the Roman aristocracy would go for cultured leisure and summertime amusement. Overlooking the sea, this villa had gardens, a large pool, and banquet halls flooded with sunlight and salty air. And yet, even now that it has a different entrance than it originally did and no longer enjoys such a scenic position, the quality of the frescoes and marbles, the complexity of the architectural layout, and even its ownership – Poppaea Sabina, Nero's second wife, would come to stay here – make it an utterly unique site within the entire Vesuvian area.

Places, works of art and lifestyles have been brought back to life, in all their color and emotion, through the wonderful illustrations of Araldo de Luca. The details, captured both indoors and outside, help make this encounter with the most famous of all buried cities, and with one of the most famous villas of antiquity, an unforgettable experience.

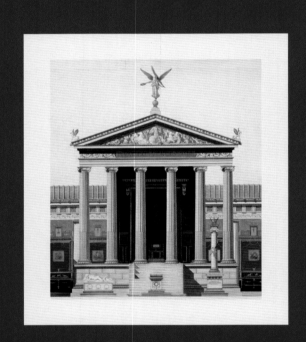

THE DISCOVERY AND HISTORY OF POMPEII

[Pietro Giovanni Guzzo]

◆

KING CHARLES AND ARCHAEOLOGY

T he discovery of Pompeii is linked to the discovery of Herculaneum several years earlier, and to the interest of Charles, King of Naples, in archaeological excavation. Ultimately, these two serendipitous findings, combined with government intervention, profoundly changed our knowledge of the ancient world. The Bourbon prince Charles (a son Philip V of Spain), who had already acquired the Farnese dukedom by marriage, won the Neapolitan crown by conquest during the War of the Austrian Succession. It was formally awarded to him as a kingdom in the 1734 peace settlement. Charles established a new dynasty and attempted to give it a distinctive character that would set it apart from the others of that era. Work for the organizational and economic development of the new kingdom targeted both agricultural and industrial activities, without overlooking social provisions for the weaker classes of the population. Charles was assisted by Bernardo Tanucci, a shrewd and trusted advisor. In particular, an energetic construction program was established to give the king and his court symbolic buildings that would also embody the power the new dynasty hoped to achieve. As part of this specific activity, plans were drawn up to build a royal palace in Portici, just east of Naples. Close to the spot chosen for the palace, two ancient statues had been discovered in the early 18th century during work to dig a well. The statues, together with other artifacts found with them, were exported by Prince d'Elboeuf, general of the Austrian army, which was occupying the Kingdom of Naples at that time. Therefore, some of these items were sent to Austria and others went to France.

When another well was dug in 1738, more artifacts were discovered and the news reached Charles, who thus decided to conduct research on a broader scale. As a result, several dozen feet below the modest houses that formed the town of Resina, Herculaneum started to come to light. This was one of the ancient cities buried by the terrible eruption of Mount Vesuvius in AD 79 as recounted – in all its drama and consequences – by the two letters that Pliny the Younger (ca. AD 61 – ca. 112) wrote to the historian Tacitus (ca. AD 56 – ca. 118).

The new excavations progressed slowly and with great difficulty, and they were conducted by digging tunnels through the tufaceous material. As opposed to the other cities around Vesuvius, Herculaneum was not buried under *lapilli* (little stones of congealed ash) and overcome by noxious gas, but was devastated by boiling mud, mixed with volcanic debris, that cooled to form a compact mass many feet thick. During this research, for which even convicts were employed, colored marble artifacts and furnishings were removed, and the wall frescoes that were deemed to be of interest were detached from the walls. Together with the valuable treasures that were found, they were collected in an area of the Portici palace, which was gradually turned into a museum. The corps of military engineers, led by Colonel Rocco De Alcubierre, directed the excavation work. Discipline was extremely strict, and workers were even searched at the end of their shifts to ensure that no artifacts had been stolen from the king's collection. The excavation site – and anything found there – was considered the property of the crown and only the members of the newly established Accademia Ercolanese – the Academy of Herculaneum – were allowed to study them and disclose the discoveries that were made.

The news that an entire city had been discovered immediately spread far and wide, arousing the antiquarian interest of all the most cultured circles in Europe. This further stimulated Charles' overall political strategy, as he also wanted to break away from papal influence. The antiquities of Rome were the age-old pride of that city and of the power – temporal and spiritual – of the popes installed there. Since the King of Naples now had equally important remains, this put him on par with pontiffs. Added to this was the news that frescoes with a wide

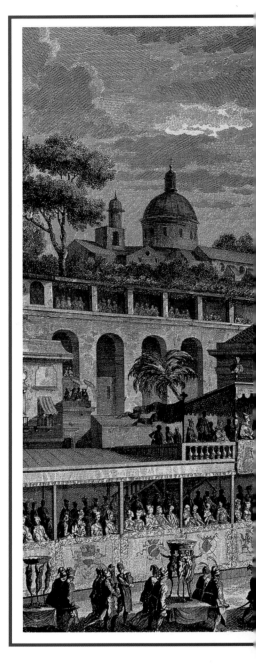

24-25

Pomp and honor accompany the transportation of Herculaneum artwork from the Portici Museum to Palazzo degli Studi in Naples at the beginning of the 19th century, as shown in this period engraving.

variety of subjects were constantly being uncovered in Herculaneum. It was widely known (based on the literary sources) that painting was probably the most highly esteemed art among the ancients – who had handed down the names of famous painters like Apelles, Parrhasius, Zeuxis and others – and yet very few paintings had been found in Rome. The most sensational finding, toward the end of the 15th century, was Nero's Domus Aurea (the Golden House) on the Oppian Hill (mistakenly identified as the Baths of Titus and, moreover, closed to the public). With its imaginative decorative motifs, the Domus Aurea influenced the Renaissance "grotesques" that were liber-

ally reproduced in aristocratic palazzos and in the Vatican Loggias. The other significant figured painting was found in the 17th century: the fresco, known as the "Aldobrandini Wedding," was an exceptional case, despite its poor state of conservation. The wealth of paintings unearthed at Herculaneum thus kindled excited hopes of finally learning about this aspect of antiquity as well. This was the main reason that the German aesthete and classicist Johann Joachim Winckelmann (1717-68) went to Naples twice, overcoming all the difficulties, reservations and obstacles that the members of the Accademia Ercolanese posed toward his requests and studies.

THE DISCOVERY OF POMPEII

This was the climate – highly favorable toward archaeological discoveries for a number of reasons – when the news began to spread about a farmer who, while working in his vineyard after part of the land caved in, had stumbled across the remains of paintings and marble statues. As a result, toward the end of March 1748, the corps of military engineers started digging in the country district of Civita, near Torre Annunziata. An important city had evidently been found, but no one knew its name yet. The city had actually been discovered accidentally 150 years earlier, several hundred yards south of the site of these findings in a place known today as the "Quadrivio d'Orfeo." At the time, work was underway to construct a canal that would be fed by the River Sarnus and would flow toward Torre Annunziata to power all the mills in the city. The canal was built along a subterranean course, vented at given intervals by air-shafts. While digging one of these air-shafts a situation similar to the one of 1748 was uncovered. However, neither the time nor the culture were yet ripe for grasping the significance of the find and benefiting from it, and the discovery was eventually forgotten.

The initial work unearthed an eruptive layer that was completely different from the one in Herculaneum. Instead of hardened mud similar to tuff, here there was a loose stratum of pumice and *lapilli* that was less than twenty feet thick. As a result, the technique of using underground tunnels was quickly abandoned, as the material offered no guarantee that the tunnels would stay in place without collapsing while the work was underway. Although this situation made it easier to extend and speed up the research, it also made the work more costly, as it involved an area that was covered with farms, including well-tended vineyards, which thus had to be destroyed and their owners reimbursed.

Within just a few years, it was clear that the Civita district had been an important settlement, drawing scholars into erudite debates. Was this Stabiae or Pompeii? The discovery in 1763 of an epigraph, complete with the city's official title (*Res Publica Pompeianorum*), finally put all doubts to rest: it was Pompeii, the city that, in time, was to become the symbol of the entire area destroyed by Mount Vesuvius. Stabiae was also quite famous and its excavation work, which was started in 1749, uncovered additional wall paintings.

Thus, by the middle of the 18th century, the three main archaeological sites buried by the volcanic eruption had been discovered, and at all three sites the excavation work proceeded under the supervision of the corps of military engineers commanded by Colonel Alcubierre, who reported directly to King Charles. The ostensible scientific assessment of the findings was handled by the guardian of the Portici Museum, first Camillo Paderni and then the Flamish sculptor, Joseph Canart. The task of studying and disclosing the discoveries was reserved for the members of the Accademia Ercolanese, whose painstaking work led to the publication of the precious folio volumes, entitled *Le antichità di Ercolano esposte*. These lavish publications, whose frontispiece bore an engraved portrait of King Charles as the restorer of once-buried antiquities, included plates with detailed engravings of the decorations and furnishings that had been collected, accompanied by explanatory texts. It was strictly through these publications that information about the discoveries was disclosed to a circle that, though quite limited, was nevertheless essential in shaping taste and culture across Europe. It was in this climate that the artistic current of Neoclassicism was established. This school of art profoundly influenced architecture and the applied decorative arts, particularly in England and France, and with the construction of the White House in Washington DC it also came to symbolize the recent political independence of the United States of America.

While quite limited, the circulation of the reproductions of the ancient Vesuvian artifacts was nonetheless ensured, although Ferdinando Galiani, secretary to the Neapolitan ambassador in Paris, proposed selling the publications for even wider circulation. However, first-hand knowledge of the artifacts, which were kept at the palace in Portici, was severely restricted, and these restrictions extended not only to those who wanted to view them in person, but also to anyone who wanted to sketch them or even just take notes about them. Moreover, the objects themselves were destined strictly for the royal collection. In some cases, they were even given as personal gifts from the king to other sovereigns, although it must be noted that this custom was not followed by the founder of the dynasty but by his successors. It has been documented that when Charles left Naples in 1759 to accede to the Spanish throne, he gave the Museum the ring he usually wore, which was decorated with a stone carved with a theater mask that had been found during the excavations. His intent with this gesture was to emphasize the distinction between personal and public assets: when he left Naples for Madrid, he could not legitimately keep what he had held as the monarch of a kingdom that no longer belonged to him.

The interest stirred by the Vesuvian discoveries triggered an enormous request for antique items, particularly paintings, which emphasized the true novelty of the discoveries. Their production process – encaustic, the technique of painting with wax, as well as other techniques – had become a topic of discussion among antiquarians, who attempted to reconstruct the phases involved using the text written by Vitruvius (1st century AD) as a reference, as it illustrated the process for preparing the layers of plaster, up to the coat that would actually be painted.

The sheer originality and scope of the Vesuvian discoveries not only triggered discussions among scholars and antiquarians, but they also led to the development of archaeological research. From then on, this research no longer addressed only sculptur-

al works and monumental architecture, as had been necessary above all in Rome. Now, the focus turned to even the minor details of daily life, represented by objects required for common everyday needs, and to the houses of obscure individuals whose names and deeds had not been handed down by ancient writers. The lack of precise references was immediately remedied by giving the houses names based on the activities of their supposed owners, names that were often overly imaginative. Moreover, within this area of renewed interest, there was also a spirit of critical comparison between all the modest everydayness that was unearthed at the foot of Mount Vesuvius and the supremely classical and imperial life that continued to mark Rome's allure.

Even Goethe followed this trend, and he did not hesitate to define the buildings in Pompeii as "dollhouses," even as he highlighted their importance as a topic of study for contemporary scholars. Nevertheless, as luck would have it Edward G. Bulwer (later Lord Lytton), published his successful novel *The Last Days of Pompeii* in 1834, two years after Goethe's death. The German master can be considered the impetus behind the transition from the excitement of the discovery to its comparative placement, not a technical level but more in terms of a widespread literary culture, just as Winckelmann had done before him. By the same token, the English lord became the providential force behind the popularity of the myth of Pompeii.

The characters, plot and sentiments described in his novel would not have come down to our own day and age if they had not been imagined against the tragic backdrop of the eruption. Bulwer-Lytton seems to have been the first person, and certainly the most famous, to bring to life – and not just for antiquarians but also for the general public – the dramatic events that destroyed Pompeii, Herculaneum and Stabiae. These events were later developed even further by the movies made based on the book.

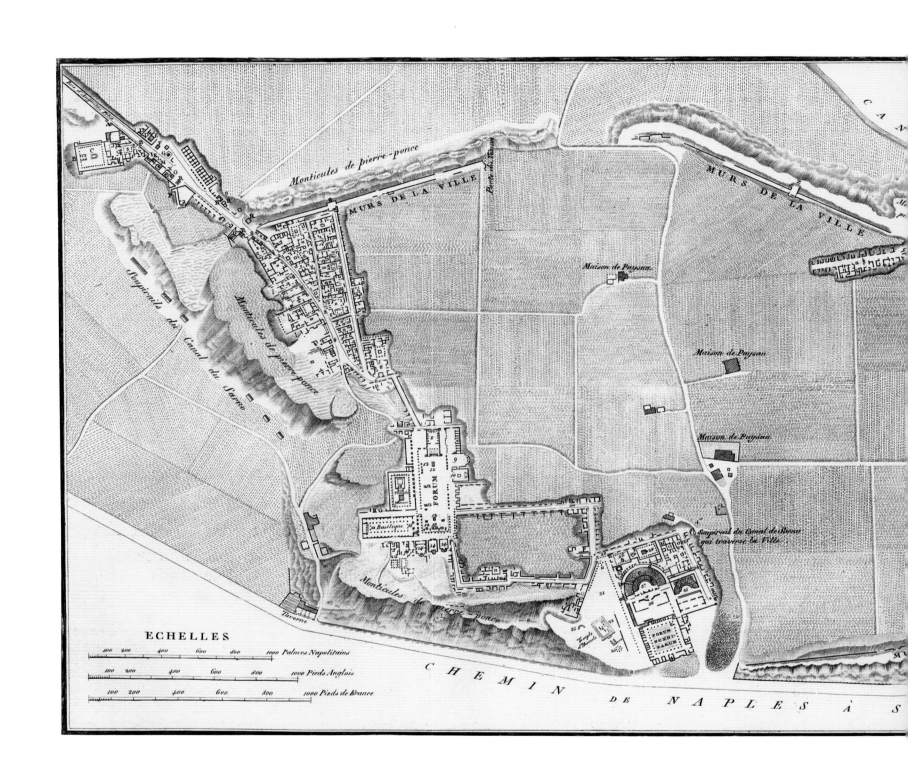

28-29

This map of Pompeii shows the status of the excavations in the early 19th century: various public buildings are visible, whereas the area with private homes is smaller (from Henry Wilkins, Vues pittoresque des ruines de Pompeii, *1810).*

29

This 18th-century washed line engraving shows the excavation work in the area around the Temple of Venus (from W. Hamilton, Campi Flaegraei, *Table no. XXXI).*

For Pompeii, the 19th century opened with the initiative of Caroline Bonaparte, the wife of Joachim Murat (appointed King of Naples by Napoleon; reigned 1809-1815), who promoted a more methodical organization of the excavations, starting the work to recover the walls ringing the city. Herculaneum, on the other hand, had practically been abandoned following the exciting discovery of the Villa of the Papyri, owing also to the difficulties in excavating the city, and the same thing happened with Stabiae.

We can follow the development of archaeological activity in Pompeii by examining the general maps that were gradually drawn up and used alongside the "romantic" views, until then the main graphic documentation of the findings. Between the 18th and 19th centuries, the quarter formed by the two theaters, the Temple of Isis, and the Soldiers' Quadriportico or Gladiators' Barracks was uncovered. The Amphitheater was known but, like the Villa of Julia Felix, it was partially reburied. To the west, Diomedes' Villa and the residence referred to as Cicero's Villa were excavated and subsequently reburied. The Consular Road was followed from the city gate of Porta di Ercolano, uncovering the houses along it, such as the House of the Surgeon and the House of Sallust.

During the first few decades of the 19th century, the excavations were extended in order to connect the theater area with the one around Porta di Ercolano. As a result, much of the current *Regio VI* was gradually uncovered, together with the entire Forum with all the public monuments that lined it, and the segment of the current Via dell'Abbondanza up to the intersection with the ancient road leading to the Triangular Forum.

The extension of the excavations conducted during the period of French dominance proceeded through the expropriation of private property, and this long and complex operation was not completed until after 1860. In fact, due to the chronic lack of funding allocated for the excavation, the government went deeply into debt with the work contractors and – like an enormous Penelope's web of property – payments were made by allotting portions of land that had previously been expropriated from others.

The main area of interest for these excavations was the exact and systematic layout of the ancient city, but the appreciation of its true extent would be left to the future generations of scholars. Instead, the individual monuments were the aspect examined most closely during this period, in addition to the furnishings and frescoes (which were detached from the walls and exhibited in the Museum, which is now located in Naples).

Among them, the temple dedicated to Isis – immediately recognized as such because of its layout, including the systems for the sacred waters, the place of the sacred serpent and the Egyptian furnishings – stirred enormous interest. The same thing happened later with the public buildings lining the square of the Forum. In particular, the Basilica attracted great attention and as a result, reconstruction and restoration work was done on much of it, mainly involving the west wall.

THE GRAND TOUR AND THE NEW BUILDINGS

The buildings used as private homes continued to represent the main attraction, particularly for those who, while not scholars of antiquity, considered a visit to Pompeii an essential part of their travels to complete their education and learn about Italy. Making a trip to Italy as part of their education was a popular habit among wealthy young Europeans, one justified by the abundance and variety of monuments and landscapes to be admired there —each of which permitted a scholarly and instructive approach to the writers of the classics. The outcome was that today we have many publications on these tours, ranging from the diaries and memoirs of certain travelers to full-fledged manuals to help readers move about, with lists of the essential places to visit. At times, they also came with footnotes on the costs of different services, from carriages to guides and from meals and accommodations. We thus have plenty of documentation to help us evaluate the powerful influence that the ancient city of Pompeii had on the cultural training of Europe's upper classes and on their imagination.

The activities of antiquarians also contributed to this, as they devoted their insight and knowledge to interpreting the findings.

Most of the names given to the buildings – public and private – uncovered during that period are invented ones. Nevertheless, many of them are still used today, as these names have now become customary. The owners of private buildings were given names taken from adjacent inscriptions. This is what happened, for example, with the suburban villa attributed to Diomedes, named after a man buried right in front of the entrance to the villa. In one case, the building was named "House of the Vestals" based on an interpretation of the function of the building. At times, the pretext for naming a building came from the objects found inside it ("House of the Surgeon") or the type of scenes painted there ("House of the Tragic Poet"), characterized by episodes recounted from the great tragic poets of Greece that in some way drew upon the Iliad, and by a mosaic of masked "actors" in satyr-like costumes.

Likewise, the famous house now known as the House of the Faun was initially distinguished by the main finding in it, one that rightfully was also the most exciting: the great polychrome mosaic of Alexander the Great in a bat-

30 and 31

These two views – the first one shows the House of Gavius Rufus and the second depicts Via dei Sepolcri – have a typical 19th-century setting. The findings and statues provide the backdrop for figures of travelers fascinated by classical civilization (Niccolini, Bibliothèque des Arts Decoratifs, France).

tle against the Persian king, Darius. The original name, the "House of the Great Mosaic," was later replaced by the current one, which in turn comes from the bronze statue found in the *atrium* and interpreted as a dancing faun.

The large number of private buildings was interspersed with buildings used as shops, taverns, bakeries and crafts shops: all of this created a unique vision of classical antiquity, particularly because of the variety of types. Knowledge about private buildings from the Roman era had been based solely on the interpretation of Vitruvius' manual of architecture and in one way, the discoveries in Pompeii coincided with literary theory. In another way, however, they diverged from it, and one example was the quarter south of the Forum. Here, the houses did not rigidly follow the principles of Vitruvius' order but instead seemed to have been adapted to fit into the narrow space between the large public square and the southern slope that clearly identifies the mountainous rise on which the city had been built.

Alongside the excavation, ongoing restoration and maintenance work was also being conducted although, as we have mentioned, most of the frescoed decorations and movable artifacts were not kept on site. The outcome was a schematic view of Pompeii and its components, and the romantic sensitivity of the period was deeply affected by the city's construction and its evocative appearance. One example of this was Théophile Gautier's successful novella *Arria Marcella*, published in 1852. Using the dreamlike pretext of the story, it blends elements admired on site and others seen at the Museum of Naples. The keystone of the story was not the variety of the decorations but the unlikely imprint, left in the hardened eruptive ash, of a woman's breast.

Gautier interpreted a need to portray scenarios – the one of the ruins and the one in the Museum – that were separate yet referred to a single, original entity.

The author thus used his imagination to add characters and situations, living beings and events, feelings and hardships, but at the same time, he avoided taking any excessive poetic license that would have horrified aloof antiquarian scholars.

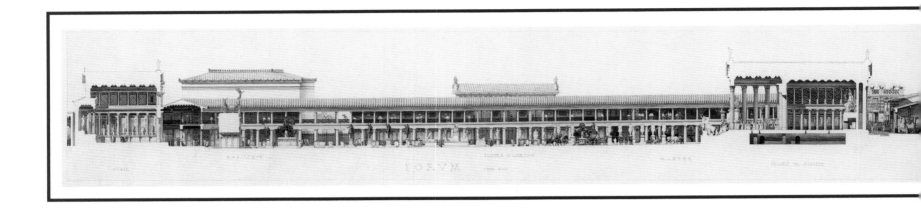

FORVM

BASILIQUE — TEMPLE D'APOLLON — MAERBE — TEMPLE DE JVPITER

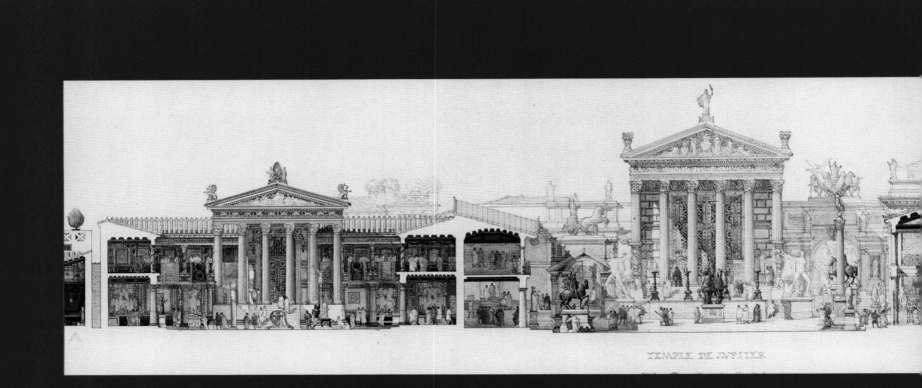

TEMPLE DE JVPITER

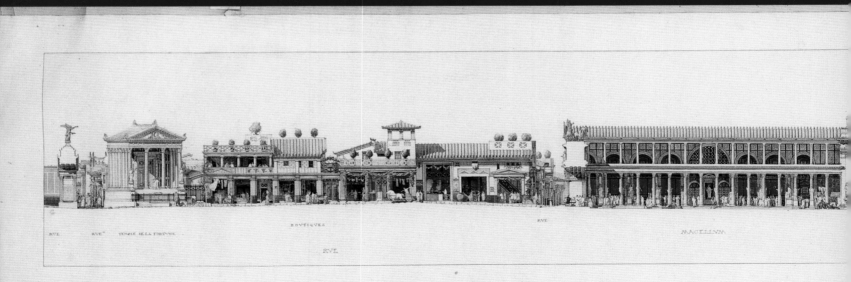

RVE — RVE — TEMPLE DE LA FORTVNE — BOVTIQVES — RVE — RVE — MACELLVM

32-33

Three front views of the Forum area, observed from several standpoints, highlight the main buildings representing the civic and religious heart of city life. From left to right: in the upper portion, the Curia, the Basilica, the market, and the Forum Baths; in the center, the Temple of Apollo, the Temple of Jupiter, and the Building of Eumachia; in the lower part, the Temple of Fortuna Augusta, the Basilica, the Macellum, the Temple of the Public Lares, the Temple of Vespasian, the Comitium, and the Office of the Duumviri. (L. Jaussely, 1910) (Ecole Nationale Supérieure des Beaux-Arts, Paris).

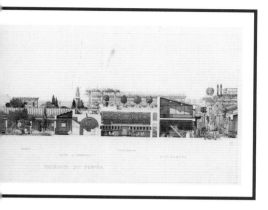

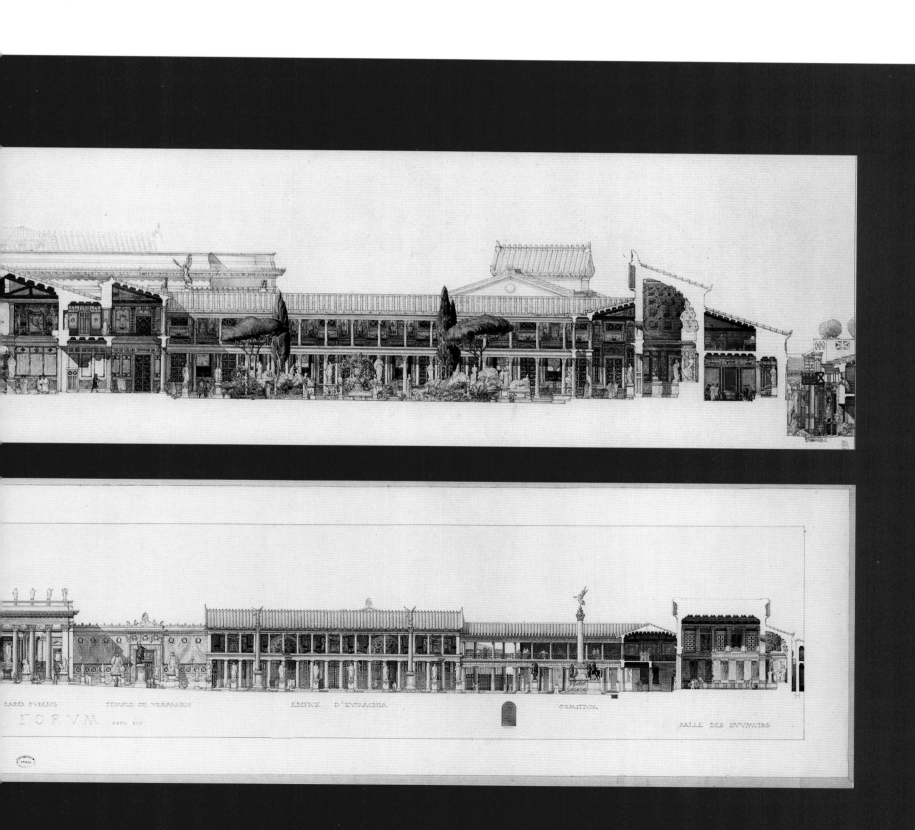

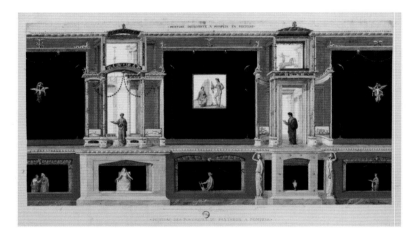

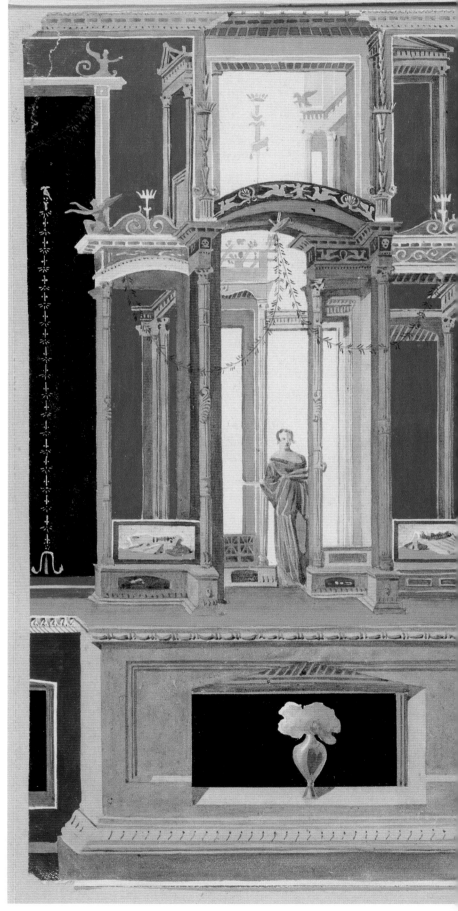

34 top
*The inset, part of a watercolor copy by an anonymous artist, reproduces
a frescoed panel from the House of the Tragic Poet.*

34 bottom
*Red and black are the predominant notes in this watercolor by
J. B. Lesueur, depicting the fresco he attributed to the hypothetic "Pantheon."*

34-35
*The elegance of the wall decorations of Pompeii's buildings is preserved in
this reconstruction showing the subjects, colors, frames, panels and niches of a
Pompeian* domus *(Ecole Nationale Supérieure des Beaux-Arts, Paris).*

BETWEEN THE 19 AND 20TH CENTURIES:
FIORELLI'S CASTS AND MAIURI'S RESEARCH

The generations of the second half of the 19th century can be characterized by their strong scientific and methodical focus. This was undoubtedly influenced by two factors. These were the fall of the Bourbon dynasty with the subsequent annexation of the Kingdom of the Two Sicilies (which included Naples) to the Kingdom of Italy, and the work done by Giuseppe Fiorelli and the engineer Michele Ruggiero, one of his closest collaborators. The first factor brought the Pompeii excavations into a circuit of relationships that was much broader than the one it had enjoyed previously, while the second acted as a systematic basis for collecting and critically analyzing the knowledge that had already been gained, hinting at a strategy for future acquisitions.

We have Fiorelli, who was active on-site from 1860-75, to thank for several aspects that may seem commonplace but that are in fact crucial. First of all, he was responsible for giving all the buildings discovered until then a unique registry name, based on an objective system of "street addresses" that was also used for the buildings excavated subsequently. Secondly, he systematically organized the excavation, which thus focused on uncovering complete buildings and not just the most richly decorated parts. Fiorelli's commitment also yielded the complete collection of the registration of works and discoveries made starting in 1748, which were united in the monumental volumes of *Pompeianarum Antiquitatum Historia*, and an accurate topographic survey of the entire city.

In addition to these strictly scientific changes, he also distinguished himself by advocating the "casting" technique and, though he did not actually invent the method, he was the one who perfected it. By pouring plaster into the hollows left as bodies – as well as parts of wooden furniture and plant roots – dissolved, he was able to reproduce the shapes of the unfortunate Pompeians killed by the eruption. More

than any other artifacts, these powerful and moving images truly bring us face to face with this catastrophe. It is also understandable that results of this kind augmented the general interest in Pompeii, which was adopted as one of the leading archaeological activities of the unified Kingdom of Italy. In reality, despite the visit of King Victor Emmanuel II, the excavations were not allocated enough resources to meet the needs for conservation and complete study, although a great deal of reconstruction and restoration work was done. This was the case with the porticoes of the Forum, the propylaeum (formal entrance) and the east portico of the Triangular Forum, as well as numerous private buildings. Among these, in 1895 the House of the Vettii became the first to be restored completely, including the roofing. Both the wall frescoes and movable treasures inside were also preserved. This undertaking filled a sweeping cultural need whose signs were evident as early as the 18th century: the availability of a physically unified and complete picture of the building structure and its original decoration. With the development of the collections and studies that were added to the compendia devoted to Pompeii in the *Corpus Inscriptionum Latinarum*, this evidence could thus be connected with the voices of the ancient inhabitants as recorded in inscriptions and graffiti: Pompeii began to live and speak once again. The words painted or carved along the walls and in the houses offered a glimpse of a broad range of moods and emotions of the Pompeians, revealing their gossip and their desires. The impetuousness of love and lust, financial calculations, coarse insults, poetic verse and sarcastic comments were all part of a normal life that became exceptional to us solely through a tragic fatality.

Together with the Archaeological Museum, the Pompeii excavations were the pride of Naples, no

The photograph documents the excavation work done on a house at the end of the 19th century.

longer the capital of its own kingdom but now one of the many cities in the new government structure. Thanks also to the work of Giuseppe Fiorelli, who became the Director General of Antiquities and Fine Arts in 1874, the operative system tested in Pompeii became the model for the work and protective measures used for all other archaeological sites in Italy. Pompeii also became the site of the first National School of Archaeology, which provided training in this new discipline to graduates who would then work for the main department.

The continuation of the excavations and of the discoveries gained extraordinary impetus from the work of Vincenzo Spinazzola starting in the 1920s. It was Spinazzola who connected the western and eastern sectors of the ancient city by completing the excavation of Via dell'Abbondanza and the residential areas south of it.

The work of Amedeo Maiuri, spanning forty years, was equally significant. With only a few minor exceptions, the current layout of the archaeological areas is exactly as it was when he left. Maiuri also championed the constant attention paid to establishing a link between the archaeological area and what we can define as the contemporary surrounding environment: the connecting streets, the modern town known by the Italian name of Pompei, which became a municipality in 1928, and facilities for visitors. These were important initiatives because the growing influx of visitors to the archaeological area required appropriate facilities for an international public from all walks of life. Maiuri also established a research trend investigating the earlier phases of ancient Pompeian life, before the last one, overcome by the eruption. The studies he conducted along the entire circuit of the city's defensive walls, in the Temple of Apollo and at various points of the city to discover the buildings' chronological sequence, retrieved much information about the city's archaic phase. For ex-

These two period photographs, both of which were taken on Via dell'Abbondanza, captured the discovery of a bronze Efebus lampadophoros (top) and the excavation of a thermopolium *(bottom).*

ample, it was possible to ascertain that Pompeii had been founded as early as the 6th century BC, as part of the interrelationships between Greeks and Etruscans.

Equally significant findings contributed to the detailed understanding of the area's last years of life. Maiuri focused on the period between AD 62, when the city suffered serious damage from a terrible earthquake, and AD 79, the year it was destroyed. His thorough review of the construction techniques, of the renewal and restoration work that can be observed, and of the general situation in Pompeii during its last seventeen years has been fundamental for all contemporary in-depth studies.

Maiuri's important personal discoveries include the Villa of the Mysteries (whose excavation had been started previously), and the House of Menander, notable because of the of silver tableware treasure found there. In addition to specific interests, the Neapolitan archaeologist also helped classify the productive and stylistic sequence of the wall frescoes, which since the 18th century have been considered the ancient Vesuvian city's most unique aspect.

Numerous scholars can be credited for the detailed technical and scientific investigations conducted during that period, continuing the initial work done on this subject by Wolfgang Helbig and Amedeo Maiuri. Even today, this work has received renewed attention from all the scientific organizations—from Australian to German ones – that have consistently studied Pompeii.

What is now one of the best-known and most frequently visited sites in the world is thus the outcome of more than two and a half centuries of research, effort,

scientific study and intellectual drive. As the successors to a long line of archaeologists, scholars, enthusiasts and inquisitive minds, it is our responsibility to continue to respect and safeguard all this.

It seems that the effect of continuing this work, conducted until then only on the ruins affected by the eruption to make them comprehensible to some extent, was to render a situation like Pompeii's more acceptable than it would have been if no one had attempted to preserve its buildings once the priority need of removing their decorations and preserving them at museums had been accomplished.

We know that Pompeii had an area of about 163 acres, of which 66 have been excavated to date. Its defensive walls covered a circuit of about 10,500 feet, reinforced by twelve towers, with seven gates, plus an eighth that was closed off in ancient times.

The urban fabric, which expanded from the original center around the square of the Forum, was laid out along two east-west *decumani* (Via di Nola, Via dell'Abbondanza) and three *cardines* (Via di Mercurio, Via di Stabia, Via di Nocera).

Within the city, there were *vici*, or quarters, clustered around their respective altars, such as the ones that would later make a ritual place of the main crossroads, known as the *compita*. Starting in the Augustan Age, an aqueduct brought water into the city, increasing its supply ensured until then by wells and cisterns. Public baths and fountains, as well as the plumbing systems of the wealthiest private homes, took equal advantage of this water supply, thus raising the average quality of life.

Though to a far lesser extent, excavations were also conducted inside Porta Nola.

THE TERRITORY AND ITS HISTORY

T|he district of the city known to modern-day Italians as Pompei was settled by humans thousands of years ago, and its long history is intertwined with the natural and environmental characteristics that are its backdrop.

The shoreline, positioned centrally on the Bay of Naples, is low-lying even today, and during ancient times it was bordered by lagoons, particularly toward the mouth of the River Sarnus, which flowed into the bay and sweetened its waters. Across from the mouth of the river in a seaward direction is the rocky island of Rovigliano, known during the classical era as *Petra Herculis* (Rock of Hercules) and once much farther from the coast than it is today.

Before flowing into the lagoons, toward the south, the waters of the Sarnus washed up against a volcanic rise (now the hamlet of Sant'Abbondio), the far segment of a higher rise: this marks the site of the city of Pompeii.

The saltpans were to the west or northwest, while the fertile plains that ringed Mount Vesuvius reaching to the plains around Capua extended toward the southeast. Further away in the same direction, the territory of Pompeii was bordered by the Lattari mountains and the Apennines.

The evidence of human activity in this broad stretch of territory dates from the 2nd millennium BC and is linked to the waterways, from Poggio Marino-Longola to Sant'Abbondio. Agriculture was the main source of subsistence, as documented by the numerous signs on the work levels. The layering of volcanic material from ancient eruptions has preserved the hollows left by plows, small channels, the separation of individual fields and posts driven into the ground to hold up canopies, and there are even tracks left by carts, livestock and human beings (in San Paolo Belsito and Nola). The entire territory is like a sandwich with different layers: the first traces of settlement, a volcanic covering, other evidence of cultivation, new volcanic debris and so on, up to the tragic eruption of AD 79. And even after the cataclysmic event, new activities were reestablished on the hardened surface that remained (for example as found in Murecine or Muregine, a nearby site.)

The oldest levels of agriculture go back to the Neolithic period, whereas the settlement distribution dates from the Bronze Age (end of the 2nd millennium BC), with major changes in the Iron Age (the first two centuries of the 1st millennium BC). Archaeological knowledge of the settlements is more extensive for the Bronze Age, but less so for the subsequent phases (limited largely to findings from burials). This has made it possible to reconstruct a countryside composed of groups of rectangular huts built using plant materials plastered with clay, with the short side set opposite the entrance in an apse shape. These mini-villages were closely linked to the cultivated areas, waterways and beaten paths that connected the different communities.

These communities fulfilled their needs with crops, hunting and freshwater fishing, as well as livestock, as demonstrated by the pens and fences next to the huts. The production of clay containers was very widespread, and metal tools were used less extensively.

The recent excavations at Poggio Marino-Longola (the upper course of the Sarnus) have added important new information about the oldest human organization and on how man interfered with the environment around him in this corner of Campania. An extraordinary settlement has been found, not only in terms of the local protohistory but also in a European context. This settlement, active from the 1st century BC to the early 6th century BC, fills the gaps in our knowledge of the period between the Bronze Age and the foundation of Pompeii. Immediately nicknamed the "Venice of Protohistory," it was composed of a series of small islands created by channeling and reclamation work. The site points to extensive knowledge of hydraulic engineering and a careful

*The multifaceted nature of Mount Vesuvius – impressive, richly verdant yet menacing – dominates the territory
around it in this engraving from the 1810 work* Vues pittoresques des ruines de Pompeii, *by Henry Wilkins.*

selection of the materials used to build dwellings. To move along the canals, the people used dugout canoes like the one found here, while to fend off humidity they raised their huts on stilts, composed of wooden supports and loose foundations made of potsherds. The thousands of artifacts, most of which are fragments (500,000 ceramic artifacts), include 600 scraps from the hand-worked bronze, iron, amber, vitreous paste, and carved bone and horn, indicating that Poggio Marino was an important center that produced and traded prestigious goods. Archaeologists have also gleaned other information about the surrounding environment: there were oak forests and enormous numbers of wild animals (bears, roe deer, deer and boars).

THE BIRTH OF POMPEII
THE SAMNITE ERA

Between the end of the 7th and the middle of 6th century BC, the inhabitants living in the huts north of the Sarnus were forced to abandon their village after a flood. They did not flee the area, but gradually migrated, as demonstrated by some of the furnishings that were discovered. For people who were accustomed to living near water and knew the course of the river toward its estuary, the rise stretching into the sea must have looked like a reassuring alternative for starting a new life: we therefore cannot overlook the possibility that the founders of the city of Pompeii included a large number of inhabitants from Poggio Marino-Longola. Materials from Pithecusa (the modern-day island of Ischia) dating from the 8th century BC have been found along the banks of the Sarnus, leading us to assume that there was ongoing contact between the first settlement of the Greeks and Asians who colonized the Italian peninsula and the people who had settled in the river valley. This contact involved the mutual exchange of products or foodstuffs, thus entailing seafaring activity and overland transit. This marked the first social and morphological change in an area that had remained more or less the same for fifteen hundred years. In fact, this economic rapport presumably meant that the people had to establish routes to connect the seafarers' landing places to the settlements, the trade terminals and, in turn, the producers of the requested goods. The organizational paths of the territory, used until then to link the settlements, were thus also laid out to connect them to the outside through an interface with the landing places. The watercraft may have dropped anchor at the entry to the lagoons, allowing the seafarers to travel up the river from the sea. It is no accident that during the historic era, the existence of a sanctuary honoring the Greek sea god Poseidon (the Romans' Neptune) was documented on an intermediate sandbar of the remaining lagoons.

The difference in importance noted in the funerary accoutrements from this period denotes a change in the internal organization of the settlements, in relation to some kind of social hierarchy with (we assume) different types of housing and their position in the villages.

It was in this context, during the 6th century BC, that the city of Pompeii was founded atop a volcanic rise overlooking the plains and forming a terrace toward the coast. In that period, the settlement – still just a village – was laid out as an organized town enclosed by defensive walls, which were built using blocks of *pappamonte*, or soft lava, that encircled the level ground for 40 acres. A powerful military presence thus oversaw the establishment of farms and sanctuaries in the area outside the city.

Fortification of the settlement was probably also motivated by the need to monitor the landing place operating at the mouth of the Sarnus and thus the traffic toward the interior, mentioned by the historical sources. The city must have had an economy based on agriculture, fishing and raising livestock.

For the very first time, the stable settlement of Pompeii shaped itself to the coastal appearance of the Bay of Naples, with signs of construction that can be distinguished from the simpler items made earlier, not only in form but also in the technology and materials used. The landscape began to take on unique characteristics due to the handiwork of man, using not only organic materials but also stone. This was followed by a parallel search for and the permanence of place names, starting with the word "Pompeii" itself. The word probably derives from the Italic *pump*, meaning "totality" (from "five," like the fingers on one hand) in reference to the districts located in the surrounding area. These people, who had established themselves based on different models and had intense contact with the Etruscans from the Tyrrhenian cities and with the Greeks in Cumae and Parthenope, decided to form an association to create a stable and well-equipped settlement. The area protected by the defensive walls was not fully urbanized: the north sector of the excavations conducted by the University of Milan have revealed areas covered with vegetation in which religious ceremonies must also have been performed. We do not have extensive archaeological documentation about what was traded with Pompeii, with the exception of Greek pottery (from Attica) placed in the archaic sanctuary under the Temple of Apollo for votive purposes. The square of the Forum had already been earmarked as such: clear of any buildings, it was a meeting place for the residents, perhaps divided into groups based on the district in which they lived, with political and trade functions.

A city was laid out around it, with an interlay of roads set in a herringbone fashion with respect to the north-south line marking off the eastern end of the Forum square, which extended northward along the current Via di Mercurio and stretched past the walls through a gate that was closed in a later period. This axis, extending into the countryside toward Mount Vesuvius, became so well established over the years that it became a point of reference for dividing fields and building farms in the sector outside the city. The earliest city of Pompeii ended to the north with another road, which went from the coast up to Porta di Ercolano and headed toward the north-south axis, following a course that has left clear archaeological documentation (a diagonal roadway between *insula* VI, 3 and VI, 4, maintained in later buildings, and part of the roadbed under the flooring of the *Casa delle Forme di Creta*, or the House of the Plaster Forms, VII, 4, 62). According to some scholars, the archaic sanctuary of the Triangular Forum was instead used as a sacred place for a "cult of commerce," for the trading of goods and watercraft of different capacities, intended for sea and river navigation. During this era, anyone sailing in the bay could see a number of well-built strongholds: Cumae with its

port of Dicearchia (modern-day Pozzuoli), Parthenope (which was to become Naples) and Pompeii. The island of Pithecusa (Ischia), the first Mycenaean and Greek trading center in the Tyrrhenian, had already seen its heyday, although the temple on Mount Vico – with its polychrome terracotta – was still visible. All around, the shore was dotted with unfortified villages as far as Sorrento, while work had started to 'monumentalize' the Temple of Minerva at Punta della Campanella.

The landscape seen from Pompeii was a mirror image: nearby, set at regular intervals there were farms, with bustling movement near the natural landing places where men and goods were transferred to other boats before sailing up the river. Many villages could be perceived only from the smoke curling up from the dwellings, because they were concealed by the vegetation and there were no defensive walls or monumental temples. Dense forests covered the slopes of the Lattari mountains and those of Vesuvius, with plants that thrived in a climate that was cooler and damper than it is today.

Between the end of the 5th century and the beginning of the 4th century BC, the city and the entire area were dominated by the Samnites, who spoke the Oscan language, as did most Campanian peoples. These warlike people came from the inland areas of the Apennines and as they grew in number, they occupied the most fertile lands close to the sea. Pompeii was fortified once again using blocks of local limestone and building proceeded inside the walls, around the Forum and in the eastern sector of Via di Mercurio, encroaching on the green areas. However, there were many areas without any buildings, as we can deduce from the historian Livy, who cites an episode from the end of the 4th century BC. When an armed Roman fleet arrived to attack the Samnite cities of this district, which had rebelled against the *Res publica*, the inhabitants of the nearby countryside took refuge inside the walls of Pompeii, leaving their enemies free to plunder their farms and crops.

The traces of the Samnites can be verified in part, although there are gaps in the chronological sequence. The city layout was generally straight and uniform in shape, and the previous constructions were not always linked with it. The alleys that mark off the city blocks follow an uneven route (northeast corner of *insula* IX, 1) or they show a lack of alignment (west side of *insula* IX, 6 and of IX, 5), due to the specific political decision of the new authorities who, for various reasons, felt it best to follow the previous layout.

The "aristocratic" dwellings seem to have been concentrated in the northwest sector (*Regio* VI), but there is no lack of sprawling homes, built by the 1st century BC, in the other city sectors. It is as if the original districts from the five preceding centuries had continued to distinguish themselves and indicate the best locations for the leading families. Until just a few years before the tragedy struck, many wealthy Pompeian families purchased the residences left behind by the Italic rulers – an unmistakable status symbol – and alongside the ambience and decor called for by current fashion, they also maintained the much older facilities and materials. For example, this was the case with the House of the Surgeon, the House of Sallust and the House of the Figured Capitals.

THE ROMAN CONQUEST

In the Roman wars against the Samnites and against Hannibal and the Carthaginians, Campania was a cruel battle theater. Nevertheless, although certain cities like Capua and Nola lost all forms of freedom, Pompeii, perhaps because it was less important, managed to keep control of its trade traffic. During the 2nd century BC, it even increased its production of oil and wine, restructured its monumental areas (the Triangular Forum and the Theater complex), and constructed new public and sacred buildings (the Basilica and the Temple of Jupiter). The social, political and urban structure underwent radical change only after Sulla's conquest in 89 BC, without touching the economic setup. Pompeii had participated in the Social War against Rome to obtain full right of citizenship, joining many other southern cities. When it was attacked by Roman troops, it was forced to surrender (signs of those ancient battles can still be seen along a section of the walls), seemingly without being sacked and devastated like Stabiae.

In 80 BC, Lucius Cornelius Sulla led a colony of his veterans there and the city became *Colonia Cornelia Veneria Pompeiianorum*, named after the dictator and the goddess he revered the most. New magistracies, new and emerging families, and a new official language were brought in, but the cultural substrate did not change. Many families thus bought back the properties that had been assigned to the veterans and created homes that were more comfortable and luxurious, following the fashions that were in style. The Amphitheater was undoubtedly built during the era of the Sullan colony, as was the Great Palaestra, under which there are traces of buildings that were torn down so it could be built.

The first phase of the Great Theater dates to just shortly before this time, and the new magistrates added the covered Little Theater to it. The city was embellished with public furnishings, statues, dedicatory and honorary inscriptions, shop signs and electoral inscriptions on the walls. The colors of the different materials used and the ones of the plaster façades were interwoven with the fluttering awnings that shaded the shops. The building types cover the entire range that was common for a city with a population of more than 10,000 people. In addition to private homes, which differed in their decorative and architectural level, and the sacred and public buildings, there were *thermopolia* (shops selling hot beverages), warehouses, and crafts and production facilities.

At the beginning of the 1st century AD, the city reinforced the aqueduct, derived from the one that stretched to Misenum to meet the needs of the military fleet on the Tyrrhenian Sea and stationed there. The aqueduct served public and private utilities, the fountains along the main roads and the growing numbers of baths, which had helped change the urban landscape. In fact, the distribution lines can be seen, with the uprights for the tanks used to maintain the water pressure.

The countryside around the city had gradually been turned into extensive farmland, and we can assume that the only uncultivated areas were the uppermost slopes of Vesuvius and of the Lattari mountains. Although we cannot establish the exact chronology, we know about the activity of a certain horseman by the name of *Corellius*, a native of *Ateste* (modern-day Este), who introduced the cultivation of chestnuts to the Pompeian area. Based on this, we can deduce that also the areas that were not used for the normal cultivation of vegetables, grains and vineyards were allocated for progressive urbanization and refined imports. To the west and southwest, from the rise on which it was built the city overlooked the port system, although the distance between them has not been determined. It has been confirmed that a frontal was constructed between the Baths of the Sarnus and the spur. Composed of a warehouse with several floors, it was used to preserve foodstuffs and products that were shipped by sea for trading.

With the *pax augustea*, the old defensive wall was no longer needed for military purposes. Building activities expanded beyond the outside walls, leading to a type of construction known as "slope houses." This can be seen in the southern segment, between the Triangular Forum and the Baths of the Sarnus, and on the western slope. For anyone arriving by sea, the Temple of Venus was another feature that also changed the city's appearance, as it stood dramatically on the rise of the city jutting toward the southwest. Built by Sulla, it overlooked the port system and the works connected to it. With its bright marble, this construction recalls Asian opulence and it represents the oldest example of this evidence in Pompeii, repeated at this point by the little Temple of Fortuna Augusta, north of the Forum. The use of marble from Luni (Carrara), exploited since the Augustan period, also spread to Pompeii and was used inside homes and flßor thresholds. The more prized marbles from the empire's eastern quarries were used to create various designs to decorate the *atria* of the most luxurious residences that can be seen from the street.

The urban furnishings confirm the ones documented elsewhere, particularly in terms of expressions of loyalty to the Julio-Claudian dynasty, honored with statues and inscriptions in public buildings, some of which were erected solely for this purpose. Alongside them, there are also similar expressions, demonstrated in the *Regiones* with cults centered on the *compita* (crossroads). The attention paid toward the central power meant that the ancient local monuments were neglected. The Doric Temple in the Triangular Forum lay in ruins and no attempt was made to restore it.

The development, particular in terms of commerce, that was experienced by the economy of Pompeii – and the rest of Italy – once it came under Rome's sphere of influence also led to the introduction of the cult of Isis, linked with Alexandria and the wheat trade. Thus, in the district that had once been the site of the ancient cult of Minerva and Hercules and later became the place where the *vereiia* (youth) would meet and train during the Samnite era, the Egyptian goddess's exotic cult appeared, with its characteristic architectural forms and rituals, completely different from those of the previous cults.

I n its last summer, Pompeii covered an area of about 163 acres, of which 103 have been excavated. Its defensive walls covered a circuit of about 10,500 feet, reinforced by twelve towers. It had seven gates, plus an eighth one that was closed off in ancient times. Its urban fabric, which expanded from the original center around the square of the Forum, was laid out along two east-west *decumani* (Via di Nola, Via dell'Abbondanza) and three *cardines* (Via di Mercurio, Via di Stabia, Via di Nocera). Within the city, there were *vivi*, or quarters, clustered around their respective altars, such as the ones that would later make a ritual of the main crossroads, known as the *compita*. The Augustan period promoted inter-Mediterranean trade, which led to economic well-being, and it was during this era that many public buildings, now part of the urban landscape, were monumentalized, including the entire Forum, the Great Palaestra (sports field) and the new temples. During the Julio-Claudian period, the local magistrates and imperial officials continued to embellish, restore and build, and until Nero's time (AD 54-68) there was constant activity to raise honorary statues, expand aristocratic homes into true *villae*, and offer inhabitants greater opportunities for entertainment and free time. Gladiator fights were held at the Amphitheater (one of the oldest ones made of stone), races and musical events were performed at the Odeion (a small, covered theater of Greek origin), comedies and dramatic performances were given at the Great Theater, and the youth associations exercised at the Palaestra. In addition to a multitude of shops, workshops and *tabernae* (shops), there were also numerous baths, the favorite meeting place throughout the Roman world. Pompeii's baths included the Stabian Baths (built during the Samnite period and thus the oldest ones); the Forum Baths near the Temple of Fortuna Augusta; the smaller Baths of the Sarnus, set high on the southern end of the hill on which Pompeii was built; and the elegant suburban baths near Porta Marina. The so-called Central Baths were still being built during the last period. This entire setting, common to many other towns in Campania, was severely damaged in AD 62, seventeen years before the tragic eruption. In the spring of that year, a powerful earthquake dealt a terrible blow to Pompeii and the outlying areas, destroying water systems, temples and houses. Seneca's description reflects his dismay, also alluding to the animals that perished in the Lattari mountains. The extraordinary marble reliefs found in the House of Caecilius Jucundus document the effects of the earthquake on some of the monuments in the Forum and on the area near Porta Vesuvio. For the thriving town, which over its long history had faced and brilliantly overcome profound political and cultural changes, this natural disturbance marked the beginning of the end. Recent studies have shown that much of the restoration work still underway on the streets and houses in August, AD 79 was not to repair damage caused by the earthquake of AD 62, but damage caused by more recent earthquakes; these must have occurred repeatedly and regularly toward the end. Many Pompeians had already left the city for good. others had probably taken shelter in their summer homes or farms (for example, the owners of the Houses of the Menander, the Vettii and the Ceii) until the masons and decorators could repair the cracks in the walls of their houses, and the paintings and the mosaics that had split. Still others (Caius Julius Polybius, the *gemmarius* – jeweler – Pinarius Cerialis) had decided to oversee the home restoration work personally and continue their business activities. There was a desire to start anew. The Temple of Isis, redone with its new colors, welcomed its followers; construction work was in full swing at the Central Baths; and the Temple of the Public Lares had been built recently with prized marbles. Even the restoration work in the houses and along the streets pointed to the drive to look toward the future. But for

This 1850 lithograph by F. Federer shows Pompeii viewed from the southeast. The Theater Quarter is visible in the foreground, whereas in the background are Mount Vesuvius and the Gulf of Naples as they appeared to travelers in the mid-19th century.

anyone arriving there, Pompeii had lost the appearance of an active and lively place. Everywhere, one could see errand boys pushing rubble-filled barrows toward the city walls, workers intent on repairing the water lines along the streets, inns with only a few patrons. Then, on August 24th, the terrible end. But not everything was left abandoned forever, as long believed. Recent findings have demonstrated the attempt to start yet again. Several hundred yards from Porta Vesuvio, a complex – whose function has not been determined yet – even revealed human footprints, impressed in the vitric ash left by the last eruptive phase of Mount Vesuvius. Before the dust had even cooled, someone returned to assess the damage and possibility of new building work, bearing tangible and unexpected evidence of life in a landscape swept away by the effects of a deadly fury.

PLAN OF POMPEII

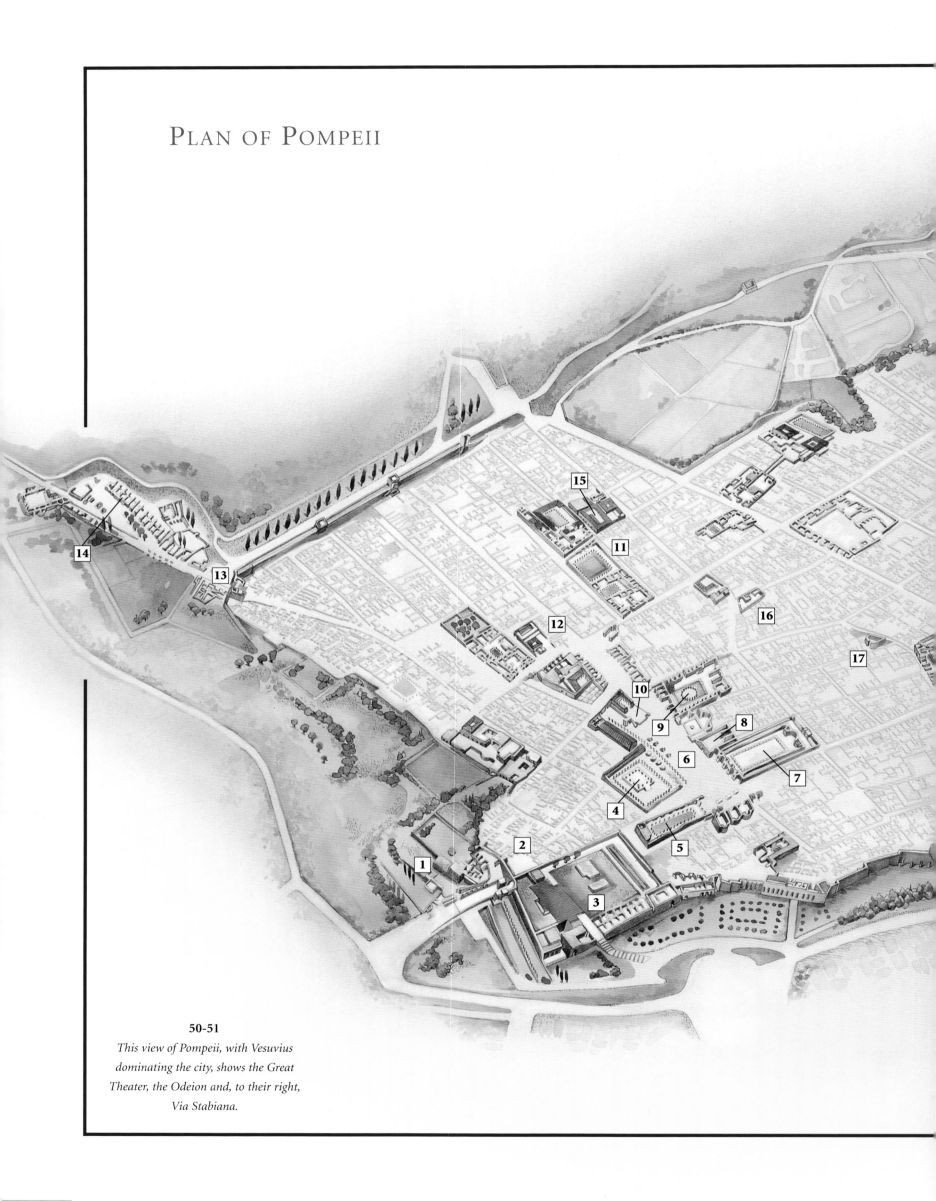

50-51
This view of Pompeii, with Vesuvius dominating the city, shows the Great Theater, the Odeion and, to their right, Via Stabiana.

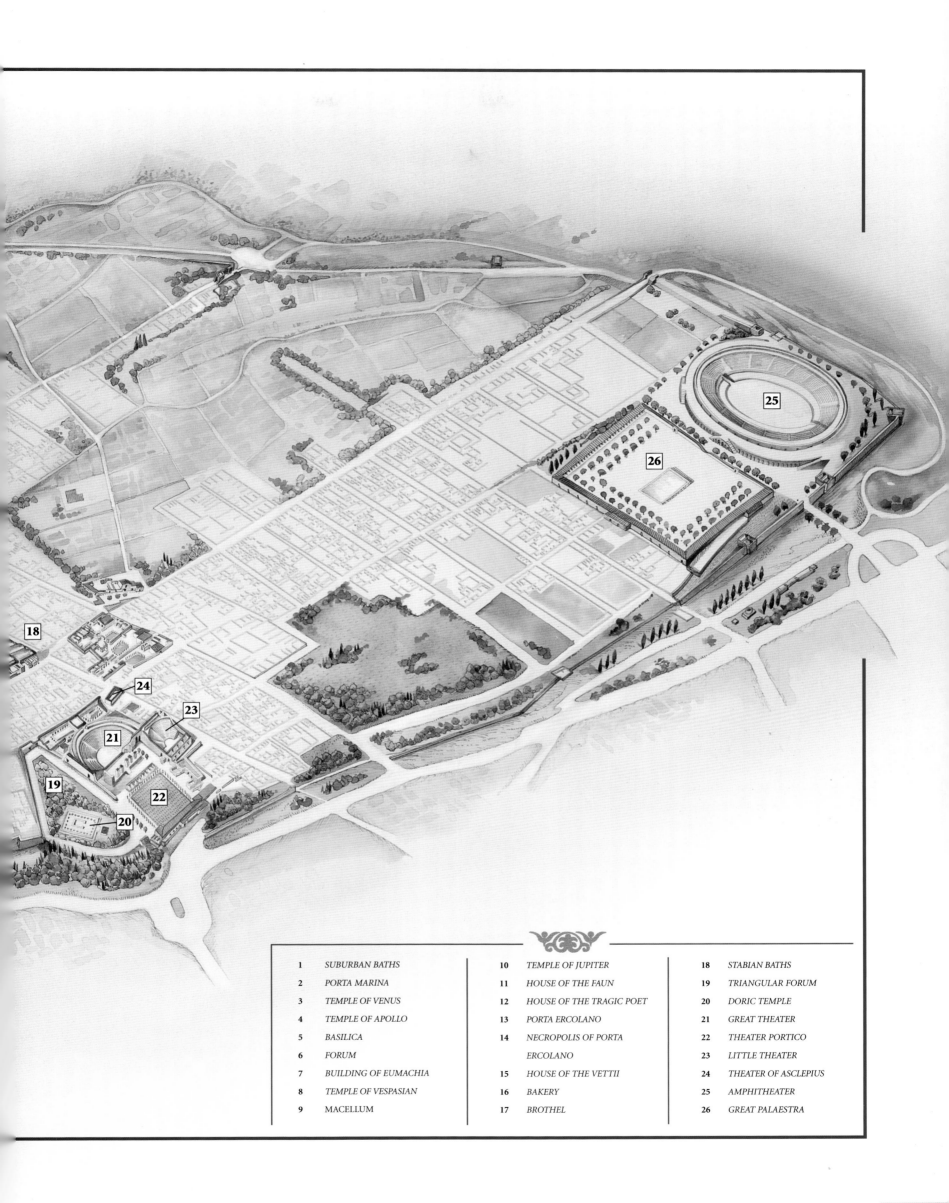

1	SUBURBAN BATHS	10	TEMPLE OF JUPITER	18	STABIAN BATHS
2	PORTA MARINA	11	HOUSE OF THE FAUN	19	TRIANGULAR FORUM
3	TEMPLE OF VENUS	12	HOUSE OF THE TRAGIC POET	20	DORIC TEMPLE
4	TEMPLE OF APOLLO	13	PORTA ERCOLANO	21	GREAT THEATER
5	BASILICA	14	NECROPOLIS OF PORTA	22	THEATER PORTICO
6	FORUM		ERCOLANO	23	LITTLE THEATER
7	BUILDING OF EUMACHIA	15	HOUSE OF THE VETTII	24	THEATER OF ASCLEPIUS
8	TEMPLE OF VESPASIAN	16	BAKERY	25	AMPHITHEATER
9	MACELLUM	17	BROTHEL	26	GREAT PALAESTRA

PUBLIC LIFE

[Elio Lo Cascio]

◆

CURRENT INFORMATION ABOUT POMPEII

In a clever book published in Britain about the emergence of Christianity in the ancient world, there is a description of a trip undertaken by two college students who use a "time machine" to go to Pompeii just before the eruption of Vesuvius in AD 79. This amusing invention, a cross between scientific data and fiction, portrays the reactions of the two young people as they face a broad variety of situations. These included buying hot drinks a *thermopolium*, seeking a slave trader to buy a couple of slaves, visiting the baths, participating in a religious procession, watching a gladiator fight at the amphitheater, and so on. The students' reactions – in the middle of crowded streets, when confronted with fouls smells or noise, and before the erotic paintings at the Suburban Baths – are ambivalent. They are the reactions of anyone who grasps both the extreme diversity and the close resemblance between life in ancient times and our own, with the impression of being in a foreign and "exotic" place that is somehow also quite familiar.

On the other hand, this is indeed the impression conveyed by the virtual reality offered by the innumerable websites devoted to Pompeii, thanks to documentation that is unrivaled with regard to the ancient world. This virtual reality evokes daily life in a city that, in many ways, is typical of the Roman world, illustrating the occupations of its inhabitants and its forms of social interaction. It gets much of its charm from the fact that it offers those living in Western Europe in the early 21st century a normal yet also highly original image.

However, there is an aspect of daily life in Pompeii that seems to reinforce the impression of familiarity: the importance and function of the written word. The thousands of messages that have been preserved on its walls, painted in red and black, were akin to the ad pages in our newspapers and to our billboards – to use a few anachronisms. They were the work of professional writers who would work at night using a ladder and a *lanternarius* (lantern bearer), and they would clean and whitewash the walls before writing a variety of messages over them. Thus, they would publish birth announcements and obituaries, official notices that banned illegal construction work, posters with electoral propaganda, notices about houses for rent and announcements of gladiator shows.

There was a class of painted inscriptions referred to as electoral *programmata* – this writing was found on the walls of Pompeian houses, generally on the busiest streets – and it promoted candidates for municipal offices. These inscriptions offer us unique insights into the most important characteristics of the political and administrative autonomy of a community like Pompeii: a medium-sized town not too far from Rome (the center of power), geographically or otherwise, nor so marginal that it did not feel Rome's decisive influence in many ways. Through these words, which sometimes listed the candidate's name as well as those who supported his candidacy, we get not only vivid testimony of how an electoral campaign must have taken place, but we can also understand the elements underlying the organization of consensus. Furthermore, we can determine just how free people were to choose from alternative candidates.

GOVERNMENT BODIES
AND ADMINISTRATIVE ACTIVITIES

As in every other Roman city, the constitution of Pompeii called for three bodies: the popular Assembly, the magistrates and the Council (*Ordo decurionum*). The first one included all adult male citizens, divided into a certain number of voting units – generally defined as *curiae* or *tribus* – which probably corresponded to the territorial districts in which the city and the rural territory was divided. However, it was not named for Pompeii, and it is thought that the city involved *vici*, or quarters. In these circumstances, the individual's vote was indirect: it merely helped determine the majority within each unit, which would then express a single preference. Every year, the Assembly had the sole task of electing the magistrates from a list of candidates, who had to meet specific requirements in terms of age and wealth, and could not be ineligible as a result of court verdicts or professions considered shameful. The magistracy offices in each Roman city varied in number and were temporary. Most of them were collective. Like the ones in Rome, they also envisaged separate areas of responsibility as well as a hierarchy among them. Once Pompeii became a colony, there were four annually elected magistrates, divided into two pairs: the *Duoviri iure dicundo* and the *Duoviri aediles*. The first two, the top-level magistrates, were responsible for exercising jurisdiction within the municipality, and their name derives from this distinctive function. However, they also had to convene and preside over the Assembly and the Council and, in general, handle the city administration and public finances, given that there appears to have been no specific magistracy such as the quaestorship. The second pair of magistrates was responsible for maintaining roads, public buildings and temples, supervising markets and organizing the *ludi* (shows and public games), and their responsibilities were thus similar to those of the *aediles* in Rome. In order to be a candidate for the magistracy of the duumvirate *iure dicundo* one generally had to have held the office of *aedile* first. In addition, it was possible to be re-elected to office several times, and there are documented cases in Pompeii of people who held the office of duumvir many times.

Every five years, the *Quinquennales* were elected in place of the ordinary *Duoviri iure dicundo*, and they were drawn from among those who had already held the latter office at least once. They had the same responsibilities as the censors in Rome: they carried out the *census*. In other words, they documented the citizens and their assets and then revised the list of *decuriones*, the members of the *Ordo* or civic council composed of a fixed number of members (in many communities, it was as large as 100). The *quinquennales* did this in order to remove the names of those who no longer met the requirements for inclusion in the list and to add the names of new participants. The admission of those who had held a magistracy over the five-year period was virtually automatic, but often this was not enough to fill the openings that arose as a result of the high mortality rate of the era. Consequently, it became necessary to appoint other people who had the right requisites, even if they had not held a magistracy yet. Due also to the fact that it was essentially a permanent body, the *Ordo decurionum* represented the effective power of the city, not only with regard to its internal administration but also for external relations, particularly with Rome. In fact, aside from ensuring the continuity of the municipal financial policies, it also guaranteed a link with the center of power through the appointment of patrons chosen from the local elite and from the capital city itself. We have little information about the ruling classes and the political management of Pompeii during the Samnite period, although we can assume that there were institutions calling for an assembly, magistrates with various responsibilities and a council. It seems certain that its transformation into a Roman city following the Social War, and above all the arrival of a large number of new settlers (several thousand adult males) when Sulla installed a colony there, must have caused enormous social upheaval. The so-called "deduction" in an inhabited area like Pompeii involved the confiscation of land for distribution to veterans and new subdivisions of the voting districts following the dramatic increase in population. A passage from one of Cicero's orations appears to confirm that during the colony's early years, there was conflict between the old residents and the new colonists, also between both sides with regard to the enjoyment of political rights. For a certain period, the old Pompeians apparently felt their rights to elect magistrates had been limited. At the same time, the old ruling class of the Samnites was eclipsed. Nevertheless, the period in question was indubitably quite short: the most important families quickly regained their preeminent position alongside the new elite of Sulla's colonists. By the middle of the 1st century BC, the old and new aristocracies had merged completely.

ELECTIONS AND PROPAGANDA

Thanks to documentation that is far more extensive and, in many ways, more informative than what has come from other Italic cities, we can study the mechanisms of consensus and popular participation in the political life of the community. We can also examine if and to what extent there was any true social changeover.

For this kind of analysis, we must use the *programmata* (posters for voters), of which about 2600 have been interpreted so far. Of these, 124 (the *programmata antiquissima*) refer to the early period of the colony and the remainder (the *programmata recentiora*) are from the city's final period. Most of the latter, probably about 90 percent are from the city's last decade, while most of the remaining 10 percent date from the period following the earthquake of AD 62 These more recent writings were painted against a white background, fully or partially covering the previous ones. As a result, it is often possible to read the less recent words that had been covered over. The *programmata* followed a stereotyped formula. They stated the name of the candidate (or candidates, as joint candidacies were quite common) and the office sought; a general presentation of the reasons to vote for the candidate(s), usually personal merits, professional capacities or moral integrity (which meant that honest administration could be expected), but there was no indication of what we would define as a "political platform"; and lastly, the formulaic invitation to vote for the candidate, *oro vos faciatis* ("I ask you to elect him"). In a little over 20 percent of the *programmata recentiora*, there is also mention of the *rogatores*, or those who promoted the candidacy. Most of the *rogatores* were individuals, who were indicated using the full or partial onomastic (name) form. Over a hundred *programmata* instead list the *rogatores* as a wide variety of groups of people and in some cases, modern scholars have rightly questioned just how serious their plea really was (some have theorized nothing short of counterpropaganda!). There were the *vicini*, in all likelihood the neighbors, various professional groups (such as the *fullones* or launderers-dyers, the *muliones* or mule drivers, the *aurifices* or goldsmiths), various types of groups such as *clientes, coloni, incolae, discentes, liberti*, as well as *Isiaci* (those devoted to the cult of Isis), *Paridiani*, the fans of the actor or mime Paris, and the *seribibi*, those who stayed out late drinking. But there were also *furunculi* (petty thieves), *pauperes* (poor), *populus, spectaculi spectantes* – almost certainly those who attended shows at the amphitheater – and the *pilicrepi*, ballplayers, not to mention the *Campanienses, Forenses, Salinienses* and *Urbulanenses*, who were probably the residents of the various districts.

The extensive and singular information gleaned from the *programmata* has obviously paved the way for a broad range of studies on the nature of the electoral campaigns. It has recently been posited that since the number of candidates in the elections for the duumvirate was always equivalent to the posts to be filled, there was no real competition involved, or that the elections may have been the outcome of a complex game of putting pressure on people. Popular consensus would thus have been channeled and guided within the individual voting districts of Pompeii by the district associations tied to the cult of the Lares of the crossroads and, later, to the imperial cult, and by their management bodies (*magistri* and *ministri*, very close to the most eminent families since they were their freedmen or slaves). Moreover, the *Ordo* chose the candidates to vote for in the case of the duumvirate, as there were only two candidates a year for two positions. However, the choice was strongly conditioned by the Council also for the candidates for the office of *aedile*. The conclusion, once again, is that a limited number of the elite held the reins of pow-er in Pompeii. As some have noted, what was determined by the elections would thus have been "support from the few," or backing by the members of a ruling class that was composed of a small number of families and was essentially stable in its composition. Several other scholars have purported that the evidence of the *programmata* would exclude any true popular participation in electioneering, given that it was directed by the individual candidates and by their supporters.

As the record confirms that the proportion of magistrates from new families was always rather high, we can therefore deduce that there was great social mobility (accompanied by geographic mobility, if it is true that new immigrants from other communities in central and southern Italy also joined the ranks of the elite). Nonetheless, we can also observe that only a few families seem to be cited in almost all stages of Pompeii's history. These families must effectively have represented the highest level of the *Ordo* and the one that, through patronage relations, exerted control over the entry of new families to the Council, although there was some leeway for outsiders. While the candidates themselves organized the electoral campaigns, this does not mean that there was no effective popular participation in the political and administrative life of the city. Not only were the elections themselves free, but based on an analytical study of the *programmata* mentioning the individual and group *rogatores*, at least these *programmata* could not have been the product of the "electoral committees" of the individual candidates but were a means by which the voters themselves, individually or as a group, could be drawn into what we can aptly define as "electoral fever" in Pompeii. This fervor was justified by the fact that the elections were indeed authentic and competitive, and the electoral campaigns focused on galvanizing popular consent: if this were not the case, we would be forced to consider the *programmata* an enormous farce and a mere ritual.

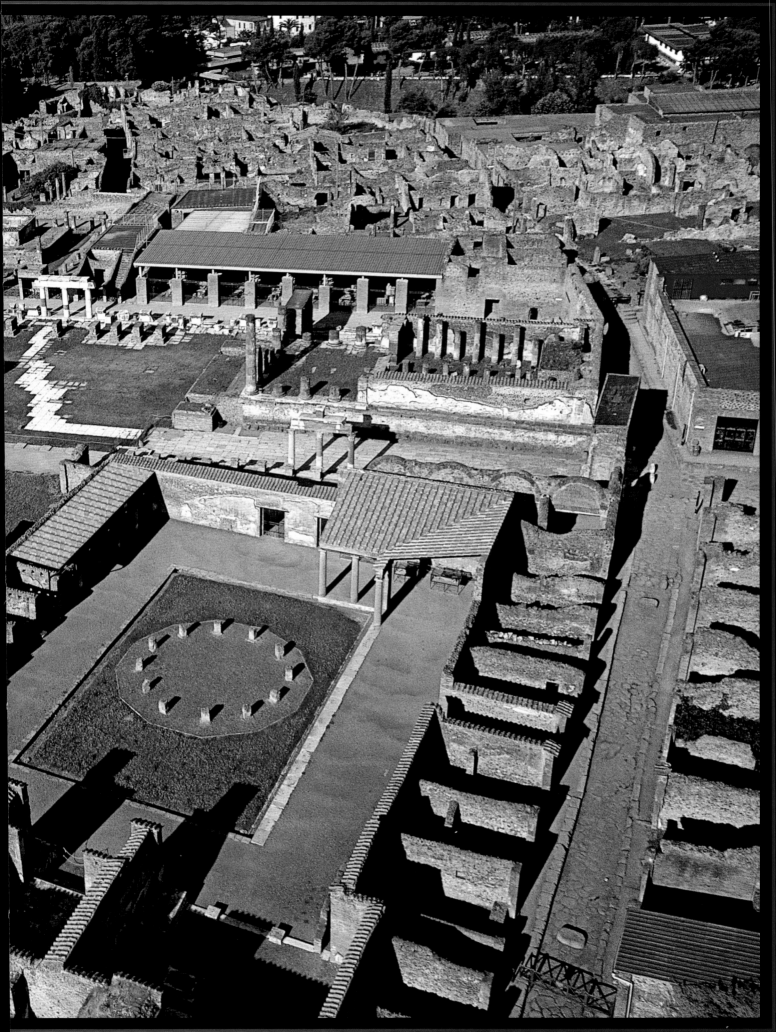

POLITICAL AND
ADMINISTRATIVE VENUES

Public life as we have described it here took place essentially in the center of town, at the Forum and in some of the buildings around it. Voting took place at the *Comitium*: to vote, the electorate would presumably enter through the five doors opening onto the Forum Square and would exit through the five doors leading to Via dell'Abbondanza. Justice was administered in the roofed building of the Basilica, at one end of the Forum across from the *Comitium*. However, private parties also conducted major commercial and financial transactions there. This type of building, which would later become the model for Christian churches, was thus used in the Roman world for civil functions. The large central area was surrounded by a colonnade and this was where business meetings were held, while the area where justice was administered was at the end of the room. This was the magistrate's *tribunal*, a *podium* that was probably accessed using mobile wooden structures, perhaps to isolate the magistrate and guarantee his safety in the event of overly heated trials. The three buildings on the short end of the Forum Square, between the Basilica and the *Comitium* (which were reconstructed following the earthquake) have traditionally been identified as the colony's administrative buildings. In effect, they were simple rooms, two of which may merely have been the receiving areas for the city magistrates. According to a fitting interpretation, the central building must have been the *Curia*, or the place where Pompeii's decuriones met, while the other two were the headquarters of the duumviri and of the aediles, respectively. According to other scholars, the central building instead housed the *Tabularium*, the city archives, and the *Curia* was in the west building, which is larger. Another building that, based on recently theories, is thought to have been connected with political activities is the Small Theater or *Odeion*, also referred to as the *Theatrum tectum* in the twin inscriptions citing its construction. It was a roofed building that could hold 1500-2000 people. The Small Theater was built in the colony's early years by the Duumviri C. Quintus Valgus and M. Porcius, two leading members of the new ruling class, both of whom were closely connected with Sulla. A short time later, these two men, this time as Duumviri *quinquennales*, also oversaw the construction of the Amphitheater, in part at their own expense. Given its proximity to the Great Theater, the *Theatrum tectum* has traditionally been acknowledged as the building used for recitation and musical performances, as the fact that it had a roof would have ensured better acoustics. Moreover, the association of the two buildings in Pompeii was apparently planned as early as the 2nd century BC, based on a comprehensive city-planning project similar to the one that can be observed in nearby *Neapolis* (Naples). More recently, however, the very opposite has been suggested: that the *Theatrum tectum* was built much later than the theater and that in a new stage in the history of the city, it was used – at least initially – as the *Ekklesiasterion*, the place used for city meetings, as was done with theaters in several Greek cities. Ultimately, the new building must have had several different functions, and its construction was probably motivated by the need felt by the new Sullan colonists to create their own space, not only to meet but also to watch their own *ludi scaenici* (theatrical shows), intended for a new community of Pompeian citizens who spoke Latin and not the Oscan language.

61

This painting from the Praedia *of Julia Felix portrays a scene of life at the Forum. Three equestrian statues stand out in the background of the porticoes (Naples,* MAN).

62 and 62-63

Built in about 120 BC, the Basilica was located in the southwestern part of the Forum area. The oldest and most important public building in Pompeii was a rectangular construction with interior colonnades along the perimeter walls. It was initially covered by a ceiling with a single trussed vault, which probably collapsed following the earthquake of AD 62.

64-65

This aerial view of the Large Theater and the Small Theater, which have the same Hellenistic architectural layout, clearly shows each cavea – the tiered seating for the audience – divided into several sectors by staircases radiating outward.

65 right

Brawny tufa telamons seem to support the outside walls of the cavea of the Small Theater by the sheer strength of their arms.

THE BATHS AND THEIR FUNCTIONS

The baths were an area in Roman cities – including Pompeii – that played a fundamental role as a place for people to socialize. The baths that characterized the Roman way of life, from one end of the Mediterranean to the other, are well known – in their progressively more complex structures and their increasingly varied functions – not only through a wealth of archaeological documentation, but also from the numerous references of the ancient authors. These range from the architect Vitruvius to Celsus and Galen, who wrote texts on medicine, Petronius, Seneca, Pliny the Elder, Pliny the Younger, Martial and Juvenal.

The custom of the baths and the areas reserved for them indubitably originated in ancient Greece. However, the habit of bathing in public and of public baths, as well as their association with the palaestra and exercise, became an exquisitely Roman element, without any significant parallels in the ancient world and few counterparts in other civilizations (the hamman, the "Turkish bath" of the Islamic world, is derived from the Roman *balnea*). This was a practice that fulfilled very different functions with respect to public baths such as the ones in Victorian England, which were created to guarantee personal hygiene to the lower ranks and the working classes. We must note, in fact, that all social groups used the baths and that the different areas were used in an egalitarian way: admission to the bath buildings cost very little, and in many cases it was completely free. The baths and the practice of pub-

lic bathing is another significant aspect of the Roman civilization, and our own ambivalent reaction toward this has been noted even in recent times. The Romans' obsession with cleanliness and hygiene has been defined as familiar and "comforting" (and it is no accident that medical concepts contributed to the rising popularity of spas), yet at the same time it has been claimed that the way these objectives were achieved is foreign to us, making the Roman world "Oriental and decadent."

However, the baths were far more than an area set aside for bathing: the Romans would spend many hours a day there, because it was also a place that offered the opportunity to socialize and relax. We could draw a parallel between the baths and modern shopping centers, as both are designed for a specific use yet people go there to enjoy social activities and entertainment. As a result, over the years these facilities ultimately focused on sectors that were not immediately related to bathing, as we can see even more readily in Rome's large imperial complexes. Gyms and swimming pools (*natationes*) began to be added for exercise, followed by porticos and gardens, nymphaeums, resting areas, music auditoriums and libraries.

As a rule, in the baths the rooms were laid out on a longitudinal axis and their layout corresponded to the different stages of the bathing "ritual." This ritual initially called for different rooms for men and women (this was the case in Pompeii), but later there were common rooms for all (some have theorized that there were dif-

Decorative stucco coffering decorated the vault of the men's apodyterium
at the Stabian Baths.

ferent hours for men and women). It generally included the hot and cold bath, the *assa sudatio* (the dry bath, which we now refer to as a sauna), the *destrictio* (scraping the body with the strigil to remove sweat and dust), the *unctio* (an oil rub). As one entered the baths, the first room was the *apodyterium* (waiting and dressing room), which had marble or bronze benches and shelves to hold clothing. This was followed by the *frigidarium*, with a pool or tub of cold water in the same room or in a roofless room next to it. This was followed by the *tepidarium*, the room used as a transition to the hotter rooms to avoid too much of a temperature swing, and next to this was the *laconicum*, the room for a bath of hot, dry air. The last rooms were the *caldarium*, with the *alveus* or tub of hot water, and the *labrum*, a basin of cold water to help bathers withstand the overheated rooms longer.

The bath buildings, including those in Pompeii, point to remarkable progress in heating techniques. The *hypocaustum* was an innovation that was supposedly introduced by an entrepreneur who worked in the Phlegrean area and was then used extensively at the bath facilities. The system used hollow flooring, made by setting the floor of the room to be heated on *suspensurae*, small brick pillars, among which the hot air flowed. This hollow space in the floor was coupled with one in the walls, thereby avoiding the need for braziers, as the hot air was formed by heating water in a nearby room, the *praefurnium*. This system could generate temperatures of up to 140°F.

The Stabian Baths were the Pompeii's oldest and their facilities, built in the 4th century, included a gymnasium. With the arrival of the Sullan colonists, a room was added for the *sudatio* and following the earthquake in AD 62 renovation work was done to ensure its accessibility. We can still see the polychrome stucco decorations of the vaults, the round *frigidarium* and the *caldarium* with an apse. The Forum Baths, which were the most centrally located ones, fully developed the "sequence layout" that was probably already in use at the private facilities of the villas in the Phlegrean area. The devices used in the men's area to avoid even minimum discomfort are striking. In the round *frigidarium* with a cupola roof, the tub has steps for gradual immersion or sitting. In the *caldarium*, which also had heated walls, the duct over the vault would trap the water from condensed steam to prevent the annoying drip of cold water on the heated bodies.

It seems that after the Forum Baths were completed, the Suburban Baths were built next to the city walls, just outside Porta Marina. They may also have been intended for occasional users, such as travelers and seamen, and featured rich pictorial decoration with amphitheatrical and erotic subjects, panoramic rooms and an elaborate heating system. But Pompeii's largest facilities, the Central Baths, were never inaugurated: ornamental and structural work was still being done when Vesuvius erupted.

68 and 69

The Stabian Baths, built in the 2nd century BC, were so called because they were located near the road to Stabiae. The complex was laid out with two separate sectors, male and female. In these pictures, we can see the same type of room, the apodyterium, *but in the two different versions, one for men (left) and one for women (right).*

70

The ornamental detailing in this pictures shows the decoration in the men's
apodyterium *at the Stabian Baths. The vault features curved stucco festoons*
that end at the coffers in which various subjects – often women – are
portrayed.

71 top

Terracotta telamons symbolically sustain the large vault of the men's
tepidarium, *decorated with polychrome stuccowork, at the Forum Baths.*

71 bottom

The men's caldarium *at the Forum Baths was covered by a vault decorated*
with stuccowork. The part of the room facing south ended with an apsidal
niche, in the middle of which was a marble fountain whose function was
to cool the room with its jets of water.

72-73
The entrance at the peristyle of the Suburban Baths was built during the early Imperial Age. In contrast to the city's other baths, at this complex the male and female sectors were not separate.

73 top
As documented by this photograph of the windowed apse of the caldarium, the intent of architecture of the Suburban Baths was to unite the constructed areas with their natural surroundings, via openings to the outside.

73 bottom
The originality of the frescoes is one of the striking features of the apodyterium of the Suburban Baths. The figures that are depicted – often erotic ones – reveal all the vitality and sensuality of Pompeian culture even today.

THE SAMNITE PALAESTRA, THE QUADRIPORTICUS AND THE GREAT PALAESTRA

The baths were not the only places where people exercised: there were also gyms and pools in separate areas. In Pompeii, the oldest area of this kind was the Samnite Palaestra, located north of the Theater between the Temple of Isis and the Triangular Forum. Based on the Oscan inscription citing the patron who donated money to build it, it can be dated to the second half of the 2nd century BC. It was composed of a columned courtyard with a pedestal in the center bearing a statue of the god who protected the palaestra. The statue was crowned by the winners of competitions (although the actual competitions probably did not take place here, given the small size of the palaestra). Another area that may also have been associated with physical activity is the Quadriporticus, dating from the end of the 2nd or the beginning of the 1st century BC, built behind the Great Theater. Given the indications gleaned from the dedicatory inscription, some scholars believe that the Samnite Palaestra hosted the Pompeian *vereia*, a military association for young people that was also found in other Samnite cities. However, it has also been thought that it was a Gymnasium in the Greek tradition, reserved for younger boys. Thus the Quadriporticus would not only have been used as a foyer for the theater – where the audience would mill about during show intervals – but it would also have been used for older boys (the Quadriporticus was later transformed into the Gladiator Barracks). The Great Palaestra was added during the Augustan period, and it was built in a clear area near the Amphitheater. It was an enormous complex surrounded by colonnades on three sides, with the *natatio* in the middle. The *natatio* was about 112 x 72 feet in size, more or less like a modern-day swimming pool, and like the modern kind, it sloped from a depth of 3 feet to 8.5 feet. The construction of the Great Palaestra should be viewed in connection with the imperial promotion of youth associations that could act as vehicle of consensus for the new regime.

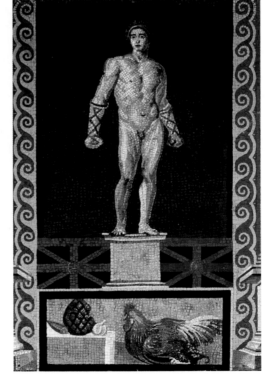

74-75

*The Large Palaestra, built in the Augustan Age, featured a rectangular plan
(463 x 351 feet). It had colonnades on three sides and was surrounded
by rows of plane trees. There was a large pool in the middle.*

75 bottom
*This mosaic, made of vitreous paste, depicts a boxer in an athletic pose.
Pictured at the bottom of the portrait, together with a pinecone and fruit,
is a rooster with its legs bound (Naples, MAN).*

THE THEATERS AND THE AMPHITHEATER

When it came to socializing and entertainment, Pompeians also had a variety of different places available for shows (*ludi*). To understand the role of shows staged in the Roman world – the Circus, the Theater, the Amphitheater – and their evolution over the years, we must always consider their close link with religion and cult. Although this link gradually weakened, it never fully disappeared. For example, this tie can be seen in the calendar set for the various types of *ludi* and in the fact that the first theater representations in Rome took place in the temples, as well as the close association between theaters and sacred buildings. Nevertheless, the cities of Campania in general – and Pompeii in particular – are also remarkable in that they built stone theaters and amphitheaters far earlier than Rome did (where the first ones were built respectively in 55 and 29 BC), owing to the influence of Magna Graecia and of Greece itself. The Great Theater of Pompeii was built at the time the layout of the Triangular Forum and the Forum was redone (2nd century BC) and it reflects the structure and appearance of a Greek theater. Part of it is set on the slope of the hill on the west side, and part was built on the terracing on the side of Via Stabiana, with the horseshoe-shaped cavea typical of Greek theaters. During this initial phase, the building could hold 5000 people. Following the first renovation of the *scaena* (theater) shortly after Pompeii became a colony, the building was restructured, enlarged and transformed during the Augustan period at the expense of two members of what was probably the richest and most influential family of the era, the Olconii brothers, who were duumviri during the same year. The goal of the project was also to enlarge the theater's seating capacity by adding more steps in the *summa cavea*. *Tribunalia* (galleries) were built on the *parodoi*, the covered passageways on the two sides of the *cavea* (seating area), to offer a direct view of the stage. These galleries were reserved for those who were staging the show and for guests of honor. Additional work was done following the earthquake. The *ludi scaenici*, the shows that were held in the theaters, were mainly tragedies and comedies. The two implied different stage props, as Vitruvius described, and the paintings in the Pompeian houses offer significant information about this aspect. The genres were also distinguished by the different masks the actors wore on stage. The tragedies and comedies that were staged were modeled after classic Greek tragedy and the New Comedy. However, they were not used directly by Latin actors-playwrights, who relied on the "scripts" of Greek-era actors (staging only a few parts of the originals) and the anthologies of texts used in the schools. *Contaminatio* was another distinctive feature of Roman theater. This involved drafting a script using different original Greek texts, and this practice can be explained by the need to adapt the repertory to the size and characteristics of the "theatrical company" that was available. Naturally, there were also other genres that were destined to become much more popular, such as the *Atellana*, essentially a popular farce with typical characters akin to those of the *Commedia dell'Arte*, the mime staging realistic plots with dialogues full of double entendres, and the pantomime, in which the plots taken from mythology would be staged strictly with gestures and musical accompaniment. The different genres implied shows that often combined dancing, acting and singing, with an important role reserved for music. These events would be staged by full-fledged all-male companies with a head comedian (*dominus gregis*), and the actors would also interpret the female roles. As popular as actors may have been, however, they did not enjoy a good reputation and were low on the social scale.

77

The bas-relief panel with theater masks, from the House of the Golden Cupids, gives us an idea of the exaggerated realism of the theater masks of the era (Naples, MAN).

78-79

*This mosaic by Dioskourides of Samos, from what is commonly referred to as the
Villa of Cicero, portrays a group of street musicians (Naples, MAN).*

80 center

*The brawl between the Pompeians and the Nucerians, recounted by Tacitus, is depicted
in this fresco from a Pompeian house (Naples, MAN).*

80-81

*This aerial view, with Mount Vesuvius standing out in the background, reveals the
amphitheater's full grandeur.*

The gladiators were even more popular, as demonstrated by the numbers of graffiti written by their fans, particularly women, who apparently appreciated their sexual prowess. Nonetheless, they were below actors in the social hierarchy, due to the fact that they were usually slaves or freedmen and only rarely freeborn citizens. Their shows were staged at the Amphitheater, which was built in the early years of the Sullan colony. The Amphitheater could probably seat about 20,000 people (according to an interesting theory, it marked the conciliation and amalgamation of the two populations). It is the oldest example of this type of building, created before the specific denomination even existed, as an "area for spectators around the arena." It was

built in the southeast part of the city next to the walls, in an area without any houses. Its location away from the center of Pompeii made it easily accessible for spectators arriving from nearby towns. The shows held at the Amphitheater were known as *munera* ("gifts"), since the magistrates offered them to the people. (It is noteworthy that not only did the city magistrates receive no recompense for their term of office, but they were even required to pay part if not all the expenses for the games they offered out of their own pockets.) These shows were mainly gladiator fights, which originated in connection with funerals as a replacement for the original custom of human sacrifice, and they became quite popular, particularly in Campania. The battles envisaged various roles, with the corresponding offensive weapons and forms of protection. At the same time, *venationes* – the "hunts" of wild animals – were held, and these were also extremely popular.

Unique evidence of the shows held at Pompeii's Amphitheater come from the *edicta munerum*, the painted announcements (about 75 have been preserved) of the shows on schedule. These announcements resembled modern-day theater playbills. They followed a standard form even in their graphic presentation: first came the name of the *editor muneris* (the person organizing and "producing" the games) in big letters, followed by the term *gladiatorium paria* (the pairs of gladiators) who would be playing, generally twenty. The announcement would also list the place and date, as well as an indication if the *venatio* would take place, or the presence of the *vela*, i.e. the cloth covering for the amphitheater to provide shade.

The gladiator fights stirred great enthusiasm among the spectators, who would express themselves in forms quite similar to our own cheering for modern football teams or other sports. And like today, this zeal could also lead to scuffles and riots.

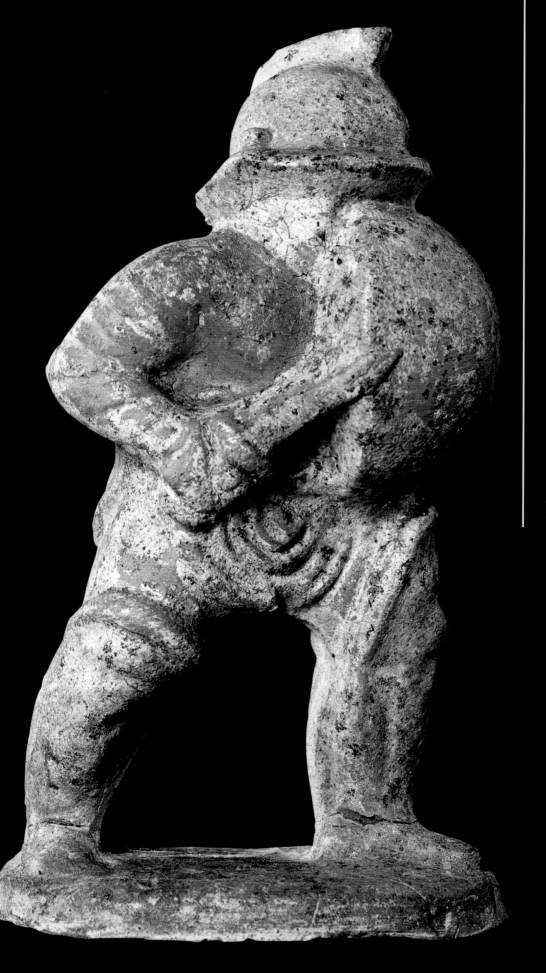

Information about one riot comes from the historian Tacitus (ca. AD 56 - ca. 120), coupled with the fresco in a Pompeian house portraying a bird's-eye view of the scene and a graffito whose interpretation is controversial. Tacitus wrote that in AD 59, a brawl broke out for trivial reasons between the Pompeians and the Nucerians who had come to watch the gladiator games organized by Livineius Regulus, one of Rome's elite. The uproar ended tragically: there were many dead and wounded among the Nucerians, who bore the brunt of it. The Roman Senate, which was responsible for passing judgment, punished the Pompeians by banning this type of assemblage for ten years (equivalent to banning *munera* at the Amphitheater) and dissolving the *collegia*, the associations the Pompeians had illegally established. It then exiled Livineius Regulus and the others held responsible for provoking the turmoil. There has been extensive discussion as to whether there may have been far more serious motivations behind a local competition that degenerated to end in

Following a long hiatus that started in about the third decade of the 5th century BC, by the mid-2nd century BC the cult of Apollo once again played a significant role. It was during this period that the old wooden temple was torn down and replaced with a masonry one on a high *podium*, set in a porticoed enclosure. If we attribute the terracotta slabs reused in the garden of the House of the Golden Bracelet to this context, then the god worshipped in this period reflects other points of reference linked with Delos. The slabs are two architectural elements, one decorated with a vine with insects and other animals, and the other composed of a series of quadrangular panels. Here, the procession of deities, almost all of whom are headless – Artemis, Nike and Apollo can be distinguished – suggests that the slab was originally a frieze from the city temple. It is important to note that one of the slabs has been interpreted as a likely reference to the punishment of Marsyas, a Silenus who challenged Apollo to a musical contest and was condemned by the god to be flayed.

The theme identifies a new connotation of the cult of Apollo, suggesting ties to Delos, which also happened to be the hub of Mediterranean trade and of the activities of the Italic *negotiatores* (traders), whose ranks almost certainly included members of Pompeii's elite. This was the period of the richest temple furnishings, as demonstrated by the two bronze statues of Apollo and Diana, which fortunately escaped the pillaging of the public buildings.

By the time the city became a Roman colony, the temple was no longer the focal point of the city's religious life, which now revolved around the cult of the Capitoline gods. Work on the temple was thus limited to the construction of an altar by several magistrates, including Marcus Porcius, a *deductor* of the Sullan colony. This deed acknowledges the importance of the cult and, at the same time, it also reflects the appropriation of the ancient rites practiced in the god's honor. The existence – documented by an inscription – of *Ludi Apollinares*, celebrated with great pageantry at the Forum with gladiator shows and stagings, and the fact that the temple was isolated from the nearby houses by building a sundial, also demonstrate the important role the cult continued to play during the early Imperial Age. This focus may well have arisen due to the importance that Augustus attributed to this god following his victory over Antony and Cleopatra.

Evidence from the Neronian period is more substantial. It was during this period that the entire decoration of the portico was redone, transforming the Ionian columns into Corinthian ones painted red, yellow and blue. The old frieze was also replaced by a new one, with a procession of griffins – animals sacred to Apollo – holding laurel festoons. The god's connection with music is also one of the reasons behind the decision to update the antiquated architectural decoration, but this time the stimulus can be attributed to Nero's fanciful artistic aspirations.

88

A segment of the Ionic portico that surrounded the Temple of Apollo is preserved at the southeast corner of the ruins, behind the copy of the statue of the archer god.

88-89

The oblong opening of the civic Forum, on the right, extended east of the Basilica, whose ruins can be recognized in the colonnade to the lower left, next to the remains of the Temple of Apollo, in the center.

THE DORIC TEMPLE

A building was constructed near the southern edge of the city walls on a terrace known as the Triangular Forum. This building, whose archaic remains can still be seen, was erected when the sanctuary to Apollo was built. It was a peripteral (having a single row of columns on all sides) temple in the Doric style, with seven columns along the front and eleven on the long sides. Its visual impact, across from the edifice on a wooden platform, based on our reconstruction of the Temple of Apollo, points to a completely different concept of monumentality. Above all, however, it recalls other models. The closest references are the temples of Poseidonia (later known as Paestum), albeit with several changes. First of all, there is the odd number of columns, in addition to other aspects of the architectural decoration that have recently been noted. However, "Greek-style" temples were also known in Latium by this time. The evocative power of a temple built in the Greek style was meant to underscore the fact that local politics were open toward the "outside world" in close geographic proximity of the area, thus guaranteeing the city's economic and cultural vitality. Therefore, it was also essential to define which deities reigned over the complex. The idea that it was dedicated to more than one deity is suggested by the fact that in the cella (shrine room), the base of one of the cult statues is shifted with respect to the central axis, thus envisaging the presence of another one. Since we are talking about the Samnite period, the two deities can easily be identified, as a series of antefixes with the heads of Minerva and Hercules, and an inscription citing a temple of Minerva, leave no doubts as to the divine pair. For the older phases as well, however, clues about the association of the two cults abound in Rome, Latium and Pompeii itself, where a small votive bronze portraying Hercules was found in an area that rested on the Doric Temple during the archaic era.

This dual cult can be linked solidly with the local history. The role of Minerva as the divine protectress of navigation is proven by the sanctuary to the goddess at Punta della Campanella, with a lighthouse that was probably built in the 4th century BC to guide sailors in their perilous navigation of the inlets of Capri. This arm of land also marked the border between the Greek area of the Bay of Naples and the Etruscan one of the Bay of Salerno. Hercules was also a common figure in Pompeii. Not by chance, he was linked to the salt-pans cited by Columella and thus played a role similar to the one at the Foro Boario – or Cattle Market – in Rome and in places of worship along transhumance routes, in close connection with the trade and preservation of meat. Pompeii was one of Hercules' stops during his travels in Campania (he was traditionally claimed as the founder of Herculaneum), and the word "Pompeii" may also have derived from Hercules' journey.

This meaning of the cult was the reason for its decline in the Roman era, when – as we will see – another sanctuary supplanted the one of Minerva as the deity connected to navigation. Consequently, given the lack of any political or ideological motivation, no renovation work was done on the Doric Temple during the Roman era to modernize its appearance, as can instead be noted at the Temple of Apollo.

A decoration of leaves frames the beardless face of Hercules in one of the antefixes from the Doric Temple; these elements were alternated with other antefixes portraying Minerva (Naples, MAN).

THE CULTS OF THE COLONY

T he new political situation created by the Roman colonization in 80 BC was immediately reflected on a religious level. Alongside the civil institutions of the Roman state, the colonies were also required to worship the Capitoline Triad (Jupiter, Juno and Minerva), which represented the state religion. The temple on the north side of the Forum was devoted to the Capitoline Triad. The temple, which had probably already been dedicated to Jupiter during the last half of the 2nd century BC, was a decisive factor in the layout of the square. The changes implemented on the cella made it possible to install statues of the three gods that, as also documented by similar groups elsewhere, were acroliths (i.e., statues made on a wooden structure, either gilded or covered with real or metal drapery, with the bare parts of the body made of stone). Only the bust of Jupiter and the head of Juno remain. The temple was extended along the front with a terrace incorporating the new altar, for reasons that have also been linked to the new electoral procedures that were conducted in the Forum and culminated at the *Capitolium*.

92

The goddess Juno, generally associated with the protection of women, was part of the Capitoline Triad venerated at the Temple of Jupiter, overlooking the Forum (Naples, MAN).

93

Jupiter, lord of the heavens and of light, is portrayed with stern features in this marble work. This statue and the one of Juno are from the temple dedicated to the god and located on the north side of the Forum (Naples, MAN).

94 and 94-95

The Temple of Jupiter, viewed respectively from the south and east in these two photographs, was preceded by a hexastyle portico, whereas eight columns rose along the sides of the cella, which held the statues of the Capitoline Triad.

96 and 97

These two terracotta statues portraying Jupiter and Juno were found in the small Temple of Jupiter Meilichios, at the south corner of the Triangular Forum. The presence of a bust of Minerva in the same place suggests that the building temporarily housed the cult of the Capitoline Triad, in the Forum (Naples, MAN).

Another cult is closely connected with this historic period and with the "personal" rapport established between the holders of Roman power and some of the gods. As a result of the close tie between Venus and the dictator Sulla, not only was the colony given the title *Colonia Cornelia Veneria Pompeianorum*, but in order to endorse the central role of the cult of this goddess, a new sanctuary was built on the southwest edge of the city. The cult was not a new one by any means, but it represented the Roman interpretation of the Samnite cult of the goddess Mephitis, which gave Pompeii's early *Venus Fisica* an astral characterization. This led to a particular iconography of the goddess that is found only in Pompeii.

It thus comes as no surprise that this new sanctuary, overlooking the port frontage, supplanted the Doric Temple and that Venus came to be considered the protectress of sailors. All that remains of the Sullan temple is the base of the *podium*, as the sanctuary continued to be central to religious life in the Imperial Age and underwent radical renovation during the Augustan-Tiberian period. At this time, it was reconstructed entirely in marble to adapt it to the new standards of opulence imposed by Augustus, thanks also to the intensive exploitation of the marble quarries of Luni (Carrara). Today, there remain very few traces of this wealth, but the centrality of the cult is confirmed by the fact that becoming a priestess of Venus was considered highly prestigious, and this rank was held only by women from the most important families. Venus would later become particularly important to Nero and, according to Dio Cassius (*Roman History*, LXII 26, 3), when Nero's second wife Poppaea died he wanted to consecrate her memory by comparing her to the goddess. During one of his visits to Pompeii – perhaps when he came to perform at the Naples theater in AD 64 – the emperor decided to donate a large sum of money to the sanctuary. This is mentioned in a graffito found in the House of Julius Polybius: *Caesar ut ad Venerem venet sanctissimam, ut tui te vexere pedes caelestes, Auguste, millia milliorum ponderum auri fuit* ("As soon as Caesar reached Venus, as soon as your divine feet brought you here, there were thousands and thousands of librae of gold"). Poppaea had also done just as much, but her gift instead went to adorning the statue of the goddess: *munera Poppaea misit Veneri sanctissimae berullum helencumque, unio mixtus est* ("Poppaea sent as gifts to most sacred Venus a beryl and a hanging pearl, and also added a large pearl").

There is precious evidence that seems attributable to this rich donation, which probably aided the temple after it was damaged by the earthquake two years before. This is the splendid gold oil lamp, which according to the indication on the bottom weighed three librae (it now weighs less, 32 ounces, because the cover has never been found), whose provenance has been traced by recent studies.

98
The Temple of Venus, destroyed by the eruption of AD 79, was still undergoing reconstruction following the earthquake of AD 62.

99
This Aphrodite attracted great devotion and was highly popular in Pompeii (Naples, MAN).

100

Associated with the figure of the emperor, the sacrifice of the bull embellishes one side of the ara *facing the Temple of Vespasian, on the east side of the Forum.*

The imperial cult

While the development of the main cults shows how politics and religion were closely intertwined, this phenomenon explicitly came to the fore during the Imperial Age, when political power transformed and exploited religious needs, turning them into a powerful tool of legitimacy.

Pompeii accurately reflects both the roots of this process and its spread through all levels. An emblematic example of this was the transformation of the college of priests of the *Ministri Mercurii et Maiae*, which united slaves and freedmen in the worship of the gods of trade (it is no accident that it was headquartered at the city *Macellum*), into the *Ministri Augusti Mercurii et Maiae* after 14 BC and, as of 2 BC, exclusively into the *Ministri Augusti*. Central to this changeover from a merchants' cult to the cult of the emperor is the assimilation of Augustus with Mercury, as also confirmed elsewhere (including an altar in Bologna and stuccowork from the Farnesina House in Rome).

This path conciliating divine worship and the emperor was accompanied by another one that got around any qualms over accepting the dynastic cult of the living emperor by replacing it with the worship of his essence, defined as *Numen* or *Genius*, depending on the social standing of the consecrators. This cult was promoted by the members of Pompeii's elite, who used this instrument to parade their approval of the dynasty that had just been established.

In all likelihood, the dedicatory inscription of the priestess Mamia to the *Genius Augusti* can be attributed to the Temple of Vespasian, which marks the start of the occupation of the eastern side of the forum with monuments, all of which devoted to the imperial cult. The temple closely follows the institution in Rome of the cult of the *Genius Augusti* at all the *compita* (aedicules located in the city quarters) in the year 7 BC, through which Augustus incorporated his *persona* with the genius of the *paterfamilias*. The same paternalistic bent arose again when he assumed the title of *Pater Patriae*, which was granted to him in 2 BC and thus expanded on the previous concept.

The altar in the sanctuary allows us to imagine the ceremonies in honor of the living emperor, which called for sacrificing a bull. Instead, the objects required to celebrate the rite are reproduced along the sides: the *lituus* (an augural rod), *mantile* (linen) and *acerra* (a box containing incense) are on one side, and the *simpulum* (ladle), *patera* (a shallow cup) and *urceus* (pitcher) are on the other. The decoration on the back, with the laurel trees framing an oak wreath, recalls the symbols that characterized the house of Augustus on the Palatine hill.

According to a brilliant theory based on metric calculation, the elegant marble cornice currently mounted on the portal of the adjacent Building of Eumachia can be attributed to this monument. This is also the monument that shows the highest artistic level in the meager panorama of Pompeii's sculptural documentation. Friezes of scrolls with small animals fan out from acanthus bushes set on piers and in the center of the architrave, and the detailed and elegant finish of the surfaces denotes the work of excellent sculptors, comparable to works found in Rome (the leading example is the *Ara Pacis*).

Eumachia, a priestess of Venus from a family that descended from the ancient Samnites and enjoyed a high rank also during the Augustan period, commissioned the Building of Eumachia, and the edifice reflects the same architectural design. The large monument (which may have been used as a venue for trade negotiations) opens up behind a columned vestibule with aedicules along the back, and it appears to be modeled after the *Porticus Liviae* in Rome, constructed by Augustus' wife Livia and his son Tiberius. The latter was dedicated to *Concordia Augusta*, or harmony among the members of the imperial family.

Eumachia also included her son Numistrius Fronto in the dedicatory inscription, which was extended to the *Pietas*. This was not only an attempt to draw a parallel with the Livia-Tiberius model, but it also echoed the capital city's more celebrated architectural example of the era: the Forum of Augustus. The niches on the façade of the vestibulum even held statues of the ancestors of the ruling family, including Aeneas, progenitor of the *gens Iulia*, and Romulus, the founder of Rome, with inscriptions at the base (*elogia*).

This model was probably copied on a more widespread level and thus the statues set against the columns on the opposite side may have presented the gallery of the municipal notables, reflected in the images of the illustrious Romans of the Forum of Augustus. The success of these statues in Pompeii is demonstrated by the fact that they were faithfully copied on the façade of a house on Via dell'Abbondanza (IX 13, 5) and were reproduced in small terracotta artifacts and in household items, such as the large lead receptacles used for water. Such great reverence toward the Augustan propaganda also conceals several voices of dissent, however, as indicated by the fresco with the caricature of the Flight from Troy, in which the obscene, monkey-like features of the main characters embody covert resistance.

The Temple of Fortuna Augusta that another local notable, M. Tullius, dedicated at the end of the 1st century BC was not built in the Forum. This is probably due to the fact that Tullius also owned the land, as explicitly stated in the dedicatory inscription. The temple held *signa* (statues) that were dedicated to the new emperor's rise to power, but we have no way of knowing if they were portraits of real people or icons of Fortuna.

102 and 103
*The statue of Eumachia, a priestess of Venus, was located in the building
the woman constructed in the Forum, perhaps for commercial purposes.
The sculpture was dedicated to the corporation of the fullones.
Shown on the right is the delicate gesture of her hand holding the
peplum (Naples, MAN).*

104 and 105

The reproduction of a lararium *and the detail of a frieze with putti and a mascaron are the subjects of these two engravings showing Pompeian findings, from* Les Ruines de Pompeii *written by François Mazois and published in Paris in 1879.*

The last to be built was the Sanctuary of the Public Lares, an enormous hall that opened completely onto the Forum and ended in a large apse. The *podium* of the apse, like the ones of the rectangular *exedrae* on the sides, must have had a rich series of statues. The building was one of the city's most luxurious, as the floor was paved with colored marble slabs creating a geometric design (*opus sectile*), the walls were also faced in marble, and the front with high *podia*, which must have sustained the columns of the portico, was made of basalt. The lavishness of this construction fully expressed the architectural taste of the Neronian period and the enormous financial resources of those who promoted the initiative. Despite the complete lack of any epigraphic indications, a comparison with other complexes dedicated to the imperial cult (which became the privilege of the wealthiest members of the freedmen class to erect), points to the fact that the Sanctuary was built by their organization, the *ordo Augustalium*, whose name has clearly been derived from the *ordo decurionum* (the municipal senate).

In addition to this building, constructed expressly for the imperial cult, virtually all public monuments held statues of the emperors in order to evoke their presence everywhere. In most cases, only the epigraphic texts or monumental bases remain, devoid of any ornamentation due to the pillaging of Pompeii's public places that probably occurred following the eruption of AD 79

Statues of Augustus were indubitably on the stage of the Theater, in the sacellum (small shrine) of the Great Palaestra and in front of the pulpit of the Basilica. We also know that a bronze quadriga was erected in his honor and set on an unusual fornix base (entrance aperture base) on the south side of the Forum. This homage may naturally have been extended to the other members of the family. A statue was erected in the Triangular Forum in honor of Marcellus, Augustus' beloved son-in-law and designated heir who died unexpectedly in 23 BC, and it was dedicated to him as a patron.

The tradition continued with the later emperors. When the *Macellum* was reconstructed by Gnaeus Alleius Nigidius Maius following the earthquake of AD 62 a sacellum dedicated to the imperial cult (probably) held the statue of Claudius. Unfortunately, only an arm with the globe remains from the statue, which portrayed the emperor modeled after the seated Jupiter. Likewise, over the years the central area of the square of the Forum was gradually filled with large pedestals, which must have been used to hold impressive monuments dedicated to the imperial family.

PRIVATE RELIGION

Streets, shops and houses reveal other aspects of religion, expanding our knowledge by encouraging the exploration of lesser known fields. Here, the broad sample offered by Pompeii has proven to be particularly valuable. A series of central figures belongs to this world of private worship, namely the Penates, the Genii and the Lares.

The Penates were part of the oldest household pantheon of the Roman world. Originally the *geni* who protected provisions (*penus*), they were given offerings of spelt and salt. Over time, their cult became interchangeable with that of the Lares and of Vesta, the goddess of the hearth. As opposed to the Lares, however, which were connected with the house, the Penates would move about with their owners wherever they went. The most famous citation on the subject is the one from Virgil: when Aeneas was fleeing the burning city of Troy, he took his elderly father and the Penates with him. The Genius was the supernatural essence inherent in each person or place, remaining nearby to offer protection. In its human function, the representation of the Genius is identified with the portrayal of the real person, sometimes even with the same physical features. The *genius* of the *paterfamilias*, a focal point of household religion, also became a point of reference for the imperial cult. For example, Augustus became the *Pater Patriae*. The Lares were also essentially protectors (*Praestites* is the attribute defining this role in general) of places or people. During the Imperial Age, they were portrayed as young dancers donning a short, fluttery tunic and holding the cornucopia and *rhyton* (a horn-shaped vase), or a *patera* (a shallow bowl) and *situla* (a bucket). Outside the home setting, people worshipped the *Lares Compitales*, custodians of the crossroads, and the *Lares Augusti*, effectively a cooptation into the imperial cult of these entities that were so entrenched in the daily religious tradition. The *Lares familiares*, originally the spirits of the ancestors, presided over the house. Their icons were worshipped in shrines, which varied in size, set in the *atrium* of the house or near the kitchen. At mealtimes, a slave would offer the Lares tidbits, placing them on a fire that was always kept lit. Depending on their location in the rooms of the house, their function would change. The cults practiced in the *atrium* represented the official aspect of private religion, whereas the cults practiced in the service rooms involved only the *familia*, or the group of servants. These *lararia* could also hold the icons of other deities to which the master of the house felt a particular tie owing to commitments connected with a public office or with his job. Aristocratic families, which displayed the most carefully tended and impressive "little temples" in the *atrium*, also enjoyed the privilege of exhibiting the waxen images of their ancestors, which could be carried in a procession during funerals.

We have not been able to determine the composition of all the *lararia*, particularly in the houses that were still being restored when Mount Vesuvius erupted. Nevertheless, there seems to be a predominant figurative element. This was the snake

106

A group of household gods with Mercury and Bacchus was part of the lararium *that decorated the* thermopolium *of Vetutius Placidus at No. 10, Via dell'Abbondanza.*

107

In the House of Menander, one of the largest in Pompeii, the lararium *was composed of a small temple with a niche, which held images of the spirits protecting the house.*

(sometimes even two of them), placed at the sides of the altar or around it for its apotropaic (designed to avert evil) or protective value as a "favorable demon," a significance also attributed to it by the Greeks. A great deal of information has come from the House of the Golden Cupids – where a shrine decorated with stuccowork held the small bronze statues of Jupiter, Juno and Minerva, Mercury and two Lares – and from the Centennial House. Here, in an *atrium* leading to one of the areas of this lovely house, which was transformed into a *caupona* (inn) with an annexed brothel and baths following the earthquake, there is a panel where the figure of the snake slithering toward the altar stands out against the countryside depicted in the background. The cone-shaped mountain is Vesuvius, as it was before the eruption of AD 79: this is the only representation of the volcano found in Pompeii. The slopes on the left are covered with vineyards (just as a sorrowful poem by Martial would recall them following the catastrophe), and alongside them is an opulent image of Bacchus, his body transformed into a cluster of bloated grapes. The patrons who frequented the inn were thus offered a "view" of the places that produced wine, the main resource of the local economy.

Sometimes the lararium represented an opportunity to paint, carve augural inscriptions and greetings, or even report important events. The one belonging to Julius Polybius, located in the kitchen, was used as a means of self-celebration. Depicted here is a sacrifice celebrated by the *dominus* and *domina*, and alongside it are the words *pro salutem redditum ac victoria(m)* (For health, the return, and victory). This clearly refers to the owner of the house, following the formula recalling the one used when the emperor departed for battle. Naturally, the deities represented most often at the *cauponae* (inns) and *thermopolia* (restaurants) were Bacchus and Mercury, as well as Fortuna, the main guarantor of successful business. It comes as no surprise, for example, that most of the *pistrinae* (bakeries) had the image of Vesta, sometimes accompanied by a donkey, the animal that was sacred to her but that was also used to turn the grindstone. Even more eloquent is the documentation from the House of the Lararium of the Sarnus (I 14, 6-7). Under the shrine decorated with the image of the sacrificing genius is a scene that is a cross between realism and allegory. To the left is a bearded male figure sitting on a tall rock, resting against an urn with water spouting from it. The water flows down to form a pale blue band: a river and its source, or the Sarnus and its wellspring on Mount Torrenone. The rest is a naive representation of reality, with a boat, people weighing products (onions?), and mules used as draft animals. It is essentially a description of the work conducted by the proprietor at the river port that was so important for the local economy, where the river god's protection was fundamental.

The houses and shops have also yielded other information on the private and public religion of Pompeii. The fresco on the façade of a house-cum-shop (VI 78-11), for example, shows us a tradition that differs little from modern ones, particularly in southern Italy. It depicts the procession of the goddess Minerva during one of the celebrations dedicated to her (*Quinquatria*), organized by a crafts guild. The figures are carrying a litter on which several workers are intently sawing wooden planks. The statue of Minerva must have been at the far left, but all that remains is the shield, while the figure standing on the right has been interpreted as Daedalus, the legendary craftsman. At his feet is his nephew Perdix, the inventor of the saw and compass, killed by Daedalus in a fit of jealousy.

A vast religious program can also be found on the façade of a workshop, not fully excavated yet, that was probably used by *Quactiliarii*, felters (based on the electoral message found there). Four busts of gods – Diana, Mercury, Jupiter and Apollo – dominate the architrave, and their sequence may suggest an intentional association with the days of Monday, Wednesday, Thursday and Sunday, considered important for this work for some reason. Two large panels along the sides illustrate the proprietor's main devotion to Cybele and Venus. The left panel in particular presents Venus in an iconography that is unique to Pompeii. As opposed to every consecrated image from the classic repertory, the goddess is shown as an opulent matron wrapped in a star-studded mantle and covered with jewelry. She is holding her attributes, the scepter and the rudder, while two cupids at her sides are offering her a palm, the cornucopia and a crown. Eros, who is also dressed, is next to her holding a mirror.

This unusual portrayal of Venus also appears in another fresco from the workshop of M. Vecilius Verecundus, which produced fabrics, as the scene decorating the lower panel clearly illustrates. Here, Venus is shown leading a quadriga of elephants on chariot shaped like the prow of a ship. She is at the helm, and Fortuna and a Genius are at her sides. The Pompeian Venus was thus a triumphant Venus – in Rome, Pompey celebrated his victory at the head of a quadriga of elephants – and she was a maritime Venus who ensured fortune to the city, symbolized by the Genius.

110 and 111
Paintings from the House of the Cryptoporticus (in situ) *and the House of the
Centenary (Naples, MAN): the serpent is associated respectively with Mercury,
represented in a niche, and Bacchus, in the form of a bunch of grapes and set next*

THE ORIENT IN POMPEII

When work to excavate the Temple of Isis began in Pompeii in 1764, Egyptology was still a fledgling field. Very little was known about the sumptuous complexes of the pharaohs, and it would take Napoleon's expedition of 1798 to shed some light on the extent of this immense wealth. The temple in Pompeii, the first building to be unearthed in the city incredibly all in one piece, thus became a "Little Egypt," a miniature compendium of a world waiting to be discovered.

The Oriental cults appeared in Campania quite early. The attraction and source of dissemination was undoubtedly Puteoli (modern Pozzuoli), whose intense trade activities led Asian groups to settle there, and these groups also brought their gods with them, spreading their cults. Like the other cities in the region, Pompeii reflected this phenomenon, and the first temple of Isis was built shortly after the one erected in Pozzuoli at the end of the 2nd century BC The history of the monument is summarized by the inscription on the lintel of the entrance, which provides valuable information: *N(umerius) Popidius N(umeri) f(ilius) Celsinus aedem Isidis terrae motu conlapsam a fundamento p(equnia) s(ua) restituit. Hunc decuriones ob liberalitatem cum esset annorum sexs ordini suo gratis adlegerunt* (Numerius Popidius Celsinus, son of Numerius, has restored at his own expense the temple of Isis, which collapsed in the earthquake.

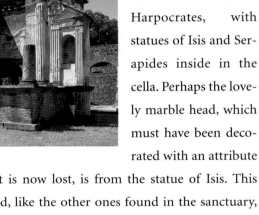

Although he is only six years old, because of his generosity the decuriones have elected him to their council). The cult of Isis was an esoteric one whose practice called for a rite of purification. Inside the tall enclosure around the temple, there was a small building whose entrance led to an underground room that safeguarded the water of the Nile (which was actually local water). This was a *Purgatorium* for the *sacra* of the cult.

The temple, set on a high *podium*, had a columned pronaos (the inner area of the portico of temple) and a very narrow cella. The two niches in front of the cella must have held the statues of Anubis and Harpocrates, with statues of Isis and Serapides inside in the cella. Perhaps the lovely marble head, which must have been decorated with an attribute that is now lost, is from the statue of Isis. This head, like the other ones found in the sanctuary, was part of an acrolith (a statue made of wood and covered with fabric; only the bare parts were made of marble). The lovely statue offered by the devout L. Caecilius Phoebus also represented Isis. Here, she is depicted in a refined archaistic model with the *ankh* (the key of life) and the sistrum (musical rattle). The temple furnishings included a slab with representations and a long text in hieroglyphics, from the Ptolemaic era, that was undoubtedly placed in the temple in Pompeii strictly to give it "genuinely Egyptian" air.

112 and 113

Rebuilt by private initiative following the earthquake of AD 62, the Temple of Isis was a separate edifice within a tall enclosure. The cult of this goddess, depicted in the acroterial head on the right, was very popular in Pompeii.
(Naples, MAN).

114-115

A fisherman with his rod and an officiant before the sarcophagus of Harpocrates (the Greek name for the god Horus) are depicted in this fanciful evocation of a landscape near the Nile. The painting was part of the decoration of the Temple of Isis (Naples, MAN).

115 bottom

This painted panel from the Temple of Isis depicts two facing sphinxes. The panel, found in excellent condition, reinterprets Egyptian themes connected with the Eastern origin of this goddess, doing so according to Pompeian artistic taste. (Naples, MAN).

However, the most intriguing part of the temple at the time it was discovered – and even now, particularly since exquisite restoration work has been done – is the rich pictorial decoration. Although it was divided into "pictures" of various sizes, it has been possible to recompose it in the National Museum of Naples. Considering the short amount of time between the reconstruction of the temple and the eruption of Mount Vesuvius, it is not surprising that the frescoes have maintained all their polychrome glory. The walls of the portico had broad red fields, set over a yellow base and separated by architectural perspectives, that were decorated with vignettes, with the priests of Isis or sacred architectural elements. On the east wall, the pattern ended at the level of a shrine, with Harpocrates portrayed against the background of a temple that closely resembles the one in Pompeii. A priest is offering him candelabras that look much like some of the ones that have been found here. Along the top is a sumptuous frieze with scrolls that enclose corollas, animals from the Nile and pygmies. An open area at the back of the temple, encroaching on the adjacent "Samnite Palaestra," was created following the earthquake. Donated by Popidius Celsinus together his father Popidius Ampliatus and his mother Corelia Celsa – as attested to by the mosaic epigraphic in the floor – it was decorated with a cycle of paintings, set in a view imitating a marble colonnade. Some of the panels show imaginary views of Egyptian land-

scapes, one of the most notable being the sacrificial scene before the sarcophagus of Osiris. Fanciful architecture, islands, rocky slopes, small figures of fishermen and ibises, statues of Isis and rich furnishings of precious pottery weave a dreamlike atmosphere that evokes the land of the Nile. The interpretation of this complex has been debated extensively. Traditionally, the restoration of the temple was viewed as a sign of the rise of the classes of freedmen during the 1st century, as it contrasts the state of disrepair of many other public buildings. Popidius Ampliatus could not hope to hold public office, as he was born a slave, and thus he ensured that his son Celsinus would have a place in society by promoting this construction work. The evidence can also be interpreted to mean just the opposite, however. Perhaps the temple does not represent one of the monuments reconstructed following the earthquake, but is instead one of the few that was not systematically plundered after the eruption. Its furnishings, its few small statues, the fact that there was no marble cladding and the smattering of worthless Egyptian-like artifacts would hardly have offset the costs involved in digging up and transporting the materials. The decision of the wealthy freedman may also have been the outcome of a political move, given that the new Flavian dynasty was closely tied to the Egyptian cults. Vespasian, proclaimed emperor in Alexandria, received his sacred investiture from Serapides and not from the Capitoline Jupiter, as traditionally done.

116-117

Fantastic landscapes and evanescent architectures come to life in the paintings from the Temple of Isis. In the photograph on the left, artwork seems to portray the sacred building itself, accessible by means of a steep and rather narrow staircase (Naples, MAN).

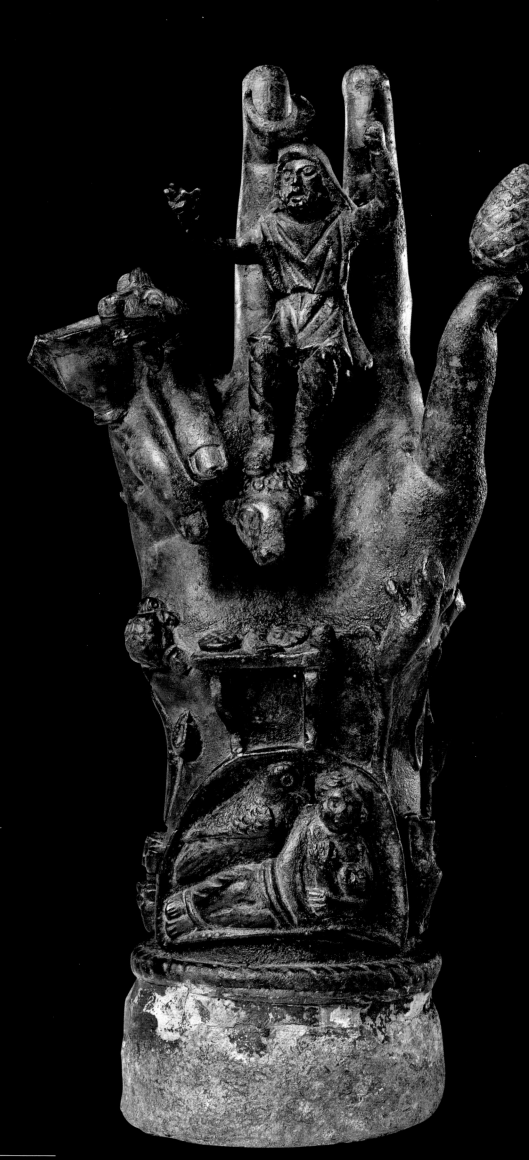

As opposed to the cult of Isis, that of Cybele is not well documented in Pompeii. Aside from the painted procession of Via dell'Abbondanza, evidence may also come from an enigmatic block of black lava stone found in a niche in *Regio* I, next to a *thermopolium*, as it may evoke the non-human form of the cult of the Pessinus goddess. Sabbatius is deity from the same area. Connected with nature, he ensured regeneration and fertility, particularly of grains. However, as a result of the religious syncretism that often occurred during the Greek and Roman eras, the god may also have incorporated Dionysus, thus taking on some of the latter's attributes.

Pompeii has given us highly intriguing documentation in which the intersection of this god's religious aspects is expressed as a collection of attributes, creating a picturesque symbiosis. A bust portrays him with a long beard and hair decorated with a trail of ivy, with a tall *kalathos* (a fruit basket with shape of a lily, often used as a symbol of fertility) and bunches of grapes, figs, plums, ears of wheat and a loaf of bread coming from it. In his left hand, he is holding poppy leaves and flowers, the attributes of Dionysus and Demeter

118 left and 119
A tangle of symbols tied to childbirth can be noted on the back and palm of this "magic hand" found in a Pompeian house (Naples, MAN).

118 bottom right
The bronze bust with angular features is associated with Sabbatius, the god of nature from Phrygian mythology connected with orgiastic rites and assimilated with Dionysus in the Greco-Roman world (Naples, MAN).

that add to this god's supremacy in every field of agriculture. Sabbatius was also considered the protector of childbirth, however, and this function is alluded to by a group of "magic hands" made of bronze that were discovered between Pompeii and Herculaneum. Two of these items have been found in only one house in Pompeii (II 1,12): the Eastern god is portrayed seated in the palm of the hand, with his ring finger and smallest finger bent in the sign of the Latin blessing. Among the different attributes that cover the hand – a scale, a caduceus, a knife and a snake climbing to drink from a small amphora resting on the smallest finger, a pine cone and so on – the figure that stands out is a mother with a child at her breast, lying in a grotto loading a table with offerings. She may represent Persephone, the mother of Sabbatius. It has been theorized that gladiators were regulars at this house, given its proximity to the amphitheater and the fact that many of them were of Phrygian and Thracian origin (*Thrax* is the term used to define a common type of gladiator and it comes from the name of the armor). As far as nascent Christianity in Pompeii is concerned, research has not provided any interesting clues so far. The time was not yet ripe, or perhaps its few followers had not officially come forward.

COMMERCIAL LIFE

THE PORT AND TRADE

Pompeii's favorable position of at the mouth of the Sarnus helped make the city an important part of Campania's articulated trade flow, which from as early as the 6th century BC was the expression of the Etruscans', the Greeks', and the indigenous population's political and economic life.

The river allowed the ships making calls in the Bay of Naples to dock easily and its course permitted communication between the inland areas and the coast. Archaic era finds and the presence of a shrine dedicated to Poseidon (Neptune), god of the sea, and used until the Augustan period, bear witness to the location of Pompeii's docking area in Bottaro, the outermost of the sand dunes that, toward the sea, bordered by the Sarnus' marshy delta.

This was probably where the fleet of *socii navales* (naval allies), commanded by P. Cornelius, landed. The episode, recounted by Livy, took place in 310 BC and it represents the first mention of Pompeii. Aside from the secondary importance of the expedition of the Roman fleet into Pompeian territory to punish the Nucerians for their alliance with the Samnites, it is significant that at the end of the 4th century BC Pompeii not only controlled the river mouth but presumably also acted as a seaport for other inland cities.

Nevertheless, the first proof of Pompeii as a port, by this time fully a part of the integrated system of Campania's landing places headed by Puteoli (modern Pozzuoli), dates from the 2nd century BC. In a passage in his *Geography*, Strabo cited Pompeii as the port city for Nola, *Nocera* and Acerra, the point of arrival for the products from the Sarnus plains and destined for export or import.

The location of the Pompeian port is still open to debate, as is the issue of whether it was a fluvial or maritime port. The question arose with the initial findings of the late 19th century because of the lack of definitive archaeological data and precise knowledge of the course of the river during the Roman era: it was probably diverted by the eruption of AD 79 and was also channeled during the Bourbon period. The hypothesis that Pompeii had an integrated port system – fluvial and maritime – for better management of local and "international" traffic is quite intriguing. The excavations conducted in several phases at Murecine (or Moregine), located on the Sarnus' right bank and well connected to the city center by Via Stabiana, have uncovered buildings and structures interpreted as warehouses and sales facilities that were part of the fluvial station of Pompeii. Specifically, the discovery of approximately 300 waxed tablets in the "*domus* of the *Triclinia*" confirms the area's association with trade. They listed the deeds of the business (*negotia*) conducted between AD 26 and 61 by the Sulpicii, the Puteoli bankers who owned the building and had come to Pompeii to take advantage of the reconstruction opportunities following the earthquake in AD 62.

The landing places were probably located in the immediate vicinity, and this was where the products from inland, transported down the river, were unloaded to be brought into Pompeii for consumption. These products were indubitably wine, oil and wheat, as well as vegetables and onions, mentioned repeatedly in the ancient sources as among the produce of Pompeii. Several frescoes from the House of the Sarnus Lararium portray a ship floating in the river, loaded with goods weighed previously, using a large scale.

Export commodities produced in the

*The fresco shown here, which is from Stabiae, represents an idealized
view of an unidentified port area, capturing the hustle and bustle
of trade (Naples, MAN).*

countryside around Pompeii and in the inland area of Nuceria – first and foremost, wine – were probably transported by river to the maritime port facilities, where they were loaded on ships headed for Puteoli, the hub for Mediterranean traffic. The discovery of buildings that were probably set up as port warehouses, with various types of equipment connected with maritime activities and amphorae for shipping purposes, al-

lows us to pinpoint the port facilities in the small coastal lagoon. The lagoon, mentioned by Columella (1st century AD) as *dulcis palus Pompeiia proxima Salinis Herculei,* was formed by the sandbar of Bottaro and the *tombolo* (a sand or gravel bar connecting an island with the mainland or another island) set farther out in one of the Sarnus delta's outlets, one of the branches of which reached the base of the Pompeian hill,

THE GOLDEN AGE OF POMPEIAN WINE

T he rise of Pompeii during the Samnitic era was due largely to the revenue generated by overseas trade, promoted starting in the 1st half of the 2nd century by the Roman expansion throughout the Mediterranean basin. This is demonstrated by the development and modernization of the city's layout and, above all, by the extraordinary wealth seen in private homes. The richest members of the city elite, which included those from

types of grapes were grown in Pompeii and around the area of Vesuvius. In addition to *Vesuvinum*, a variety of the prized grape known as *Gemina minor*, Pliny the Elder and Columella also cited *Murgentina*, a type indigenous to Sicily that was successfully transplanted in the Pompeii area, where it was named *Pompeiiana*, and the less valuable *Vennuncula*. Other varieties from Pompeii included *Holconium*, mentioned by

other cities in Campania and from the Italic communities, settled in Pompeii to take advantage of the opportunities offered by its trade. They thus became the leading figures as producers and probably also traders of these commodities. Wine was indubitably the main agricultural resource of the Vesuvian area, although since there is no significant information on the territory's productivity and the size of itse population, the volume of production cannot fully be estimated. Various

Pliny the Elder, and *Rubellianum*. These two varieties were named after two important Pompeian families that presumably became wealthy on the handsome profits they earned from the wine trade. Pompeian wine, which was sufficient to meet the needs of the city population, became popular in various areas around the Mediterranean starting in the 2nd century BC. Amphorae from Pompeii have been found in Spain (Ampurias) and at numerous sites in Morocco,

In the triclinium of the House of the Vettii, winemaking cupids pour appetizing nectar from an amphora to a cup, which a host offers to a guest

The variety of amphorae discovered in Pompeii testifies to the city's economic prosperity between the 1st century BC and the 1st century AD (Boscoreale, National Antiquarium).

and in the French region of Saône et Loire. The proceeds that the Pompeian aristocracy earned from the wine trade in turn allowed them to purchase items and commodities from the provinces; this is extensively documented in archaeological excavations dating from this period, with coins from *Massalia* (Marseille) and *Ebusus* (Ibiza). In addition to shards of Spanish pottery, used to transport the area's famous honey, there was also a significant number of amphorae from overseas containing wine and oil, as well as a more infrequent number that contained olives and African fish sauces. The wines that Pompeii would continue to import until its destruction – undoubtedly insufficient to meet local demand – underscore the level of well-being achieved by the city's social elites, who could afford to buy even the most expensive provincial wines. This explains the presence of thirteen Rhodian amphora seals, found during the excavations in the area of the Basilica. The amphorae were used to transport wine mixed with seawater, which was quite popular among Italic consumers. Exports of Pompeian wine to the provinces climaxed during the 1st century BC. The wreck from Anthéor, France (between Cannes and St. Raphaël), which occurred shortly before the Sullan colony was established in Pompeii, yielded a series of amphorae with stoppers made of pozzolan clay bearing a seal in Oscan letters (*M.C.Lass.*). This seal designated two brothers, M. and C. Lassii, from an important Pompeian family that was in the wine business for several generations. In the middle of the 1st century BC, the Lassii were related to the *gens* Clodia of Pompeii who, like the Holconii and Rubellii, gave their name to *Clodianum*, the wine produced on their estates around Sorrento. Nevertheless, the most significant evidence of Pompeian wines comes from Africa, owing to the presence of numerous Italic *negotiatores* from Campania in the colony as well as the re-establishment of the colony of Carthage. Here, in the big deposit of Roman amphorae on the hill of Saint Louis that have been dated between 43 and 15 BC, many seals and amphora handles bear the name of L. Eumachius, father of Eumachia, the famous priestess of Venus. Half a dozen examples of other Pompeian seals were also found in Carthage, together with a painted inscription that mentions the wine of Mount Vesuvius. While more substantial in terms of quantity, Pompeii's concurrent oil imports had different implications than wine. During the Roman era Campania was quite famous for the quality of its oil, but it did not produce enough to supply the constant flow of exports. It may not even have produced enough to meet its own needs. In the Pompeii area, fewer farms produced oil than wine and the export of Pompeian oil has never been proven. It is likely instead that, in order to satisfy the local demand, the city was forced to import oil from other areas of Campania, starting as early as the Republican Age.

It is widely known that the Augustan period marked a turning point in the economic relations between Italy and the provinces, characterized by the decline in Italic exports for reasons that are still being debated. By this time, even the presence of Pompeian wine was limited to a few military sites in Gallia and Britannia, and we cannot exclude the possibility that it circulated outside regular market routes, under the direct control of the imperial authorities. Its increasingly limited penetration in overseas regions was offset – at least in part – by the enormous Rome market, as the city was a megalopolis with a population of nearly a million inhabitants by the early Imperial Age. To meet Rome's demand for wine, large quantities were brought in from Pompeii and the Vesuvian area. Nevertheless, the intensification of Pompeii's importation of wine from Campania and the provinces, particularly Greece, fish sauce (*garum*) and oil from Baetica (a Spanish province) does not bear out the theory of a decline in the quality of life among the Pompeian aristocracy. A significant demonstration of Pompeii's entrepreneurial spirit can be found through its establishment of *garum* production. *Garum*, a sauce made of fish fermented and pickled with salt, was a basic condiment for the Roman cuisine and it resembles Vietnamese *nuocnam*. The production was bolstered by the presence of the *salinae Herculeae*, mentioned by Columella. Based on personal experience, Pliny the Elder judged the quality of Pompeian *garum* as equivalent to that of Leptis and Clazomenae, which were famous in the Roman world. Of the

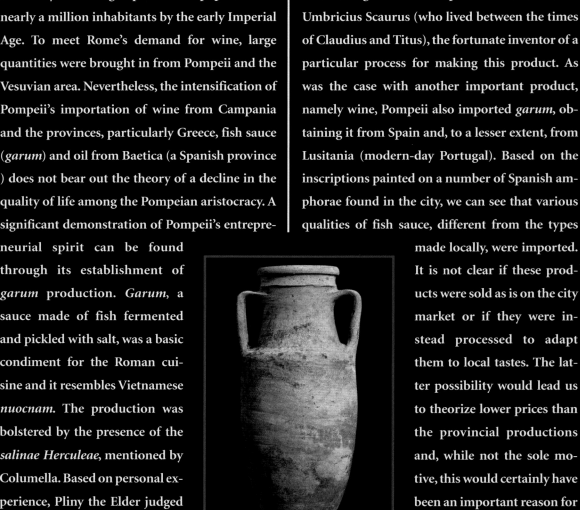

different varieties that existed, the inscriptions on the amphorae from Pompeii indicate a prevalence of the most valuable types: *liquaminis flos* and *gari flos*, both of which were made with mackerel. As further evidence of the changed economic rapport between Italy and the provinces, it does not appear that Pompeian *garum* was sold outside Campania or, in any event, north of Rome. Its limited circulation was no impediment to earning handsome profits, however, as can be theorized based on the fact that prestigious members of the city elite were involved in producing and perhaps even selling it. One example was the famous A. Umbricius Scaurus (who lived between the times of Claudius and Titus), the fortunate inventor of a particular process for making this product. As was the case with another important product, namely wine, Pompeii also imported *garum*, obtaining it from Spain and, to a lesser extent, from Lusitania (modern-day Portugal). Based on the inscriptions painted on a number of Spanish amphorae found in the city, we can see that various qualities of fish sauce, different from the types made locally, were imported. It is not clear if these products were sold as is on the city market or if they were instead processed to adapt them to local tastes. The latter possibility would lead us to theorize lower prices than the provincial productions and, while not the sole motive, this would certainly have been an important reason for their success on Italic markets. The earthquake of AD 62 marked a crucial moment in Pompeii's socioeconomic history. The city itself bore the most serious damage and required major reconstruction work, while the same catastrophic effects apparently did not affect the production facilities of the rural areas. Although they are inadequate for reaching any definitive conclusions, the archaeological findings from Rome seem to confirm that, following the earthquake, Pompeii's wine business proceeded on the same level, if not greater. To the very end, the city was able to import wines from other areas of Campania and Latium, alongside those from other regions in Italy, Spain and Greece. Likewise, the city imported oil from North Africa and Baetica, as well as *garum*. The production and sale of wine and, to a lesser extent, of *garum* – almost exclusively involving Rome and the main cities of Campania by this time – remained the principal economic resources of Pompeii's elite. An important clue to the importance of Pompeian wine in the city's final years can be gleaned indirectly from information on Rome's wine supply after AD 79. The eruption of Mount Vesuvius, which buried the villas on its slopes under twenty feet of lava, prevented any kind of cultivation for many years. It took more than a decade, and the conversion of vast areas to vineyards, to bring the wine production of south-central Italy back to its previous levels.

126 and 127 bottom left
Findings indicate that amphorae like this one were used in Pompeii during the 1st century AD. They featured a large cylindrical body and probably came from North Africa. The first one contained oil (Naples, MAN) and the second one held wine (Boscoreale, National Antiquarium).

127 right
Perhaps a merchant originally from the Greek island of Lesbos commissioned this work, portraying the ship he owned, for the external wall of his house in Pompeii. The goddess Aphrodite, the protectress of good sailing, is portrayed at the helm (Naples, MAN).

128

This fresco, from the realty complex (praedia) *of Julia Felix, depicts piles of coins next to a bag, with* instrumenta scriptoria *in the lower register (Naples,* MAN*).*

129

The bronze coin of Nero (AD 54-68) depicts the Temple of Janus, in the Roman Forum, with closed doors to symbolize peace in the Empire (reverse) (Naples, MAN*).*

CURRENCY AND FINANCIAL ACTIVITIES
POMPEII, A PRIVILEGED OBSERVATORY

The eruption of Mount Vesuvius, which sealed the outlying areas under a pall of ash and *lapilli*, has given us a virtually complete snapshot of a day in the life of Pompeii. The city has thus come to represent a privileged observation post for reconstructing the history of the entire area of ancient Campania. As far as currency is concerned, the importance of the documentation, in terms of both quality and quantity, offers us a solid basis for reconstructing the city's socioeconomic context, financial situation, and commercial trends. At the same time, it also offers us a key to understanding the monetary aspects of the Roman economy during the early Flavian period. In sharp contrast with the documentation from other ancient sites, Pompeii is represented by findings, for the most part discovered out of context, or by deposits. These deposits, referred to as "storerooms," were established progressively over the years or as a result of emergency situations following extraordinary and traumatic events, and they are the outcome of a rather deliberate selection dictated by the desire to hoard. This Pompeian observation post has also posed several serious flaws due to various aspects tied to the specific situation of Pompeii itself, and these flaws must be taken into account in order to avoid creating a distorted view that does not accurately reflect the original situation.

First of all, it must be noted that at the time of the eruption, many of the buildings were completely or partially abandoned and were being restored following the damage caused by the quakes during the last period (AD 62-79). Moreover, the proprietors took some of the assets kept in the homes and the cash from the shops when they fled, as demonstrated by several *arcae* (safes), which were found empty, and by the stashes that those fleeing had with them. This documentation was further depleted by pillagers and by the work that the central government in Rome conducted following the eruption in order to recover any valuables. Added to this is the damage caused by the wartime bombing in 1943, not to mention the fact that the archaeological excavations are still underway. Likewise, valuable information has been lost about the coins found during the initial excavations, from 1748 through the entire 19th century, as the coins were added to the collection of the National Museum of Naples without any indication of provenance. Consequently, only detailed research of the bibliographic sources and archives has made it possible to arrive at a partial identification.

Despite all of the foregoing problems, there remains an enormous documentary basis that has given us the picture of a diversified and varied monetary scenario. We know that three metals were used in the coinage: they were gold, silver, and alloys of base metals, conventionally indicated as bronze, although the proportions differed depending on absolute values and the specific function. Bronze currency was used as the circulating medium for activities and trade on a common day-to-day level, and this has been determined by its predominance at commercial facilities and not on large amounts of evidence. This information matches Roman accounting practices in the Imperial Age, which was based on the *sesterce* (the largest bronze face value). It is also reflected by the prices of foodstuffs or everyday items, which were quantified in bronze coinage in the epigraphic evidence from Pompeii. It has been confirmed that precious currency and silver in particular, which predominated over gold, played a role as a value and/or exchange reserve linked with more important transactions. Thus is testified to by the prevalence of liquid assets hoarded in homes, found on site, and on the bodies of those who attempted to flee from the eruption. The coinage in various metals is further distinguished by the varied evidence of the chronological stages. As far as bronze is concerned, the volume of coins in circulation during the city's last eleven years represents a very large percentage of the entire money supply, worth nearly half of the currency of the 81 years of the Julio-Claudian period and of the Republican Age. The latter include a fairly large nucleus of bronze token money from Greek cities, which sketches out the large trade network that extended from the cities of Campania across the Tyrrhenian and Mediterranean, from Sicily to Massalia (Marseille) and over to Spain, with Ebusus (Ibiza) playing a pre-eminent role.

130

Clockwise from the top left, an aureus, or gold coin, from the Republican Age (41 BC), portraying the head of Octavian (obverse); three aurei of Augustus (27 BC-AD 14): the first one shows the head of Augustus (obverse), the second one has a bull with its horns lowered, ready to attack (reverse), and the last one depicts Winged Victory seated on a globe (reverse) (Naples, MAN).

131

Clockwise from the top are an aureus of Augustus with a triumphal quadriga (reverse); an aureus from the Republican Age (41 BC), with Fortune holding a plow and a cornucopia (reverse); an aureus struck by Augustus, with Gaius and Lucius Caesar in togas (obverse) (Naples, MAN).

Top, on the left is a bronze coin of Nero showing the emperor addressing three soldiers (reverse); right,
a bronze coin of Tiberius showing the emperor seated on the curule chair (obverse). Center, on the right
is a bronze coin of Vespasian (AD 49-79) with the figure of Equity (reverse); below, on the left is a bronze
coin of Claudius (AD 41-54) showing Minerva with a helmet, lance and shield (reverse), on the right
is a bronze of Augustus, on which the wording M. SANQUINIUS Q.F. III VIR AAAFFAN includes the acronym
for Senatus Consultum (reverse) (Naples, MAN).

Clockwise from the top left are a bronze coin of Nero engraved with the head of the emperor wearing
a laurel crown (obverse); a bronze coin of Claudius (AD 41-54) with a portrait of the emperor (obverse);

134
*From top to bottom: a silver coin from the
Republican Age (43-42 BC) with an axe and*
simpulum *(reverse); two silver coins from the
Republican Age, the first one (32-29 BC) shows
Mercury seated on a boulder holding a lyre (reverse);
the second one (31 BC) depicts a warship with
oarsmen (reverse) (Naples,* MAN*).*

However, the evidence of silver coinage
shows a discontinuous trend, with two well-de-
fined peaks. The first one was during the late Republican Age, with a concentration of the legionary issues of Mark Antony, and this fully reflects the historical and political events of the
city: the foundation of the colony, the intense
program of construction work and so on. There
was a sharp decline in *denarii* during the Julio-
Claudian period, which seems attributable to
the effects of the Neronian reform of AD 64 that,
by reducing the weight and purity of precious
coins, triggered an 18.5 percent drop in their intrinsic value compared to Augustan values. This
led to people to melt down pre-reform pieces
and keep the clearly worn Republican coins in
circulation alongside Mark Antony's legionary
denarii, which were made of a base silver alloy
and thus had little intrinsic value. The high concentration of *denarii* came during the Flavian
period, hand in hand with the price trend of
bronze. This flow of currency appears to be related to the slow and partial post-earthquake reconstruction, which does not seem to have received great financial support from the central
government. At the same time – at least over the
medium term – this surely did not mark a period of complete recession. Instead, it seems to
have acted as a factor that accelerated a process
of socioeconomic transformation of the population, with the renovation of many areas of Pompeii and the rise of new groups whose success
was tied more to industrial and commercial activities than to land rent.

135
Above, a bronze coin from the Republican Age with the two-faced head of Janus (reverse); lower left, a silver coin of Nero, showing the emperor's head with a laurel crown (obverse); right, a silver coin from the Republican Age (43 BC), engraved with a vase and a lituus *(reverse) (Naples,* MAN*).*

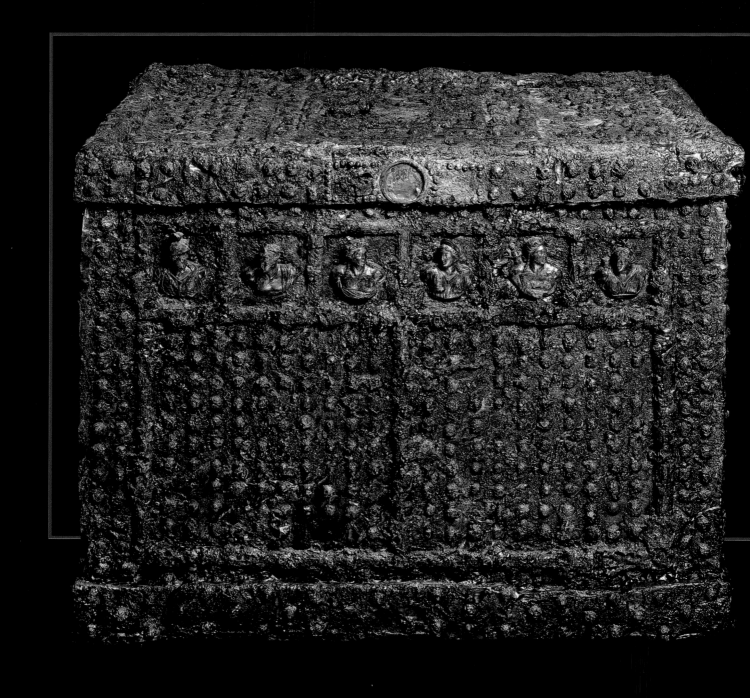

136
The surface of this safe (arca) is decorated with a dense array of raised
nails and six bronze tiles portraying busts of various figures
(Naples, MAN)

137
The arca found in the peristyle of Villa B of Oplontis is a wooden safe
covered with iron, bronze, silver and copper decorations.

THE FINDINGS

Only limited importance can be attributed to the coins found in public buildings, comprising only small amounts of bronze token moneys and the hoards found on those trying the flee the city. These coins sketch out a general situation and are not related to the functions of these structures. The picture offered by the homes is instead far greater in scope. Only a small percentage of the documentation is represented by divisional coins scattered on the floors of the houses: these coins were not carefully preserved or taken when the people fled. Most of the examples come from the hoards found near skeletons and stored in bronze or wooden boxes and in leather or fabric bags, or they are composed of stores kept in bronze-decorated wooden boxes or in terracotta moneyboxes, closets or ordinary jars. The distribution seems to match the function of the rooms, with a concentration in the areas used for social purposes, principally the *atrium*, followed by a much smaller concentration in the *tablinum* and the peristyle. However, there have also been findings in the private areas, servants' quarters, gardens, underground areas and cellars of several particularly prestigious residences. There also appears to be a significant relationship between cash flow, the social status of the owner and the type of residence, although here as well the specific situations differ. Judging from the contexts that were intact when they were discovered, the amounts of liquid assets were rather limited. The largest rarely exceed 4000 sesterces – only in one case does the sum go over 9000 – while most come to between 1000 and 3000 sesterces. The most modest ones amount to just 200-500 sesterces. This sketches out a situation of sharp differences, with a concentration of wealth in a limited social class. This picture is rounded out by the findings from trade facilities, workshops and businesses that produced and sold products: contained in large terracotta jars (*dolia)* or piled up on the sales counters – or elsewhere – this represents the currency kept "in the till." This essentially coincides with sporadic currency, as it offers a better representation of the effective circulation of the money supply in daily use than the piles of money hoarded in homes for years.

THE ACCOUNTS OF CAECILIUS JUCUNDUS

The considerable supply of money that was found is due to the fact that there were numerous shops and workshops in Pompeii and its region. It is also linked with the intensity of the cash flow of certain activities, and is not related to price levels. Particularly as far as foodstuffs were concerned, these prices were generally rather low. Among trade activities, only public foodservices document a more intense movement of cash: at the *thermopolium* of Vetutius Placidus on Via dell'Abbondanza, the large amount contained in the *dolia* – 1385 coins, all made of bronze – must have been the daily proceeds, or at most the takings from the previous few days. Instead, the amount of cash from the sales of food and everyday goods seems to have been far more modest:

the numerous shops dotting the various *Regiones* document a widespread infiltration of coinage, but one that was limited in quantity. For example, the box found at the *Macellum* (the main food market), with proceeds from the sale of staples, contained 1163 bronze units of small denominations, bucking the trend seen elsewhere of a predominance of *asses* (low-value coins). The stashes of money found at production facilities were, however, quite different in amount. The last receipts of the important laundry business (*fullonica*) of a certain Stephanus (I 6,7), amounting to 1089.50 sesterces, documents an intense circulation of cash, if we consider that it cost just 4 sesterces to wash a tunic. The till of a bakery on Via della Abbondanza (IX 1,3) held 9 *aurei* (gold coins), together with 433 bronze units, indicating a large amount of available cash. This is probably not attributable to sales revenue but to the fact that the

bakery needed to purchase large quantities of wheat, since the business not only made and sold bread but also ground flour. Aurei can also be found in the shops of craftsmen who worked and sold metals, above all precious metals (*gemmarii*). In this setting, the presence of gold establishes the function as a value and/or exchange reserve tied to the provision of raw materials, among which wheat and metals played a major role. We must round out this picture by citing the production of wine and oil, documented by the farms in the suburban area and the land around Vesuvius – for example, the villas of Oplontis or Boscoreale – owned by important families whose substantial liquid assets, composed mainly of gold coins, seemed to be used to run the facilities. Lastly, the level of liquidity found in Pompeii is lower than what the city's economic relations would have required, as evidenced by the development of the use of credit. This is proven by the archives of the banker (*coactor argentarius*) Caecilius Jucundus, listed on several wax tablets: 137 documents represent the receipts (*apochae*) issued in front of witnesses for payments made during auctions. We know which assets were auctioned in only a few cases: wood, linens, slaves, and a mule. Sixteen other documents deal with the collection of municipal taxes. They include receipts issued by a public slave for the payment of several fees, such as the one on pastures (*pascua*) and the one for the right to sell goods (*mercatus*) during the markets that were held in Pompeii every Saturday. These markets, given the auctions conducted at the same time, promoted exchanges and the circulation of money. The amount of capital involved points to a

Wax tablets, like the ones shown here from the House of Caecilius Jucundus, were
the medium used for bookkeeping (Naples, MAN).

medium-low level. The figures come to a few hundred sesterces; the average price was about 7500 sesterces, and the largest sum was 38,078 sesterces. This business was conducted between AD 52 and 62 (only one document, in the name of his father L. Caecilius Felix, is dated AD 15) and it deals with a set of procedures, guarantees, interest and the duration of loans. If analyzed in detail, this alone would take up an entire book. The Sulpicii, a family of moneylenders (*fenatores*), carried out a complementary activity in Puteoli, a port and more important market than that of Pompeii. A comparison between Jucundus'

archives and those of the Sulpicii reveals two different areas of transaction. In the first case, we have the local and municipal one, while the second one involves the ruling class – the patrician and equestrian ranks – where credit seems to have been used for large-scale businesses. This diversified lending activity proves to have been of vital importance, not only in order to recover and add to the circulating capital required for market needs and to promote the spread of coinage in sectors from which it was excluded, but also to increase the development of investment, an important incentive for production activities.

THE FORUM MARKET

The Forum in Pompeii was indubitably a place teeming with life. Not only was it the hub of the city's political, administrative and religious life, lined with many civil and religious buildings, but it was also its commercial heart, which must have had many more structures than the ascertained number of *tabernae* set up in it or nearby. Simply by stepping inside the *Macellum*, we can immediately understand not only the lively trade that went on there, but also how society regulated the supply of goods and foodstuffs during that period. The building was constructed during the 2nd century BC but was completely redone and expanded at the beginning of the Imperial Age. Its main entrance was at the northern end on the eastern side of the Forum. However, two other side entrances also connected it with Via degli Augustali to the north and with the Alley of the Hanging Balcony to the south, so it could be reached easily from several directions. It served as a general marketplace for meat, from livestock to wild game, and for fish and other food products. It was composed of a large rectangular courtyard enclosed by porticoes, with a *tholos* – a twelve-sided pavilion with a conical roof sustained by twelve pedestals – set in the middle. Beneath the pavilion was a fountain that was connected by a gutter to a drainage ditch, in which numerous fish scales have been found. On the south side of the complex, there was a row of eleven shops that sold a variety of goods. On the north side, many bones from sheep and wild animals have been discov-

A lively fresco from the Praedia *of Julia Felix shows the city's busy trade along the porticoes of the Forum*

ered. The division of the far end of the *Macellum* (the eastern one) is quite interesting. Set in the middle and preceded by steps, there was a sacellum that was built in the Imperial Age and was probably devoted to the cult of the Caesars, given that a statue fragment was found there. This fragment, a hand holding a globe symbolizing supreme power, may be from the statue of an emperor that was set against the back wall. Along the side walls of the sacellum there were also four niches, and the solemn statues of a couple were found in two of them. Perhaps they were Pompeian notables who had paid for renovating the complex. She is portrayed as a veiled priestess, while he is portrayed as a nude hero, following the style of the Claudian-Neronian period. One pro-

posal theorizes that the statues represent Alleius Nigidius Maius, duumvir in AD 55, and his daughter, a priestess of Venus and Ceres. North of the sacellum there was an area whose function is not clear. It seems to have been used for ritual banquets, based on the paintings that decorate it (they depict cupids dining amid musicians) and on the presence of the low altar for sacrifices and libations. However, the purpose of a tall marble *podium*, set against the back wall and accessed by stairs, is unclear. It may have been used for public auctions. The area south of the sacellum, also decorated with the bases of columns at the entrance, was reserved for fishmongers, given that along the walls there are sloped marble counters with water runoffs. The artwork on the walls

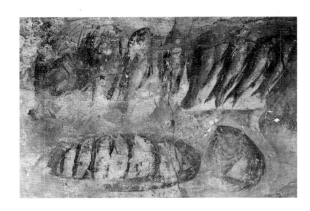

portrays the River Sarnus and the coast, the provenance of the products that were sold there.

Along the northern and western sides of the colonnade, we can still see the wall paintings that decorated the construction. The upper register features panels with still-lifes referring to the food sold there and portraying poultry, game, fish and jars with processed foods such as *garum*, a thriving industry in Pompeii.

In effect, the *Macellum* is the monumentalized representation of a place used for provisions, one whose construction concept is part of the broader layout of the Forum itself. Its function, which is clearly evident also through its relationship with the adjacent installations, reflects the desire to make even this structure fit in-

to the decorative architectural program advocated by the new imperial policy. We have observed that the *Macellum* was built in the Forum, and this was only natural, because it represented one of its hubs. During ancient times, the Forum was originally built as a place used for the market and for trade. This function, which was handed down over the centuries, then came to be associated with the role of social representation, taken on in each city during the early Imperial Age.

Thus, great importance was attributed to the side of the *Macellum* leading into its main entrance in the Forum, with two doors separated by a wall acting as a backdrop for a marble base with two marble columns. A large number of statue bases set along its façade created a full-fledged gallery of famous figures, while the columns of the Forum colonnade in this segment were particularly monumental in appearance. As opposed to the

other ones, these were fluted and decorated with Corinthian capitals. Between the columns and the façade of the *Macellum*, there was a series of shops that became deeper and deeper moving to the north, thereby aligning the construction with this space, since it was set at an angle with respect to the Forum. This area thus acted as an architectural link and, naturally, it also served a practical purpose as a place to sell wares. Given the gallery of statues outside the complex and the sacellum inside, it also became the perfect setting for political propaganda. In the place that was the most popular daily attraction, the general populace was entranced by the impressive construction with its sumptuous marble and paintings. Thus +the people felt that they were somehow a part of the grandeur tied to the supreme imperial power, even when simply buying a handful of sardines.

We have already commented on the logical link between the *Macellum* and the surrounding areas. First of all, it was connected to Via degli Augustali, where the north entrance led directly to a series of shops set up on the outside on the longer side. Likewise, on the southern end the entrance from the alley of the Hanging Balcony linked it to several shops that recent excavation work has identified as places where *garum* was produced. Lastly, in the Forum beyond the Temple of Jupiter Capitoline, the natural complement of the *Macellum* was the Forum Olitorium, the vegetable market. This was located in turn across from the *horrea*, the granary that was also used to store household goods that were being traded or that had been lodged as collateral.

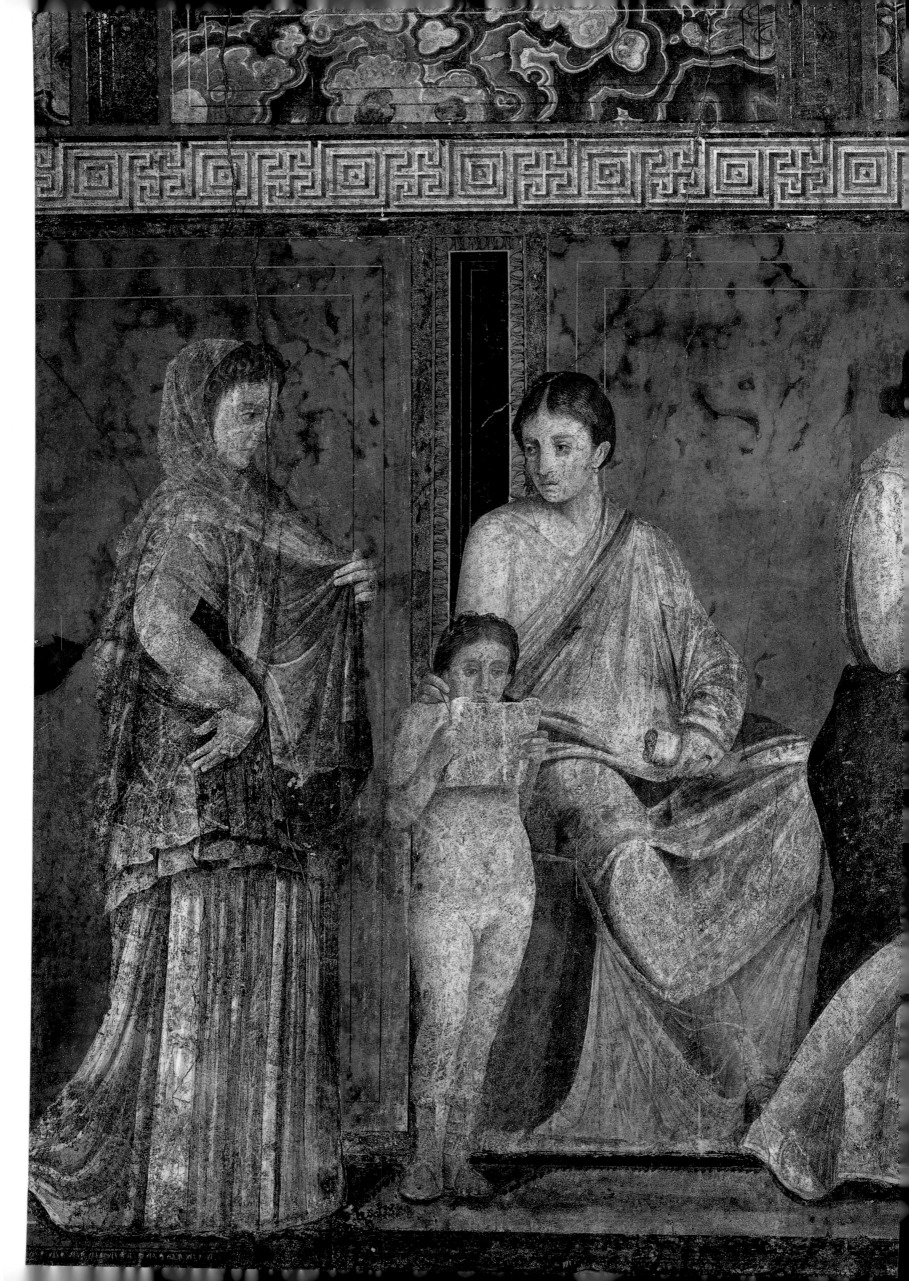

142

*These two frescoes from the Macellum depict two
different shops, one selling fish, above, and the other
for poultry, below.*

142-143

*In the aerial view from the northeast end
of the Macellum to the center, the base of the tholos
is clearly visible.*

THE MENSA PONDERARIA
AND THE TRAVELING VENDORS

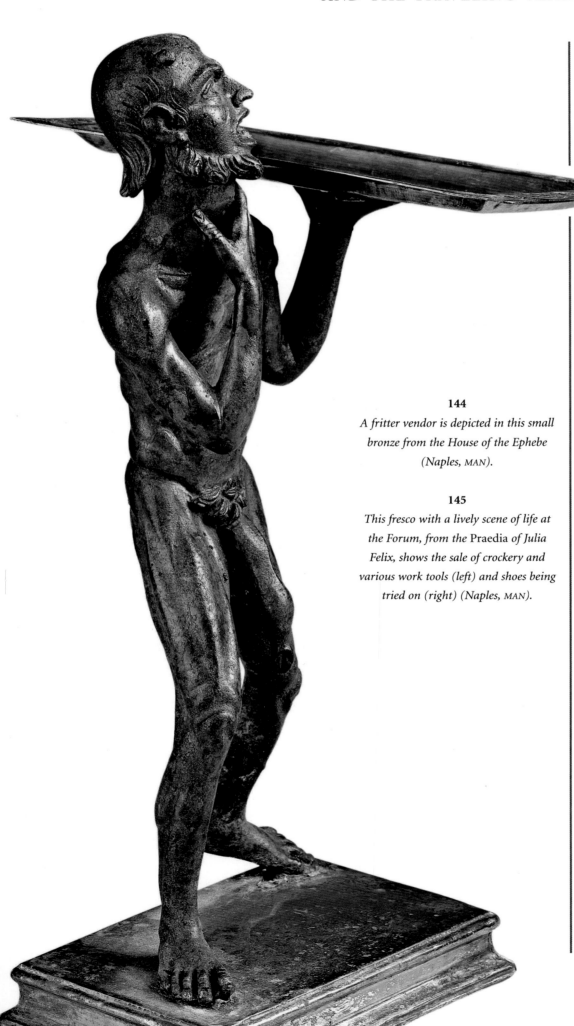

144

A fritter vendor is depicted in this small bronze from the House of the Ephebe (Naples, MAN).

145

This fresco with a lively scene of life at the Forum, from the Praedia *of Julia Felix, shows the sale of crockery and various work tools (left) and shoes being tried on (right) (Naples, MAN).*

The fact that the most important business was conducted at the Forum is also demonstrated by the existence of an unusual construction, the *Mensa ponderaria*, on its western side. This was essentially a public office that officially monitored weights and measures, and it could be used for purchases and sales made in the square. It already existed in Pompeii during the pre-Roman period and was composed of two slabs set on top of the other, each of which had round cavities that differed in width and depth to correspond to the various measures. The cavities, marked in the Oscan language, were similar to the kind used in the Greek world, with a hole on the bottom to let out the product that had been placed in it to be measured. It seems logical to think that they were used so that magistrates could check the accuracy of the shopkeepers' assessments. During the Augustan period, with the reform that standardized the weights and measures used locally to set up a general system, the cavities were enlarged to comply with the new Roman system that had gone into effect.

This is noted in an inscription along the front of the lower slab, commemorating the Pompeian magistrates who standardized these measures in about 20 BC.

Thus, the places used for selling food were organized in a very significant way, and within the Forum this corresponded to the other places reserved for different types of trade. However, alongside the permanent posts there were also mobile ones, represented by traveling retail vendors as well as temporary installations set up on market days.

Several inscriptions offer valuable information that helps round out this picture.

Based on some of the graffiti found in the Basilica, we can establish that there were traveling beverage vendors, who mainly sold wine to the crowds busy handling their different transactions. There were also bums or parasites, ever present to beg money or favors, as the inscriptions here also document. Other texts on the south wall of the Temple of Apollo (*CIL* IV 1768s.) cite the place where two vendors of flatbread (*libarii*) set up their stand. In this case, we do not know if they were there illegally or "with the permission of the *aediles*," as instead noted in several similar inscriptions referring to sales areas near the Amphitheater, where stalls were set up during shows.

In our reconstruction of life under the Forum porticoes, archaeological findings, such as the many portable ovens found in the city, are of assistance. They must have been used to make *panis clibanicius*, sweets that were sold on street corners. Likewise, the small bronzes of the *placentarii,* found in the House of the Ephebe, recall these traveling fritter vendors, who would hawk their delicious wares and wander through the streets trying to entice passersby to try them.

However, nothing gives us an idea of the bustling trade of the era as much as the scenes portrayed in several paintings that have a photographic accuracy. In the one found in the House of Attius Aniceto, which depicts the brawl that broke out between the Pompeians and the Nucerians in AD 59 at the Pompeii Amphitheater and then spread to the city streets, we can easily pick out the peddlers who set up tents or stands to sell their products near the gladiator shows. At the Julia Felix complex there is a series of paintings generically identified as "Daily Life in the Forum," and they offer additional details about the sale of goods and other activities that took place there.

In fact, amid the porticoes and the bases of the statues that decorated the square, we can see people selling pots, pans and other everyday items. Then there are shoe salesmen, carts pulling merchandise, laden pack animals (perhaps brought there to be sold), beggars receiving alms from matrons, scribes ready to offer their writing services to the illiterate, and people hawking multicolored fabrics, bread and sweets, fruit and vegetables, and hot food. There is even a school group that looks on while a teacher punishes a lazy student by flogging his backside, in a scene reminiscent of the poet Horace's *plagosus Orbilius.*

And there's more: people intent on recording legal deeds on tablets, probably in connection with the *patronatus,* craftsmen selling and repairing metal implements, people reading the *acta diurna,* the news of the day written on long papyrus rolls tacked like posters to the statue bases, cobblers fixing shoes, perfumers giving their patrons a whiff of their fragrant products … in short, a jumble of people and activities, just as we would imagine on a typical market day. An inscription (*CIL* IV 8863), we learn that that the Pompeii market was on Saturday, as it was in Nuceria, while it took place on Sunday in Atella and Nola, on Monday in Cumae, on Tuesday in Puteoli, on Wednesday in Rome, and on Thursday in Capua.

This clearly suggests that in order to go to these markets, the traveling vendors or even potential buyers would move from place to place according to their possibilities and needs.

SHOPS

While a large concentration of businesses could be found both near and inside the Forum, we must also note that shops and businesses were essentially located all over Pompeii. Naturally, most of them were along the main streets and in the center of town. Many shops were directly connected to the large aristocratic residences by *atriums*, and people often used the rooms at the sides of the entrance, opening them onto the street as shops. These shops were run by the family of the house or were rented.

Nevertheless, most of the shops were run by the common people, who used the space as both a business and home. This house-cum-shop setup had rather small rooms and, in some cases, also a back shop as well as other rooms or privies.

In general, the height of the room was exploited, creating a halved room (*pergula*) using a wooden beam mounted halfway up the wall. It was accessed using wooden ladder, often preceded by a few masonry steps. We can easily imagine that these lofts were used to hold beds, wardrobes and the bare necessities in terms of furnishings. Instead, the lower street-level floor served as a shop area and as a result, it was used mainly for merchandise.

A truly ingenious system was used to open as many rooms as possible onto the street while also maintaining – in such a limited amount of space – the privacy of home life during the hours the shop was not open for business. A set of wooden planks would slide into a grooved track across the entire width of the threshold of the room and in the architrave, leaving just enough space for the leaf of a small door, without a track. Mounted close together, these planks effectively created a wall. Once closed, the door latch would hook into the last plank, which had a fastening device. The door was hinged on the end of the threshold and, by means of the pins that fastened it to the jamb, it could swing open and closed like an ordinary door. This meant that at night, the room could be closed completely while also leaving enough room to enter and exit through the door comfortably. In the morning, the planks would be slid off the track to open the room along the entire storefront in order to display all the merchandise to passersby, without worrying about where to store the leaves of big and cumbersome doors. We should also point out that at the edges of the sidewalks, there are often holes that were used to block the stays of the awnings that, sustained by posts, were mounted outside the shop. Thus, the goods could be displayed on the sidewalk, shading them from the sun or a sudden rain shower while also effectively increasing the display area. To date, 614 shops have been counted in Pompeii, although in some cases it has not been possible to specify exactly what they sold.

These shops were used not only as places of business, but often also as small workshops in which a broad variety of work was conducted, typical of an orderly and well-organized society.

146-147

A fresco from the Praedia *of Julia Felix depicts customers buying bread from a stand (Naples,* MAN*).*

THE TRADES DOCUMENTED IN POMPEII

An inscription written in a facetious and rather contemptuous tone about a poor unfortunate who had tried his hand at every possible way of making a living, lists a series of trades the man had attempted. Before ending with a sarcastic and obscene comment (which we will omit), this inscription notes: "You failed eight times, but you'd be capable of failing sixteen. You worked as an innkeeper, you had a pottery shop, you worked as a butcher, then a baker and then a farmer, you then started selling little bronze items and you even worked as a second-hand dealer; now you've started making earthenware jars....". The documentation written on a city wall is a gold mine of information about the crafts of Pompeii and the surrounding areas. (It is in *Corpus Inscriptionum Latinarum* (*CIL*; designated inscription IV 10150.) The electoral inscriptions, in particular, cite a fair number of professional associations or at least work colleagues involved in supporting the candidates. Based on the assumption that some of the associations were also established as legal entities, attempts have been made to pinpoint the headquarters or places where the members met. Not all of these have been confirmed, however, and as a result it is preferable simply to indicate the businesses involved in many cases. To back this epigraphic evidence, we could also point to the large numbers of work implements found

in houses and *tabernae* but, again, we must move along the lines already cited. In terms of trades connected with agriculture, we have the *agricolae* or farmers, the *aliarii* or garlic sellers (although some sustain that the term refers to dice players), the *caepari* or onion sellers, the *lupinari* – also referred to as *lupinipoli* – who sold lupines, the *pomari*, who sold fruit, and above all the *vindemitores*, who harvested grapes. It is known that there were countless vineyards and winemaking facilities inside the city walls and in the surrounding countryside. The grape harvest, which is also expressly mentioned in the inscriptions, was also the subject of the famous pictorial frieze along the walls of the main room in the House of the Vettii. The production of wine, a mainstay of the Pompeian economy on a par with oil, is discussed in another chapter of this book (see Eliodoro Savino § The Golden Age of Pompeian Wine, pages 124-127.)

The *piscicapi*, or fishermen, exploited the resources of the sea. Numerous fishing implements, such as trammels, hooks and more, have been found at the port of Pompeii in Bottaro, the little village where many of the fishermen were based. In the city, there are also many little painted scenes and graffiti with images portraying fishing activities. This area was also the point of reference for the *nautae*, the seamen who performed various jobs.

148
Cupids with a goat carry flowers to prepare perfumes in the pictorial frieze from the main hall of the House of the Vettii.

149
The mosaic with polychrome inserts from the caldarium *of the House of Menander gives us a glimpse of marine life.*

By contrast, there is no explicit epigraphic evidence of hunters, but they appear repeatedly in graffiti sketches left in many Pompeian houses and in several paintings that depict both hunting scenes and still lifes with ground game and wild fowl, thus indicating that the practice was quite common. This is also confirmed by all the bones of wild animals found in the city. On the other hand, there is definite evidence of the *gallinarii*, who raised and sold poultry and barnyard animals.

There have been many findings of aviaries, used to breed thrushes and other fowl as food, for example in House VII 7, 16. At *caupona* I 8, 15-16, in particular, there is a painting portraying a procession of fowlers (*aucupes*). The area's large cattle were so famous that the *mons Lactarius* (now known as the Lattari mountains) was named after them, and they were led to pasture by the *armentari*. We also know from the sources (Seneca, *Natural Questions*, VI 27, 1-2) that there were large flocks in the area, obviously supervised by shepherds, who may also have been the ones who prepared *caseum* or cheese, an item that was always present on "shopping lists."

The timber from the forests on Mount Vesuvius was used as raw material by the *lignarii* for their numerous and varied products, and a specialized category of woodworkers known as *lignarii plostrari* made wheels and carts. A painting found outside a shop on Via di Mercurio shows the *lignari* celebrating their festival, carrying images of Minerva and, their patrons, on a baldachin (*ferculum*) in a procession. Deposits of lumber and carpentry items have been found near Porta Ercolano. A painting at the entrance to building VI 14, 37 instead shows a carpenter intent on sawing a beam, assisted by his errand boy. The carts were the main work tool of the *muliones*, carters who not only transported goods but also worked successfully as drivers, as indicated by an inscription. Their *stationes* were located near the main gates of the city, and from here they would take their agile gigs, ready to transport customers to nearby towns. There were also *saccari*, or porters, to transport goods.

Bread was prepared by *pistores*, while *clibanari* and *libari* were the ones who made cakes and flatbread.

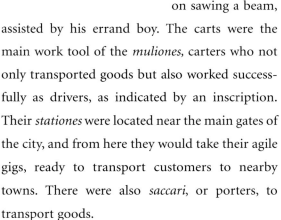

150-151
A cat snatches a bird and, in the lower register, ducks swim in a pond with birds, fish and shells in a mosaic from the House of the Faun (Naples, MAN).

151
A fresco from a shop on Via di Mercurio shows a procession of woodworkers carrying a baldachin with images of Minerva and Dedalus (Naples, MAN).

There were various categories of artisans involved in making textiles, dyeing and washing fabrics and clothing, and preparing mats and hides, also a fundamental part of the Pompeian economy. They were the *lanifricari*, who would degrease and card the freshly shorn wool, the *textores* or loom workers, the *infectores*, who were responsible for dyeing new fabrics and clothing, and the *offectores*, who redyed faded clothing. The *fullones* (a generic term that covers various workers in this sector), were responsible for degreasing and washing fabrics, while the *vestiarii* made clothing and the *sagari* made twill. The *quactiliari* handled the production of felt, the *tegettari* made mats and the *coriarii* worked hides and leather. Alongside the *quactil-*

iarii, the *sutores* also made shoes. In one of their shops (VII 1, 40-41), in addition to several work implements, a graffito was also found, commemorating the upgrade of some of these instruments. Other suppliers of personal services included the *unguentari*, who made perfumes. This trade is also portrayed in the frieze in the main room of the House of the Vettii: several nurseries have also been identified near the Amphitheater, and their plants were used to make scented ointments. Other ointments were used for medicinal purposes. Like the *unguentari*, the *tonsores* (barbers) and *unctores* (massagers) were also connected with the baths, where they would work as *fornacatores*, responsible for the heating system, and as *perfusores*, the bath attendants for those who could not immerse themselves completely in the tubs. The *dissignatores* assigned seats at the theaters. Lastly, at the service of the wealthiest, mainly members of the *familia*, we also find *ianitores* or doormen, as well as *arcarii*, who administrated assets.

The *argentarii*, like the famous Caecilius Jucundus, were full-fledged bankers. The funerary monument of one of these *argentarii* was found outside Porta Nocera, and there is plenty of evidence of people, like Faustilla, who practiced usury. The *aurifices* or goldsmiths, the *caelatores* or chasers, and the *gemmarii* worked with precious materials. The frieze from the House of the Vettii also portrays the various production processes of valuables, and two workshops that handled gemstones have been discovered near the Amphitheater, going north along Via di Nocera.

The liberal arts were the arena of sculptors and bronze workers, and studios have been found in what is known as the Sculptor's House and in the villa of Siminius Stephanus outside Porta Vesuvio. There were also numerous painters who decorated houses. One, Lucius, left his name written in the summer *triclinium* of what is known as the House of Loreius Tiburtinus. A painters' workshop has also been identified on Via di Castricio, and the production and sale of paint was handled by at least three factories. The *programmatum scriptores* also worked with paint. They were the workers who painted the city walls with electoral posters, notices of gladiator shows, messages and various signs The names of many of them are known and for some of them, it has even been possible to pinpoint where they lived.

There were also different teachers who often conducted their business in public places, such as the Forum. Evidently, their work wasn't always adequately compensated, given that one of them in the *Campus* felt obliged to invoke the gods to bless those who had paid the fees he charged for his lessons.

152

The activities of a coppersmith's shop are illustrated in this marble bas-relief sign (Naples, MAN).

153

Work tools are depicted in bas-relief on the shop sign of a lignarius *along Via Stabiana.*

However, the *librari*, or scribes, were more readily satisfied, as they were undoubtedly paid for each job. The real technicians were the *architecti*, who supervised construction work, and the *mensores* or surveyors, whose most important instrument was the *groma*, found in shop I 6, 3 together with other bronze items sold there. The depiction of the *groma*, together with the plumb line and the alignment balls, can also be seen on the funerary relief of Nicostratus, which was found – recycled – at the necropolis of Porta Nocera and is now at the Museum of Boscoreale. Various types of surgical implements, like pots and scales for medicinal potions as well as other tools used specifically by *medici*, have been found extensively in many settings in Pompeii, first of all the House of the Surgeon. Unfortunately, it must be noted that the medical profession has not been investigated as extensively as it deserves.

154 top and 155

Aeneas, whose leg has been wounded, leans on the weeping Ascanius as the Iapyx, the doctor, treats him and Venus brings medicinal herbs. The fresco is from the House of Siricus (Naples, MAN).

154 bottom

A scraper, wax tablets, a double inkwell, a quill and an unrolled papyrus, depicted in this fresco, represent the instrumentum scriptorium, *or writing implements, of ancient Roman world (Naples, MAN).*

The shops of the thermopolia *had receptacles for food. In this one, located along Via dell'Abbondanza, in the background we can also see the well-tended* lararium. *The inset on the right shows the* agathodaemon *serpents tasting the offerings.*

There were also numerous inns and *thermopolia*, places that served readymade food and, above all, wine, which in winter was diluted with water kept hot on a burner that was always lit. Thus, instead of coffee, tea or spirits, this was the pick-me-up enjoyed at all hours of the day. At the same time, there is frequent mention (the most numerous citations along with those of the *fullones*) of the innkeepers, or *caupones*. Likewise, there were also many restaurants and hotels throughout the city, above all in the historic district, near the city gates or the Amphitheater. It was commonplace to rent lodgings on the top floors of houses, but some large property-owners, such as Julia Felix and Alleius Nigidius Maius, had also allocated entire real-estate complexes for this purpose and advertised the fact with posters.

We also know that around the city there were workshops that manufactured tiles and bricks, although they have not been located yet, while a workshop that made oil lamps has been identified in House I 20, 3. An oven to make glass items was found in the *insula occidentalis*, under the rooms occupied by the school of archaeology set up by Fiorelli. The *fabri*, and some of their workshops, are equally well documented.

There were also other intriguing trades, like the *putianus* or well-digger, the *veterarius* or second-hand dealer and, naturally, the *sortilogus* or soothsayer.

The words (*CIL* IV 9839) written by Marcus Epidius, who sold hardware and other small items, on the sides of his shop window on Via di Castricio gives us a sense of the spirit of commerce in Pompeii: "I swear on my head: I'll never offer credit. I was cheated by Annius Atimeto and I won't give anyone else credit!"; "I hate the poor. Anyone who asks for something for free is foolish. When you hand over the money, you'll get the goods."

AGRICULTURAL PRODUCTION

Sources materials emphasize the wealth of the vineyards in the territory close to Pompeii, and archaeological and epigraphic findings fully confirm this. However, it should not be forgotten that since ancient times Mount Vesuvius' eruptions must have made the fields adjoin the city quite fertile, as the authors acknowledge (e.g., Strabo, *Geography*, V 4, 7 - C 247). In fact, archaeological findings have shown that in the countryside around Pompeii and on the first ledges of Vesuvius' slopes there was a myriad of small and large estates. These were the prerogative not only of small producers but also of important Roman capitalists or wealthy Pompeian families who had their land cultivated by their servants. For example, the House of Menander had accommodations for a large number of slaves who were employed in the district by day to cultivate the fields.

In addition to food products documented by findings and, above all, crops famous far beyond the local area for their quality, there was wine, oil and numerous other products worth mentioning. First of all, there was cabbage, mentioned by Columella (*De Re Rustica*, X 135s.) and described by Pliny (*Natural History*, XIX 140) as follows: "They are larger in size [than those of other regions], with a thin stalk at the roots and large leaves. They are rarer and narrower, and their main quality is their tenderness, which also does not survive in cold weather."

When it came to onions, Columella (XII 10, 1) also expressly recommended the Pompeian variety, and in fact they can frequently be found on the many "shopping lists" scratched onto various walls in Pompeii. Some have even been unearthed, for example in the *Lupanare*. Garlic was also consumed in large quantities: one graffito lists the purchase of 250 bunches. Other graffiti include two typical vegetables commonly found on the "shopping list," beets and pennyroyal. "Carbonized" seeds of melons, pumpkins, fava beans, peas, chickpeas, lentils and lettuce have also been found, while chicory, turnip greens, yellow carrots and basil have been identified through pollen studies. Hemp seeds have also been found: hemp, linen and byssus, the last made from the filaments of a bivalve shell, were raw materials used in weaving.

In terms of fruit, abundantly depicted in the various still lifes, figs led the way, even though the local variety was named after the nearby city of Herculaneum (Pliny, *Natural History,* XV 70). Fresh or dried, they have been found almost everywhere in Pompeii, including the *Macellum,* alongside grapes, chestnuts and plums. There were walnuts, hazelnuts, almonds, apples, pears, cherries, apricots, peaches and pomegranates, whose juice was used to make an enjoyable beverage and medicinal extracts.

Grains were also plentiful. An inscription from a farmhouse north of Pompeii mentions

Figs, one of the most renowned agricultural products of the Vesuvius area, are exquisitely depicted here in an elaborate wicker basket in this fresco from Poppaea's Villa at Oplontis.

that barley and fava beans were grown, and an analysis of the pollen has also confirmed that barley was grown in the area. Another inscription, this one found in a house in Pompeii, notes 200 *modium* of wheat, or about 50 bushels, for the date of July 13. In the same house, another graffito dated June 25 notes the sale of lees for 32 *asses*, so we can assume that the first amount also refers to the sale of goods produced on the farms. Another graffito mentions the transport of a fairly large load of hay. Large quantities of spelt, a typical local crop, were also found, while the many country villas that have been explored have constantly demonstrated the presence of barns and large granaries. All this leads to the inference that there was a local production of soft and durum wheat.

A large quantity of forage, composed of oats mixed with fava beans, was found in a loft above a stall in the House of the Chaste Lovers. An analysis of the grasses mixed with this material has made it possible to determine that the oats came from a field in which the crops were rotated, an ancient farming practice that alternated the production of grains and other crops so the land could "rest."

160
A Silenic mask gazes from a garden with lush vegetation in the detail from a
fresco from the House of the Golden Bracelet.

161
In the Praedia *of Julia Felix, which included apartments for rent, eating areas,*
bath facilities, pools stocked with fish, and furnished garden areas, a large space
was set aside for ball games, played by pilicrepi, *or ballplayers.*

162-163

The bakery of Modestus, located in the very center of town, was one of the largest in Pompeii. In addition to numerous millstones for grinding wheat, the main room at the bakery also had a massive brick oven.

163 top

In the atrium of the caupona of Sotericus on Via dell'Abbondanza, there were five dolia set inside a masonry counter, and a marble labrum was set on a round table, also made of masonry.

We have already seen the variety of crafts conducted in Pompeii, and it is interesting to take a closer look at some of them to understand their organization and technologies.

To start, we can enter one of the 35 bakeries to date identified in Pompeii. In the inside courtyard, on the floor composed of large stone slabs, grindstones made of volcanic stone were set up to crush wheat. They were composed of a mobile part shaped like an hourglass (*catillus*), which was set with the lower tub on a fixed conical part (*meta*) that matched it perfectly. The wheat was placed in the hollow of the upper receptacle of the *catillus*. Donkeys or mules, for which the flooring was designed, would drive the mobile part of the grindstone, crushing the wheat kernels that would drop toward the bottom by gravity, turning them to flour that was collected on a surface lined in lead. After being blended with water, the flour was mixed in a hand-operated kneader that worked much like the kind still used today, with rotary blades and resistance wedges along the tank that kept turning and blending the dough. In a special room next to the oven, the dough was turned out onto counters composed of wooden boards set on stone piers. It was generally shaped into round loaves scored in wedges. Once the entire surface of the board was covered with loaves, the board was lifted and passed through a slit on one side of the oven, to be placed directly on the counter in front of the opening of the oven. Here, the worker used a wooden paddle to place each loaf in the cooking chamber. When necessary, he would moisten the end of the paddle with water from a tub set at the foot of the oven, in order to keep the heat from ruining it. The wood-burning oven, made of bricks assembled to form a false vault, was essentially the same as the kind still used in the area today, particularly for baking pizza. However, it differed from the modern type above all in terms of the flue, which was set outside the heating chamber, across from the counter holding the unbaked loaves. We have the end-product of this fast-paced work process, which followed a complete cycle and used a production line, in the form of a number of charred loaves of the famous bread whose fragrance was praised in ancient times. An inscription (*CIL I 8903*) beckons travelers to taste the bread of Pompeii, putting off their stopover for a good glass of wine until they reach Nuceria.

Fabric producers, dyers and launderers played a very important role in both the economic and social life of Pompeii, and their significance is underscored by the magnificent Building of Eumachia, the operating headquarters of the fullers' guild, built in the middle of the Forum. It must also have been used as a sort of negotiations market for various types of goods, and this is probably where the *auctiones*, or auctions, which are frequently mentioned on the wax tablets, took place.

A total of eighteen *fullonicae*, or laundries, have been counted, in addition to the thirteen *officinae lanifricariae* that treated raw wool, the seven *textrinae* where the wool was spun and woven, and the nine *officinae infectoriae*, where it was dyed. As soon as the wool was shorn, the grease (*oesypum*) was removed in lead boilers over an open flame, and the degreasing process was done using ammonia-rich urine or soda, which was then eliminated through long rinsing. After drying in the sun, the wool was then carded with iron cards and was spun with a spindle before being woven on a loom. Various weaving shops, particularly during the city's last years, were set up in old houses, such as House of the Figured Capitals and the Houses of the First and Second Columned Cenacolo (room), where a large number of slaves were also employed, pointing to the growing importance of this production.

The cloth was then boiled in lead boilers with colorants, but before the actual dyeing process could begin the workers had to treat the different dyes, which were made from plants (such as indigo and saffron) and animal substances (e.g., purple), as well as minerals and textile fibers. At the end of the process, the fabrics were washed again and then fulled.

The *fullonica* run by Stephanus on Via dell'Abbondanza had five oval pounding basins. The cloth would be trampled by foot and placed to soak in water with urine or soda. There were also three large communicating vats, placed on descending levels for each rinsing phase. Between them, there were passages with stairs to allow the workers to go into the vats to do their work. The cloth, which was hardened by the process, was then treated with fuller's earth and rinsed again in a large central vat. After it was dried on the roof of the building, which was built horizontally for this specific purpose, the cloth was then pressed with a special press.

164 and 165

A pillar at the fullonica *of Veranius Hypsaeus is painted with scenes of the laundry business, such as the workers trampling the cloth in basins with their feet, and delivering the product to the customer (Naples, MAN).*

166-167

The same pillar also shows another scene on the left, with a worker carding wool and another one preparing a wicker cage, used to treat the cloth with sulfur. Note the owl, the protectress of the fullones (Naples, MAN).

168-169
The frieze with cupids and psychai *from the main hall of the House of the Vettii offers an exquisite portrayal in miniature of the various phases involved in the fullers' work.*

169 bottom
The main room at the fullonica of Stephanus, on Via dell'Abbondanza, is taken up by a large vat for washing cloth, which was then laid out to dry on the buildings flat roofs.

The launderers' activity is also depicted in the frieze in the House of the Vettii, whereas a pillar of the *Fullonica* of *Veranius Hypsaeus* (now in the National Museum, Naples) features paintings with the different details of the fabric preparation and finishing processes that took place in the shop.

The only tannery found in Pompeii (I 5, 2) has a series of six compartments split up by dividers. In three of them, a pipeline brought tannin directly to one of the three earthenware jars at the end, so that two workstations could use it. In a back room, there were fifteen round vats lined with *cocciopesto*, or crushed potsherds, with two openings, one to add the tanning agent and the other to drain it. Of them, only three tanks – the smallest ones – were used for non-vegetable tanning, i.e., with alum, which was better suited for thin leathers.

The felt workers (*coactiliarii*) produced cloth by rubbing and pressing hare pelts or "dead" wool, treated with coagulants made using boiled vinegar. Their work is depicted in a painting at the entrance to the workshop of Verecundus on Via dell'Abbondanza, which also made rather costly clothing. A graffito (*CIL* IV 9083) cites a *tunica lintea aurata,* a garment made of linen with inserts made of spun gold.

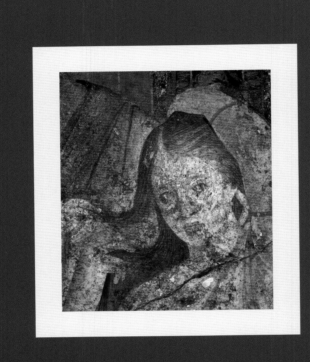

PRIVATE LIFE

◆

SOCIETY: PUBLIC AND PRIVATE

THE ELITE AND PRIVILEGES

L ike many other cities in ancient Italy, following the Punic Wars Pompeii underwent rapid economic development that was reflected in intense building activities and the luxurious houses of the Samnite aristocracy. The decisive factors in this development were the influx of families from the more highly developed Campanian towns (punished for backing Hannibal) or from cities in south-central Italy and, in particular, the predominance of a slave-oriented production system over the older and more familiar forms of dependence. Roman Pompeii was also a prosperous and lively community, one without much dissension but marked by enormous inequality within its ranks. This hardworking, well-to-do city, where many had the opportunity to emerge rapidly, was nonetheless a municipal society of Roman Italy, founded on the intensive exploitation of slave labor and on the patronage of the ruling classes. In Roman society, social status and rank were closely connected with how one had earned his wealth: in Pompeii, the aristocracy based its power mainly on farming, but it also dealt in trade and crafts that were often managed through slaves and freedmen. Perhaps it would be more correct to refer to aristocracies using the plural form, as there were enormous differences even within the elite in terms of wealth, ethnic origin and social traditions. The ancient Samnite families showed a remarkable capacity to adapt and survive. Some of them held public roles throughout the entire life of the city, such as the *gens Popidia.* Others, like the *gens Audii,* seemed to disappear when the city was colonized, only to reappear in the Imperial Age.

172 and 173
The marble statue of Livia, the wife of Augustus, was found
at the Villa of the Mysteries and is now in the Pompeii
Antiquarium. The sculpted portrait of a man comes from
the House of Vesonius Primus (Naples, MAN).

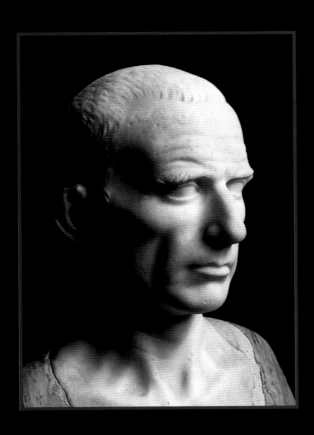

Among several of these newly arrived *gentes* and families, shrewd marriages, which were quite frequent during the early Imperial Age, created a widespread network of relations. These were alliances among structurally similar groups in which the ethnic factor quickly lost ground. Likewise, the adoption of members of the elite by these new families appears to have been done for the purpose of a controlled changeover of the aristocracy, and there are plenty of examples of this. The Clodii were related to the native families of the Lassii, the Gelli and the Holconii; the Lucretii were related to the Decidii, the Epidii and the Satrii; the Maccii married into the Epidii (both were local families, but on different levels). As the names indicate, the two adopted sons were from the Mamii and Velasii families, respectively. The last phase in the life of Pompeii, in which men from rather modest families or families with slave origins emerged in the political life, reveals the symptoms of an ongoing social transformation whose depth and underpinnings are difficult to assess. Caution is a must in examining a type of commerce that was always tied to farming, with problems of liquidity and the seeming lack of true entrepreneurial figures. What is certainly striking is the interest in profit, exhibited even in the words done in mosaic found in the *atrium* of several houses, such as the one of P. Vedius Siricus (VII 1 25, 47), duumvir in AD 60: *Salve lucrum* (Welcome to Money!), words that powerfully evoke the concept of *lucrum facere* (making money) cited repeatedly in Petronius' novel *Satyricon* (mid-1st century AD). Within the municipal elite, there are different characteristics from one city to the next. The most important families usually had considerable resources and a lifestyle similar to the one of the rich Roman senators, which whom they were tied by an intricate network of relationships. Blood relations with the Roman aristocracy were quite rare in Pompeii, but relationships of

amicitia and *clientela* are well documented, ranging from Cicero, the owner of a storefront in Pompeii, to the Roman nobleman Livineius Regulus, who was expelled by the Senate between AD 37 and 47. The nobleman was the one who, in AD 59, organized the games at the Amphitheater that became infamous because of the fighting that broke out with the Nucerians. There is also another odd aspect: there are no known Pompeian aristocrats in the senatorial order. One almost gets the impression that their sole interest was in any

tablinum *of the House of Marcus Lucretius Fronto. It depicts a lavish
construction with porticoes on two floors and delightful hillsides in the
background.*

production activity that would gain them wealth, a position with the political leadership, and a demonstration of status. Many of the other notables had political ties of *amicitia* with important people, but they did not have boundless resources, nor could they aspire to prestigious marriages. With the exception of privileges connected with their offices, for most magistrates and decuriones daily life probably differed very little from the one led by their ordinary freeborn fellow citizens. This is amply demonstrated by the differ-

ences in acts of patronage, which for most of these notables was limited to the sum connected with the office they held. In other cases, however, this patronage was quite pompous, such as the construction of the Odeion and the Amphitheater during the Sullan period by C. Quintus Valgus and M. Porcius, the renovation project with extensive work in marble undertaken by the Holconii and by Celere and Rufus during the Augustan period, and the parades and splendid games A. Clodius Flaccus put on.

PLEBS *URBANA,* SLAVES AND FREEDMEN

The different groups declaring their support for candidates to public office give us a very lively and uncommon idea of how Pompeii's different *plebs urbana* were set up. There were "categories" connected with different trades, as well as de facto associations distinguished by the type of lifestyle and by the emergence – possibly – of a fledgling awareness of class, if this is how we are to interpret the reference to the *pauperes* (the poor) as a group supporting the candidacy of a man named Modestus for the office of *aedile.* This is the area of "stable poverty" of pre-industrial societies: men – but also women prevalent in certain sectors such as inns and taverns (*cauponae*), textiles – involved in different crafts activities and minor trade. There is no lack of street peddlers or of homeless people who would take on odd jobs. The Pompeian plebs would earn what they needed to survive (based on the graffiti, labor must have had a low incidence on prices) and these people would gather together in associations, often based on the métier they plied, to gain a level of social dignity they were otherwise denied. This dignity focused on decent funerals, enjoyable meals, and collective participation in public life. The plebs included *ingenui* (born freedmen) of humble birth, who seem to decrease among the craftsmen during the Imperial Age, as well as a majority of *liberti* (manumitted slaves). Certainly most of the toughest work at the shops of the *fullones,* the *coriarii,* the *garum* shops and the textile workshops was done by slaves. This was the typical structure of Roman society during the early empire, in which juridical conditions diverged from social differences and the breaks in society were essentially vertical. For freeborns and slaves, there were parallel steps (but on different levels) for climbing the social ladder: in short, freeborns and slaves, *ingenui* and freedmen were present – without every truly mixing – on the various levels of social life. Slavery left a deep mark on Roman society. In Pompeii, as in every Italic community, even people with a modest income owned at least a slave or two. From a legal standpoint, the position of these men and women (and the slave trade was quite profitable) was a condition of total personal dependence. They were so utterly devoid of any form of freedom that in the literary sources a slave is defined as "an instrument with a voice." In effect, their limited personal and property rights were not acknowledged until the Imperial Age. From a social standpoint, their condition was instead defined by how they were used. A privileged minority lived close to their masters: they would handle negotiations for them and run their shops and crafts enterprises. In short, their living conditions were essentially akin to those of a freeborn person. Paradoxically, the economic and even juridical subjectivity required for these tasks gave these slaves a better chance to move up in society than the kinds of opportunities offered to the plebeian *ingenui.* In Pompeii, we can see from the records of the "banker" L. Caecilius Jucundus the many slaves acted in deeds and although they had no legal capacity, they stood in their masters' stead in stipulating various contracts. Caecilius himself used his slaves to manage his dealings. The slaves of the imperial house were particularly fortunate. Likewise, the position of public slaves of the colony was also a privileged one, as they were allowed to carry out rather important tasks. One example is Secundus, who in AD 53 was indicated as a *servus coloniae.* Slaves who were educated or received sufficient training to administer their masters' assets were in the minority (for example, M. Vesonius Primus' treasurer). They were often the first to be manumitted, but even as slaves they were often accepted – alongside the most fortunate freedmen – into the religious colleges tied to the imperial cult of Fortuna Augusta or Minerva Augusta.

177

In this fresco, Phaedra, the wife of Theseus, is assisted by a young girl who seems to offer her material favors in a very intimate manner (Naples, MAN).

This fresco, discovered in Regio V 2,4, *recreates the*
atmosphere of a rich banquet, illustrating the lavishness
of entertainment as well as the servants' various tasks
(Naples, MAN*).*

Nevertheless, most of the slaves were members of the lower social classes, in which their juridical statute of dependency points to an even more oppressive position. In the urban *familia*, they were full-fledged household servants who were subjected to a work pace set more by their masters' whims than by the principles of good business management. In Pompeii, they lived in a marginal section of the house, which was isolated from the residential part and was of inferior building quality. The working conditions of slaves employed for particularly exhausting manufacturing activities were even worse, although they were slightly better than those of rural slaves, who were exploited intensively. The harsh treatment of the latter group is proven by the practice of closing them up in large rooms (*ergastula*) at night

and of often keeping them in chains. This is documented by the structure of several rustic villas as well as the shackles for 14 people (one-fourth to half of the total number of slaves working there) found at a villa near Gragnano. Discovered among the agricultural equipment and tools from the shop of the ironsmith Junianus in Pompeii there were also four pairs of slave shackles (*compedes*) with double iron rings, which must have been quite common and widespread. Nevertheless, there is no evidence of particularly inhumane conditions, nor do there seem to have been significant problems of this nature.

Manumission, which turned the slaves into freedmen or *liberti* and was experienced by many as a kind of rebirth, could be done formally, simultaneously giving the slave freedom and citizenship, through a testament, registration in the census lists or a simulated trial. Otherwise, it could be done informally in the presence of witnesses, by letter, during a banquet – but with limited effect in terms of civil and public law. Like slaves, the freedmen did not constitute a social class. Most of them – the ones who managed to gain their freedom by reimbursing their masters for the manumission tax and who then struggled to free their male or female slave companion – were poor laborers at workshops and small stores.

Freedmen had always been excluded from the Roman magistracies and as of AD 24, the *lex Visellia* also excluded them from holding municipal office. Nevertheless, their elite managed to fill public positions through the functions of the imperial cult, with the colleges of the *Augustali* and the S*eviri Augustali*. In any event, they were required to pay an honorary sum that would go toward public works, and they would lavish money on organizing banquets, rites and charity work, obtaining special honors and publicly paid funerals. There are several examples of this group, which was halfway between the *Ordo decurionum* and the plebs. N. Popidius Ampliatus was an *Augustale* who strove to get a position for his son –

A domina, *devoted to the art of painting, is the center*
of attention for other women and for her servants
(Naples, MAN*).*

just six years old at the time – among the decuriones by reconstructing the Temple of Isis. C. Munatius Faustus, who was granted the *bisellium*, or the seat of honor at the theater, and Vettius Conviva, one of the owners of the lovely House of the Vettii, were also *Augustales*. Several descendents of the freedmen's families (who were thus born free) ultimately held municipal offices, particularly during the city's last years. The most evident example, albeit certainly not the only one, was C. Julius Polybius, who was born into a family of imperial freedmen.

And yet, these figures were characterized by an underlying ambiguity. Although they were free citizens, they had to pay their patron *obsequium* – which represented a personal dependency at least on a moral level – and *operae*, or the material obligations established specifically in the deed of manumission. Other bonds involved the system of inheritance and marriage relations. More often than not, the copious examples of freedmen who managed profitable commercial and artisan activities (Stephanus, L. Vesonius Primus, L. Popidius Dionysius, the freedmen of Umbricius Scaurus, etc.) masked the patrons' properties and represented a convenient way for them to move their investments. In other words, the freedmen continued to manage the same activities just as they did when they were slaves, doing so with greater freedom but also at a greater risk. Only special terms, for example by becoming the

master's heir, could create a condition of autonomy and an independent position of wealth and prestige. The numerous freedmen involved in important economic or intellectual activities include the architect M. Artorius Primus, L. Ceius Serapio, the oldest known *argentarius* in Pompeii, and perhaps even the banker Caecilius Jucundus. Even in these more fortunate cases, the integration of these free men in society was only partial and as far as social relations were concerned, the memory of the initial stigma was never completely removed. Judging from *Satyricon* (set in Campania), the municipal aristocrats did not like to mix with freedmen, nor do *mésalliances* (marriages between people of different classes) seem to have been common in Pompeii. The freedmen instead seemed to model themselves after their patrons' fashions and lifestyles, following their marriage customs and quest for social prestige. The unofficial title of *princeps coloniae* (first in the colony), attributed to duumvir Cn. Alleius Nigidius, recalls the one of *princeps libertinorum* used by Fabius Eupor to refer to himself in an electoral poster. One of the characteristics of the freedmen was the desire to hand down their image and memory to posterity, with lavish tombs and a portrait inside the tombs. The most striking example of this can be seen in the tomb that the freedwoman Naevoleia Tyche built at the Porta Ercolano necropolis during her own lifetime for herself and her spouse.

LADIES AND SLAVES:
THE WOMEN OF POMPEII

There is no doubt that during the period about which we know the most concerning Pompeian society, the condition of Roman women was evolving toward a substantial level of emancipation, to use an anachronistic term. In the late Republican Age, women gained new rights. For example, they had a certain amount of independence in managing their wealth, they could inherit from their husbands and their guardianship was eased somewhat. By the early Imperial Age, they could essentially select their legal guardian and change him at will. This substantial independence stemmed from the rather liberal form of marriage that came to predominate by this time – known as *sine manu* ("without handing over") – whereby the woman remained in her father's *manus* and, upon his death, became his heir and an independent property-owner. However, it was limited by other factors, such as the age difference of the spouses (in the upper classes, the difference was often more than ten years), the difference in tasks, and the persistence of the traditional prestige surrounding the woman of just one man. As part of the general Romanization of Italy that started in the 1st century BC, this was also the condition of women in Pompeii. And if we are to judge by certain elements, including the portrayal of women next to writing implements (such as the famous portrait purported to be Sappho), in both Rome and Pompeii many women must have been educated. The names of women also appear in relation to production activities. Some of the bank accounts of L. Caecilius Jucundus belonged to women, and based on the graffiti we know that there were female usurers as well as owners of *cauponae*. There were also women involved in the business world. As far as their private lives were concerned, based on the funerary epigraphs we can glean a rather traditional situation: stable families, few children (one or two in the known cases, among the elite). Mésalliances (marriages between people of different ranks, or between *ingenui* and *liberti*) were rare. In the epigraphs, even slaves used the marital language of free citizens, despite the fact that their unions had no legal effect.

182 and 183

These two female portraits are also part of the pictorial cycle of the Villa of the Mysteries. The mysterious gaze of the priestess, portrayed from behind, is followed by the intense look of the domina.

We can cite several of the women of Pompeii and what little we know about them. There were Audia, daughter of Numerius, who lived in the Samnite era and died at a very old age (the indication of 112 years is probably an exaggeration); Aesquilla Polla, the bride of a certain Herennius, who died when she was just 22; Fadia, the wife of M. Tillius Rufus, who came with her husband from Arpinum and was the mother of a duumvir. We can also mention the aristocratic ladies who held a public role through the cults, such as the priestesses of Ceres Lassia, her niece Clodia, and Alleia Decimilla, whose son, already a decurio, died at the age of 17. Others include the priestesses of Venus (the most important priesthood), honored by the city for their munificence: Mamia, who built a temple to the *genius Augusti* (implying at least the emperor's consent), and Eumachia, who during the reign of Tiberius had an important building constructed in the Forum and named it after herself. This woman, the patron of the *fullones*, also symbolizes a woman from the elite ranks who was involved in extensive economic activities, on a par with Nero's wife Poppaea Augusta, who owned workshops for *figulinae* (terracotta items) near Pompeii. As far as freedwomen are concerned, we can mention Vertia Philumina (the wife of Sullan colonist M. Octavius, a freeborn), Clodia Nigella, *porcaria publica* (a woman encharged of swineherds), the freedwoman of Clodia and a priestess of Ceres, and Poppaea Note, the freedwoman of Priscus and the owner of small public baths. The graffiti also commemorate some of the lowly workers who would otherwise have been relegated to obscurity, such as the thirteen slaves from a small fabric workshop that was neither domestic nor industrial: marked next to the women's names are the weights of wool spun by each one and the length of the wefts they wove, the product of their day's work.

A maenad and a satyr, with ornaments alluding to the sylvan world, are depicted making advances to each other. Their features resemble those of ordinary Pompeians. The fresco is from the tablinum *of the House of Caecilius Jucundus (Naples, MAN).*

Impudicitia (sexual compliance) was a crime for a freeborn but a moral duty for the freedman and an absolute duty for a slave: this phrase from rhetorician Seneca effectively sheds light on the terms of the Roman mentality. And while the daily lives of slaves followed the dictum that what is pleasing to the master is no source of disgrace for the slave (*Satyricon*), here again women were the ones who were subjected to the most striking contradictions. Often destined to raise the children of their masters, they were closer to them in their everyday lives and, sometimes, even in their sentiments. These women were often freed before men were and only in rare cases could they also become the concubines or even the wives of their masters (although not in the senatorial aristocracy). However, like their male companions – and far more frequently – they were also sexually exploited by the *dominus* for his own pleasure or for that of the members of his family, or even for a type of commercial prostitution. The unusual dedication inside a gold bracelet (*armilla*) in the shape of a spiral with the head of a snake, found recently at Muregine still on the arm of its owner, killed when the building collapsed during the eruption, states "From the master to his slave" (*Dominus ancillae suae*). This certainly gives us food for thought, as it points to a relationship close enough for the girl to receive a valuable personal bauble as a gift, yet it also emphasizes the legal distinction in no uncertain terms.

Those who worked as prostitutes in Pompeii were slaves and women from the lowest classes. As noted in the graffiti, they would sell their bod-

ies for paltry sums: one or two *asses* (a measure of ordinary table wine cost one *as*, while Falerno wine cost four *asses*). The price of 16 *asses* charged by Atticé, according to a graffito on a seat outside Porta Marina, is certainly exceptional.

Many erotic paintings known as *Veneris figurae*, which appear to have served as showy advertising put up near the places used for these sexual relations, realistically illustrate the different services, and numerous graffiti allude rather explicitly to these transactions, citing names. One example is Eutychis, whose name is carved at the entrance of the House of the Vettii, who charged two *asses*. Various places whose number has not been confirmed (fewer than what was theorized in the past) were devoted to this activity, such as the brothel (VII 12, 18-20) that had rooms with masonry beds. It was located off the main road but in a central spot that was well trafficked and easy to reach, just behind the Stabian Baths and next to a secondary entrance to the baths. Prostitution was often practiced at inns and restaurants open to the public (particularly at the *cauponae*, such as the one of Sempronia Asellina), in the *cellae meretriciae*, which were single rooms with masonry beds, or in rooms in private homes. In the latter case, this profitable activity could be related to room rentals to slave dealers, or to management of the business by slaves or by the master's freedmen. A series of clues, the *Veneris figurae* painted in the servants' quarters of private homes, as well as explicit graffiti lead us to think that even the owners of wealthy city houses and of a rustic villa in Carmiano exploited their own household slaves for prostitution.

The sinuous lines created by the encounter of the bodies of a satyr and a nymph, captured in a mosaic in a cubiculum in the House of the Faun, create an atmosphere of spontaneous sensuality (Naples, MAN).

GOLD AND BEAUTY

On the morning of August 24, AD 79, many Pompeian women – gardeners, innkeepers, priestesses, slaves who served in the houses, including the *ornatrices*, or personal hairdressers of the era – had already started going about their usual activities. That day, however, the ladies who were accustomed to taking care of every curl and modeling their gowns with a matching belt before leaving the house or receiving visits, did not have enough time to do this. Starting at 10 o'clock, the unexpected catastrophe compelled them solely to seek shelter, collecting – or wearing – their most valued possessions. On any other day, part of the morning would have been devoted to styling their hair, a traditions began to count for very little as of the 1st century BC. Starting in the Augustan period, practices changed: the imperial consort of the period would underscore the political changeover by launching a new hairstyle. From the Palatine, the news about curls and hair length flew on the wings of Mercury: in a flash, everyone copied the trend set by the imperial family for all the provinces. The same held true for men but, as everyone knows, women's affectations have always been the ones that attract attention. Sometimes fashion was set by emperors' wives: first Livia's, and some other times it was Poppaea's hairstyle that became the most popular. During the summer Mount Vesuvius erupted, the ladies of the Flavian dynasty set the trend of diadems of false curls. Each woman would take up the fashion and follow its dictates according to her budget, using personal skill to make up for any lack of resources. The *ornatrix*, wielding a hot iron (*calamistrum*), would curl the *coma*, devoting hours to the hairdo. For special occasions, women would not limit themselves to styling their hair: waves and braids were held in place with large pins, embroidered ribbons covered the spot where false curls were fitted into the hairdo, and precious netting decorated ladies' heads, leaving a few wispy curls peeking out. The fashion of the gold filigree "bonnet" must have been quite popular until just a few years before the eruption (AD 50-70). This is how the woman referred to as Sappho was depicted in the frescoed medallion found in 1760. It is also worn by Ariadne, as portrayed in the work from the House of Meleager, and by the bare-breasted prostitute at the banquet table in a painting from Herculaneum (in the Museum of Naples). Paintings and statues from Pompeii have left us an enormous range of images of women with typically southern features, i.e., brown hair and brown eyes. Blond hair was quite rare around the Mediterranean and was considered very beautiful. As a result, wigs made of real hair, cut from the "barbarian" women of northern Europe, were always in great demand. These wigs cost a fortune, despite the fact that red and blond (*flavus*) were considered colors more appropriate for prostitutes than for other women. In any event, hair coloring was quite common, although these dyes were not always used in moderation or applied by experts. Ovid notes this in his *Amores* I, Elegy XIV, verses 1-44. "Did I not say to you, 'Stop dyeing your hair?' / And now you no longer have any hair to dye. /…/ Why, fool, do you set your mirror down so mournfully? /…/ You yourself poured on the poisonous mixture.

186
A winged psyche *smells a scent on her hand, between two perfumer cupids at the House of the Vettii.*

187
The girl, perhaps a bride, is doing her hair. Detail from the megalography in the Second Style at the Villa of the Mysteries.

POMPEIAN WOMEN BEFORE THE MIRROR

The women would daub on their makeup themselves, trusting in the advice of their perfumer and, above all, in the products imported from the Orient and from Alexandria. Pompeii was just a short distance from Puteoli and Baiae. The finest products on the market were easily available and were purchased for Julia Felix, for example, and for the matron who took refuge in the Gladiators' Barracks. Eye shadow, blush, foundation, brushes, spatulas and mirrors: the toilette of a 1st-century lady was as time-consuming and costly in Pompeii as it was in Rome.

Before putting on their makeup, the women would first try to get rid of blemishes and make their skin silky. There were home remedies, handed down for generations, as well as "cultured" advice offered by poets and writers. Pliny the Elder relied on his encyclopedic sources of information and listed thousands of them in his *Natural History*, leaving out things like cost and the availability of the ingredients. One of his suggestions included the famous donkey's milk used by the empress Poppaea, considered an excellent treatment for getting rid of wrinkles and whitening the skin (*ibid.*, XXVIII, 183). To get rid of unsightly spots, the choice was either calf's dung mixed with oil and rubber, or bull bile with niter and donkey urine added to it: "a cure-all"! (*ibid.*, XXVIII, 185-186). He also considered a mixture of salt and "Hercules' ants" (perhaps the hardiest) to be effective in treating "scaly" dermatitis (*ibid.*, XXX, 30), while one of the many remedies he suggested for getting rid of puffy red eyes was a mixture of cuttlebone and human milk (*ibid.*, XXXII, 71).

Aside from the results of the various beauty masks and mudpacks, women would start their makeup with foundation, using a thick layer of ceruse blended with fat to give the skin a whitish color. To achieve a rosy tone, the basic cream would be mixed with wine lees or red Selina clay, which was sold in tablets. As blusher, the women would brush vermilion on their cheeks. For their lips, they would apply "lipstick" made of plant and mineral extracts, such as red algae and cinnabar, and kept in small containers. They would use slender points dipped in lampblack or antimony powder (*stibium*) to extend their line of their eyes and their eyebrows. Some would also add a few artificial moles (*splenium*), just like the "damsels" of the 18th century. When it came to eye shadow, the favorite colors were green and light blue, made by crushing malachite and azurite into a powder, for a mix of colors that certainly could not have gone unobserved!

The gold circle is at the center of a silver mirror, found at the House of Menander (Naples, MAN).

The purple maenad, depicted as a herm, is one of the series of similar figures decorating the House of the Cryptoporticus

190
*This marble Venus wearing a
"bikini" and gold-painted jewelry
is untying one of her sandals
(Naples, MAN).*

191
*The silver mirror, from the House
of Menander, presents a repoussé
silhouette (Naples, MAN).*

The objects used to store creams and liquids varied in both shape and material: pyxides, boxes and seashells in amber, glass, ivory and silver could be found on ladies' toilette tables. A restored wooden beauty case with the original ivory appliqués, from the Vesuvian area and now at the Museum of Naples, shows us the enormous care with which the box's owner put away her balsam jars, bone brushes, the comb and the small plates used to mix colored powders with oily substances. Caterina Sforza, renowned as the Renaissance inventor of luxury face powder – rice powder and crushed pearls – was not familiar with the skill of her ancestors. For a special evening, women in the Roman world would crush crystal and sprinkle the sparkling powder over their faces to give their skin an opalescent sheen. Before stepping out, they would use a handheld silver or lead mirror to admire the results of their work.

The women's portraits discovered in Pompeii do not show made-up faces, or at least not with the showy features suggested by the descriptions, comments and methods for preparing cosmetics documented by the literary sources. Nevertheless, the enormous documentation of implements and containers confirms that this was a well-estab-

lished habit. This application can be verified through a number of small marble statues of Venus found in the city. The bare-breasted one from the garden of House II 9,3 shows the goddess leaning her left elbow on a small pillar, and her eyes and eyebrows are heavily lined in black. Her hair has traces of yellow paint: the most beautiful of the goddesses, like Helen of Troy, was imagined as a blond. On another armless statue, originally set in a niche in the interior garden of the house (I 11,10), the eyes are rimmed in black, whereas the goddess' hair is tinted a rusty red. The so-called "Venus in a Bikini" (25 inches tall), found in the *tablinum* of Julia Felix, instead represents the most intriguing example of statues painted with gold. The goddess is shown removing one of her sandals before bathing, and there are traces of red on her hair and lips. This is the copy of a Hellenistic prototype, known through other specimens in terracotta and bronze. The grace of her movements and the beauty of her body are emphasized by the short-sleeved corset with suspenders, done in a chain motif, that cross in the front and go down to cover her pelvis with a star design. The corset, as well as her bracelet and necklace, are painted entirely in gold.

BATHS AND PERFUMES

Bathing was handled differently. Few families had comfortable home baths. Most homes didn't even have a latrine and people would to the public baths to wash. In Pompeii, as in the rest of the Roman Empire, there were many different and delightful baths. Women could use a separate area, but the most recent ones (and the ones being built) did not have separate facilities. The most fortunate matrons could enjoy their baths and massages at home, cared for by slaves who would cleanse their skin with ash lye (*creta ful-*

of 1st century BC), reused in a *tablinum* floor during the city's last years (VI 15,14). The face is not a cheerful one and the woman was quite well-to-do, given her jewelry, but the physiognomic research is accurate and – a true rarity – we can see a some of her teeth between her slightly parted lips. Based on material documentation, a great deal of attention was paid to removing body hair. We know that for their legs, women would use a sort of gummy wax that resembles the type used even today in the Arab world. For their armpits

lonica), a plant-based soap (*struthion*) and abrasive substances. Lastly, they would rub on balsams and ointments to perfume the body or simply to soothe any irritation. Many Pompeian women would use little sticks to clean their ears (*auriscalpium*). We don't know how many took care of their teeth (toothpicks, or *dentiscalpia*, were used). The recommended methods for dental hygiene were mouthwashes using lemon and "toothpaste" made of pumice powder, mastic and sodium bicarbonate. In general, realistic paintings do not show open-mouthed smiles: the only exception is the mosaic portrait of a woman (end

and for facial hair, they instead used tweezers much like ours, some of which were made of gold and were entrusted to a slave responsible for this patient task (*alipilius*). The way the Romans put on perfume was completely different from what we do today. Cologne and toilet water are made using alcohol, which was only introduced by the Arabs in the 7th century. The very word "perfume" comes from the Latin *per-fumum*, meaning "through smoke": this was the oldest way of honoring the gods with odors that were emanated by burning prized plants. Therefore, in the Roman world we refer to balsams and ointments, as

scrape off sand and sweat. These ointments were produced to meet all tastes: Pompeian lilies were used to make *susinum,* delicate jasmine blossoms yielded *iasminum,* and royal ointment or *rhodium* was made of a base of saffron oil and was

nied by her slave, would go before an open cabinet displaying a variety of prepared bottles to make her selection, testing the perfume on her hand. In all likelihood, these frescoes were drawn from real life. In Pompeii, the presence of a full-

more highly prized. They could be found in the perfumeries of major cities. Prepared ointments or the natural material from which these aromatic substances were extracted followed the same sea routes as exotic spices. Pepper, cinnamon, myrrh, incense, cardamom, and nard came with caravans from the Orient (india, Mesopotamia, Syria) and Egypt, then by merchant ship to Puteoli and, and from there they were brought to the various destinations. A group of Cupids and *Psychai* from the House of the Vettii in Pompeii illustrates the entire workmanship cycle of a scented ointment, using the most common procedure

fledged workshop is demonstrated by the House of the Garden of Hercules (or of the Perfumer), where large numbers of flowers and olive trees were grown. It is also proven by inscriptions mentioning a guild of *unguentarii.* Glass bottles in every shape and color can still speak to us about roses and myrtle, because even today they hold minute traces of their contents. It seems impossible: thousands of human beings vanished and massive columns were shattered, and yet those pieces in blown glass – elongated in blue, green, yellow – were left intact in all their precious and expensive fragility.

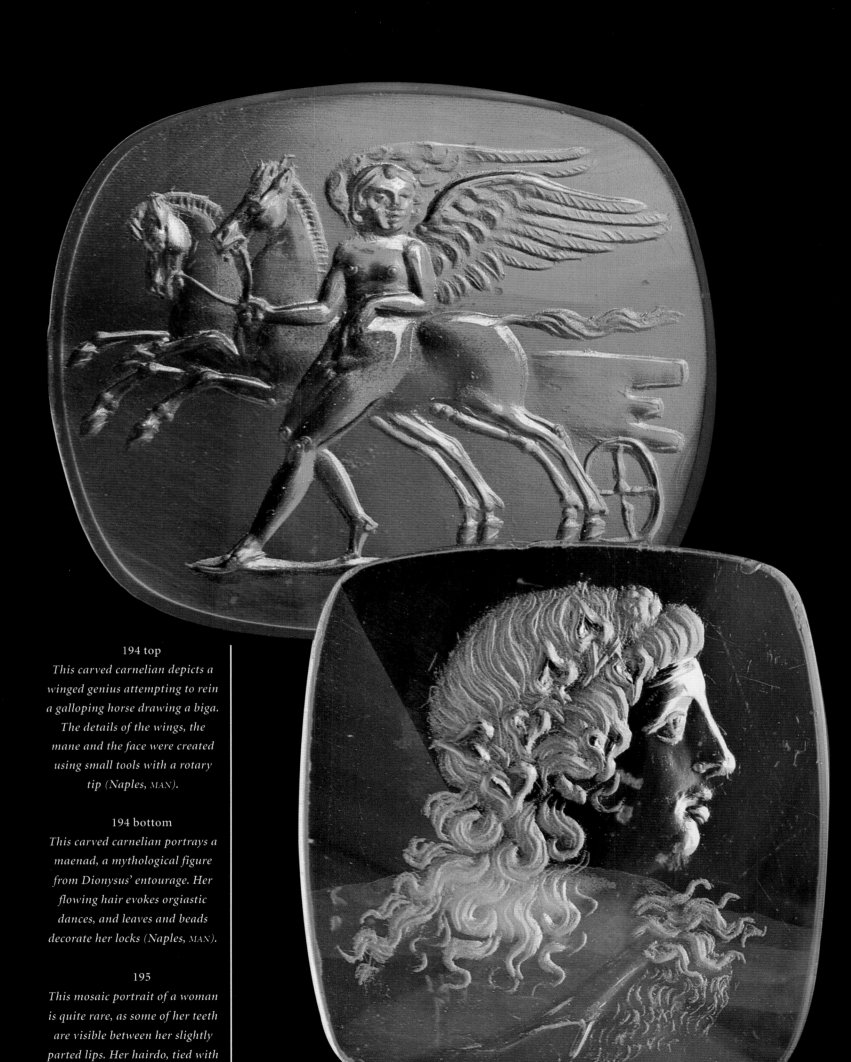

194 top
This carved carnelian depicts a winged genius attempting to rein a galloping horse drawing a biga. The details of the wings, the mane and the face were created using small tools with a rotary tip (Naples, MAN).

194 bottom
This carved carnelian portrays a maenad, a mythological figure from Dionysus' entourage. Her flowing hair evokes orgiastic dances, and leaves and beads decorate her locks (Naples, MAN).

195
This mosaic portrait of a woman is quite rare, as some of her teeth are visible between her slightly parted lips. Her hairdo, tied with a ribbon at the nape of her neck, was popular during the 1st century BC. From a tablinum in Pompeii (Naples, MAN).

A TRIP TO THE GEMMARIUS

Much jewelry was buried by the lava. Many pieces survived as sets enclosed in purses or boxes, often to be found with the victims themselves. The precious collection from Pompeii and the outlying areas (about 900 pieces) is important because of the information it has yielded. Based on recent studies rings appear to be the most common item, and both men and women would wear more than one. They would often have a stone set in them. For example, the poet Martial poked fun at a certain Carinus because "he wears six rings on each finger… and never takes them off, either at night or when bathing" (*Epigrams*, XI, 59). There were also crescent-shaped earrings, with pendants, bracelets (*armillae*), necklaces, generally chains with links of different sizes and, very rarely, diadems. However, necklaces made of glass paste were more common, as they were not as expensive. In the Roman world, there were different areas of specialization: the *margaritarii* traded pearls, the *auratores* gilded different materials, the *gemmarii (sculptores)* were experts in rings and gemstones, the *caelatores* crafted chased metalwork, and the person who fashioned gold items was known as an *aurifex* (at Pompeii, evidence of the latter three trades has been found in inscriptions).

Valuables could be purchased from specialized shops, but the most demanding matrons could have the collections shown to them at home. The *gemmarius* Pinarius Cerialis must have been quite well known in Pompeii. He lived along a quiet side street near the central Via dell'Abbondanza, just a short distance from the popular Amphitheater. He had his studio on the east side of the two-story house (damaged by the bombs dropped in 1943), in one of the three rooms that opened onto the interior portico, and he kept his gems in another room next to them. In the summer of 79, he had put his precious stones in a wooden box, but when one of the stronger quakes struck the city, or when Pompeii was plunged into darkness although it was daytime, Pinarius left everything where it was and fled the building. There are 114 gems of different types and three iron implements with ivory handles: he probably personally carved the most valuable items, leaving the ones that were less elaborate and costly for his assistants to do. Different workmanship techniques can be seen and some of the stones appear to be used, so he may also have been a gem trader. In this assortment of carnelians, amethysts, agates and one sardonyx, 79 were uncut and were barely even polished, while 29 have lovely decorations. In particular, six cameos and several carnelians were carefully carved with a variety of subjects: a *biga* with two galloping horses and a cupid trying to stop one of the horses by the reins, the silhouette of a maenad with shoulder-length curls held in place by an ivy wreath, the sea god Neptune holding a trident in his hand and resting his foot on a rise. Aside from its inherent value, each stone tells us its own story. Each of them – particularly the rarest kind – were attributed with different values, for example to ensure the fidelity of one's beloved, invincibility and so on, although they would all be worn together to ward off the evil eye. Moreover, they give us information on their provenance and trade, as well as the fashions and lifestyle of a given era.

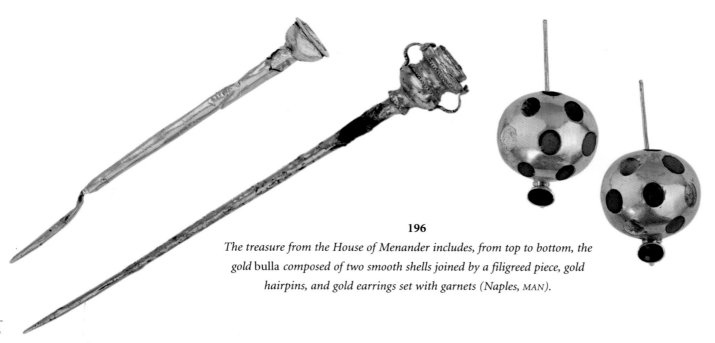

196

The treasure from the House of Menander includes, from top to bottom, the gold bulla *composed of two smooth shells joined by a filigreed piece, gold hairpins, and gold earrings set with garnets (Naples, MAN).*

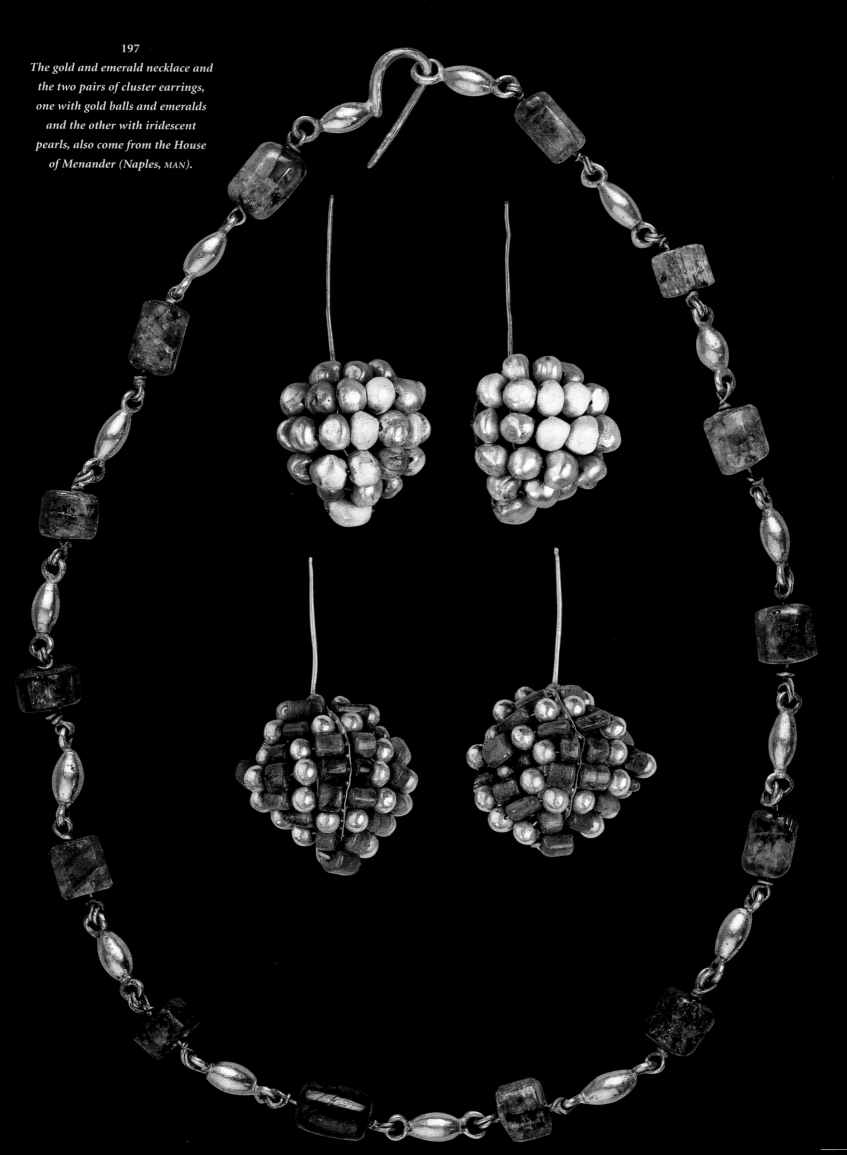

197
The gold and emerald necklace and the two pairs of cluster earrings, one with gold balls and emeralds and the other with iridescent pearls, also come from the House of Menander (Naples, MAN).

The remains of wooden boxes holding stones and work tools were found in another house in Pompeii (II 9, 2). We don't know the name of this *gemmarius*, who lived on Via di Nocera in the southeast quarter of the city. A "stone-holder" – a device to grip the gem while it was being carved – was found there. The anonymous craftsman used a pedal-operated lathe to turn a small pointed metal rod.

Other Cupids and *Psychai* painted in the House of the Vettii portray – as is the case with other trades – work phases and the required tools: from the producer to the consumer. In this case, the goldsmith's shop shows the casting furnace and a cupid covered with rings, seated on a stool and pounding a jewel on an anvil.

In the middle of the scene is the sales counter, with jewelry displayed in three drawers, while an *aurifex* uses a small scale to determine the price of the precious item for the elegant lady who, seated comfortably, is waiting before him.

198-199

Cupids work as goldsmiths make jewelry at the House of the Vettii.

199 bottom

*The bracelets (*armillae*) are made of gold, but they differ in value: the two hemispherical ones are the most common types, while the one composed of a disk, which bears the repoussé figure of the goddess Selene and is set between the jaws of two snakes, is rarer and more valuable (Naples, MAN).*

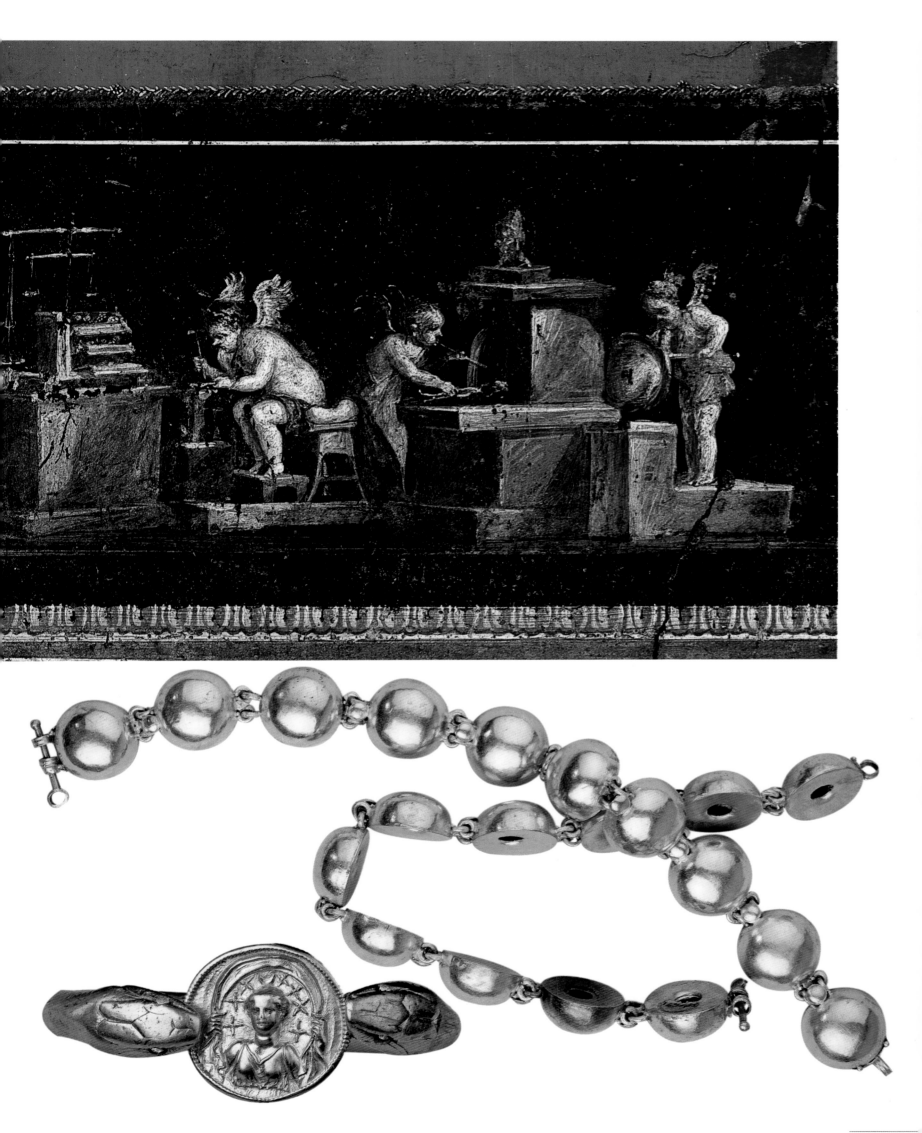

EROS PORTRAYED
SCANDALOUS ANTIQUITY

As opposed to Rome, where the ongoing archaeological findings never repudiated the solemnity of the outdoor ruins, the discovery of the cities destroyed by Mount Vesuvius were a source of considerable embarrassment for the early excavators. The gradual revelation of daily life in the Imperial Age opened a completely new field of study to science, yet at the same time it offered a glimpse into the secrets of each household, violating the privacy of hundreds of private lives. As a result, those who entered boudoirs, brothels and shops centuries later and found themselves looking at countless portrayals of nudity and erotic scenes felt discomfited and troubled. What had happened to the austere "Romanness" of tradition, full of matrons and valorous *consoles*? How could one exhibit in a museum – before religious, women and children – marble groups like the one found in Herculaneum, depicting the god Pan about to penetrate a goat? Particularly in Pompeii, which was studied more extensively because it was easier to excavate, each corner seemed to reveal a population intent on spending its time in licentious banquets and sexual performances. Quite a few thought they had unearthed a latter-day Sodom or Gomorrah, the biblical cities destroyed by divine fury because of their inhabitants' corrupt ways. Charles III, the Bourbon King of Naples and the Two Sicilies, had no doubts about the matter, putting under lock and key the works that could offend the sense of modesty of his day and age. In observing the monarch's instructions and abiding by their personal moral standards, the excavation supervisors had the frescoes considered obscene detached from the walls. They set aside

and, in some cases, even destroyed all the objects that had to do with ancient eroticism, avoiding any annotation of their provenance in a modern *damnatio memoriae*. In the rest of Europe, there were Secret Cabinets that collected artwork considered erotic, but at the Museum of Naples, transferred from the palace in Portici with the addition of the Farnese and Borgia collections, by the middle of the 19th century people were not even allowed to look at paintings like Titian's *The Danaë* and statues like the *Callipygean Venus*. Rediscovered in 1860 thanks to Garibaldi, what was forever destined to be known as the "Pornographic Collection" faced additional bans and closing in the decades that followed. Gradually, it became permissible to exhibit a few pieces in public as certain taboos began to fall: this is the case with mythological deities, considered artistic expressions tied to the taste of the era. However, the exhibition of the findings from the Vesuvian area was far more troublesome, and they also had to be reclassified, catalogued and studied like "ordinary" documents of the past. The subject of recent research and publications, it was not until the year 2000 that they formed part of a new section in the National Museum of Naples. Even today, for most visitors of the Museum and those who wander through the streets of Pompeii, it's difficult to observe the ancient erotic representations without prejudice. The subject of sexuality crosses all cultures and is experienced and interpreted according to changing standards. Our modern distinction between heterosexuality and homosexuality, for example, had no meaning in the Greek and Roman world, where acceptable or unacceptable behavior was

The three Graces (Euphrosyne, Aglaia and Thalia) are generally portrayed in the nude, gently embracing each other. They symbolized gracefulness and wisdom (Naples, MAN).

part of social structures that judged interpersonal relationships according to different standards. Moreover, during the historic era to which we refer, terms like "obscenity" and "pornography" (derived from the Greek for "writing about prostitutes") were used in different contexts and did not provoke the moral and religious judgments that were later applied. Excesses were criticized even then, and when historians wanted to condemn the behavior of an emperor, they would point to his unrestrained sexual behavior. Physicians, legislators and philosophers also preached moderation, but the field of moral value systems was gauged in relation to age, gender and social status. In any case, the implication of sin was unknown to the Roman world, which considered sexuality – and its representations – a natural fact without of any kind of inhibition. Obviously, there are no differences in the immediate impulses, reflections and reactions. All we need to do is read the graffiti and painted words left on the walls of Pompeii (collected in the *Corpus Iscriptionum Latinarum*) and we find passion, jealousy, oaths and delicate sentiments that may not help us fully understand the motivation for so many material documents, but they manage to create a direct link with the men of

each epoch. In those words, written freely or in metric verse, we can find expressions reminiscent of Catullus ("May you always be in bloom, O Sabina / May your beauty be your guide and long may you remain a young maiden," *CIL* IV, 9171), of Shakespeare, ("May he who loves prosper; but may he who knows love not, die. / May he who impedes love die twice," *CIL* IV, 4091), of the Romantic poets ("Nothing in this world can last forever / When the sun has spent its glory, it plunges into the sea. / The moon wanes although it was full before. / The fury of the winds often turns to a gentle breeze," *CIL* IV, 9123), and of D'Annunzio ("…Imagine that the bed is a meadow and let me be your steed," *CIL* IV, 9246b). We can recognize the same epithets and the same oaths used by Juvenal in his *Satires* and by anonymous authors on the walls of modern metropolises and in highway restrooms, including personal boasts ("Successus, the weaver, loves Iris, the waitress at the inn, who instead is heedless of him. And the more he begs her, the less she listens. The writer of these words is his rival. Farewell!" *CIL* IV, 8259). No place in antiquity has left as much evidence of its private life without any hesitation about revealing its innermost secrets.

POMPEII, *VENERIS SEDES*

L|ong before the dictator Lucius Cornelius Sulla linked the name of the city with the goddess Venus, the inhabitants already worshipped a *Venus Fisica*, the symbol of the generating power of nature. Therefore, it comes as no surprise that there are plenty of images of the most alluring goddess throughout the houses of the city. We can admire her, nude and bejeweled, as she reclines on a shell sailing the seas, in what has naturally come to be known as the House of Venus in the Shell, and she is portrayed with Mars in many other city residences. However, it was not this close link, emphasized by the poet Martial – *Pompeii, Veneris sedes* (*Epigrams*, IV, 44) – that stimulated the Pompeians to portray her in so many erotic subjects. It was quite common to exhibit paintings and sculptures in private and public places, portraying not only Olympian gods and mythological figures famous for their love affairs, but also anonymous people. In all the Vesuvian towns blanketed by the eruption of AD 79, there are countless examples and, presumably, they were also frequent in Rome and other cities. The fact that sim-

ilar findings elsewhere are scarce, however, has drawn attention to the number found in Campania. The mythological scenes are found in the most luxurious residences, in different rooms (*cubicula*) and alcoves, and also in the rooms where clients were received (*tablina*), guests were entertained (*triclinia*) and people would stroll around the internal gardens (*peristilia*). Some of the most frequent subjects depict Venus and Mars, in flight or seated (her) and standing (him), accompanied by cupids, showing the god of war touching his companion's breast (House of Cupid Punished), or they are portrayed in the alcove before the two lovers were discovered by Vulcan, the goddess' husband (House of the Citharist). Mythology offered thousands of opportunities to portray the naked female body being seduced: the nymph Daphne trying to avoid Apollo's amorous attempts (House of M. Lucretius), Ariadne, the daughter of Minos, the king of Crete, surprised by Dionysius after Theseus had abandoned her on an island (House of the Citharist), and Leda with the Swan (House of the Golden Cupids).

202

Perseus, with winged sandals, saves Andromeda from being sacrificed. The fresco of the celebrated myth was found in the peristyle of the House of the Dioscuri.

203

The loves of Mars and Venus are often portrayed in Pompeii. In this fresco, the goddess – half-naked and bejeweled – predominates, while merry putti play with the weapons of the god of war (Naples, MAN).

204-205

A shell is used as a boat for Venus. Reclining between two putti as the wind fills the sail, the goddess of love flaunts her beauty. She is wearing gold jewelry around her neck, around her ankles and in her hair (House of Venus in the Shell).

The models used for the composition were often famous paintings from the Hellenistic era, which at times lost certain artistic touches and simply provided the structural layout. The final effect depended strictly on the skill of the copyist or whoever used the original as inspiration. In the case of many paintings, in the features of the famous lovers (like Venus and Mars in the House of the Wedding of Hercules) we can easily glimpse the features of ordinary Pompeians. Copies of paintings by famous artists were considered a "must" to be exhibited proudly, particularly by those who enjoyed considerable wealth but could not boast of the highest social extraction. The names and works of the great painters were as well known as Homer's poetry and Menander's comedies. A message written on one of the walls in Pompeii notes, "If you haven't seen the Venus painted by Apelles, look at my girl (*mea pupa*): she has the same glow" (*CIL* IV, 1824).

It was also quite common to find images of couples composed of the god Pan and a nymph, or satyrs and maenads. This was the retinue of Dionysus (Bacchus for the Romans) and the sylvan gods, ideal for places where, for centuries, the main activities were agricultural and pastoral. The setting envisaged rocks, trees and natural shelters that fostered encounters dictated by instinct, without any cultural mediation. As a rule, what is portrayed is the moment just before the sexual act, which generally involves a display of force: the satyr – with a tail and animal-like ears – surprises the nymph, who is sleeping in the nude and cringes in fear, in a type of role-playing where the woman pretends she's asleep and then appears to avoid a tussle, initially refusing these advances. A rather fluidly executed mosaic instead portrays a *symplegma* (tangle), in which the bodies of the two figures (Satyr and Nymph) are entwined and it probably filled the central part of a floor (*emblema*). The different figures are sometimes portrayed in a passionate kiss, like the one between Cupid and Psyche, or the Cyclops Polyphemus and the Nereid Galatea, in which the woman is shown from the back, her gown falling to the ground to show off her buxom figure (House of the Ancient Hunt). Other kisses and advances appear in frescoes on the subject of banquets. In this case, the leading figures are ordinary people – aristocrats, of course – who are lying on the couches typical of the era and let down their reserve. The festive atmosphere, the effect of the wine and the air of promiscuity favor advances, jokes and lewd comments. We know that half-clothed dancers and musicians were often on hand to provide entertainment, while silver cups and goblets were engraved with explicit heterosexual and homosexual encounters. The masters of the house were well aware of the erotic arousal that a *coena* (dinner) could inspire. For example, the owner of the House of Menander tried to mix gastronomic delight with sensual pleasure, exhibiting his silver dinnerware with the cup (*kantharos*) depicting the intimacy between Venus and Mars, while the dining room of the House of the Moralist was painted with phrases asking participants not to give in to excesses – in every sense – in their behavior. The frescoes portraying nameless couples could also represent husband and wife. Etruscan art has handed down many examples of this type, depicted on the sarcophaguses, and in Pompeii there is no lack of material evidence of marital love (funerary epigraphs, tombs prepared for a couple and household reliefs, like the husband and wife sculpted in the tufa capital in the House of the Figured Capitals). In general, however, passion and sexual attraction were more frequent outside the bonds of marriage, particularly among men, as they were not bound by fidelity and had relationships with slaves, prostitutes and young girls, practices that were fully tolerated by Roman society. Brothels and obliging backrooms overflowed with small paintings showing realistic sex scenes, done by artisans for a pittance. The purpose was to stir clients and patrons, rather than to illustrate the type of performance offered (although we can't exclude this possibility).

The representations discovered in the *apodyterium* (dressing room) of the Suburban Baths, recently opened to the public, are unprecedented in Roman and Greek iconography. In the Pompeii's last months of life, they were covered with other, mannered decorative paintings, perhaps to follow the more austere dictates of Emperor Vespasian. At a certain level on the south wall, seven erotic scenes had been painted

small paintings portray group sex scenes (three and four people) multiplying the most common "positions." Surprisingly, number VIII shows a naked man with a laurel wreath on his head and a *volumen* in his hands. If he weren't naked, he could easily be a poet or man of letters in the customary pose (House of Menander). However, another trait pokes fun at this scholarly attribution, as the subject has evident malformation of

on eight numbered "boxes" (on the east wall, the numbers that have been preserved go to XVI, but the plaster above it collapsed). Holes that match up with the painted boxes indicate that, in all likelihood, there were shelves with containers for the personal effects of the people who went to these lovely baths. Frequented by both men and women without separate areas, they demonstrate a moral liberalism unheard until then: the

the testicles (bilateral hydrocele). This is the same illness jeeringly mentioned by the poet Martial (XII, 83) in his description of a man who, at the Baths of Nero in Rome, displayed his naked body in public. The intentions of the owner of the establishment during the Julio-Claudian period are not entirely clear. Some scholars theorize that the numbers written under these complex sexual acts refer to the upper

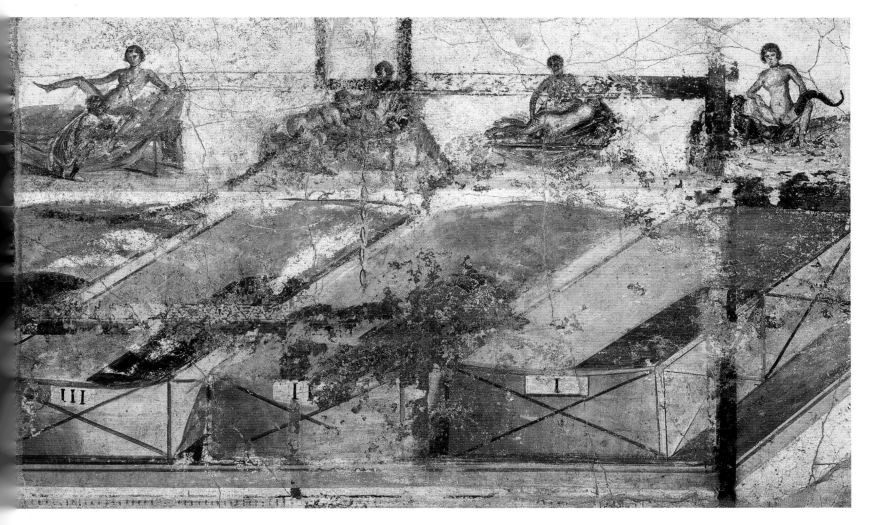

level, where there were rooms set aside for prostitutes. According to others, the scenes were extraordinary devices to attract customers and, at the same time, they were an entertaining way to help people remember where they had put their clothes. Manuals are known to have circulated in Roman houses, describing samples of *Veneris figurae* – as the various types of coupling were commonly defined – and perhaps this number-ing repeats classifications that were also known widely in Pompeii. Moreover, the illustrations of the *figurae* did not decorate only the places used for bodily pleasure, like the Baths. The poet Ovid noted, "In our houses, just as the figures of ancient heroes painted by an artist are in full view, in other places there are small paintings depicting erotic positions and a variety of embraces." (*Tristia*, II, verses 521-524).

In any event, the figure of the poet had nothing to do with paid sex, and laughing over others' physical defects was not considered uncouth. In fact, portraits of pygmies or dwarfs – in graceless erotic displays – aroused gales of laughter. At the foot of Mount Vesuvius, the Egyptian civilization was evoked in many houses, just as it was in Rome. The exotic fashion of making miniature replicas in one's garden of the landscapes described by merchants and travelers became popular among the more cultured classes during the Republican Age. In Pompeii, in the *Praedia* of Julia Felix and other residences, references to the Nile and the Pharaonic deities abounded. The goddess Isis, in particular, had many followers because of her magical and saving powers. The pygmies, who were thought to come from Egypt (or India), were portrayed as little statues in comical poses, in decorations on terracotta oil lamps, in mosaics and in many erotic scenes, where the unlikely intercourse would take place on boats adrift amid crocodiles, or outdoors in public while someone plays the flute.

210 top

In the summer triclinium *of the House of the Ephebe, a painted scene depicts intercourse outdoors as others look on and a woman plays a double flute.*

210-211

In Pompeii the exotic allure of the Nile, with its animals, was common, as was the presence of dwarves and pygmies, depicted in this fresco of an orgy (Naples, MAN).

211 top

Two men and a woman have chosen a somewhat unstable boat on the Nile for their erotic encounter, heedless of the dangerous crocodiles infesting the river (Naples, MAN).

While these portrayals were met with laughter and lewd comments, in real life other deformities elicited horror. A malformed child, who was eliminated at birth, was known as a *monstrum* and was considered a sign of divine rage, as were hermaphrodites, those who had the traits of both genders. According to a fable explaining their origin, a creature was generated by Aphrodite (Venus) and Hermes (Mercury), as the term itself indicates. The handsome Hermaphroditus aroused the passionate love of Salmacis, the nymph of Lake Salmacis. When Hermaphroditus rejected her, she resolutely clasped the young man's body to hers, dragging him into the water so they would never be separated again. The gods granted her wish and thus

formed a being that was half-man and half-woman. With all due respect to Venus and Mercury, no one wanted a son like that, yet his representation had a powerful influence on the creativity of many artists. In Pompeian houses (never in the temples), marble statues of Hermaphroditus were displayed (House of Loreius Tiburtinus or of Octavius Quartus), as were paintings with sylvan figures trying to rape or pull away from him as soon as they discover his dual nature (House of Epidius Sabinus). The taste for representing the unusual, the irregular, reflected the influence of Greek art, but people nevertheless kept their distance from the unorthodox.

212 left

Hermaphroditus is an ambiguous being generated by Hermes and Aphrodite. Half male and half female, this creature is both attractive and repulsive. In this painting, Hermaphroditus tugs at the beard of an old satyr (Naples, MAN).

212-213

Discovered in the House of the Dioscuri, the fresco shows the wild god Pan drawing back in disbelief: the object of his desire, with the seductive breasts of a woman, proves to be a monstrum *(Naples, MAN).*

*As opposed to divine loves, earthly ones were often depicted explicitly, like this one
from a secluded room in the House of the Centenary.*

*This picture shows one of the mythical couples poised in flight against a precious red
background (made using cinnabar). It is from the same room as the famous cupids on
a black ground, from the House of the Vettii.*

Another aspect of ancient sexuality that we have not fully understood yet is the presence of bedroom paintings illustrating explicit erotic encounters and intended for visual stimulation, as well as silver mirrors, small paintings with doors and oil lamps with erotic scenes, expanding on the allusions from the "night stand" or "toilette." In a consumer civilization like ours, we tend to tire of things quickly and it is hard to imagine the erotic potential of gazing at the very same image forever. And yet for the Pompeians (and the Romans), this is exactly how it must have been. In the bedchamber of the Palace of Capri, Emperor Tiberius never tired of admiring the painting by Parrhasius depicting the daring performance of Atalanta and Meleager (Suetonius, *Life of Tiberius*, XLIV), while in Pompeian houses, the owners did not mind pausing to gaze at lovely female nudes, often depicted from behind or wearing jewelry and a *strophium* (a sort of bra). However, it was not a widespread habit among women to go naked even before their own husbands, and the great love poets praised the modesty and reluctance of young girls. Ovid offered Roman women advice on how to make the most of their assets even in the heat of intercourse, yet various authors condemned the diffusion of erotic objects and paintings, which were thought to promote immodesty. Exhibition, combined with a dose of voyeurism, was evidently considered very exciting. This would explain the wall writings boasting of personal prowess and performance, and the paintings suggest intriguing atmospheres, showing slaves near the bed, doors ajar so one could peek inside, and so on. We are delving into the topic of a refined and seductive game, one present in cultured and aristocratic milieus where transgression was exhibited with nonchalance. Confirmation of this comes from the small paintings that decorated the *cubicula* of Villa della Farnesina in Rome (at the National Museum of Rome in Palazzo Massimo), thought to be the residence of Augustus' daughter Julia.

THE FASCINUM

The presence of so many objects and images in a provincial environment nonetheless points to a freedom of expression that was more "vulgar" compared to Rome or Naples (*Neapolis*). Most people worked as traders and farmers, while the aristocracy of the Imperial Age was largely composed of former slaves who had become wealthy (freedmen). They thus shared tastes, an argot and habits that eschewed the formalities and reserved attitudes that were essential in other cities.

Nevertheless, the display of virility, emphasized in every corner of Pompeii, was common to all the ancient – and other – civilizations. The origins went back years and were tied strictly to the fertility of the land. With his enormous member, the god Priapus, protector of doors and gardens, acted as a scarecrow for private plots of land, and at the same time he propitiated the harvest. The phalluses reproduced on the paving blocks of the city streets, the bronze ones in bizarre lamp holders that hung from the ceilings of shops and inns, and the ones painted behind the main doors of aristocratic homes (House of the Vettii) were considered a sort of "lucky charm," an amulet against the *fascinum* or "evil eye" of envious people. As opposed to the modern-day excavators, who were shocked by so much display, none of the Pompeians were surprised, much less offended by them. The apotropaic or protective value of the phallus was recognized by everyone, mothers and children included, and it did not conceal any erotic mischief.

Among the many representations, the words on the oven of the bakery annexed to the House of Pansa draws amused grins even today: *Hic habitat felicitas* ("Happiness lives here"). Sculpted in red stone, a triumphant male member seems to represent a successful trade, good products on sale (made from wheat, the epitome of fertile lands) and – why not? – the sexual prowess of the owner.

216

The phallus was thought to ward off the evil eye and was also a symbol of prosperity. This relief in travertine with the inscription Hic habitat felicitas *("Happiness lives here") is from a Pompeii bakery (Naples,* MAN*).*

217

The painting at the entrance of the House of the Vettii shows Priapus weighing his enormous member on one plate of a scale, while the other one holds a bag full of money.

218-219

Eggs, game and bronze ware testify to the eating habits of the era.
From the Praedia *of Julia Felix (Naples,* MAN*).*

ON POMPEIAN TABLES

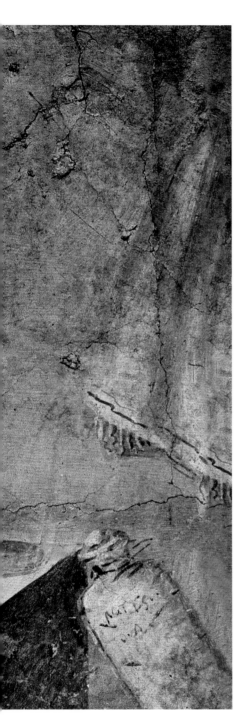

The first vegetarian manifesto may well have been written by the poet Ovid during the Augustan period. In his *Metamorphosis* (XV, 62, 80), he maintained that it was a "crime to burden one's table with meat," given that a garden can produce all the fruit that exists. In reality, the Romans – and the Pompeians – enjoyed meat immensely. The variety offered by a well-stocked market during the Imperial Age was certainly more original than what we find today. In addition to pigs – according to Pliny the Elder, pork had about fifty different flavors – there were chickens, geese, turkeys and hares, and dormice and donkeys were also widely appreciated. And then there were other tidbits worthy of a king, such as flamingoes, swans, and parrot tongues. Sought-after specialties included game, given that it was virtually nonexistent, and veal, because cattle represented a workforce that was too valuable to slaughter. Certain animals were bred in the city for food: in several domestic stalls (House of the Ship *Europa*), there were pigs, sheep and chickens, while cages for thrushes and other birds have been found elsewhere. Just as today, bread was the most important part of the

Pompeians' diet. Different than the modern variety in softness, bread could be purchased in various shapes and flavors, from the "toasted" army bread for the legions to the more costly type made with milk, oil, pepper and poppy seeds. The fresco from the *tablinum* of House VII 3, 30 (at the Museum of Naples) depicts a man wearing a white tunic distributing bread to three people standing before him. On the counter, there are several round loaves as testified also by carbonized remains. This scene may have portrayed a donation by a baker who had been appointed to a public office. Pompeii must have produced high-quality bread, because writings on the city walls recommend its consumption and the façade of the House of Caius Julius Polybius on Via dell'Abbondanza calls for people to vote for him in the elections because "he supplies good bread." The first paleoecological studies done on skeletons have made it possible to calculate that an estimated population of 20,000 inhabitants consumed nearly 32,000 pounds of grain every day. If we consider bread as the leading grain product, we arrive at a calculation of a total of 15,000 loaves produced daily by the city's 35 bakeries.

218 bottom

The fish shown here against a pale blue background seem to dart between open shellfish. This fresco is from the House of the Chaste Lovers.

219

The cast of a loaf of bread shows the most common shape: a round loaf cut into wedges (Boscoreale, National Antiquarium).

Barnyard animals, vegetables, eggs, legumes, fruit (mainly figs and grapes) were the most common-place foods. Fried foods were very popular (small animals were dipped in a batter made of flour and eggs and then fried in oil or lard). Nevertheless, the one product found on every table in Pompeii – and in Rome – was a local specialty known as *garum*. This sauce, made of fish guts and remains steeped in salt, was also exported. Once it was filtered, *garum* was used as a condiment for almost all food, from meat to fruit. The thickest kind was known as *allec*, and the *flos* (flower) variety, made of pieces of mackerel and mullet, was considered a real delicacy. Sauces, spices and condiments always accompanied food on Roman tables, and they were characterized by daring mixtures, for a sweet-and-sour combination typical of contemporary Oriental cuisine. This abundance was also determined by the predominance of boiled meat: while it could be used to make soup and meatballs, and it also kept longer, it lost most of its flavor. The methods used to cook vegetable soups, boiled vegetables (vegetable purée was known as *olus molle*), spit-roasted meat, mushrooms and snails were just like the ones we use today. As to other dishes, however, modern tastes are quite different, particularly with regard to the "pies" that have been handed down to us in ancient recipes.

220 top left
In this fresco, a theater mask can be noted over game that has been hung
to make it tender (Naples, MAN).

Honey was used extensively. In addition to sweetening wine, it was also an important ingredient in numerous dishes, and also it helped preserve meat and fruit. Both red and white wines were produced. Since the wine was not fermented, it was kept in large terracotta jars (*dolia*) that were buried, and it was treated with seawater if it had to be transported. As a rule, it was not served pure but mixed with water. However, it could also contain pepper, aromatic herbs and fruit, thus becoming syrupy in consistency. Amphorae for personal use or for trade have been found in many houses in the city, and one that was discovered in the House of the Four Styles was marked *try(ginon)*, or wine "black as ink." During the day, it did not take long to eat: breakfast or *ientaculum*, eaten at the start of the day, was a piece of bread or some biscuits dipped in milk or water, or perhaps some leftovers from supper. Toward noon, people would eat something light as they stood in the snack bars of the era, the *cauponae* and *thermopolia* located around the city. For all pocketbooks – the smallest homes did not have kitchens – these taverns would offer hot and cold beverages, dried fruits and nuts, olives, bread and various kinds of cheese and, presumably, a few prepared dishes. Sometimes, a break at the *caupona* was also an opportunity to enjoy a game of dice in the backroom or go off with one of the maids, who would offer her favors for a few *asses*. People on their way to the baths, those who remained at the Forum for religious and public ceremonies, purchases or business, and those who went to the Amphitheater for a day of entertainment would probably buy something from street peddlers, who would set up their portable stoves to make flatbread, fritters and cakes. Dinner, or *coena*, with an appetizer and one or more hearty dishes, was served late in the afternoon. Naturally, the hours as well as the types and amounts of food were not the same for everyone. For example, the slaves who worked in the city and the countryside, shop hands, and the lowliest workers had to settle for very little, as did conscripted soldiers, who were given a few librae (pounds) of bread a day and a piece of fruit. Onions, turnips and other roots may have supplemented their diets. Those who worked near the sea ate *pectunculi*, saltwater mollusks, while the amount of wine – of low quality – was increased only for religious or city celebrations. The diet of slaves who worked in the homes of their masters – secretaries, cooks, administrators, guardians and so on – enjoyed a better diet, as they were allowed to eat leftovers from the banquet tables or were even given a smaller portion of the same dishes their masters ate.

220 right
The smiling face of the bronze satyr, from the House of the Centenary, savors
the spurting wine (Naples, MAN).

221
This fresco, with a still life and colorful roosters, decorates a wing
of the House of the Vettii.

The evening meals served in the rich *domus* and *villae* outside the city were on a completely different level and they often represented a status symbol. The wall paintings and mosaics depict an assortment of fish, fruit and game, in the varieties consumed traditionally. However, the most delectable dish can be seen in the fresco of a *triclinium* in Poppaea's Villa in Oplontis: it looks like a Sicilian *cassata*, ready to be served, with a red crust of almond paste and a filling made of ricotta with a handful of candied fruit in the middle. These dishes were prepared by expert slaves for an elite class that would serve food in chased silver tableware and sometimes invited musicians and dancers to entertain at their banquets. At dusk, the triclinia in the House of the Faun, the House of Menander and the House of the Vettii would welcome guests who, leaning on one elbow, would recline on the characteristic couches arranged around three sides of a set table. Slaves would see to their every need, even cutting up the food into small pieces, so that the spoon (*cochlear*) was the most common utensil. Nevertheless, people would generally eat with their hands, using knifes and special implements for snails and shellfish. Each one had his or her own cup, in the Greek style, and would draw wine from large bronze or silver kraters.

The meals started with appetizers (*gustatio*), which were rather substantial dishes, and generally eggs. Then came a first series of meat and fish courses, followed by a *mensa secunda* (as Cicero's "second course") with fruit and sweets, washed down with plenty of sweet or aged wines. The pride of the cook – and the host, of course – included dishes like suckling pig stuffed with ground meat, nuts and vegetables, or saddled bream (typical of the Bay of Naples), morays, which could cost thousands of sesterces, and seafood that, like today, was the highlight of the banquet.

222 top

This veiled wicker basket with fruit and thyrsus (Bacchus' floral staff) is from a painting in the Second Style that decorates the main hall of Poppaea's Villa at Oplontis.

222 bottom

The dessert pictured on the table, decorated with dried (or candied) fruit looks like the handiwork of a modern chef (Poppaea's Villa at Oplontis).

222-223

The fresco with a symposium decorates the triclinium of the House of the Chaste Lovers. Note the two seated couples who continue to drink, while a woman, donning a mantle and about to leave, tries to raise her kantharos for one last drink, with the slave's help.

224

The frescoed picture shows a lovely glass vase filled with fruit, an amphora and a jar full of olives; a halved pomegranate stands out on the counter (Naples, MAN).

225

The glass cup, painted in one of the rooms in Poppaea's Villa at Oplontis, holds pomegranates and reveals the decorators' excellent artistic level.

Shellfish farming was first started in this area by Lucius Sergius Orata. Using clay tiles, he set up an oyster farm at his villa in Baiae toward the end of the 1st century BC, conducting this business in private pools or lakes and earning enormous amounts of money. In fact, the name of the nearby Lake Lucrino comes from *lucrum* or profit. The banquets held by Lucullus and the ones described sardonically in Petronius' *Satyricon* were famous, and we can easily image these kinds of banquets being held in Pompeii. Nevertheless, many Latin writers have left us interesting infor-

mation about the meals that were enjoyed on different occasions. Seneca, the Stoic philosopher who was surrounded by luxury, maintained that bread, figs and cheese sufficed (*Epistulae ad Lucilium*, XI, 87,3). Pliny the Younger (*Epistulae ad familiares*, I, 15) went a little further, at least in his preparations, to entertain his friend Septimius Clarus: three snails and two eggs with salad (appetizer), boiled barley or a similar grain (first course), wine sweetened with honey and cooled with snow, served with olives, onions and other tidbits as the last course. Perhaps – at least in

writing – one would stress his own moderation and portray the excesses of others. *De re coquinaria* nevertheless remains the most important Roman cookbook. It is attributed to M. Gavius Apicius, who lived during the reign of Tiberius and is known from later editions. Several suggestions, reinterpreted appropriately, are still acceptable for that crossover of tastes proposed by today's famous gourmets. Naturally, we wouldn't eat rotten fruit and *garum* as the Pompeians did, but dishes like chicken with olives or suckling pig cooked with different herbs would

certainly be welcome on modern tables. In the early morning hours of the city's last day, people were thinking about food as usual. During the pauses between quakes, one person had set a ladder against a tree in the garden to pick some fruit (House of Julius Polybius), another one had filled a big pot with water and placed a lid over it (Asellina's *caupona*), and someone else had put chicken bones on the fire. A plate of beans and onions was found in a brothel (VII 12, 18): it was left on the table, untouched, when the person fled suddenly to meet a fate we'll never learn.

226

*Found at the House of the Faun, the mosaic was originally in the middle
of a floor (emblema). It shows the most highly prized Mediterranean
seafood, which was enjoyed by the Pompeians (Naples, MAN).*

227

The pictorial detail of the tablinum *in the House of Marcus Lucretius
Fronto shows fish hung together or slipping from an overturned basket.
The frieze running beneath it features fanciful floral motifs and birds.*

DAILY LIFE ON THE WALLS OF POMPEII
THE IMPORTANCE OF THE GRAFFITI

The discovery of a wealth of perfectly preserved wall inscriptions is one of the most interesting features of the documentation from ancient Pompeii; they are a unique resource for reconstructing the society of the Early Roman Empire. If considered individually, they are seemingly of little importance; if taken as a whole, the inscriptions are so significant that they paint an extraordinary picture of the daily life of the era.

The graffiti, scratched directly onto the plaster walls with a stylus or some other sharp implement, such as a nail, are generally inscriptions. Often fragmentary, they were created on the spur of the moment, for no reason other than to express a feeling, an emotion or an impromptu thought. Unlike inscriptions on marble, bronze or other durable materials, graffiti are the product of spontaneous inspiration dictated by a particular circumstance and, moreover, without entailing any costs. Thus, they are private or semi-private in nature and cover an enormous range of topics, reflecting every aspect of life itself. Their chief value lies in the fact that they are first-hand documents through which the modern reader can *immediately* connect with the ancient writer, without any interposition – amendments, censorship or changes – of a cultural nature or stemming from social convention. Being unfiltered in any way, they express unhindered the writer's spontaneity to those who read his message, even two thousand years later.

From a narrower cultural standpoint, they are invaluable for understanding the literacy levels of the different social classes. The forms and styles of writing, the handwriting, the languages that were used, and the grammar and syntax draw an accurate picture of the different systems of verbal expression. At the same time, they provide a close approximation of the actual spoken language, which at times differs notably, in the use of words and constructions, from the affected or formal language of the writers known to us through the tradition of written texts. Inversely, however, these graffiti also allow us to see the influence that the official authors and poets of the era had on popular culture, on occasion also giving us different versions of texts that have been handed down by codices. In some cases, it is even possible to glean which texts were studied at school.

Going beyond these cases, important though they are, and glossing over their valuable contribution to the study of origins and forms of names and words (onomastics), these graffiti – virtually glimpses into everyday life – allow us to recapture the problems and aspirations of an entire lost world, something that would otherwise be impossible.

It is probably pointless to try to arrange the graffiti in set categories in relation to the different aspects or areas of studies they enable us to examine. Paradoxically, it would be more appropriate to emphasize their overall value as documents of a community's "civilization," including the relational models linked to the cultural and social climate of the times. These inscriptions, so far removed from the great events

The popular Via dell'Abbondanza was the perfect place for inscriptions with electoral messages as well as more personal ones.

and the deeds that mark the key moments of history, simply capture brief and secondary episodes – perhaps even commonplace ones – of past lives, and yet they clearly sketch out a picture of the life behind them, shedding light on it.

One of the topics that is echoed most insistently in the graffiti is love, sometimes longed for with tender, lyrical accents or even in a poetic form. More frequently, however, it is presented in its crudest and, one would venture to say, most brutal aspects. Without going into this in great depth, it is nonetheless worth noting that these inscriptions, which may simply seem obscene, provide a clear idea of the rapport between men and women, the incidence of pedophilia and homosexual encounters, the characteristics and prices of prostitution, and the various forms, times, places, customs and circumstances that characterized sexual relationships in the society of this era.

The graffiti are often written in a metric form and they have even helped in the discovery of poets who were otherwise unknown, such as Tiburtinus, a Pompeian writer who was quite familiar with the tradition of Greek poetry. Toward the middle of the 1st century BC, though of limited means, Tiburtinus had already embarked on the poetic path that would later lead to Catullus and the *poetae novi*.

S ome of the verses left on the walls of Pompeii take on delicate existential overtones with a universal meaning, often with a melancholy air. More often, however, they portray a spirit open to hope, as in the case of this anonymous composition scratched onto the wall at the entrance to a shop along Via dell'Abbondanza (*CIL* IV 9123):

Nothing can last forever.
The sun that shines above plunges into the sea and the moon becomes a sickle, although it was full before.
The fury of the winds often becomes a gentle breeze.

In other cases, these verses show genteel irony, pondering man's weaknesses as in the following couplet, found at the *caupona*, or tavern, of Euxinus on Via di Castricio (*CIL* IV 9847):

The fair lass taught me to loathe the dark-skinned ones.
I'll hate them if I can, and if not ... I'll love them reluctantly.

In still other cases, the truth of some misdeed is shrugged off with a laugh, as in the couplet written outside the main door to a house (VIII 7, 6), which may also have been an inn, near the city gate of Porta di Stabia (*CIL* IV 4957):

We wet the bed; of course, we're unpardonable.
Guest, you want to know why? There was no urinal!

Some have the tone of a full-fledged complaint, such as the couplet found at tavern I 2, 24, also located near this gate (*CIL* IV 3948):

Host, may you pay for your swindling.
You sell us water, and save the good wine for yourself.

Few of the graffiti have a metric composition, however, and they are expressed more simply in the type of Latin defined as "vulgar." Nonetheless, they give us intriguing information about the habits of the times, and this is the case of several announcements. The following, found outside Porta di Nocera (*CIL* IV 3864), states:

"If anyone lost a mare loaded with baskets on November 25, contact Quintus Decius Hilarus, the freedman of Quintus, or Lucius Decius Amphio, the freedman of Lucius on this side of the bridge over the Sarnus, in the storeroom of the Mamii." Another inscription with just the opposite tone, painted on a wall along Via dei Teatri, announces (*CIL* IV 64 with addenda):

"A bronze container has disappeared from the shop: anyone who brings it back will get a reward of 65 sesterces; the reward for information about the thief, so I can catch him, is 20."

Even ordinary "shopping lists" provide valuable information about humble daily needs, as well as the current prices of products. This is the case of the graffito written on a column of the Great Palaestra, perhaps by a passing traveler (*CIL* IV 8561):

"In Pompeii [I bought]... a pound of lard, three asses; wine, one as; cheese, one as; oil, one as; bread, two and half asses; pork, four asses." The anonymous writer was evidently drinking table wine. A

graffito at the entrance to Hedone's tavern, annexed to the House of the Wounded Bear in the center of Pompeii (*CIL* IV 1679 with addenda) tells us,

"*Here you can drink for just one* as; *for two asses you'll drink better wine; for four you'll drink Falerno.*"

Again, on the subject of money a small, sad comment discovered in a room of House I 8, 13 gives us insight into the world of loans and usury, as well as its costs and rules (*CIL* IV 8203):

"*On July fifteenth I pawned earrings to Faustilla for two denarii [equivalent to 32 asses]. From this amount, she deducted one-thirtieth as interest for the monthly usury of one as.*" We should note that, based on what we can glean from another graffito in this room (*CIL* IV 8204) written just a few days earlier, on July 4, Faustilla received another bitter pledge, this time a cape with a hood. However, another Pompeian managed to squirrel away a small fortune playing dice, and seemingly without plying other methods to give luck a helping hand, a practice that was evidently quite common at the time (*CIL* IV 2119):

"*In Nuceria, I won 855 and a half denarii playing [dice], and without cheating!*"

It is amusing to read the curses that, like greetings, idlers would leave in public meeting places, first and foremost the Basilica. The outbursts of a sponger, whose main preoccupation seems to have been wrangling a supper invitation, are un-derstandable, given the writings he left behind (*CIL* IV 1937):

"*I salute anyone who has invited me to dinner.*" Likewise, he scrawled barbs against those who failed to do so (*CIL* IV 1880):

"*Someone at whose table I do not dine, Lucius Istacidius, is a barbarian to me.*" The ones seething with dark malice toward an unfortunate victim are more troubling (*CIL* IV 1820):

"*Chius, I hope your ulcerous sores open again, so that they burn even worse than before.*" Even death failed to spare this poor fellow from his rival's sarcasm (*CIL* IV 1852):

"*Pyrrus salutes his colleague Chius. I regretfully heard you're dead. Farewell, then.*"

We could continue for hours with our examination of these documents that covered the city walls in astonishing numbers. Even the Pompeians themselves were not indifferent to them, for we find unconventional writings such as:

"*I am amazed, o wall, that you have not yet fallen into ruin under the weight of the nonsense of so many writers*" (*CIL* IV 1904 with addenda; see also 2461, 2487).

These graffiti represent an element that, with the quick flashes offered by these short but incisive signs, brings to life the pace of society in that era, and the sense of an entire civilization. At the same time, they manage to bridge the centuries, showing man in his existential dimension as he comes to grips with the deceit, disappointment, joys, sorrows and hopes of life as it has always been.

Necropolises in the Roman Era
FUNERARY RITES AND BUILDINGS

"The life of Pompeii is reconstructed through its houses and tombs," wrote the great archaeologist Amedeo Maiuri at the start of the excavation work on the necropolis outside Porta Nocera. This observation couldn't be more appropriate because, as a whole, the Roman necropolises in Pompeii constitute a virtually unique complex in their extension, typological variety, state of conservation, wealth of decorative elements and information on the lives of the deceased – whose age we can often ascertain. We learn too, the honors conferred to them, the priestly or political offices they held and the work they did. If we add the fact that we even know where some of them lived – like the garum producer or trader Umbricius Scaurus and the politician Obellius Firmus – then we can also establish connections and evaluate the type and level of residence in relation to the type chosen for their final resting place. Thus, we can easily understand how important these elements are in studying the city and reconstructing all aspects of its social life. As a rule, funerary edifices were built to help perpetuate the memory of the departed, and they were erected along the main roads leading out of the city, past a 100-foot clearance area around the city walls in which burials were forbidden. However, this ban was often ignored and there are many cases in which, through a special decree of the decuriones, the most illustrious citizens were allowed to build their tombs within this strip of land. It was the funerary monument rather that the person's lifetime home – merely a transitory abode – that handed down the memory of the deceased to posterity. As a result, anyone entering or leaving the city would pass a row of sepulchers, some of which monumental and others more humble. But all of them were enduring signs of a person and of a family. Inside the tombs, the site of each burial was often indicated with a stone insignia, the stylization of a human bust that is referred to as a "columella" in the "Pompeianistic" tradition. Buried at the feet of the columella was a vase containing the ashes of the deceased (generally a clay jar, although in some of the richer tombs it was made of glass, sometimes protected inside a container made of lead or marble). It was often covered with a stone slab that had a hole so that liquid offerings could be poured onto the ashes. The practice of inhumation, adopted in the preceding Samnite period, was replaced by cremation of during the Roman era. The deceased would be dressed in ceremonial clothes and placed on a pyre, which would be lit once friends and relatives had called his or her name aloud for the last time (conclamatio). Once the blaze subsided and any flames were put out with water and wine, the ashes and what remained of the bones were put in the cinerary urn, which in turn was placed in the ground or in a niche. A banquet (silicernium) was served near the tomb, and this was followed by nine days of purification. At the end of this period, another banquet (coena novemdialis) was held near the burial, and libations of water, wine, milk and the blood of a sacrificed animal would be poured over the site where the cinerary urn was buried. Offerings were brought to the tomb on the anniversary of the person's death (parentalia) and on the feasts for the dead (feralia), with a nine-day period consecrated to mourning that ended on February 21. Of the various types of funerary edifices documented in Pompeii, the simplest one was also the most common. This was the type set inside an enclosure composed of a simple masonry structure circling the burial area. In some cases, there were no openings, so the only way to access the tomb was by climbing movable wooden steps or blocks jutting out from the front of the en-

This marble statue of a woman was set discreetly along the edge of Via Nucerina, almost as if it were protecting the sepulchers along the road.

A series of podia *delimits the road of the Porta Nocera necropolis. Excavated starting in 1954, today they represent the largest group of tombs discovered in Pompeii.*

closure. Inside it, the tombs were aligned along the walls. In the more complex versions, the front of the enclosure featured an entry fornix or a façade with a pediment, with cornices decorated in stuccowork, such as the tomb of Veius Atticus at the Porta Nocera necropolis. The fornix was present from the Late Republican era through the last years of the city, and was used generally by the middle and lower classes. Its use has also been documented for the ruling class starting in the Neronian period, generally in the version with a pediment façade such as the tomb of the duumvir Marcus Obellius Firmus at Porta Nola. Another very widespread monument was far more complex and sumptuous. This type, also found among the Greeks, was documented in Pompeii starting in the Sullan period and was particularly popular until the Claudian period. It is composed of a rather tall *podium*, either smooth or decorated with pilasters or half-columns in relief,

sometimes with a niche on the front surmounted by a form of crowning. Some of the *podia* contained a funerary chamber. In the oldest examples, the crowning was sometimes composed of sculptures (for example, the lions on the tomb of the *Stronnii* at the Porta Nocera necropolis). However, this structure was almost always an aedicule, generally with two or more columns on the front (like the "Tomb of the Garlands" at the Porta Ercolano necropolis). In some cases, it was shaped like a tholos (beehive tomb) with statues of the owners of the monument, creating a "self-representation" paralleled by the tradition of displaying portraits of the leading family members in the *atrium* at home. This type of funerary building is seen frequently, above all at the Porta Nocera necropolis, and despite its monumentality, it was not used exclusively for citizens from the ruling

classes and has also been documented for freedmen. A variation of the preceding type is the fornix monument, in which the *podium* is crossed by an arched passageway. This type is found only at the Porta Nocera necropolis and dates from the late Republican-Augustan Age. All the cases in which the owners have been identified involve the families of freedmen. The altar-type tomb, already quite popular in Italy and in the Roman world during the Late Republican period, consists of a quadrangular *podium* that can hold a funerary chamber, surmounted by a pyramid with steps and an altar on top. There are 16 specimens in Pompeii, including cases that are uncertain, given that they are only partially preserved, but that in all likelihood come under this category. Ten of them are at the Porta Ercolano necropolis and they date mainly from the Neronian-Flavian periode. This one is distinguished by the same form as the aedicule funerary monument,

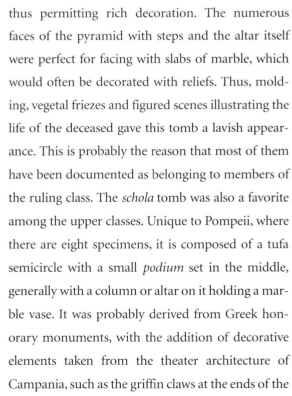

thus permitting rich decoration. The numerous faces of the pyramid with steps and the altar itself were perfect for facing with slabs of marble, which would often be decorated with reliefs. Thus, molding, vegetal friezes and figured scenes illustrating the life of the deceased gave this tomb a lavish appearance. This is probably the reason that most of them have been documented as belonging to members of the ruling class. The *schola* tomb was also a favorite among the upper classes. Unique to Pompeii, where there are eight specimens, it is composed of a tufa semicircle with a small *podium* set in the middle, generally with a column or altar on it holding a marble vase. It was probably derived from Greek honorary monuments, with the addition of decorative elements taken from the theater architecture of Campania, such as the griffin claws at the ends of the

This altar tomb, located in the Porta Ercolano necropolis, conveys a sense of austere elegance created by the simplicity of the lines defining its shape.

semicircle. The examples uncovered to date, almost always from the Augustan or Claudian period, are present in all the necropolises unearthed in Pompeii. All of them are distinguished by the fact that they are located just outside the city gates and thus on public ground, which required a special order issued by the decuriones, and by the fact that they have been linked with magistrates or public priestesses. The niche tomb represents a rather simple form that can nevertheless take on a monumental appearance, as the rectangular or semicircular niche could be painted with wall decorations. The smallest and simplest examples belonged to the lower classes, and this type is documented in Pompeii only in the Neronian-Flavian period. In addition to the cylindrical tombs – the one of Veia Barchilla, Porta Nocera, represents a category quite widespread in Roman Italy, the most famous being that of Caecilia Metella on the Appian Way, and the type with a funerary column

on a quadrangular base, rare in Pompeii – there are two other distinctive funerary monuments worth mentioning. These are the one of the priestess Eumachia and the one of the Flavii, both at the Porta Nocera necropolis. The first one, from the Tiberian-Claudian period, is composed of a broad terrace delimited along the back and part of the sides by a high wall. The entrance, lined with dedicatory inscriptions, opens along the front. The monument itself is set in the middle, and it is composed of an impressive *exedra* (receiving room) whose upper part must have been divided into a series of niches separated by half-columns and embellished with sculptures. The crowning was decorated with a relief frieze. Unfortunately, however, only a few fragments remain. Located to the rear is the entrance to the funerary chamber, whose layout follows the one of the *exedra*. To

accentuate the theatrical appearance of the monument, the architect set the monument between two existing aedicule tombs placed on *podia*, creating a very dramatic complex that is unrivaled in Roman funerary architecture. Analogies can be drawn with nymphaeum architecture, particularly the one built by Herod Atticus at Olympia. The tomb of the Flavii consists of two funerary chambers with vaulted roofing, set along the sides of a fornix that crosses the entire monument. It is distinguished by the two rows of small niches aligned in two orders along the entire façade. The lower row holds funerary insignias, while the upper one holds busts portraying the deceased. Based on recent studies, this building, which is unique in the funerary architecture of this region, has been recognized as a type of funerary architecture of urban Rome defined as the "house façade" and it was used solely by freedmen. We have already mentioned the importance of statuary, which was meant to exalt the prestige of the figures and *gentes* represented in the necropolises. Generally, the figures were shown standing in a toga-wearing arrangement if the deceased being portrayed was a man, or as Pudicitia if it was a woman. In Pompeii, the statues of a seated elderly couple and the one of a young woman in military garb, all from the Porta Nocera necropolis, are unique. Made mainly of gray tufa or white limestone and then covered with painted stuccowork, they were produced locally and often show coarse craftsmanship. However, since they were placed upon aedicules or in tholoi, they were far enough from the observer to conceal their poor quality. At the same time, however, this did not detract from their celebratory function that, if anything, was enhanced by this elevated position.

VIA DEI SEPOLCRI AND OTHER NECROPOLISES

Via delle Tombe outside Porta Ercolano – or Via dei Sepolcri, as it was named during the period of the excavations – was one of the main roads outside Pompeii and it led north toward Herculaneum and Naples. Discovered at intervals between 1763 and 1838, this necropolis was one of the first areas of the city to be excavated. As a result, it long represented the starting point and one of the most fascinating parts of a visit to Pompeii, as well as an endless source of inspiration for innumerable sketches and watercolors by artists and travelers such as Robert Hubert (fl. 1760s), Jakob Hackert (fl. 1790s) to François Mazois (fl. 1810-20) and Giacinto Gigante (fl. 1830-60). What is striking here is the frequent use of altar tombs, all belonging to citizens from the upper classes, although not always from the city's ruling class. On some of these tombs, we can still see the marble facing with relief decorations. One example is the tomb built by the freedwoman Naevoleia Tyche to commemorate and honor her husband Caius Munatius Faustus, who held the office of *Augustalis* (priest appointed to the cult of the emperor). Because of his virtuous conduct toward the general population, he had been granted the right to a seat of honor at the theater, symbolized by a large chair (*bisellium*). The slabs of white marble cladding the altar are covered with a frieze with acanthus scrolls around it. On the front, the epigraph is surmounted by the portrait of Naevoleia, while sculpted below is a scene representing largesse, an explicit reference to Munatius' virtues, as cited in the inscription. The *bisellium* is depicted on one side of the altar, while the other side shows a ship entering port with its sails unfurled. This may allude to the soul reaching Hades, although it is more likely to be a reference to the trade that helped Munatius amass his fortune. By the time they were discovered, many of the sepulchers had already been pillaged in ancient eras, but many still had their cinerary urns. Most were made of terracotta or glass, but there were also some in precious materials, such as the famous "blue vase," an amphora in cameo glass with scenes depicting the grape harvest. There were only a few funerary accouterments with the ashes and in addition to bronze coins, the offering to Charon in order to be ferried across the Acheron to the Underworld, there were a few ointment jars and several oil lamps. The one with a gold ring set with a cut gemstone is unique. Excavation of the area south of the city walls of Pompeii proceeded mainly during the 1950s. This work was conducted next to the site studied at the Fondo Pacifico in the nineteenth century, uncovering a substantial part of the necropolis outside Porta Nocera, currently Pompeii's largest with over 70 tombs. "*And I can finally leave the city through the ancient Porta Noceria.... And just outside the gate, beneath the thick pall of ash and lapilli there appear the first tombs, lined up along the sides of the street. After the famous Via dei Sepolcri outside Porta Ercolano, this is the second most important street of the Pompeian necropolis."* These words, written by Amedeo Maiuri in May 1954, reflect a legitimate touch of pride over the fact that he had had the opportunity to undertake this impressive excavation. The tombs are set along the street that intersects the one exiting the city almost at a right angle and then diverges gradually from the city walls, heading east toward Nocera. To the west, it must have been connected with the street that exited through Porta di Stabia to lead to the city of Stabiae. This must have been a well-traveled thoroughfare, as we can deduce based on the numerous inscriptions carved onto the tombs citing elections – mainly those of Nuceria – and announcing gladiator shows in various cities throughout the region, such as Atella, Nola, Nuceria,

Herculaneum, Puteoli and Cumae, and even the distant town of *Forum Popilii* in the Agro Falerno. The tombs in the area of this necropolis that has been unearthed – and there are more than 70 of them – are mainly the kind with an aedicule set on a tall *podium* and enclosed tombs, either plain or with a pediment façade. The first type includes the monument that was built, perhaps following the earthquake of AD 62, by the freedman Publius Vesonius Phileros for himself, his family, his patron Vesonia and a friend, Marcus Orfellius Faustus. However, once the tomb was finished Vesonius had such a se-

rious argument with this friend that he added another epigraph on the front of the monument, with a long tirade against the man who had proven to be a false friend. The tomb that, as indicated in the epigraph on the front, was built by Marcus Octavius and his wife Philumina for themselves and their descendents, also dates from the 1st century BC, during the pre-Augustan period. Above the tall *podium*, the aedicule is shaped like a small tetrastyle temple containing the tufa statues of the owners and a figure that is almost certainly one of their sons in military garb. While it has a large number of important buildings, the Porta Nocera necropolis does not appear to have been used extensively by the upper class. In fact, based on the titles in the extant epigraphs, only a small percentage of the tombs belonged to upper-class citizens (magistrates and priestesses), just the opposite of what we can observe at the Porta Ercolano necropolis. Instead, the tombs of freedmen – documented as such – are concentrated in this necropolis. This may simply be due to the locations of these necropolises. The ones of Porta Ercolano and Porta Vesuvio are next to *Regio* VI, which was a residential part of the city and was thus inhabited by the more prestigious families, whereas the one of Porta Nocera is next to *Regio* II and the southeast end of *Regio* I, areas that were inhabited predominantly by the middle and lower classes, as we can glean from the smaller number of large houses with an *atrium* and

peristyle. The necropolises near the other city gates are not nearly as extensive, although this may be due to a lack of large-scale exploration, but they include the tombs of prominent city figures. One of the most striking tombs near Porta Vesuvio is the one of the young Caius Vestorius Priscus, who died at the age of 22 shortly after embarking on a career in politics that had already gained him the position of *aedile*. In terms of type, it is an altar tomb, yet it is unique because of the rich paintings decorating the inside walls of the enclosure and the base holding the altar, with scenes portraying both the public and private life of the young politician. Vestorius is portrayed in his house, speaking to people who may

be members of his family, and he is also depicted seated on the magistrate's chair (*sella curulis*) set on a platform, as he carries out his political duties. The scenes depicted here are a banquet and a gladiator fight offered by Vestorius, commemorating the young man's generosity. The animals may also refer to this type of event if we interpret the scene as a *venatio* held in the local amphitheater. A rich array of silver dinnerware is depicted, reflecting the man's status. The garden that is portrayed may also have been one of the areas he used for entertaining, as this was an essential part of the home of any well-to-do citizen. A very close parallel can clearly be seen between the pictorial cycle of this tomb and

238-239

In this fresco painted on the tomb of Vestorius Priscus at Porta Vesuvio, three pygmies
are portrayed sailing on a boat.

the instructions that Trimalchio (Petronius, *Satyricon* LXXI) gives for his own tomb, pointing to a common attitude. A tomb must look like a viridarium, there must be scenes portraying gladiator fights and other scenes showing the generosity of the deceased, there must be images connected with his business (in the case of Trimalchio, ships with their sails unfurled to signify the trade that had made him successful). As we have seen, these parallels can also be found on other funerary monuments at Pompeii, such as

the ship with unfurled sails and the scene of *largitio* (largesse) at the tomb of Munatius Faustus at Porta Ercolano, as well as the gladiator fights depicted on the tomb of Clovatius near Porta Stabia, and on the one that may be attributable to Festius Ampliatus, also at Porta Ercolano. These opportunities to compare the literary sources and epigraphic documentation against the archaeological evidence from Pompeii and its necropolises reveal the enormous potential for research the Vesuvian cities offer.

239 bottom

This image, one of the many painted on the tomb of Vestorius Priscus, depicts a gladiator fight – perhaps in reference to an offering the deceased had made to the Pompeians while he was an aedile *– to commemorate his largesse.*

LIFESTYLES

◆

HOUSES AND SOCIETY

The fascinating and adventurous story of the discovery of Pompeii began in March of 1748, and from the very first excavation campaigns, the interest of researchers, scholars, and visitors focused primarily on city dwellings. Apart from rare exceptions like the Temple of Isis, the public and sacred buildings were found in ruins. This was due to the restoration work still under way following the earthquake of AD 62 and the seismic instability that followed, and also to the fact that their valuable items were pillaged or recycled over the years following the eruption.

In contrast, to the excavators' eyes most of the homes looked simply as if their owners had just left them for a short time. They were intact in their lively decorative schemes, paintings and floors, with their gardens embellished with statues and fountains, and furnishings set out in the various rooms. The way we see Pompeian homes today obviously reflects the wealth of their last owners. Nevertheless, their appearance is also the outcome of the transformations that influenced the field of Roman residential architecture between the 4th century BC and the 1st century AD.

As compared to our own homes, which essentially open to the outside, the different types of Roman houses had one feature in common: they created a separation between the indoors and the surrounding area. They had high walls, whereas small windows – often just slits – opened onto the streets at a considerable height from the ground. Likewise, our modern way of living is also mainly devoted to our private lives, which we separate from work and business. With the exception of only a few sectors of society, today only a minimum number of rooms are used to welcome guests, and they are furnished to reflect the homeowners' tastes.

In contrast, in the Roman world the home was an important means for conveying the owner's status. In a famous passage from his tome *On Architecture* (VI, 5, 2), the architect Vitruvius noted that in designing a house the first thing to consider is the patron's social status. As a result, this created a type of residential construction that was tied to the social hierarchy, with the holders of public office or citizens with economic power at the top. These people were obliged to receive a daily throng of visitors, or *clientes*, in a specific area of their homes. The purpose of this habit was to create a close bond between the *patronus* and those who went to pay their respects. Thus, the *clientes*, who were freedmen, received help and protection, whereas the *patronus* expanded his consensus and power with the *clientes*, over whom he thus gained control for electoral and economic purposes.

Particularly in Pompeii, we can see how the home became a way for the owner to present himself. During the city's final years, in which the economic aristocracy was represented mainly by former slaves (freedmen), people felt an even greater need to show off the status they had achieved. Thus, any passerby could peer through open doors to see how the main rooms of a house were aligned, with the garden toward the back. And based on the size, decorations and value of the furnishings set out for all to see, they could gauge the success and, consequently, the power gained by the person who lived there.

At the bottom of the social pyramid were the ordinary citizens, and as they had neither these obligations nor any notable assets, they would open their modest homes only to friends and family. Between these two extremes, there was a series of intermediate categories that, for economic reasons, needed to keep up social relations on various levels, and this led to a wide variety in the types of homes in terms of the size and number of the rooms.

242-243

In one of the paintings comprising the pictorial decoration of the tablinum *of the House of Marcus Lucretius Fronto, a magnificent example of the Third Style, a row of lavish villas overlooks an airy seascape. Paintings of this kind were meant to convey the patron's tastes and, more importantly, his social status.*

Consequently, the need to receive visitors was clearly a decisive factor in the architectural layout of the houses. It created a distinction between the areas reserved for the family's private life, with annexed privies and sometimes a small heating system, and the areas that were open to outsiders at particular times of the day. These were the *atrium* and, starting in the 2nd century BC, the peristyle – the internal courtyard. In addition to these two areas, which were passageways used by family members and visitors alike, there were also other rooms in which guests were received, depending on their importance, the type of discussion to be held, and even the time of day and the season. This effectively created a hierarchy of rooms and areas that ultimately led into the interior of the home. As a result, architecture, furnishings and decorative apparatuses were at the service of social competition, and the fact that one could choose from a broad range of rooms was a mark of great distinction.

Polychrome mosaics set in geometric black-and-white frames decorate the floor of the atria *at the Houses of Paquius Proculus and Cuspius Pansa, in accordance with a style documented in Pompeii during the Augustan Age.*

The houses of Pompeii also reflect these general characteristics of Roman residential architecture, although they were adapted to local resources and needs. Within their range of types, however, it has been possible to recognize an ideal model that can be found on the various social levels, and it is defined as the "*atrium* house," either with or without the addition of a peristyle. This type of residence, the oldest example of which is the House of the Surgeon built in the second half of the 4th century BC, is also the most common in Pompeii. In its traditional form, it features an entrance, composed of a corridor that could vary in length, opening onto a large room – the *atrium* – that was either square or rectangular. At times, this was followed by a small *hortus* (garden), with several rooms set along the sides.

The term "*atrium*" (from *atrum*, black) may have derived from the fact that there was a fireplace whose smoke blackened the walls. It was originally the dining area and the center of family life, as also proven by the presence of a sacred shrine (Lararium) used by the *paterfamilias* to worship the domestic deities. The *atrium* subsequently lost this role and became a passageway linking the other areas of the home. In some cases, it was transformed into a monumental area, with statues, to welcome *clientes* and celebrate aristocratic pride. There are five different types in Roman residential architecture: the *atrium Tuscanicum*, the *atrium tetrastylum*, the *atrium Corinthium*, the *atrium testudinatum* and the *atrium displuviatum*. The first four types have been documented in Pompeii. However, in the urban area there are no known examples of the *atrium* displuviatum, which was characterized by the four roof sections sloping to the outside, with a central opening protected by a raised canopy but open on the sides to let light in. However, it has been theorized that one was built in the House of

the Surgeon. The Tuscan, tetrastyle and Corinthian *atria* featured an evenly shaped aperture (square or rectangular) in the roof, the *compluvium*. The roof would slope toward the *compluvium* so that terracotta gutters could drain rainwater into a corresponding tank or *impluvium* in the floor, with two channels leading away from it, one toward the underground cistern and the other beneath the sidewalk toward the street as a water runoff.

The Tuscan and tetrastyle *atria* were particularly common in Pompeii. The Tuscan *atrium*, commonly considered the oldest type, was composed of wooden crossbeams holding flat and bent roof tiles, so that the weight of the roof was borne by the side walls. The tetrastyle *atria* was instead characterized by four columns at the corners of the *impluvium*, and they clearly played a dual role: static and aesthetic. The Corinthian *atrium* was developed during the 2nd century BC and its rows of columns around the *impluvium*, as seen at the House of the Dioscuri and the House of Epidius Rufus, clearly show its Greek origins. Lastly, the testudinated (roofed) *atrium* had a conventional double-pitched roof that was completely closed, and it can be recognized in all Pompeian houses that did not have a cistern set in the middle of the room. Along the walls of the *atrium*, there were several rooms of different sizes: the *tablinum, alae* and *cubicula*. The *tablinum*, the largest and most important room in the *atrium* area, covered the back wall near the entrance. In Pompeian houses, it was built in three forms, depending on the appearance of the back wall. The back wall could be entirely solid, have a large window if the house extended beyond it with the *hortus* or the peristyle area, or be removed entirely to be transformed into a passageway.

The *alae*, which were average in size, were the rooms along the side walls of the *atrium*, and they were followed by the *cubicula,* which were smaller.

This traditional layout of the "*atrium* house," influenced by the Greek world, was transformed by the addition of the peristyle. This columned portico marked off a garden area (in place of the original *hortus*), and the numerous rooms used for receiving guests and dining overlooked this area. The addition of the peristyle went hand in hand with a changed home life, because it created a new hub in which the family members would cross paths with visitors. Among the many rooms located in the peristyle section, we can identify the *oeci,* new receiving areas with refined pictorial decorations for guests to admire. Starting in the final decades of the 3rd century BC, it became customary to eat meals "in the Greek style," while reclining on a couch (*kline*). This led to the need to create a room for this purpose, and it was generally rectangular. This room came to be known as the "triclinium," so called because of the three couches placed in a horseshoe arrangement around a table that held food and plates. In its most complete and sophisticated form, this type of residential construction was the manifest expression of the Pompeian aristocracy, and it can be seen in the grandeur of the Tuscan *atrium* of the House of the Faun and the tetrastyle *atriums* of the House of the Silver Wedding, the House of the Labyrinth and the House of Obellius Firmus. In some cases, for example the House of the Faun and the House of the Labyrinth, two other *atria* were set alongside it so that the two areas of the home could be accessed separately and without any obstacles.

With the exception of the *cubicula* (rooms used by the servants or reserved for storage), the other rooms around the front part of the house also played a specific celebratory role. The *tablinum* held the family archives, as underscored by the presence of a wall closet in the House of Menander, and it was also where the marriage bed was set up for the wedding day, as mentioned by the literary sources. The *alae* were used instead to hold wax or wooden images of the family forefathers, exhibited when funerals were held.

In deference to this celebratory penchant, and as documented extensively by the findings, the bronze or marble portrait of the proprietor would often be set on a pillar placed next to the entrance to the *tablinum*. Otherwise, two massive coffers would be placed along the side walls of the *atrium*, bearing witness to the family's financial resources. The *impluvium* area would often be decorated with marble furnishings such as a *cartibulum* (a two- or four-legged table) to display valuables, and there were also statues and fountains.

To highlight one's social status even further, a single porticoed garden sometimes wasn't enough, even if it was quite large. As a result, two or more would be created in a row, like the two at the House of the Faun and the House of the Figured Capitals, and the three at the House of the Citharist. Likewise, extra rooms were added for private meetings, as were triclinia, where the amount of sunlight would vary depending on the season. These internal gardens were embellished with sculptural elements and sophisticated water displays, testifying to Pompeian society's lofty decorative tastes in the 1st century AD.

This type of residence, which is quite distinctive with its abundance of areas, sometimes monumental, clearly represents the minority in Pompeian buildings. The houses of the middle classes represent the largest category, with countless varieties. Characterized by an increasingly marked development of the top floor, these houses have a smaller *atrium* and an *impluvium* that was sometimes modestly decorated with a fountain and a statue. The *alae* and the *tablinum*, the most important rooms in this part of the home, came to be utilized strictly for family life, and they were used, respectively, as a dining room and as a simple area to receive guests. The peristyle – when present – was not complete but resembled a courtyard, with three porticoes (House of Julius Polybius), two porticoes (House of the Ancient Hunt) or just one (House of the Prince of Naples) set around a modest green area. The love for furnishing gardens in various forms can also be observed in this range of homes and the House of Marcus Lucretius is an important example. Here, the owner arranged Dionysian herms (square pillars supporting a sculpted head) and statues around a circular pool, aligned with the *tablinum*.

In contrast to the bigger houses, in the homes that had very little space available for a green area, such as the House of the Small Fountain and the House of the Bear, we can observe the ingenious solution of placing a lively polychrome mosaic fountain, shaped like a shrine, against the back wall to create a line of perspective with the entrance, *atrium* and *tablinum*. The less well-to-do classes of Pompeian society lived in yet another type of house, generally using the top floor. These homes were even smaller, generally no more than 1000 square feet, and since they had to be adapted to a limited amount of space used essentially for private purposes, their layouts do not always match specific types. Among these, we can cite a series of houses that can be recognized particularly in *Regio* II in Pompeii, along Via Nocera. They have been defined as "row houses" and they center around a small testudinated (roofed) *atrium*, which sometimes had steps with a catwalk to an upper floor. These houses had two rooms on the sides of the entrance and others with privies along the back, where there was also a small *hortus*.

There was an even more modest type, where the living quarters had to be concentrated on the top floor so that the rooms on the ground floor could be used for various types of business and trade activities.

Nevertheless, this type of *domus*, which we can consider respectable popular housing, was not the poorest place to live. There was certainly a class of people, including freedmen, who could afford only a simple loft without a privy, fitted with a small window overlooking the street. The loft, set over the person's work area, was accessed using stairs with stone steps at the bottom and the remaining ones made of wood. These lofts, concentrated along the most crowded streets of Pompeii, were referred to as *pergulae*, and a maxim that Petronius wrote gives us a very good idea of what it meant to belong to a subordinate class living in such accommodations: "But he who is born in a *pergula* cannot imagine a house for himself." (*Satyricon* 74, 14).

248-249

The west side of the peristyle at the Praedia *of Julia Felix, one of the largest and most breathtaking in Pompeii, is delimited by a magnificent portico with an open summer* tablinum. *In the center, a canal stocked with fish was crisscrossed by three small bridges.*

THE FOUR STYLES

In the Roman world, the taste for covering walls with paintings could be found in every level of society. Anyone who could afford a "proper" home would turn to specialized workshops ready to satisfy any request – with the quality of the paintings depending on how much the homeowner could spend. The walls could be covered entirely with paintings, with the exception of the areas used for the privies and the servants' quarters. In these areas, the walls would simply be whitewashed or, at most, decorated with barely outlined geometric motifs

The wall paintings were not merely ornamental, and with their colors and rich figures they represented the main form of room décor. In the Roman world, neither the living quarters

nor the rooms used to welcome guests had the abundance of furniture we have today. Even the dining rooms had only couches and a table in the middle. What marked the function of the rooms, underscoring their luxury and importance, were the pictorial decorations in particular and, to a lesser extent, the floors. Architecture and frescoes thus complemented each other and their evolution is an extraordinary source for understanding the tastes, fashions and techniques they express. Because so many pictorial decorations have been preserved in the Vesuvian cities, and at

Pompeii in particular, this has made it possible to conduct in-depth research on the subject and these works continue to provide new fields of research. The wall paintings were first studied by August Mau in 1882, and he classified them into the so-called "Four Styles," establishing a chronological sequence for the decorative motifs that, while perfected over the years, remains the basic reference for anyone interested in studying ancient Roman painting.

The First Style consists of a stucco imitation of masonry structures and veneers, composed of horizontal rows of large panels and rectangular blocks, done in relief or incised and then brightly painted to imitate the variety of colors typical of precious marble. This decoration, of Greek derivation, became popular in Pompeii in the 2nd century BC and was used extensively to decorate public and sacred buildings as well as the homes of the upper classes.

At the House of the Faun, we can admire the marvelous refinement of this type of decoration, above all in the entrance: this not only has the usual rows of slabs and blocks but also has a bracket used as a support for the façade of a temple and its colonnade. Another excellent example can be seen in the *atrium* and *tablinum* of the House of Sallust.

250

Enormous polychrome panels, painted to imitate precious marble cladding, embellished the atrium *of the Villa of the Mysteries. They were done using the technique typical of the First Style.*

250-251

August Mau drew up the classification of the Pompeian styles – the one shown here is a painting in the Second Style from the
Villa of the Mysteries – at the end of the 19th century. His studies were based on Book VII of Vitruvius' On Architecture.

Perfectly inserted in the room's geometric division, the austere architectures that decorate a cubiculum *at the Villa of the Mysteries are an excellent example of the Second Style.*

In addition to being a natural development of the First Style, the rise of the Second Style between the late 2nd and early 1st century BC may also have been fostered by its close link with theater-stage design, as noted in a well-known passage from Vitruvius (*On Architecture* V, 6, 9). It is a more complex style that sets perspective views of landscapes and artwork (paintings and statues) between the architectural elements, creating the illusion that the wall itself "breaks up."

Some of the most striking evidence of this style in the Vesuvian areas can be seen in some of the rooms of the Villa of the Mysteries and Villa A at Oplontis. Here colonnades, gates, shrines and houses with several floors, complete with balconies and terraces, are set side by side on the wall, while imaginary windows overlook bucolic landscapes and gardens.

In the same cubiculum *at the Villa of the Mysteries, a* trompe l'oeil *door in the Second Style attracts the viewer's attention, suggesting further dilatation of the rooms: other evanescent architectures can be discerned beyond the portal.*

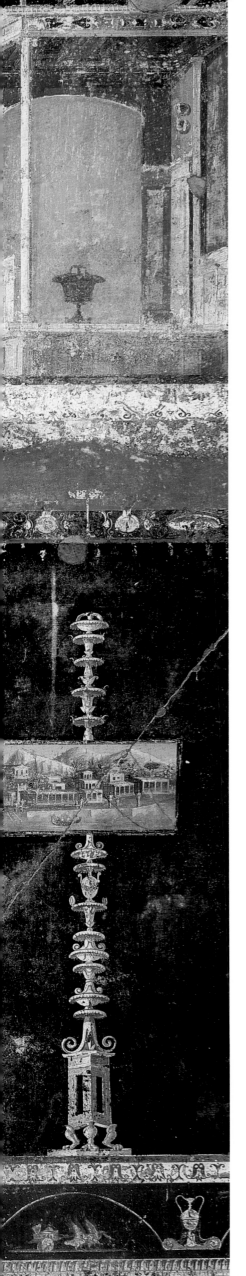

Pictorial evidence between 20 BC and AD 40-50 reveals the emergence of a new system of wall painting. The architectural illusionism of the Second Style was abandoned and the wall now called for a rigidly tripartite field, with a base, middle zone and upper zone. In particular, the middle zone included large rectangular panels with a single ground, separated by architectural and vegetal elements. This tendency gave the wall surfaces "solidity," while the viewer's attention was drawn to the middle panel. A fundamental innovation that would later be developed in the Fourth Style was the rise of figured representation, placed in the central panel of the middle zone in the form of a large painting, medallions or simple figures outlined in the field of the panels. One of the

best examples of the final phase of this style can be seen in the refined decorative program of the House of Marcus Lucretius Fronto.

The Fourth Style became popular in the Vesuvian area shortly after the middle of the 1st century AD, inspired by the artistic trends in Rome and influenced by Nero's imperial palaces. Two main schools of composition have been identified: the first one is referred to as *scaenae frons* and it is considered a development of the Third Style.

This first type, rarely seen in the Vesuvian area (e.g., the Palaestra of *Regio* VIII) was inspired by stage design that, as we have noted, was a fundamental part of the Second Style. It is presented as a composition that covers the entire wall with complex architecture and sweeping views, with full-length figures in the foreground. Instead, there is extensive documentation of the frescoes that are part of the second school, which developed directly from the preceding decorative system. The middle zone is divided into panels, in which there are pictures with various subjects or isolated figures, marked off by borders and separated by elaborate architectural views. The upper zone is divided with complex pavilions and architectural theatre wings, embellished with fantastic figures and decorated with stucco molding. The House of the Vettii, in particular, is an important example of this style, with its wealth of fantastic architectural perspectives and mythological figures.

256

In the spirit of the Fourth Style, fantastic architectural perspectives create illusory, surreal ambiences, alternated with large "narrative" paintings with a mythological theme. The close-up shown here is part of the decoration of the exedra at the House of the Vettii.

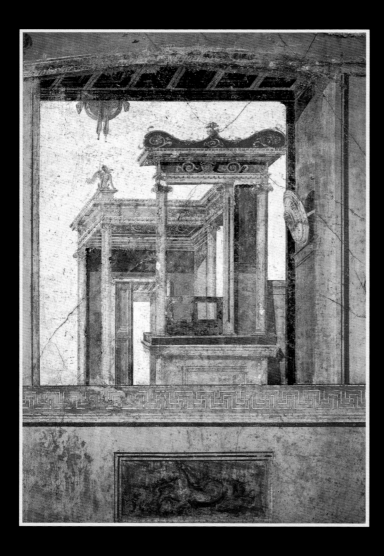

256-257

On the east wall of the exedra of the House of the Vettii, airy theater wings with masks flank the central painting, depicting the Torment of Ixion.

HOUSEHOLD FURNISHINGS
FURNISHINGS AND DÉCOR

Today, the choice of furnishings for a home depends on a number of variables tied not only to financial resources but also to changing tastes and ideological choices. Therefore, it should come as no surprise that the furnishings of the houses and gardens of Pompeii offer a unique observatory for reconstructing the mentality of many generations of Pompeians. Stepping into each of these households allows us to understand the social, economic and cultural level of its inhabitants, not only through the actual size of the home but also through the choice of furnishings. However, each era corresponds to the specific needs guiding these choices, which either accumulated in the subsequent periods in the life of the house or were wiped out completely by radical renovation, often because the property changed hands.

The Pompeian documentation obviously offers extensive evidence of this last process and of the final stage of its development, and whenever possible we must attempt to extrapolate the oldest data and the changes that occurred over the years.

The picture that is gleaned from this would be far richer if two factors hadn't come into play to make it incomplete in many cases. First of all, the lack of attention paid to the original contexts has detracted from our knowledge of many of the furnishings from the houses excavated in the 18th and 19th centuries. For a large number of objects there is no indication of specific provenance and as a result, there is no way to establish a link among them. In addition, the reconstruc-

tion work that was ongoing in many fully or partially uninhabitable homes following the earthquake of AD 62, has added to the confusion in reconstructing the original furnishings. Few furnishing items remain from the Samnite homes. Some of the noble houses dating from this period were uninhabited when Vesuvius erupted and the excavation work has yielded few artifacts. Therefore, we must rely on their architectural decoration to get an idea of the tastes of the owners in that period. Evidence of this can be found in the elegant façade capitals, with a characteristic "sofa" shape, and in the even more refined ones with figured subjects. Some of the most significant examples come from the House of the Figured Capitals, so named because of the pair of capitals decorating the panels at the entrance. Here, on the side facing the street, two pairs of Satyrs and Maenads sketch out the lifestyle chosen by the owner, who together with his wife is portrayed in a half bust on the side facing the interior of the home. This is the same kind of pattern we find repeated in many Etruscan sarcophaguses and urns, with a clear allusion to the banquet. Love and joie de vivre are the messages conveyed by these capitals, and they closely follow models that originated in the world of Greek palaces: Pompeii is adorned in the Greek style, demonstrating that the city grasped and assimilated the figurative language and behavioral structure suggested by Eastern *luxuria.*

The message conveyed by the House of the Faun is even more sophisticated. Here, the little bronze statue of the Satyr, set in the *impluvium* of the *atrium*, recalls these same ideals in a form

that is seemingly less personalized. However, if we accept the suggestive theory that the owners of the house during this period were named Satrii, the choice of an "icon" of this kind to represent them assumes the meaning of mythical descent. There was also a Dionysian touch in the aristocratic homes of the later period. Two small bronze statues portraying a Satyr and a Silenus, also Hellenistic, found in the *atrium* of the Villa of the Papyri in Herculaneum, point to the importance attributed to this element to symbolize a penchant for living in the Greek style. The furnishings of a Pompeian house always show this reference, which in the ancient periods may have stemmed from direct relations with the Greek world. In the Roman period, however, this reflects a taste that had been fully assimilated by this time. The décor of a Roman house depends on the extent and the way in which those choices were adopted in the various eras by the different social classes. Given the fact (as we learn from Vitruvius) that the Roman house in the late Republican and early Imperial Age also served in part for the upper classes' public purposes, then its furnishings had to be appropriate for this function, for example, in the distribution of the rooms and their wall and floor decorations.

258
On the surface of the two small pillars found at the House of the Golden Cupids, bas-relief decorations portray subjects evoking mythical sylvan settings (Naples, MAN).

259 left
The bronze statue of the dancing faun was originally set on a pedestal in the impluvium *of the house that was named after this sculpture (Naples, MAN).*

259 top right
A centaur predominates in a marble oscillum (a shield that would sway in the wind to ward off the evil eye) (Naples, MAN).

THE SCULPTURAL DECORATION OF THE ATRIUM AND TABLINUM

The *atrium* and the *tablinum* are the most representative areas of the house. It was here that the doors would be opened in the morning to welcome *clientes* obliged to offer the patron their *salutatio*. Therefore, we find portraits of the owners in these spaces, based on a custom that came from the Greeks, as documented by the statues in the houses at Delos, but was adopted in the reduced form of the herm, in response to this desire for self-representation. A classic example is the herm found in the house of L. Caecilius Jucundus. In this portrait, the person's features – his hooked nose, jug ears and the wart on his chin – show a naturalistic balance. The person portrayed here is not the banker, who worked during the Claudian and Neronian periods, but is probably the patron to whose generosity Jucundus owed his ascent in society. The portraits of Vesonius Primus and Cornelius Rufus can be given a similar placement. Two bronze herms, male and female, were found at the House of the Citharist and they portray the owners. Also found in this house, but on the top floor, were two portraits of figures tied to the imperial house (existing in other replicas). They have been identified as Marcellus, Augustus' beloved nephew designated as the heir to the throne, who died prematurely in 23 BC and to whom the city of Pompeii dedicated a statue in the Triangular Forum. Ancient ties with the imperial family, which were no longer valid due to a changeover in the dynasty in power or because the house itself changed hands, made the two portraits obsolete.

In the House of the Golden Cupids, a portrait was found in the peristyle. It depicts an anonymous figure also found in another image at Herculaneum. The portrait was done in the Augustan period, while the house was renovated following the earthquake. Its presence in the peristyle seems inconsistent with the rest of the sculptural decoration, almost as if it were a way of reusing an outdated work of art. There is a complete lack of portraits datable beyond the Claudian period and this is particularly significant, as it reflects a change in taste. The social transformation that took place with the rise of the freedmen class in the middle of the 1st century AD in Pompeii, and in the rest of the Roman world, led to choices other than portraits, tied to a tradition of displaying the images of one's ancestors (*imagines maiorum*) in the *atrium*. Cicero himself asserted his lack of noble ascendants when he boasted of the absence of "smoky images" in his house. Other

furnishings used in the *atrium* for entertainment purposes include the *cartibulum*, or rectangular table. One of the oldest specimens is the one decorated with winged lions found in the House of Cornelius Rufus, a splendid piece of Greek craftsmanship, as clearly demonstrated by the baroque tangle of tendrils. Varro (*De re rustica* 5, 125) tells us that these supports were used to show off the household silver. The fact that this was considered a status symbol, just as it is now, can be seen at the tomb of Vestorius Priscus. In order to symbolize his social prestige, one of the subjects he chose in addition to the one depicting him in his public office as *aedile* included the representation of a laid table, showing off a rich set of bronze tableware. In examples from the Augustan period, such as the House of Meleager, the decorations include the cornucopia, a symbol used often to express the *aurea aetas* (Age of Gold) achieved by the new dynasty but that was also chosen by the owner, perhaps to publicize the fact that he was well-to-do. The round table, found disassembled and without the tabletop in the House of the Theatrical Pictures, is a veri-

table collector's item: written on the upper side of the three lion's feet is the name of the original owner, P. Casca Longus, the tribune of the people who was the first to strike Julius Caesar on the Ides of March. The table, evidently confiscated by Octavian, must have ended up on the market and was purchased by a Pompeian. Tables with just one leg in the form of a decorated pillar were also quite common. In this case, a figure with a pointed hat and long pants often appears next to a Sphinx and a herm of Bacchus, Hercules or other figures. This figure has traditionally been identified as Attis, the young man with whom Cybele fell in love. However, the theory that this is a portrayal of a vanquished Eastern barbarian is more convincing, based on widely propagandized iconography as the symbol of the "victory" of the factions in the Augustan figurative culture. At times, the figure holds a *cyathus*, a type of ladle used to pour wine into cups, a task carried out by a slave known as *a cyatho*. In this case as well, the image has a dual meaning, taking up a theme of political propaganda and expressing personal luxury.

260
Two herms from the House of the Citharist, found in the atrium, probably portray the owners of this residence *(Naples, MAN).*

261 top
Four winged lions supported the surface of this white marble cartibulum *(Naples, MAN).*

261 bottom
The elegant tapered bronze tripod with ithyphallic satyrs decorated the Praedia *of Julia Felix (Naples, MAN).*

262-263

This view of the atrium *and* tablinum *of the House of Marcus Lucretius Fronto clearly shows the effect achieved by combining wall paintings with architectural decorative elements and furnishings.*

263

The fountain from the House of Menander is composed of a bronze basin resting on a marble pedestal (Naples, MAN).

With the furnishings of the *atrium* we come to the Augustan period, a period that marked a radical evolution in the way people lived. The reason for this change was the arrival of running water once the Serino aqueduct, built by Augustus, was completed. Like all the coastal cities as far as Misenum, Pompeii benefited from this and the improved standard of private life is evident from the ensuing transformation of the furnishings. Water displays became the new status symbol, shown to entertain passersby and add a touch of life to gardens. Since the *impluvium* was no longer needed to collect rainwater, it was lined with marble. It was often connected to a base holding a statue or to a pool spouting water. There were many different ideas. At the House of the Little Bull, water spewed from the mouth of a bronze bull into a pool decorated with leaves and small animals, and then flowed into the *impluvium*. There would often be a statue-fountain of a Faun or Silenus (House of Obellius Firmus, House of M. Gavius Rufus, House of M. Lucretius), while in other cases a marble vase or a *krater* was connected directly to the *impluvium* to become a miniature garden with flowerbeds along the sides.

By this time, the *atrium* had lost its specific function and centrality, not only from a practical standpoint in terms of providing water and light, but also as an ideological fulcrum expressing social status to the outside world. This is also demonstrated by the changed function of the *arcae* (safes), which continued to be kept here. Once used to distribute *sportulae* (gifts in kind) that the patron gave his *clientes*, they now came to express the homeowner's financial well-being. This is demonstrated at the House of Siricus, where the words SALVE LUCRU(M), done in mosaic on the floor, accompanied the display of the safe (of which the block of lava stone on which it must have been mounted is all that remains). This message was reinforced by the *cartibulum* (the prized table), which again was decorated with the globe and cornucopia that, as we noted, had a dual meaning. The famous painting of the god Priapus had a similar meaning but a different visual impact. At the threshold of the House of the Vettii, the god guaranteed the wealth of the residence with his enormous phallus resting on the plate of a scale, counterbalanced by a bag full of money – whose amount was immediately confirmed by the fact that there were two safes in full view along the sides of the *atrium*.

IN THE TRICLINIUM AND THE GARDEN

The showiest symbol of luxury displayed in the *triclinium* was a series of statues, connected to each other to be used as clothes stands, lamp holders or tray holders. The ostentation of this type of item, which has also been confirmed by specimens found in Morocco and Egypt, is also cited extensively in the sources. Lucretius (*De Rerum Natura* II, v.24 ff.) clearly insults the useless luxury they express, recalling "the golden statues of children whose right hands hold lit torches to illuminate nighttime feasts." The fact that this choice matched the tastes of the era is demonstrated by the five bronze statues found in Pompeii. The specimen found outside Porta Vesuvio, an Ephebe vaguely inspired by the models of Polyclitus – although here the oversized head ignores the sculptor's rule of creat-

ing strictly harmonious relationships – was embellished in silver leaf. The two vines found together were used to hold oil lamps. The one from the House of Cornelius Tegete, found wrapped in cloth near the summer *triclinium*, served the same purpose, and this was probably how the one from the House of the Citharist, an Apollo that held a lamp in place of the usual lyre, was also used. The bronze found at the House of Fabius Rufus instead held a tray on supports with rich vines. A recent addition to this series is the sculpture of the House of Julius Polybius, which was inspired by a type of Apollo from the Greek "Severe" period but elaborates its formal traits with contrived stiffness. The extensive restoration work done on these bronzes nevertheless underscores the great value they were given. We can consider these ranks

of luxury servants as the distant forefathers of the numerous statues of blacks, traditionally found in the furnishings of the colonial homes in the United States, which characterized many 19th-century décors and were used for different functions, including lamp holders.

Four bronze statuettes found in a wooden box added a more eccentric touch to the *triclinium* of the House of Cornelius Tegete. All four statues are obscene representations of an old man with an enormous member who is shouting to advertise the items offered on a valu-

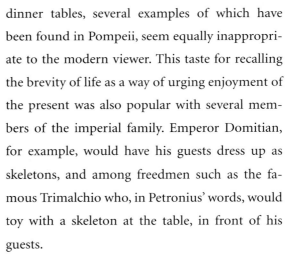

able silver tray. This theme was probably considered refined due its provenance – Alexandria – and its visual impact is indubitably powerful, but today it is difficult for us to understand how it could be appropriate at banquet. The small skulls and skeletons that would be placed on the dinner tables, several examples of which have been found in Pompeii, seem equally inappropriate to the modern viewer. This taste for recalling the brevity of life as a way of urging enjoyment of the present was also popular with several members of the imperial family. Emperor Domitian, for example, would have his guests dress up as skeletons, and among freedmen such as the famous Trimalchio who, in Petronius' words, would toy with a skeleton at the table, in front of his guests.

The open area inside the house could differ in shape and size, depending on the amount of available space and what the family could afford: from a peristyle (courtyard) to a simple viridarium (garden), it was the center of the social life of the home. Originally, it was a dynamic space that maintained the functions and layout of the Greek

*The famous statue of Apollo Citharedus, which decorated the garden, can be seen
in this outdoor view of the House of the Citharist.*

265
*In this mosaic symbolizing the transience of life one can distinguish a skull,
mason's tools, a scepter and a haversack (Naples, MAN).*

models, used as gymnasiums and palaestrae. As demonstrated by recent studies, however, this living area that opened onto the rooms used to receive and entertain guests soon became a privileged ambience in terms of furnishings.

The model that inspired the furnishings came from the *otium* (leisure) villas of the late Republican Age aristocracy. With its wealth of artwork, the Villa of the Papyri in Herculaneum offers the best and most complete example. Nevertheless, as opposed to what was achieved in these villas through detailed study that strove to create a well-balanced series of sculptures set in the appropriate spaces and to tailor these choices to an ideological and artistic plan (Cicero's letters offer extensive information on the subject), the "miniature villas" lose the uniformity of a balanced project and frequently end up being poor imitations. This limitation is often a fundamental aspect of Pompeian garden sculptures, as documented by their smaller size.

266 and 267
The peristyle of the House of the Citharist temporarily held the bronze statue of Apollo the Citharist, after which the house was named. However, the original – now at the National Archaeological Museum of Naples – was probably used to hold oil lamps. The insertion of powerfully expressive eyes made of vitreous paste gives this austere and magnificently proportioned work a lively yet gentle touch.

In fact, only a few of the Pompeian sculptures were life-sized. One of these is a marble statue of Apollo discovered at the House of Menander, documenting the presence of sophisticated sculptures that were freely inspired by classic models, but it is difficult to determine the statue's original position. Nonetheless, this work lacks a sense of balance, given the stiff position of the body and the arrangement of the hair, inspired by archaic Greek sculpture, and the supple form of the body drawn from more recent models. Moreover, the griffin and laurel wreath betray the work's decorative purpose, which fully reflects the revival of Augustan classicism.

A statue of Diana from the same period was found in an aedicule set on four columns in the peristyle of House VII 6, 3, complete with an altar. It was a type of private sanctuary, such as the one dedicated to Hercules, that the poet Papinius Statius (*Silvae* III,1) noted at the Villa of Vedius Pollio in Sorrento. Similar ones devoted to Hercules and Isis have also been found.

Reproductions on a smaller scale were much

more frequent, as documented by the numerous images of Venus, from the figure of Venus crouching to the one in which she is tying her sandal, getting out of the bath, and so on. Instead, there are none portraying the matronly Pompeian Venus documented in paintings – an eminently local type – as this would have been difficult to reproduce in statuary due to a lack of models to copy. As a result, models drawn from a cultural tradition were preferred. The images of men of letters were also small, from the terracotta statuettes of Antisthenes (from House I 2,16) and Pittacus of Mitylene (from the *Praedia* of Julia Felix) to the little busts of philosophers assembled in galleries. The richest one series (from House IX 5,6) presented Demosthenes, a bust alleged to portray Seneca, Epicurus and a woman, perhaps Leontion, the philosopher's student and companion. Even Alexander the Great, whose deeds were commemorated in the mosaic of the House of the Faun in a monument worthy of his glory as leader, is portrayed with youthful features in a small bronze that was being restored by a shop on Via del Foro.

A beautifully crafted marble statue of a stag being attacked by dogs was found in the garden of the House of Stags at Herculaneum. Here again, however, the version of this scene proposed at the House of Camillus in Pompeii is merely an unexceptional replica in both size and craftsmanship. A similar subject, with dogs attacking a boar, can be seen in the bronze group that decorated the fountain of the House of the Citharist, but here as well, the violence of the struggle is lost in static modeling. Nevertheless, it is mainly from the complexes that we have been able to recover and preserve – in some cases even restoring their ancient functions before it finally became necessary to conserve them elsewhere – that we have gained an integrated view of how the sculptures were arranged in Pompeian gardens. Therefore, we will take a closer look at some of these.

The House of Marcus Lucretius had a viridarium located behind the *tablinum* and it opened onto an elevated floor, intentionally creating a theatrical effect that was noticeable even from the exterior. In the fountain set against the back wall, a miniature waterfall flowed from a marble statue of a Silenus into a round pool that was surrounded by small statues of animals spurting water. Around them, there were miniature replicas of elegant sculptures: a group portraying Pan with a goat, an *Aposkopeion* Satyr (using his hand to shield himself from the sun), a Satyr removing the thorn from Pan's hoof, and Dionysian herms.

The House of the Vettii and the House of the Golden Cupids have peristyles with the most important reception rooms opening onto them. In the peristyle of the House of the Vettii, cupids poured water into rectangular pools in front of them and in the middle of the columns, in a layout in which symmetry predominates. This decorative system bars any access to the central garden, favoring the refreshing effect of a number of gushing fountains. Sophisticated subjects are developed in the paintings that decorate the rooms around the peristyle, and they are suggested by the figure of the seated scholar portrayed on the south wall of the portico.

The peristyle of the House of the Golden Cupids is even more crowded and its sculptural decoration has a surfeit of references. The world of the theater is present with a small and rather ordinary herm of Menander as well as a number of marble *pinakes* (small pictures) of theater masks, and there are *oscilla* (hanging figures) swinging between the columns. Herms of Dionysus, Jove and Eros decorated the interior space of the garden, while other reliefs, including several "antiques," were set in the south wall. The furnishings can be dated to the period prior to the earthquake of AD 62, as proven by the extensive restoration work done on the sculptures. Their small size and the fact that the arrangement is best viewed from the south portico – the reliefs with the theater masks face this way – suggest an overall panorama, created to be viewed from this perspective. The other portico was probably used instead as a passageway.

The ideological perspective of these private collections cannot be interpreted using the same parameters governing the furnishings in the villas of the aristocracy of the late republic. There, choices were made piece by piece, seeking a sense of balance between the function of the rooms and the meaning of the subject being depicted. Instead, the limited space of the urban peristyles, coupled with the entertainment function the sculptural furnishings were meant to fulfill, determined not only the choice of Dionysian subjects but also the enormous attention that was paid to their arrangement. A pleasant overall view was the most important objective.

270 and 271 bottom
The two oscilla *portray a centaur with its arms tied behind his back and a helmet at his feet, from the House of the Golden Cupids, and a man armed with a sword and shield (Naples, MAN).*

271 top
The rectangular marble relief, originally at the House of the Golden Cupids, portrays theater masks set facing each other (Naples, MAN).

272

The mouth of the marble fountain may depict Oceanus: a lead
waterspout is visible between the figure's lips (Naples, MAN).

273

The head of a maenad portrayed on an oscillum is decorated with leaves
and berries, symbols that evoke the cult of the god Dionysus (Naples, MAN).

The leading example is naturally the House of Loreius Tiburtinus. Here, the layout of the garden along the lines of two canals set in a "T" widens the perspectives and enhances the concepts being evoked. As a result, the choice of sculpture is broader and more varied. Mythology is alluded to by young Hercules strangling snakes, the Muses evoke the theater, to Egypt, represented by sculptures of the Nile and the Sphinx. In short, it was a miniature park created as a visual path rather than a walking itinerary. Even the theme of the garden sanctuary, of which we have mentioned several other examples in Pompeii, can be found here in the aedicule, which held a statue of Diana and acted as a link between the two

the Sileni call to mind the Dionysian world, and groups of fighting animals recall the world of nature. The long canal evoking the *euripi* (waterways) that were so popular in villa architecture (the one at Hadrian's Villa in Tivoli is a leading example) was naturally a reference canals. In viewing this setup, which brings together a plethora of cultural suggestions but without any sort of uniformity, we can't help but compare it to the house of the freedman Trimalchio, described by Petronius with such biting sarcasm.

274 top and 275
The two sculptures in white marble, both from the House of Loreius Tiburtinus, respectively represent a sphinx that holds a bronze Gorgon's head between its paws, and a cupid holding a comical mask. The sculpture decorates a small waterfall in the garden (Naples, MAN).

274 bottom
One of the two canals, supplied by a fountain, that crossed the green area to form a "T" in the garden of the House of Loreius Tiburtinus.

HOUSEHOLD ITEMS

ompeian houses have yielded an enormously varied repertory of both valuable and everyday tableware. When the first 18th-century excavations started to uncover all this evidence of daily life, not everyone felt it important to examine and conserve these artifacts: antiquity was considered a superior entity whose study was not supposed to contemplate whether "the Ancients used cutlery or not." Despite this reluctance, however, so many everyday items were discovered that, using an innovative approach for the period, an exhibit was set up in one of the rooms of the Herculaneum Museum, recreating an ancient kitchen fully equipped with pots and pans, plates, cutlery and more.

This ethnoanthropological curiosity did not correspond to conscious scientific interest, either at that time or throughout most of the excavation work. As a result, no project was implemented to guarantee the conservation of all the objects, including the roughest and most fragmentary ones, and to record – for the most peculiar items – their exact provenance and the set of objects found with them. As a result, of the household items of Pompeii we are now familiar with all the silver vases, a large number of bronze ones, numerous glass ones and an enormous quantity of oil lamps, but there are very few terracotta vases and even fewer pieces of what is now referred to as "common pottery" because of its simple form and lack of decoration.

Two large sets of silverware have been found. The first (now in the British Museum) was discovered toward the end of the 19th century in a villa at Boscoreale, hidden under an oil mill. This was a rather "dark" period for the study and con-

276 and 277

The treasure found at the House of Menander includes 118 pieces of silver weighing over 50 pounds. Visible on the left are a mediolus *and a cup with scenes of nature and rural life; on the right is a* kantharos *with olive branches laden with fruit, symbolizing the fertility of the land (Naples,* MAN*).*

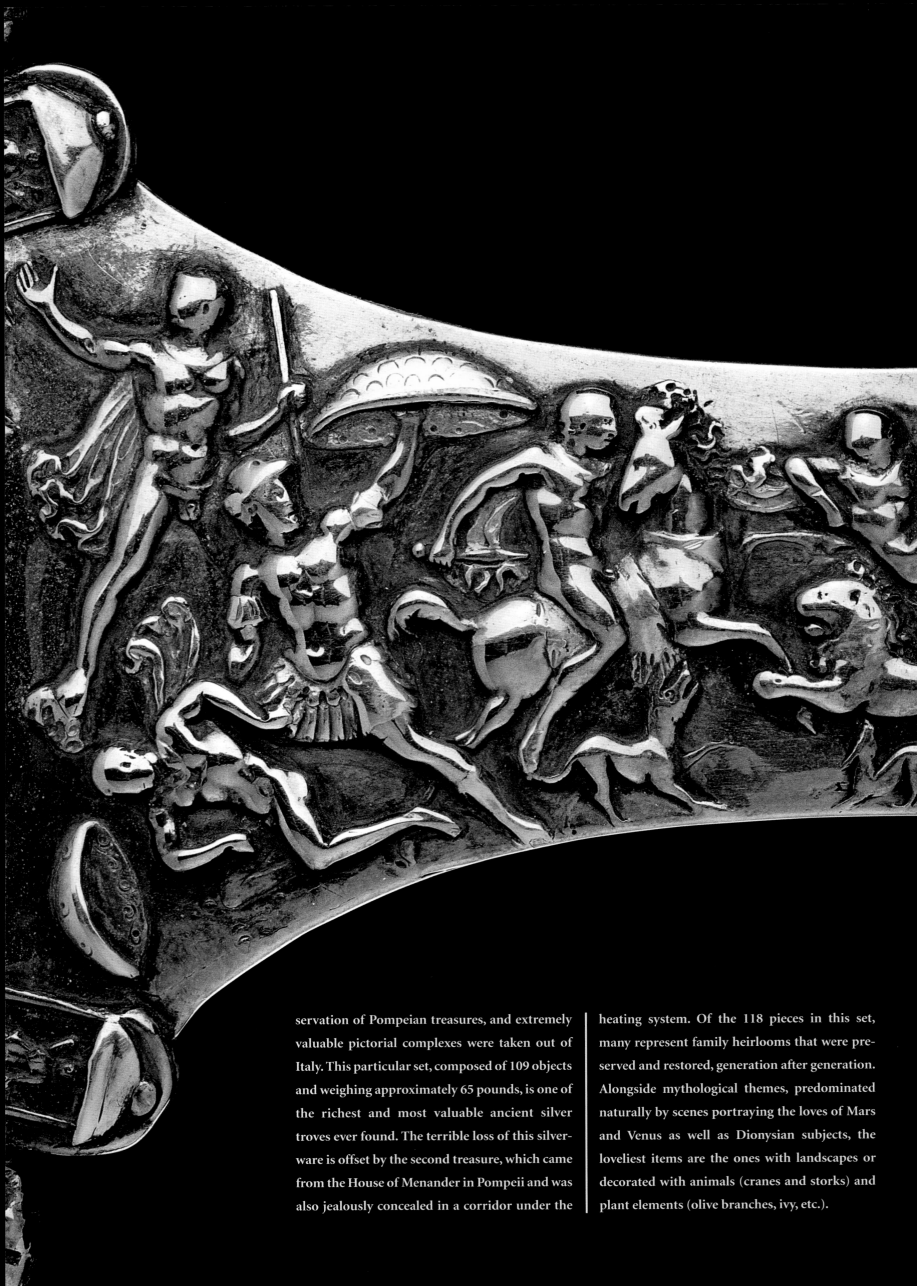

servation of Pompeian treasures, and extremely valuable pictorial complexes were taken out of Italy. This particular set, composed of 109 objects and weighing approximately 65 pounds, is one of the richest and most valuable ancient silver troves ever found. The terrible loss of this silverware is offset by the second treasure, which came from the House of Menander in Pompeii and was also jealously concealed in a corridor under the heating system. Of the 118 pieces in this set, many represent family heirlooms that were preserved and restored, generation after generation. Alongside mythological themes, predominated naturally by scenes portraying the loves of Mars and Venus as well as Dionysian subjects, the loveliest items are the ones with landscapes or decorated with animals (cranes and storks) and plant elements (olive branches, ivy, etc.).

278-279
The handle of a silver patera from the treasure
of the House of Menander depicts hunting scenes.
The gilding of some of the details gives the decoration
a lively touch (Naples, MAN).

The bronze items also include antiques, such as the Greek pitcher from the 5th century BC, found at the House of Julius Polybius, with a dedication to Hera of Argos engraved on the lip. It would be almost impossible to trace the journey that brought this item to Pompeii. Others date from the Greek era, including many particularly elegant bed decorations. Most of the documentation involves tableware, which is more finely decorated, and kitchenware, which often gives us a fascinating look at ancient cooking methods, such as the different "cake" pans in animal shapes. There are also many other items made of bronze – stools, braziers, double-chamber food warmers – that reveal the level of technological advancement stimulated by the population's sophisticated eating requirements.

280

The bronze oinochoe with the head of Silenus at the lower part of the handle graced a Pompeian table (Naples, MAN).

281 top

On the bronze oinochoe found at the House of Julius Polybius, the handle starts from the back of a winged sphinx and ends on the body of the vase with a Medusa's head (Naples, MAN).

281 bottom

This bronze pyx was used to hold ointments and balsams (Naples, MAN).

282-283

*The panel made of vitreous paste, from the House of Fabius Rufus, shows a scene of
Dionysian abandon; Hermaphroditus can be seen on the left (Naples, MAN).*

Glass was slowly becoming more important and one of the most famous production centers was nearby Puteoli, where there was a glassmaking district located around a *clivus vitrarius.* (glazier's slope). In addition to items made of pressed glass with *millefiori* or mosaic decorations (the worthy forerunner of Venetian murrhine glass), Pompeii has also yielded notable specimens of cameo glass, made with two layers of glass – blue on the bottom and white on top – in which elegant figures were carved. Examples include the famous vase with the harvesting cupids and the panels from the house of Fabius Rufus. Glass was used for everyday purposes and was probably also made on site to produce astonishingly clear vases and glasses, which are also documented by frescoes decorated with vases filled with fruit, as well as windowpanes.

283

The famous Blue Vase offers valuable evidence of the cameo-glass workmanship technique. A layer of intensely colored glass was overlaid with a layer of opaque white glass; the latter was carved following the lines of a specific design in order to create a contrast between the pale reliefs and the dark ground (Naples, MAN).

284 left and 285
The clay vase, decorated with grapes, a lizard, stairs and a tortoise in relief, was used for offerings during magical rites associated with the Eastern god Sabbatius (Boscoreale, National Antiquarium).

284 right
The body of this clay oinochoe is decorated with six figures relating to the myth of Iphigenia (Naples, MAN).

Nevertheless, pottery was the most commonly used material and the crockery production that has been found attests to the far-reaching trade in which Pompeii was involved. Thus, it is not surprising that there are more examples of ceramics produced in the East than the competing type produced in Gaul. Here again, the influence of trade with the East, of which Puteoli was the beachhead, has given us the key to understanding this scenario. As far as common pottery is concerned, there was a broad range of containers that served special purposes. For example, there was a special jug, produced in Pompeii that has been interpreted as a *fritillus*, the jar used to shake dice. There were also perforated vases used to grow plants with the layer technique, and these were probably produced in the city as well. Some vases were used for agricultural purposes, such as the ones with several holes used as drinking troughs for chickens, and the closed type with spiral stairs inside, which were used to fatten dormice.

If we study these forms and compare them with the revealing texts of ancient agrarian writers, also examining the forms that are traditionally produced even today, we can start to understand the fascinating link between ancient practices and the modern world.

THE PICTORIAL TECHNIQUE
HOW A FRESCO IS CREATED

O f all the many "gifts" the cities buried by the eruption of Mount Vesuvius have given to humanity, one of the most remarkable in many ways is undoubtedly the evidence of ancient pictorial art. The original productions and masterpieces of great artists, known through the literary sources, have been lost, as this artwork was executed mainly on wooden panels. The paintings placed in the middle of the frescoed walls of Pompeii and Herculaneum portrayed subjects and models from the Greek tradition, which were spread through "copies" that were repeated over and over, yielding different results depending on the skill of the copyist. This copyist was known as the *pictor imaginarius,* who specialized in executing figured themes but did not participate in creating the decorative context in which the painting would be inserted.

Very little is actually known about how the painters, who were certainly called upon as a group to fresco a house, organized their work. During the first two hundred years following the discovery of the Vesuvian cities, the problem was never tackled. At first, there was an attempt to recognize the models from which the figured subjects were drawn. At the same time, however, scholars also tried to place the substantial mass of decorative apparatuses into some kind of order based on chronological sequence and on examples of taste and fashion: in other words, they attempted to identify the "styles" of Pompeian painting. The in-depth research done over the past several decades has instead focused on the technical and organizational aspects of the work done by the frescoers, and the recent findings in Pompeii along Via dell'Abbondanza (*insula* IX 12) have contributed significantly to discussions about this problem. Scholars have noted that the decoration not only of a single room but even of a single wall was done by several people, and that a group effort was thus involved. This has also been established by the fact that, when working on plaster, in order for the work to turn out well and "take," it had to be done before the plaster dried, to avoid absorption of the pigments, which were mixed with lime. The physiochemical studies conducted recently on paintings *in situ* as well as those preserved in the Naples Museum have confirmed that there are no organic substances in the pictorial medium, which proved to be composed of calcium carbonate and was executed as a fresco. The a procedure that came to light following the excavation of a room (*oecus*) in House IX 12, 9 was the one used whenever the walls of houses in these ancient cities were frescoed, or in any event, when walls with more complex decoration were involved.

286
The elegant simplicity of nature encounters the sophistication of gilded decorative elements in this portion of a fresco from the Hall of the Cupids at the House of the Vettii.

287
Small paintings with subjects portrayed against a black ground are harmoniously alternated with red panels in the decorative apparatus in the Hall of the Cupids at the House of the Vettii, done in the Fourth Style.

In the decoration of the back wall of the colonnade of the Temple of Isis, a long black frieze marked the connection between the central and upper portions. It extends in a sequence of curled scrolls, in which corollas are alternated with Egyptian animals and pygmies (Naples, MAN).

289 top
Faux marble, portrayed with a keen sense of realism, acts as the upper frame for the magnificent megalography done in the Second Style, which was discovered in the triclinium at the Villa of the Mysteries.

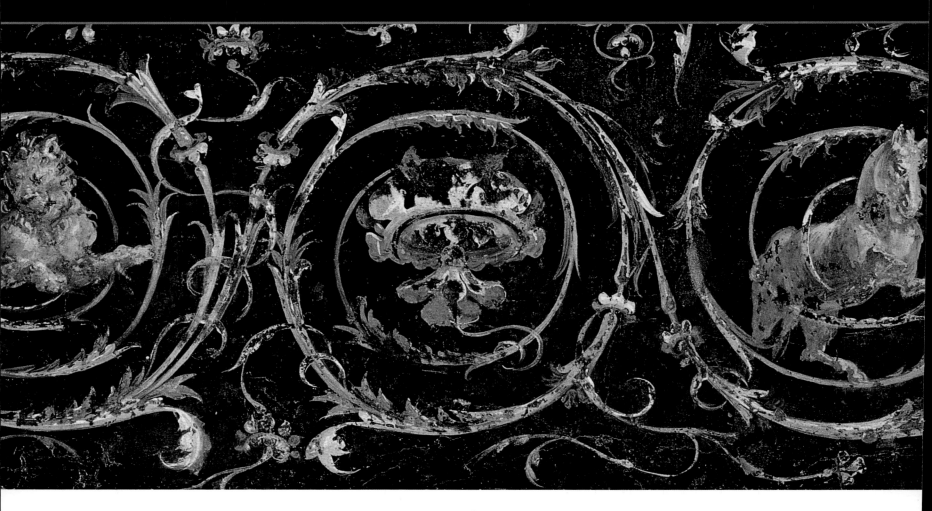

Here, using charcoal two painters rapidly sketched out the preparatory drawing (*sinopia*) of the decorative structure they were to complete, starting from the top. This last example that was discovered, as well as other known cases such as the north wall of the *triclinium* (c), the north and south walls of the *cubiculum* (h) of the House of the Lararium of Achilles (*Casa del Sacello Iliaco*) and the north wall of the *oecus* of House I 11, 17, clearly demonstrate that the work proceeded in this order. Thus, in all the cases mentioned here – in contrast with the upper and middle areas that are complete in every detail – not only are the base areas devoid of decoration but they also have no plaster over them. When executing the preparatory drawing, which could also be done by incising, the more detailed elements of the decoration were left out, such as leaves, volutes, lotus flowers and ribbons. These were the elements through which we can distinguish the hands of different artists and they were done freehand, also using the *fresco secco* technique – in other words, on a colored ground that was nearly dry in the case of the smallest detail work or the finishing touches. The pigments for these touchups were not dissolved in water but were diluted, to varying strengths, with lime. This explains the per-

fect bonding with the underlying plaster, due to simultaneous "taking" and carbonation.

By comparing elements from a single room, even if they have been detached and displayed in museums, we can easily see that the same subject could be treated with greater or lesser precision, and by a faster or slower hand. These are differences that, once the work was completed, were almost indistinguishable on the wall as a whole. Moreover, rather than these differences being flaws, they give the frescoes the liveliness typical of manual work.

And yet the ancient painters used various expedients to make their work easier, such as mechanical reproduction instruments like perforated templates, proportion compasses and molds. They used the first to reproduce repeated motifs like "carpet borders," plant scrolls, ovolo molding, palmettes and other types of frames. With the proportion compass or sector, they could enlarge or reduce decorative elements, setting their points of reference in the selected size and then using them to trace the design in the new proportion. Also molds were used to make the stucco molding that always finished the top of the wall decoration: these molds were made of wood or terracotta, and in many cases the module can be recognized perfectly.

WORKSHOPS AND PAINTERS

This wealth of experience, the availability of the required work implements, and knowledge of the methods for using different pigments certainly could not have been improvised. Moreover, given the results we can observe in Vesuvian paintings, the level of coordination among the different members of the team of decorators could not have been achieved this systematically if the team members had come together only when there was a job to complete. There must have been an organization of some sort. While it cannot be compared to the kind seen in the Renaissance workshops, characterized by the role of a master who imparted a "manner" to which his collaborators adapted, the organization undoubtedly envisaged the role of a *pictor et praepositus pictorum* (a role known to us through the funerary inscription of one of Emperor Hadrian's freedmen). In other words, this person served as the head of a group of painters, coordinating and checking their work, and acting as the go-between in handling transactions with the customer. The *pictor imaginarius* was not part of this group, which may also have hired other workers, depending on the size of the job. The *pictor imaginarius* was instead a more independent figure who would step in once the decorative work was finished, executing his picture in the field that was left free for this purpose, or he may have worked at his shop, doing his painting on a panel that would then be placed on the wall. The Vesuvian cities provide examples of paintings executed outside, done on panels, such as the one with *amorini* (infant Cupids) found in Herculaneum, and also ones that must have been placed in the hollows left for this purpose in House VI 15, 14 or in the façade of the *Praedia* of Julia Felix. Other examples include the paintings waiting to be put up, found sitting on the floor, such as the famous little paintings in the Third Style discovered in Herculaneum and now in the Museum of Naples, and the

fragment with Dionysiac elements found in the *atrium* of the *Praedia* of Julia Felix and "hung on the wall with an iron hook" (also in Naples). The interest in conserving not only paintings but also fragments can be noted in Pompeii at the House of Castricio, which has a fragment with Second Style masks inserted in Fourth Style wall, and at the House of the Four Styles, where a Third Style winged figure was inserted in the oldest decoration of a wall and maintained with an antiquarian flavor. The fact that the *pictor imaginarius* would step in after the decoration of the accessories was completed is demonstrated by one of the Pompeian discoveries we mentioned above. Here, the draft of the painting of the wall that was already completed, except for the base, was carefully executed in detail, whereas it was completely absent on the east wall, where a segment was waiting to be colored.

The attempt to identify "masters" and "workshops" in Pompeian painting thus came about nearly 200 years after the first discoveries were made. Once the search to identify the great Greek originals on which the Roman copies were based had waned, scholars focused on seeking the original proposals and solutions of local "masters," among whom the leading figure needed to be pinpointed. Instead, it was not a matter of finding the great masters but identifying the craftsmen of a provincial city. An attempt was made nevertheless to recognize workshops and a leading figure. Based on in-depth studies, ten workshops were identified, including the ones that worked at the Houses of the Vettii, the Naviglio and the Dioscuri. Other studies attributed the four main paintings in the House of the Tragic Poet and the House of the Citharist to four different masters, while in 1955 the artwork in the House of the Dioscuri was attributed to seven different artists. An analytical study of the entire decorative context of the House of the Vettii, conducted about

Two cups, one containing powder to make light-blue paint and one for white, have been preserved almost perfectly intact (Naples, MAN).

twenty years later, marked a turning point for the research method being used, acknowledging that the variations were also due to the different functions of the rooms or the different personalities of the painters themselves, working simultaneously. Proceeding along these lines, a workshop of painters, active following the earthquake in AD 62 above all in the southern part of the city, has been identified between *Regiones* I and II. They have been named the "Painters of Via di Castricio," and the workshop is characterized by a somewhat clumsy and coarse taste, the use of a limited palette and the repetitiveness of the decorative motifs, even in different sizes. This group of the painters favored still lifes with fish, birds and landscapes, medallions with portraits or still lifes, vignettes with peacocks or griffins, twisted candelabras, hanging garlands, the combined use of yellow and red panels, and carpet borders against a contrasting ground, and so on. When necessary, however, they were also capable of executing more demanding decorations. Moreover, since the decoration of the latrine in the House of Julia Felix is extremely simple, scholars think that within a given atelier there were craftsmen with different levels of skill. Nevertheless, in the search to identify workshops it is important not to confuse stylistic affinities with typological ones, taking into consideration a work team composed of a large number of people. Consequently, it is easier to identify a "style of the times" rather than a "workshop style." Although several scholars completely deny the existence of stable groups of workers, the decoration of the Temple of Isis has recently been attributed to the workshop of the House of the Vettii. The workshop of the House of Marcus Lucretius Fronto has been identified through particular details, and these decorators may have been the same ones who worked on the House of Caecilius Jucundus, the House of the Blacksmith, the House of the Orchard, and the Thermopolium (I 8, 8). The problem of the workshops of decorators in the Roman world, naturally involves the in-depth analysis of the decorative elements and of the main figures in the paintings. However, this approach also examines the techniques used to apply the layers of plaster and execute the preparatory drawings, with an analysis of brushstrokes, fingerprints and even the marks left accidentally by the artists' fingernails. This information can yield fascinating results if it is compared systematically against the evidence that is still available.

THE COLORS

Findings such as the shop of the Attii, open on Via di Stabia, where numerous remains of colors – mainly yellow and white – were discovered, the workshop (I 9, 9) where 150 little pots with different colors were uncovered and the recent ones we have already cited (*insula* IX 12) clearly demonstrate that the colors were produced on the spot, or were at least refined, altering the tones, at the time they were applied. One of the items found in the hall being painted was a pannier containing a double set of pots with colored powders: orange, white, blue, yellow, black, red and green. The duplication of the colors demonstrates that there must have been two painters using them. While these sets of colors contained an organic binder, making them suitable for finishing touches done using the *fresco secco* technique, others found in a deposit were almost pure (without any traces of calcite), indicating that they had not been dissolved in limewater because they were ready to use for true fresco painting. Moreover, the presence of a marble pestle, lumps of red pigment, and a large seashell containing the remains of lime confirm the theory that any changes in color tone were made at the time the paint was applied.

The pigments used in the Roman world were mineral and organic in nature: Pliny the Elder and Vitruvius left detailed descriptions about how pigments and dyes were prepared for construction, weaving and cosmetics. There was a broad range of yellows. *Sil atticum,* superior to other yellow ochers and almost as sought-after as silver, contained iron, silica, aluminum, calcium, calcium carbonate, manganese, magnesium and various impurities. However, hydrous iron oxide, mixed with silica and clay, is what mainly gives ocher its yellow color. Moreover, one of its properties is that it turns red with the loss of hydration, which is what happened in Pompeii on the overheated walls following the eruption. *Sil,* first used by the famous Greek painters Polygnotus and Micon, looked like mud. Reds were found in a natural state, such as *rubrica,* but they were also made by calcining yellow ochre, cooking it in terracotta pots without any cracks or chinks that would have dispersed the heat and negatively affected the quality of the results. According to Vitruvius, the best production area was Sinope on the Black Sea, but Egypt, the Balearic Islands and Lemnos were also excellent sources, to which Pliny adds Africa and Cappadocia. Other varieties of red obtained from minerals were *minium* and *sandaraca,* while the plant variety was *cinabris.* There were also artificial products, made by mixing elements of different origins such as *cerussa usta,* from a blend of minium or red lead and artificial sandarac, or *sandyx* (*cerussa usta* mixed with *rubrica*), as well as *syricum* and *spuma argenti.* One of the colors that Pliny defines as *floridi,* or more costly, is cinnabar, a splendid, brilliant red like the one seen in the background of the hall in the Villa of the Mysteries, in the hall (q) of the House of the Vettii, and in some of the rooms in the House of Augustus on the Palatine Hill. It char-

292

This detail from Scene IV of the megalography from the triclinium *of the Villa of the Mysteries portrays a Silenus playing a lyre.*

293

This disk, frescoed on an ocher wall in an ala *of the House of the Vettii, portrays a Gorgon's head.*

294

A candelabrum topped by an Isis-related figure, one of several that decorated the portico leading to the ekklesiasterion, *the large room thought to be the Isiacs' (worshippers of Isis) meeting hall (Naples, MAN).*

294-295

Various Dionysian symbols are placed on a staircase with a light-blue background, while a panther fights a serpent at the foot of the steps. The fresco is from the Praedia *of Julia Felix (Naples, MAN).*

acteristically turns black when exposed to sunlight, and this is what happened in the *atrium* of the Villa of the Mysteries. Perhaps this unique discoloration feature is what made the use of cinnabar so rare. Other colors considered *floridi* include *armenium* (azurite), *crysocolla* (or malachite and thus green), indigo and purple, which were not used alone but were mixed with binders. The preparation of *caeruleum aegyptium* was quite complex. This sky-blue color was made from a mixture of sand and Cyprus copper, which was then coarsely shaped and dampened in order to be agglomerated into little balls for firing. Other artificial colors were *coelon, lomentum* and *vestorianum puteolanum,* the latter produced since the end of the Republican Age by Caius Vestorius, a friend of Cicero, who had brought it to Campania from Alexandria. Nonetheless, all of these were less expensive than natural blues like *cyprium* (azurite) or *scythicum* (derived from lapis lazuli). Likewise, minerals like malachite, glauconite and celadonite were used to make

green pigments, and they were found in various places (although Vitruvius maintained that the best kind came from Smyrna). For white, calcium and dolomite were used for the most part, and the black found most recently in Pompeii was carbon derived from plants. According to Pliny, Polygnotus and Micon also made *atramentum* (the dark color) or vine black from lees, but we know that the type made by burning bones or ivory was also used. The cost of the colors varied depending on quality: 1.50 to 8 sesterces for one libra (equivalent to 11.8 ounces) of yellow ocher, 2 to 8 sesterces for red ocher, 32 sesterces for Egyptian blue and 44 for

Vestorian blue. The price went as high as 120 sesterces for purple. A ceiling of 280 sesterces was set for cinnabar, and this makes it easy to understand why the palette of these ancient populations was somewhat limited and why certain colors were seldom used. One of the unique aspects of the ancient frescoes is the polish of the surface. It looks so finely burnished that some scholars attributed this feature to the presence of wax in the blends of colors, while other thought it was due to the addition of clayey substances such as kaolin, which can then be polished easily. However, the studies that were conducted rejected both of these hypotheses, theorizing that the painted surface was rubbed with marble dust. According to Vitruvius' description, after the ground color was applied it was finished and smoothed to give it the compact look of marble. This procedure, which broke through the surface layer of the calcium carbonate, made the color penetrate the plaster better and was also used to draw the moisture to the surface so the painter could continue his fresco work. Studies done on the surface of the frescoes from the House of Livia on the Palatine Hill have confirmed the presence of grains of alabaster smoothed by buffing. This operation was performed with tools like the *liaculum,* a long and narrow spatula used to flatten the painted surface. According to Pliny's writings, alongside the brushes with bone handles and pig bristles, paint pots, mortars and mixing bowls, these and other tools were part of the painter's personal wealth. And as demonstrated by the furnishings from two tombs, one discovered in France and the other in Germany, no painter would ever part with them.

296-297

The wall fresco visible on the west wall of the oecus at the House of the Golden Bracelet reproduces furnishing elements that were very popular in Pompeii: large vases with handles, birds, fruit, oscilla and two theater masks.

298-299

On the walls of the exedra at the House of the Vettii, large panels in yellow ocher, alternated with panels with architectural views, are the background for the portrayal of mythological scenes, such as the one of the child Hercules strangling snakes.

300-301

This object – a group of seahorses emerging from short candelabrum with vines and a panther extending from it – looks decidedly "Baroque". In their coloring and movement, the panther is rendered with extraordinarynaturalism.

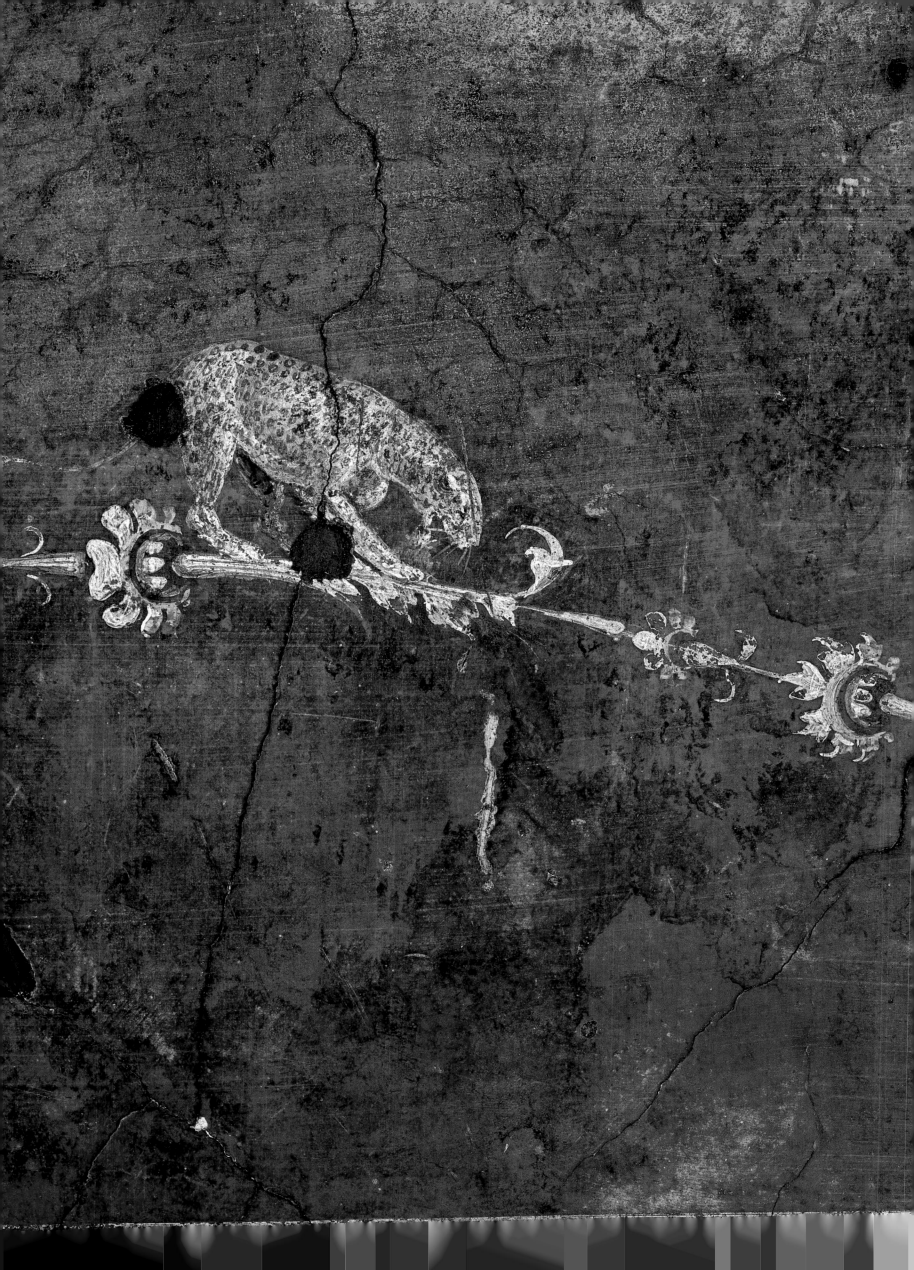

FLORA AND FAUNA
THE VESUVIAN AREA IN AD 79

When Mount Vesuvius erupted in AD 79, it buried not only Pompeii but the entire territory around the city: in addition to covering streets and houses, the shower of *lapilli* covered fields, woods, marshes and beaches in a thick layer. The area involved was enormous, and it was from here that the inhabitants of Pompeii obtained many resources vital for their survival, such as food, medicine, furnishings, textile fibers for clothing and construction materials. Consequently, learning more about these natural resources can help us sketch out the economic and social history of Pompeii as well as its everyday life. The archaeological excavations helped lift the pall that covered Pompeii and its districts. How-ever, modern research techniques have made it possible to examine the traces left by the ancient natural environments and compare them against classical writings and the iconography of the period, in order to arrive at a correct interpretation. A single datum has no meaning when considered individually but, when correlated with other data, may become significant. Deer antlers found in a house could be a hunting trophy, not proof that deer lived around Pompeii.

Nevertheless, if we are sure that beech trees were plentiful in this territory during this period, if we know that deer feed on beechnuts, if children scrawled figures of deer on the walls of their houses, if numerous antlers have been found and they bear the signs of butchering, and if we also know that in the year 1400 deer roamed the Aragonese hunting reserve (which stretched from the sea to the opposite slope of Mount Vesuvius), then we can reasonably assume that deer were present in the area in AD 79. Thus, this cross-referencing of archaeological, geomorphological, climatic, floral and faunal data allows us to sketch out the significant features of the ancient Vesuvian habitat between the sea and the mountains. Once we have established these traits, it becomes easier to understand why Pompeii was famous for its wine and its *garum*. It is no surprise that the fabrics found in its houses include a type made of broom fiber, or that that we should find traces of reeds impressed in the plaster of partition walls. The faithful portrayal of plants in numerous frescoes has made it possible to determine how much the Pompeians knew about botany. The identification of the burnt remains of parts of plants (leaves, wood, seeds) and the recognition of pollen deposited on the ground before the eruption, traces of crops, such as the outlines of flowerbeds, plowing furrows, the bottoms and "balks" (hollows that once held plant roots), set against the other elements described above, permit an accurate reconstruction of how crops were planted in ancient times. We can also trace where the trees and shrubs were located and, as far as trees are concerned, their approximate age. By cross-referencing all the available information, including literary references, we can also determine when certain species – now considered indigenous to the Vesuvian districts but actually more recent imports – were introduced, such as the peach, the apricot and the lemon.

302 and 303

These two paintings are part of the frescoed decoration of the triclinium *of the House of the Golden Bracelet: the deft execution of these works unites images inspired by the plant kingdom and details alluding to the animal kingdom (Archaeological Superintendency of Pompeii).*

The same obviously holds true for fauna. If we compare this portrayal of the local species against various types of findings – such as bones, shells, stalls and clay receptacles for small household breeding – this tells us about the animal populations typical of the different habitats and the most widespread type of breeding. In other cases, however, we can also discover which exotic animals were known to the Pompeians or were imported by them. Thus, we know that they were familiar with elephants,

tigers, panthers, hippopotamuses, cobras and mongooses from far-off places through drawings ("cartoons"), while the discovery of several cat skulls in the Imperial Villa of Poppaea in Oplontis demonstrates that this animal was a newcomer to the Vesuvian area and was still a precious rarity. One of the most intriguing discoveries concerning the importation of exotic species is the skeleton of a macaque, a small monkey that some traveler evidently brought from very distant lands.

CROPS AND LIVESTOCK

I f we could get a bird's-eye view of the Vesuvian region as it appeared in AD 79, what would surprise us most would be the shape of Mount Vesuvius, quite different than it is today: it had only one peak and was covered with woods.

The sea washed over a much more jagged coastline than the one we see today and it had a rich variety of fish, which are depicted time and again in mosaics and frescoes. In addition to the large number of shells from different species, some of the most interesting finds include the carapace of a sea turtle and coral branches, the latter used for apotropaic or medicinal purposes.

The mouth the Sarnus – the modern-day Sarno – also looked different, flowing to the sea at the Rovigliano reef and forming a broad marshy area. The ratio of buildings to nature was obviously inverted as well, so that as opposed to the tentacle-like urbanization that now stretches unbroken from Naples to Salerno, we would have seen endless woods, alternating with cultivated fields and dotted with towns set quite far apart. Moving from the sea toward the mountains, we would have seen an alternation of many different landscapes, each of which was characterized by unique plant and animal species. Classical writers also cite the availability of fresh water close to a sea abounding in fish, the area's extremely fertile soil and the excellent exposure of the hillsides and mountains slopes to sun and wind.

The saltpans and marshes that rimmed the coastal area and hosted a wealth of sedentary and migratory birds, mainly stilt birds, were followed by broad plains marked by a number of country villas and crossed by the meandering Sarnus. Pompeii was set on a rocky hill, with roads radiating from it toward the inland or along the coast.

The alluvial plain formed by the Sarnus was often subject to flooding, particularly in the lower part. This made the soil particularly wet and heavy, and thus ideal for certain crops such as fibrous plants for textiles and vine trees.

The river was clear and full of fish, including a large bivalve mollusk, the *Anodonta cygnea*, that yielded freshwater pearls, and its waters were navigable. Its shores were covered with the lush vegetation typical of riverbanks, with forest species such as willows, poplars and alders, as well as grassy species and shrubs typical of wetlands like reeds, cattails and, in the areas sheltered from the river current, even waterlilies. This vegetation was also the habitat of many aquatic animals. A forest typical of wetlands covered the middle of the plain, between the city and the sea, with ash trees, elms and alders, as well as a variety of mammals, including foxes and boars.

A broad belt of vegetable gardens also circled Pompeii just outside the city walls, and they were planted with cabbage, broccoli, asparagus, artichokes and legumes – particularly peas, fava beans and lentils – as well as lettuce, fennel, radishes, carrots, garlic and onions, so the Pompeians were able to enjoy fresh produce. The particularly fertile soil in the area also permitted several harvests during the year. The fields were

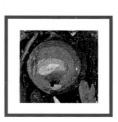

306 bottom

Close-up of a fresco from the House of the Golden Bracelet, showing a lush orchard.
(Archaeological Superintendency of Pompeii).

rotated, generally every three years: grain would be planted the first year, followed by leguminous plants (fava beans, peas, chickpeas), and for the third year the field would be left to "rest," by planting grassy species used above all as animal feed, such as alfalfa.

In ancient writings, the Vesuvian hillsides were described as a particularly rich and luxuriant area that enjoyed an excellent exposure, the right wind intensity and direction, and very fertile soil. According to the ancients, it was the ideal place to own extensive farm property with the comfortable homes, referred to as "country villas," that dotted the delightful areas around Mount Vesuvius.

Given their excellent exposure, the lush hillsides were ideal for the extensive cultivation of barley and wheat, the latter of the finest quality used to make white bread. Spelt farming was virtually abandoned, because these kernels, protected by a tough skin, required complicated hulling operations.

Grape growing was extremely important, and the land at the foothills of Mount Vesuvius produced the most prized grape varieties. Particularly suited to the rich volcanic soil, they were grown using arbor or row-training systems. In contrast, the calcareous soil of the Lattari mountains was better suited for olive trees.

This differentiation between the various crops was also reflected in the work tools that characterized the country villas on the two mountainsides. In the ones on Mount Vesuvius, grape presses prevailed, while an abundance of grinding stones and oil presses were found in the villas located in the Lattari mountains.

Orchards also thrived in the piedmont soil. Given the problem of preserving fruit, preference was given to species that dried well, such as apples, pears, figs and plums, or to nut trees (almonds and hazels). Along the irrigation channels, there were always species that were useful for working the fields, such as reeds, willows and elms, as their foliage was fed to cattle.

307

The theme of nature in a domestic vision is the leitmotif of the frescoes from the House of the Orchard. This painting
in the Third Style portrays a tree laden with figs, the image of abundance and fertility.

To the north, the lower slopes of Mount Vesuvius, often dotted with country villas, were intensely cultivated, with oak woods that gradually changed over to beech forests toward the peak. These forests were populated by mammals, and in addition to wolves and boars, stags and roe deer were also quite common. Property boundaries were usually marked by rows of pine trees or cypresses, or quickset hedges of plants for bees or types with berries, such as blackberries. The large hillside properties also had wooded areas, providing timber for everyday use, in which pigs were allowed to run free to crossbreed with boars.

To the east, the Vesuvian plains were ringed by the calcareous Sarno mountains, off in the distance, and near the sea by the roots of the Lattari mountain chain – also calcareous – covered with meadows, and dotted with forests of beech trees and silver firs. The Lattari area was used as grazing land, a fact confirmed by the numerous country villas

found on these slopes that were equipped for dairy production.

We must also note that about two thousand years ago, breeding criteria were different than they are today: while sheep and goats were raised above all for their wool – the Pompeii market was particularly prosperous – and milk, with cattle used as work animals. As a result, not only was there little meat in the daily diet, but the main sources of meat were game and pig farms.

308-309

This hunting scene, from the House of Marcus Lucretius Fronto, combines varies types of animals that were present in the area around Pompeii, setting stags alongside more exotic species like lions. The general effect that is thus achieved makes the fresco highly incisive.

PLANTS AND ANIMALS IN TOWN

ncient Pompeii had a number of gardens, and their location was revealed by the treetops that stood out over the high walls encircling them. They were spread throughout Pompeii, much like what we find in modern urban areas.

As in a modern city, in fact, the gardens in the old center, which were mainly ornamental, were quite small, with the exception of the richest houses such as the House of the Vettii or the House of the Faun. The largest park areas were located on the outskirts of town, and while some were cultivated for commercial purposes (for example, the Perfumer's Garden), others were used as depots (the *Garum* Workshop), and still others were purchased by well-to-do people who preferred to live surrounded by full-fledged parks, complete with fountains and water channels (*euripi*). On the outskirts of town near the Amphitheater, there were vegetable gardens, orchards and vineyards, some of which were quite large.

The *viridaria* (pleasure gardens), which were usually located in the oldest part of the city, were quite small, generally no more than 1000 square feet in size, and they were located in the very center of the house. They combined the desire for a pleasant area for enjoyment with the need to collect rainwater to convey it to underground cisterns. The construction of the aqueduct subsequently filled this need, making it possible to create much larger gardens that were decorated with spectacular water displays.

Species we can define as ornamental were grown in the *viridaria*, but during this era these gardens also represented a sort of "home pharmacy": wormwood, juniper, roses and the "coronary" or garland plants – which were used to make wreaths to offer to the gods – were also used as medicinal plants. Flowerbeds, marked off by a narrow channel and sometimes by reed trellises or small wooden planks, were often divided by dirt paths.

Sometimes, the gardens were also the homes of small pets. In addition to the ever-present field mice, there were often turtles, which must have been quite common in the surrounding countryside. There were also dovecots for breeding pigeons and, in some cases, also special clay containers used to fatten dormice or purge snails. In the vegetable gardens, vineyards and orchards, located mainly in the quarters around the Amphitheater, people grew vegetables (garlic, onions, lettuce and cabbage, to name some of the most common) and fruit trees (hazel, peach and fig trees). The family ate the produce or sold it at the city market. However, people also planted gardens for production purposes and for handicrafts, such as nurseries and gardens with perfume essences.

310 and 311
The theme of birds drinking from a fountain is commonly found in the frescoes of Pompeian triclinia. *The one on the left decorates a wall of the House of Venus on the Shell, and the one of the right is from the House of the Golden Bracelet (Archaeological Superintendence of Pompeii).*

The floor of the entry to the House of Cuspius Pansa is decorated with a mosaic that reproduces the image of the entrance to the house, protected by a guard dog.

Some of the Vesuvian area's ancient vineyards have now been replanted in keeping with the indications deduced from excavations and the agricultural texts of the era, using original grape varieties that have been identified by studying the shapes of the leaves and the bunches of grapes depicted in the frescoes. There were many public park areas as well, such as the field of the Great Palaestra, closed on three sides by a double row of plane trees, the oak copse that was supposedly in the Triangular Forum, the fields near the Baths, and the trees linked with places of worship. Among the latter, one of the leading examples is the "Complex of Magic Rites," dedicated to Sabazius, the Thracian-Phrygian god of vegetation. Poplars and mock privet (*Phillyrea angustifolia*) were grown in the garden. Poplars, whose leaves have different colors on the surface and under-

side, represented the duality of being, while the mock privet commemorated the sea nymph Philyra, who bore a monstrous son, Chiron, fathered by Cronus. Overcome with anguish, she asked to be transformed into a tree. As we noted, water for irrigation was drawn from wells and cisterns, and subsequently from the public aqueduct. Among the different uses of landscaping in private areas, we can cite the Nursery, the Perfumer's Garden, the park of Loreius Tiburtinus, the House of Julia Felix, the House of the Vettii and the House of the Chaste Lovers. The Nursery (II, 9, 4) was shaded by a beech tree and an alder, which sheltered 160 cuttings arranged in eight ridges of soil that divided the entire area. These tree cuttings were from hazels, peach trees, plum trees and apricot trees – smaller species that were suitable for little gardens. A much smaller number of cuttings came

The garden in the central courtyard of the House of the Golden Cupids creates an interplay of decorative plants and artifacts such as herms, tablets and fountains.

from olive trees, beech trees, oaks and pines. In the Perfumer's Garden, essences that could be used to make balsams and ointments were grown, particularly olives as they provided the oil used as a vehicle for perfumes. The olives were picked and pressed while still green. The oil was used to steep essences, particularly those of roses, myrtle and violets. The only example of a garden built over a large area, and thus not enclosed within the architecture of the house, belonged to Loreius Tiburtinus. This private "park," uncovered during the 1940s, was planted when the aqueduct was still in operation and it was decorated with fountains and water displays. The park itself was shaded by species adopted for decorative purposes: vines, big and mid-sized fruit trees such as almonds and quinces, as well as plane trees that were

linked in a single perspective with the ones of the Great Palaestra (now replaced with cypresses). Another large park area belonged to Julia Felix. Divided by dirt paths, it was planted with fruit trees. The produce, probably the inspiration for a fresco found in the house, was used by the owner for her business or was sold at the city market. Some of the interior gardens were smaller but well tended, and they were indubitably appreciated by visitors. In the *viridarium* of the House of the Vettii, discovered during the mid-19th century, the geometric design of the flowerbeds, divided by dirt paths, are still preserved. Likewise, in the garden of the House of the Chaste Lovers, excavated several years ago along Via dell'Abbondanza, the layout of the flowerbeds was still perfectly visible. Complex research – involving the collection and identification of pollen, seeds and wood preserved in the soil – al-

lowed archaeologists to reconstruct the first example of a garden area in all its natural and architectural aspects. The *viridarium* was laid out in perspective to accentuate its depth and be viewed from the rooms overlooking it. The flowerbeds, perfectly symmetrical and divided by dirt paths, were fenced off with braided reeds, while the back wall was concealed with festoons of vines. In the garden at the House of the Chaste Lovers, plants were used for ornamental purposes and were placed in a strictly symmetrical arrangement. Some species also had therapeutic properties (rose, juniper, mugwort, polypody) or were used to weave votive wreaths (rose, *lychnis*).

Chirping birds and barking dogs could be heard everywhere, despite the noise of work tools, the cries from the market and the daily chattering of people of all ages. Some aristocratic homes had stalls with donkeys and horses, many children played with turtles (certainly at the House of Julius Polybius), stray dogs could be seen wandering through the streets, while others were raised as watchdogs or hunting dogs, and still others were used simply as pets. We know that their owners would put a collar on them, as seen from the mosaic in the vestibule of the House of the Tragic Poet (with the words *cave canem*). This method of keeping the dogs under control was fatal to many of them during the eruption: it prevented all means of escape. At the House of Menander, there are no traces of the horses for which the gig, iron bit and bronze buckles must have been used. Only the watchdog was left behind to share the fate of the residents surprised by the cloud of lethal gas.

314 top
A wall decorated in the Second Style, with three openings that originally had shutters, separates the villa's
atrium *from the* peristyle, *where the pluteus decorated with rectangles of red plaster and part of the Doric
columns supporting the roof are visible.*

THE VILLA OF THE MYSTERIES

This villa, very important in the history of pictorial decoration, was built outside Porta Ercolano, just beyond Pompeii. Its layout dates from the 2nd century BC, with later transformations completed in several stages through the Augustan period. The earthquake of AD 62, which seriously damaged the rooms, was a decisive factor in the decision to transform the building from a residential villa into a farm, as demonstrated by the state of near-abandonment of the master quarters. The original entrance led directly to the peristyle with the service quarters on the sides, and a grape press was reconstructed in one of these rooms. This is followed, in sequence, by a magnificent Tuscan *atrium*, the *tablinum* (with the master quarters on the side), and a large hall with an apse and picture windows facing the bay. The Villa of the Mysteries is famous above all because of the discovery of one of the most important and complete pictorial apparatuses of the entire Vesuvian area, done mainly in the Second Style. The room that has made the villa famous is a *triclinium* frescoed with a megalography (large-scale image) datable to the 1st century BC. It is a copy of an original Greek work from the 4th or 3rd century BC, redone in a lively style by a local Campanian painter.

The work was originally interpreted as a woman's initiation to the Dionysiac rites, in connection with her preparation for marriage, although several later archaeologists identified it as an initiation to the Orphic mysteries or as the representation of a Satyric mime. Nevertheless, the first interpretation is considered more accredited. The megalography has ten scenes covering the walls of the entire hall. Entering from the left, sep-arated from the entire composition by a secondary door, is a female figure identified as the lady of the house who, already initiated into the cult, is observing the ceremony.

Starting from the left wall the scenes are: (1) reading of the ritual by the young Dionysus; (2) a group of four women intent on a sacrificial ceremony; (3) pastoral scene with a Silenus, Satyr and Nymph; (4) a frightened woman running away; (5) the Silenus grasping a cup from which a Satyr is drinking while a third figure lifts a mask; (6) the marriage of Dionysus and Ariadne; (7) a kneeling Bacchante uncovering the phallus, the symbol of fertility in Dionysian ceremonies, while a winged figure raises a *flagellum* to punish her; (8) the punished woman hides her face in the lap of a seated woman; (9) a naked Bacchante dances in ecstasy; and (10) the toilette scene.

We do not know the details of the "mystery" cults and the initiation ceremonies for their followers. These rituals were undoubtedly restricted and not everyone was admitted. There must have been a ceremony that, at the end, included a vision of the deity or, in any event, of the exclusive sensations tied to the cult of a saving god who promised a better life or at least salvation in the world beyond. In the Greek world, there were various "mystery rites" but the most common ones involved Dionysus (the Roman Bacchus). Through the drunken bliss of wine and perhaps the use of hallucinogens, the freest and most uninhibited of the gods gave people a motive to shirk routine and unleash their wildest behavior. This was also one of the reasons his cult was often eyed suspiciously – and was even openly opposed – by traditionalist authorities.

314-315

In the center of this photograph, four of the sixteen Doric columns of the peristyle, set on a tall pluteus, can be seen through the large opening. The opening, visible on the upper right, allowing light and rainwater into the central pool, or impluvium, *of the Tuscan atrium.*

A complex, sumptuous overlay of architectures decorates the walls of a double-alcove cubiculum *in the villa, according to the taste for realism typical of the Second Style. Though they did not actually exist, the structures portrayed here are "likely" nonetheless.*

317 top

An elegant floor decorated with mosaics embellishes a room linking the tablinum *and the* triclinium *with the megalography of the mysteries. On the wall, a geometric decoration in faux marble frames panels with human and mythological figures.*

317 bottom

A lively floral festoon breaks up the static appearance typical of the Second Style, crisscrossing the strictly linearly composition that decorates an oecus *(living room) of the villa, overlooking a* viridarium *(garden) on the side.*

318 top

The nine scenes of the megalography of the mysteries occupy the entire middle band of the room. The work preserves all its original vivacity and exquisite workmanship. A talented Campanian artist, who replicated part of an original Greek painting that was lost, painted the 29 life-sized figures of the cycle against the background of costly cinnabar.

318 bottom

The climax of the initiation to the mystery rites is reached in scene VII: the kneeling initiate uncovers the phallic symbol representing fertility, while the winged figure holding a whip prepares to strike her.

319

A Silenus offers a cup of wine to a young satyr behind him, who bends over to drink. Another satyr in the background holds a theater mask on the Silenus' head.

320

Though set at the end of Scene VII, a winged figured intent on striking the initiate turns a rather melancholic gaze towards the next episode in the megalography, where the young woman being scourged cries out in pain at the stroke of the whip.

321

Big, expressive and intense eyes animate the face of the female figure across from the Bacchante in a dionysian dance in Scene VIII. This figure also seems to look towards the young woman, on her knees, who cries out as the whip falls.

322

Along the sides of the entrance, the Hall of the Mysteries presents two figures that are seemingly separate from the sequence of scenes. The woman on the left is probably the domina who, engrossed, watches the events as they unfold; on the right, a winged cupid observes the toilette of the new initiate.

322-323

In scene VII, the whipped girl sobs and is consoled by another woman. In front of them, a Bacchante begins her frenzied dance.

THE HOUSE OF THE CHASTE LOVERS

The evocative name of this complex of buildings comes from a banquet scene that decorated the triclinium, portraying a couple in a tender embrace. Located in Regio IX, about halfway down Via dell'Abbondanza towards Porta di Sarno, the House of the Chaste Lovers was composed of various rooms, including a bread oven on the north side. Several skeletons were found on site, including those of mules used to drive the mill.

324 top

The compartments of the decorations in the Third Style from the House of the Chaste Lovers present slender architectures marked by powerful perspective, decorated with oversized plants motifs and tiny human figures set in a fantastic environment.

324-325

In the decoration in one of the halls in the building complex, a group of cupids is involved in a reckless and bizarre race on goat-drawn bigas. On the day of the eruption, a team of painters was at work in the House of the Chaste Lovers.

325 bottom

A shady triple portico enclosed the garden of the house, originally planted with rosaceae and cupressaceae. Part of the white-painted room where the painters were at work is visible beyond the colonnade.

THE HOUSE OF MARCUS LUCRETIUS FRONTO

Marcus Lucretius Fronto was a member of one of Pompeii's leading families, which moved to the city during the reign of Augustus. Though modest in size, the house boasts of paintings befitting the respected status of its owner, who had embarked on a brilliant political career. This was the home of a cultured man; furnished simply, it was rich in intellectual stimuli suggested by the paintings, done in the final Third Style. At the time of the eruption, the restoration work being done on the house had moved to the garden, as demonstrated by the presence of an amphora full of lime found under the stairs nearby.

In the middle band of the frescoes in the final Third Style that decorated the tablinum of the House of Marcus Lucretius Fronto, the main paintings with mythological subjects are set next to small paintings with a black background, hung from candelabra and portraying sumptuous imaginary villas overlooking the sea.

326-327

In this general view from the north, the tablinum, connected with the peristyle, opens to the left of the atrium featuring an impluvium and a cartibulum with lions' paws. Immediately to the right, two small doors lead to two cubicula, whereas the large doorway that follows leads to the vast triclinium.

328

Against the backdrop of an imaginary Delphic temple, Orestes kills Neoptolemus on the altar of the sanctuary of Apollo, while Hermione is shown in despair at the foot of the altar. This episode, inspired by Euripides' Andromache, *is the subject of the mythological painting that occupies the center of the west wall in the winter* triclinium *at the House of Marcus Lucretius Fronto.*

328-329

In the middle of the north wall of the tablinum, *winged Eros, with his quiver, is ready to shoot his arrow before the eyes of the servants, shown in a mannered pose. Dark-skinned Mars, wearing a helmet with a thick crest, is bending over Venus with clearly amorous intentions.*

330 and 335

*A cupid with a cornucopia and Narcissus, nearing the fatal moment in which his
beauty and vanity would attract the gods' mortal punishment, are portrayed in
the* cubiculum *east of the* tablinum *of the House of Marcus Lucretius Fronto.
The deep yellow background can also be found in another alcove in this residence.
The decoration in the Fourth Style was part of the restoration work done on the
room, possibly after 62 AD.*

331-334

*A fantastic setting, characteristic of the final Third Style, unfolds along the upper
band of the decoration of the* tablinum. *An* oscillum *hanging from the
architrave, a griffin as an acroterion on a door half-opened to darkness, and an
exaggeratedly long brazier give an indefinable intellectual tension to the entire
scene, which is replicated – mirror-like – on the sides of the brazier.*

336 top
A Gorgon's mask takes up the center of the mosaic that decorated the floor of the cubiculum (Naples, MAN).

336 bottom
The tepidarium of the House of the Centenary has a striking floor mosaic depicting sea creatures, centered on an octopus.

337 top
Decorations in the Fourth Style on a red ground, and erotic paintings on a black ground embellished the alcove in the western part of the house, the cubiculum of the procurator.

336-337
The garden of the House of the Centenary, viewed here from the south, is enclosed by a peristyle with eighteen columns, with a fountain in the middle. The wide area occupied by the ruins of the house is dominated by what remains of the double architectural order that characterized the façade of the master's quarters, on the left.

338

The walls of the nymphaeum of the House of the Centenary were decorated with lively polychrome paintings. In this inset, a marble basin supported by a winged creature is shown in a lushly verdant setting to the right of the fountain.

339

A maenad suspended midair seems to hover in the space illuminated by a golden light as she holds a tray with offerings in her left hand. The fresco is from the decorative apparatus of a triclinium in the house.

340 top and bottom right

The triclinium, *with well-preserved frescoes portraying mythological subjects, was the dining room of the* procurator, *who supervised the servants at the House of the Centenary.*

340 bottom left and 341

The apartment of the procurator *included a large* triclinium *decorated with mythological paintings done in the Third Style. The fresco on the left, inspired by Euripides'* Iphigenia in Tauris, *shows Pilas and Orestes, who is seated in the middle, whereas Iphigenia is visible on the right. In the right-hand page, Hermaphroditus, portrayed between a maenad and a Silenus, holds a torch and a* kantharos *(Naples,* MAN).

CAVE CANEM

The timelessness of everyday life: in this famous mosaic with the warning Cave canem, *a barking dog, nearly life-sized, discouraged any ill-intentioned visitors from crossing the threshold of the House of the Tragic Poet (Naples,* MAN*).*

343

A mosaic in black and white tesserae, set in the middle of the lavish atrium *of the House of the Tragic Poet, frames the marble* impluvium. *Nearby there is also a curb connected with the underground well. Visible beyond this is the* tablinum *and, in the background, the* lararium *and two columns of the peristyle.*

THE HOUSE OF THE TRAGIC POET

The House of the Tragic Poet is an Italic domus: *in this layout, the most important rooms are situated along the same axis, with a Tuscan* atrium. *The building, located in Regio VI, at the northern edge of the city, belonged to a man named Aninius. He was the member of a family from Pompeii's new emerging class, composed of well-to-do figures who were not of noble descent. Though the layout of the house dates back to the 2nd century BC, the decorative work was entirely redone after the earthquake of AD 62.*

344-345

A musician playing a double flute occupies the center of the scene in the lively mosaic that decorated the floor of the tablinum, *portraying the preparatory phases for a satyric drama. On the left, actors dressed in goatskins listen to the instructions of the "tragic poet", after whom the house is named, who is seated on the right (Naples,* MAN*).*

The house is named after the poet Menander, portrayed seated in the center of the exedra on the south side of the peristyle.

In the mosaic decorating the atrium of the baths of the house, a trident separates two sea creatures facing each other.

347 center

Two Doric columns made of tufa and plastered around the base precede the atrium, viewed here from the tablinum.
The vestibulum can be seen in the background.

THE HOUSE OF MENANDER

348 top

In the painting that opens the series of works on the fall of Troy, in the wing to the west of the atrium, *Laocoon and his sons succumb to the monstrous serpent that came from the sea.*

348 center and bottom

Under the Trojan paintings in the atrium, *architectures painted in the Fourth Style and set against a blue and white ground complete the decoration of the room.*

Troy's fate is sealed in the final scene of the cycle decorating the atrium. On the left, Menelaus brutally seizes Helen by the hair, while on the right Cassandra is torn away from the xoanòn, the wooden statue of Athena.

THE HOUSE OF THE BEAR

The House of the Bear was located in the center of Pompeii, just north of the brothel. It was given this name because of the mosaic of a bear on the threshold of the house. The house was connected to a caupona, *or typical Pompeian tavern. The tavern was managed by the servant Hedone, who informed patrons about the quality of wine according to price: one* as, *or coin, would buy mediocre wine, while the famous Falerno cost three* asses.

350 top and bottom
At the House of the Bear, the theme of Venus on the shell can be seen in the apsidal basin of the fountain (top), exquisitely executed using the polychrome mosaic technique. The complete structure of this remarkable work (bottom) is visible beyond the atrium *with the* impluvium, *in the background, where the garden opens up.*

351 top
Gorgon heads, like this one inscribed in a concentric frame of lozenges and rectangles, comprise the mosaic decoration along the sides of the fountain.

351 bottom

The friendly greeting HAVE contrasts with the subject of the mosaic decorating the threshold. A gravely wounded bear bleeds profusely from its right side; after breaking the lance with its teeth, it is trying to remove it with one of its paws.

352 and 353

The floors at the House of the Bear show sophisticated decorative solutions, achieved by placing pieces of marble with different textures or cuts in a black-and-white marble frame.

THE HOUSE OF THE FAUN

354

In the triclinium *that can be accessed from the right wing of the* atrium, *Bacchus, portrayed as a winged child on the back of a cat, drinks from a large clear cup (Naples,* MAN*).*

The House of the Faun covered an entire block in Regio VI, *in the northwest part of town. Its origins go back to pre-Roman Pompeii, and thus prior to the conquest of the Samnites by Lucius Cornelius Sulla at the beginning of the 1st century BC. Until AD 79, the building was carefully maintained by its owners, almost as if it were a historic "memorial" of some kind. The house has yielded extraordinary findings, including the bronze faun after which the house is named, and numerous furnishings.*

359

In the middle of the large Tuscan atrium *of the House of the Faun, the copy of the bronze statue after which the building was named is set in the middle of the magnificent* impluvium, *finished with polychrome rhombuses done in* opus sectile.

355-358

Two tragic masks, set in a mirror image, offset the lively still life with festoons of fruit and leaves that acts as the setting for this extraordinary mosaic from the atrium *(Naples,* MAN*).*

360-361

Originally located in the exedra with two columns that separated the peristyles of the House of the Faun, the most extraordinary mosaic from the ancient world – composed of 1.5 million tesserae – portrays Alexander the Great attacking Darius and his troops, in complete disarray (Naples, MAN).

THE HOUSE OF THE VETTII

The Vettii, wealthy landowners who sold the produce grown on their estates, could afford to restore their entire house with top-quality material following the earthquake of AD 62. This accounts for the building's excellent state of conservation when it was discovered in 1894 in Regio VI, in the northwest part of the city. The building's attribution to this family has been confirmed by the seals that were found bearing the names of two of the owners, very well-to-do freedmen who were members of the city's emerging class that had only recently been emancipated at the time of the disaster.

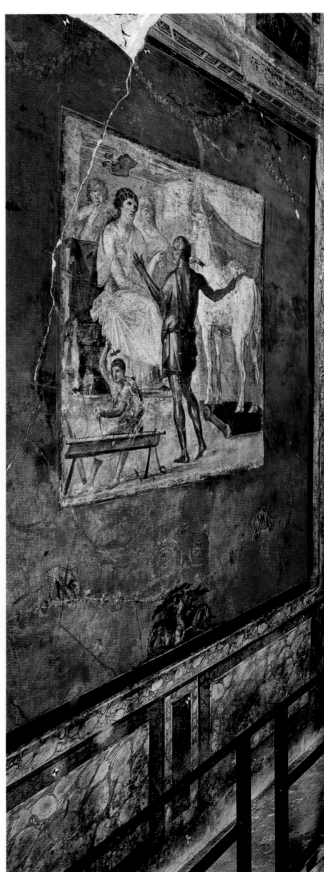

362 top

The wealth of this house is demonstrated not only by the valuable frescoes inside, but also by the decorations found in the garden. Marble herms alternated with bronze cherubs that pour water into small fountains.

362 bottom

The subjects of the wall frescoes of the exedra, framed by yellow ocher panels, are inspired by mythological episodes.

362-363

The walls of the triclinium *are decorated with complex architectural scenes, in the middle of which there are large paintings, with red backgrounds, depicting mythological episodes.*

363 top

The Tuscan atrium *of the House of the Vettii. The* impluvium, *which was devoid of cladding when the house was excavated (1894), has been restored and can now be seen as it once appeared.*

364

*The central painting on the east wall of the triclinium portrays the sacrifice
of Ixion. The gods Mercury, Juno, Vulcan and Iris can be recognized.*

365

*Portrayed on the north wall is the arrival of the wooden cow, the trick that
Minos' wife Pasiphaë used so she could mate with a bull.*

366 top
King Pentheus, shown here shortly before he was killed and torn apart by maenads, is one of the two iconographic subjects decorating the exedra.

366 bottom
The painting in the middle of the south wall of the same room depicts Dirce's agony: after capturing the bull, Amphion and Zethus tie the woman to the animal's horns.

366-367
The famous scene in which young Hercules strangles the serpents, as Alcmene, Amphitryon and Jupiter look on, predominates in the middle of another wall of the exedra.

368-369
This detail is from the scene in which several cupids gather flowers and make garlands. Here, two of them are carrying baskets of petals and buds.

369
The portrayal of a contest between charioteer cupids, driving bigas drawn by stags, stands out against the black ground that characterizes the famous frieze in the triclinium, known also as the "Hall of the Cupids".

370

On the walls of the triclinium, *one of the small paintings with mythological scenes shows a stag being sacrificed to Diana.*

371

Three psychai *gather petals in the lower panel on one of the walls of the Hall of the Cupids. Above it, a tall panel is decorated with scrolls set amidst candelabra.*

OPLONTIS

[Stefano De Caro]

◆

THE PEUTINGER TABLE

The *Tabula Peutingeriana* or Peutinger Table is a map of the Roman Empire's main roads in the 3rd century AD, although its first edition probably dates from Agrippa's *Orbis pictus* (Augustan period). Alongside the map by the Anonymous Geographer from Ravenna, an itinerary derived from it, the Table is the only ancient document that cites the name of *Oplontis*. It designates a place about six miles from Herculaneum where a road branched off from the coast road to Pompeii, *Nuceria* (Nocera) and *Salernum* (Salerno). This branch in the road served the Sorrento peninsula and led to *Stabiae* (Castellammare di Stabia), *Surrentum* (Sorrento) and, lastly, the *templum Minervae* on what is now known as Punta della Campanella. On the Table, the name Oplontis is accompanied by the outline of a large building, the kind used elsewhere on the map to indicate places famous for their baths. After more than 250 years of excavation work in the Pompeii area and often-random research in the area around Torre Annunziata – which researchers pinpointed by calculating the mileage of the Peutinger Table in modern distances – we now know that there was no city in this territory during the Roman era. There was, however, a series of villas and other buildings that dotted the road between the lower slopes of Mount Vesuvius and the sea.

We have little information about the area's remote past. There are scattered traces of what may be an Iron Age necropolis, located not far from Torre del Greco, and of another one from the same period at Boscoreale. In any event, there is nothing that sheds any light on the meaning of the name "Oplontis." Moreover, of the thousands of inscriptions and graffiti found in Pompeii and Herculaneum, not one has yielded any confirmation. Thus, we must simply accept this toponymic in-

formation and move on to mention the different interpretations that have been suggested over the years. These range from the Greek *oplon* or "weapon," and thus the figurative meaning of a "place where ships were rigged," to "rich place" from the Latin *opulentus*. Even "poplar grove" has been suggested, from the presumed Latin form of *opulus/populus*, the tree used to train grapevines. None of these theories is entirely convincing, but at the same time we cannot agree with the speculation that Oplontis is a distortion of the Greek *apololotes* or a gloss used by whoever drew up the *Tabula* to indicate "the (place) lost" in the eruption of AD 79.

This debate over the name, meaning and topographic placement of Oplontis was long the main preoccupation of early scholarly research. The first documented discovery of the remains of the villa on Via Sepolcri (now known as Villa A or Poppaea's Villa) undoubtedly came at the end of the 16th century. While digging the canal planned by architect Giulio Cesare Fontana to channel water from the River Sarno to Count Muzio Tuttavilla's new mills in Torre Annunziata, workers happened upon – and cut through – the entrance to the villa. There is no extant information about that finding, nor does it seem to have piqued the interest of contemporary scholars, just as the even more momentous fact that the canal had crossed the entire city of Pompeii, continuously running into the city's workshops, had likewise had no impact whatsoever. The time simply wasn't ripe for archaeology, but the presence of these walls alongside the canal remained impressed in the local memory.

Thus, in 1785, when the Bourbon regime had begin to promote archaeological research throughout the territory in the wake of the excitement over

A veritable roadmap of the Roman Empire, the Peutinger Table is a priceless document for pinpointing forgotten sites and conducting archaeological studies there. In the area that corresponds to the modern-day Vesuvian coastline, the Table has the only ancient citation of the place name "Oplontis". The meaning of this toponym has been interpreted in various ways, none of which provides satisfactory answers. The Peutinger Table is in Austrian National Library, Vienna.

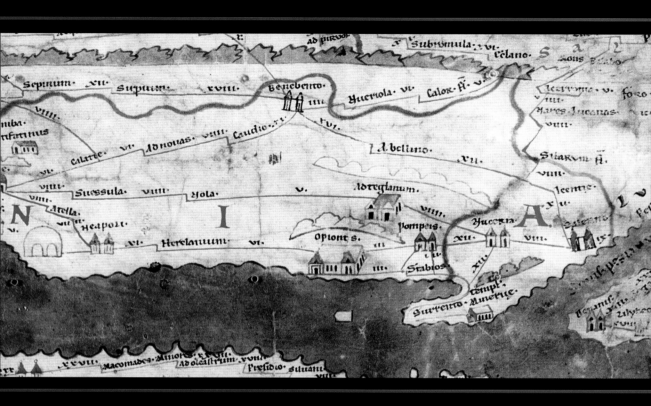

the excavations at Herculaneum, Pompeii and Stabiae, it was no accident that Francesco La Vega, the military architect in charge of the excavations, attempted his first dig. It was in the town of Mascatelle, next to the ruins near the canal supplying the Royal Weapon Factories' new facilities. Using the excavation methods tested at Herculaneum, the volcanic stratigraphy of the site (with deposits over 14 feet deep from the year AD 79 alone) was examined with a system of tunnels, and one of them was used to explore a portico along the large pool. The excavation did not yield the hoped-for results and La Vega soon abandoned the work (April 23, 1785), recovering only a decorated marble cornice.

Between 1830 and 1831, a further attempt was made to excavate the site – this time secretly. It was undertaken by none other than Wilhelm Zahn, the renowned German artist and author of the famous *Die schönste Ornamente und merkwürdigste Gemälde aus Pompeji, Herkulaneum und Stabiae* (the first volume was published in Berlin in 1827). Zahn, a friend of Johann Wolfgang von Goethe, was active in Pompeii as early as the 1820s, and in 1830 he and Goethe's son were invited to observe the excavation of the Pompeian house that was to be named after Goethe, and which would later reveal the "Great Mosaic" depicting the battle of Alexander and Darius. The covert excavation work at Mascatelle was mentioned in an 1839 report by the guardian Michele Rusca who, referring to the various sites with antiquities at Torre Annunziata, noted that the most interesting site was the one of Mascatelle, where Mr. Zhan [*sic*!] "was attempting clandestine research."

Unfortunately, we have no other information about the episode, but we can guess that news about the incident reached the government and that the excavation site was closed as a result, doubtlessin causing somewhat of a diplomatic brouhaha.

*During the 1970s, the last phase of the excavations uncovered the large pool, which
had been added during the final phase of the villa's development, as well as the statues
that embellished its edges. The pool was originally part of a more extensive complex
with internal gardens, service rooms for banquets, bathrooms and kitchens.*

A few years later, between 1831 and 1834, the Bourbon General Vito A. Nunziante undertook archaeological exploration at his own expense, working through his assistant William Robinson, an English major in the service of the Bourbon dynasty. Robinson examined the ancient thermal area he had discovered while building hydrothermal facilities tapping the local springs near the source of the Oncino. In fact, Robinson, a well-educated man who was in close contact with William Gell, a fellow countryman and renowned scholar of Pompeii, was the first to theorize that the site was none other than the *Oplontis* of the Peutinger Table. The news of this important discovery was promptly

reported in 1834 by Raffaele Liberatore in the kingdom's "Civil Annals."

Nevertheless, the moment of greatest impetus for the Oplontis excavations came in 1839. Even the events leading up to it were momentous for the history of the Vesuvian excavations and are worth examining. Several years before, Michele Rusca, who had been the supervisor or technical assistant at the Pompeii excavation site and was a veteran captain of the Swiss mercenaries, fell into disgrace with his superiors for misappropriation in Pompeii, for which he was held responsible. As a result, he was demoted to "assistant custodian" and transferred to the Museum of Naples. In

1838, the General Directorship of the Excavations decided to send him to Pozzuoli, where work had been started to excavate the Amphitheater under the supervision of Carlo Bonucci, who had also been removed from Pompeii. However, Rusca lived in Torre Annunziata, and both his family and property were there. As a result, he decided to write to the Minister of the Interior, Nicola Santangelo, to convince him to review his decision, proposing an interesting alternative. Rusca mainstained that since he lived in Torre Annunziata, he was very familiar with the sites where ancient artifacts had been discovered. Thus, why couldn't the Minister restore his post in Pompeii or – by naming him extraordinary commissioner – appoint him to research and supervise the monuments he knew, including the "most interesting and enticing one" of Mascatelle?

Showing a good measure of common sense, the Minister decided to accept the old captain's proposal and on February 18, 1839 he granted him the coveted permission, although he banned any meddling in Pompeii".

After a few mishaps with the local police, the excavation work finally got underway with the usual tunneling system. Villa A was crisscrossed in every direction, but Rusca was unlucky: he found no precious or interesting objects and practically grazed rows of marble statues (in some places by

*The long colonnade of the Villa B emerged from the ashes during the excavation work,
which gradually revealed the layout of the site. It included at least two large residential
complexes, or villas, that were separated by a road in ancient times.*

less than a yard). In the end, all he was able to hand over were some rusty nails and a few tiles stamped with trademarks. Disappointed and under pressure over expenditures for Pompeii, the Minister closed the excavation site. However, since the site proved to have two complexes divided by a public road, the decision was made to expropriate the area for future public use, following a request filed by the landowners themselves, since the property could no longer be used. This proved to be a farsighted decision, not only because it laid the foundations for the most important excavation in the area (which would be undertaken 130 years later), but also because it miraculously saved the

site from the massive urbanization that later mushroomed around it.

In fact, subsequent findings of this kind in the area around Torre Annunziata between 1800 and 1900 were far less fortunate. They included the *villa maritima* of Caius Siculius cut in 1841-42 by the trench for the Portici-Pompeii railway trench (now the area of Villino Vecchi-Suore di Cristo Re); the country villa found shortly before the outbreak of World War II during the construction of low-cost housing, east of what would later be named Villa B; the *villa maritima* at the "La Perla" work yard on Via Marconi (the 1960s); the colonnade found on the Fattorusso estate, along the same canal of the Sarno just east of Villa A.

Finally, in 1964 the Superintendent Alfonso de Franciscis, urged on by a group of local scholars who formed a committee, started the excavation work at the site of Villa A (or Poppaea's Villa), taking advantage of money available from the Development Fund for Southern Italy. The discovery of the splendid paintings done in the Second Style, followed by the series of sculptures in the gardens, gave enormous impetus to the initiative. This continued in the decades that followed with the opening of the villa to the public and with the excavation (starting in 1974) of what is known as Villa B (or the villa of Via Murat), several hundred yards from the first villa.

At this point in the research, just where or what is Oplontis? While we still don't know what the word means, findings on the local spring water seem to confirm the indication provided by the symbol on the Peutinger Table, pointing to an important spa center. It was probably a settlement that arose around the villas, gradually adding semi-urban facilities (streets, service buildings). It would thus have been a sort of *vicus* of Pompeii, akin to what occurred in Baiae (in relation to the city of Cumae) and in Stabiae, reestablished in this form after Sulla destroyed the city in 89 BC.

LIVING *PER VILLAS*

E|ven before the Social War, Pompeii's Samnite aristocracy had started construction work for both residential and production purposes outside the city walls, in the area northwest of the city, as demonstrated by the oldest phases of the Villa of the Mysteries, the Villa of Diomedes and Cicero's Villa. The Social War and the establishment of the *Colonia Cornelia Veneria Pompeiianorum* brought an extraordinary increase in the number of new villas built in the form of small and medium-sized production units. The aim was to exploit the farmland expropriated from the ancient Oscan owners and assigned to Sulla's veterans; in fact, Villa Regina in Boscoreale is probably an example of this. Particularly along the coasts and in the territory of the vanquished city of Stabiae, construction led to buildings with features that distinguished them more as luxury residences. This process was so intense that during the Augustan period, even the area at the foot of Mount Vesuvius looked completely like the "uninterrupted settlement" the Greek geographer Strabo described for the entire coastline around the Bay of Naples, from Cape Misenum to Cape Atheneum.

Although geographically located in Campania, the roots of this settlement model couldn't have been more Roman. In fact, they can be traced to a specific moment – just after the Second Punic War – when the aristocracy of the capital decided to make the fertile river plains and delightful coastline of the Bay of Naples an extension of Rome itself. While the expropriation of the *ager Campanus* (Campanian lands) and the development of the port of Puteoli (Pozzuoli) marked the first "political" phases of attention to this region, it was Scipio Africanus' decision to build his villa of *Liternum* (near the mouth of the River Clanis) that actually started a growing trend. Within just one century, owning a residential villa in Campania became all the rage for the entire Roman aristocracy, starting with Scipio's own daughter Cornelia, mother of the famous Gracchi brothers, who decided to educate her sons according to the ideals championed by the Greek *paideia*. In fact, the area's physical distance from Rome made it possible to cultivate the Greek lifestyle, language and culture without incurring the wrath of those who championed the strict traditions of the forefathers, so a type of "domestic" Hellenism could be enjoyed virtually at the outskirts of the capital city. Starting in the 2nd century BC, number of settlements grew up, inspired by these new ideals and pursuing *voluptas, luxuria* and *amoenitas* (pleasure, luxury and beauty). Those who came to their villas on the Bay of Naples, between Cumae and Dicaearchia (the older, Greek name of Pozzuoli) and particularly in the city of Neapolis, could encounter the Greek pedagogues of illustrious scions like Tiberius and Caius Gracchus, the great Sulla himself in Athenian garb, or the poet Virgil debating with Epicurean philoso-

378 and 379

The perfect proportions and majestic perspectives of the great aristocratic villas inspired these two views from the Imperial Age, in which the motif of the portico in the north garden of Villa A can clearly be recognized (Naples, MAN).

phers. In fact, these were extraordinary, delightful opportunities to cultivate cultural *otium* and become fully immersed in Hellenism.

The other reasons that made it stylish to own a villa in Campania – plenty of water for spa treatments, the possibility of monitoring business at the port of Puteoli, and the vast stretches of farmland – were less cultural but no less important, and they reflected the ever-present Roman principle of coupling *decus* and *utile* (beauty and the profitable).

From the small inlet of Baiae, which looked almost like a lake at that time, this villa-owning trend quickly spread throughout the entire area around the Bay of Naples. It became the quintessence of elegance with a concentration of the Late Republic's leading names: Marius, L. Cornelius Sulla (as already noted), Pompey the Great, and then Julius Caesar, Cicero, Hortensius Hortalus, Lucullus …. From the rolling hills down to the sea – and even jutting into the sea – the seaside villas vied with each other in the luxury of their gardens and stepped terraces. A new building technique made it possible to construct many of the daring abodes on the water, as mortar mixed with water could be made with the local pozzolan (*pulvis Puteolanus*). This was an extraordinary discovery that would later be exploited extensively by Roman engineers to build ports and river bridges.

The natural resources of this corner of Campania sparked thousands of ideas for the Roman aristocracy in its growing quest for pomp and comfort. For example, the entrepreneur Caius Sergius Orata invented ostrich farms and the heating system (hypocaustum) for baths using *suspensurae*. According to Pliny the Elder, this natural creativity was stimulated by enormous greed, because Orata "earned large profits from his invention" (*Natural History* IX, 168).

Lastly, the most exclusive status symbol was a pool. For several writers who condemned its use (Cicero, for example), this was the folly of the rich and the ostentation of parvenus, but for those who enjoyed its benefits, it was an amusing way of underscoring one's social prestige.

With regard to fish and the seaside villas, the sources report a number of extravagances. The orator Hortensius, for example, raised a moray eel in the pool of the villa in Bauli (near Baiae) and he was so smitten with it that he supposedly wept when the it died. The behavior of Antonia, Drusus' wife, was even more peculiar, for at this same villa she "put earrings on a moray of which she was particularly fond" (Pliny, *Natural History*, IX, 172).

In any event, from Augustus on, the court and its entourage would go to Baiae for golden holidays. The monumental remains of the baths, which are evident above the town even now, may have been part of the *Palatium*, the imperial palace that, with the passage of time, expropriations and inheritance, came to include several luxurious resi-

dences. All the Julio-Claudians went there to enjoy its luxury. For some, like Caligula, the enchanting locality was tied to the exploit of a bridge of boats extending to Puteoli (to outdo the one that Persia's King Darius built across the Hellespont), while in Nero's case, it was even linked to matricide. And while Tiberius preferred Capri for his villa of delight and forgetfulness, not one high-ranking figure failed to be captivated by the charm of the Bay of Naples, which managed to radiate a climate of *voluptas* to the nearby towns as well.

Obviously, only the elite of the Roman aristocracy could afford a villa next to the imperial court, but in the rest of Campania real estate must have been less expensive and the atmosphere just as pleasant. On the slopes of Vesuvius and along the coast from Naples to Stabiae, a favorable situation occurred after the Sullan colony was established. Many veterans

were willing to transfer for cash the share of land assigned to them so that they could stay in their hometowns, and this meant an opportunity for purchasers to obtain not only a holiday villa but also a profitable farm. We know that Cicero himself bought a villa near Pompeii, and that others were later purchased by Seneca's friend Lucilius and by Emperor Claudius (he bought the villa where the young Drusus died after choking on a pear he had thrown in the air and caught in his mouth). The lyric poet Caesius Bassus (the target of Persius Flaccus' sixth satire), and Antonius Agrippa, son of Felix, the Roman Procurator of Judea, also bought. (Antonius Agrippa and his wife Drusilla perished in the eruption of AD 79.) None of these villas has been identified, but we can get an idea of their sophistication from the splendid paintings in the Third Style (in the National Museum, Naples) from the famous villa at Boscotrecase, attributed to Agrippa and built between 21 and 17 BC.

In this process of settlement *per villas*, the coastal area of the modern-day municipalities of Torre Annunziata and Torre del Greco, up to Herculaneum, was certainly very desirable. This was not only because of the enchanting beauty (*amoenitas*) of these spots – beyond the marshes at the mouth of the Sarno, the coastline rises in altitude and affords a marvelous view of Capri and the Sorrento peninsula – but also because the area was well equipped.

This is confirmed by the work done immediately after the colony was established in order to renovate the road leaving Pompeii through Porta Ercolano. This was undoubtedly undertaken to modernize the road network in general for military purposes and to ensure control over the territory. At the same time, however, it must certainly have been dictated by the need for infrastructure in this area of the bay, due to the important real-estate investments being made here by the Roman aristocracy.

POPPAEA'S VILLA

Villa A at Oplontis offers us a significant example of this drive to add new villas to old farm property. The oldest part of Villa A was built next to a villa with a press (82), which may date prior to this. In the north garden, in AD 79 there was still an old olive tree from this *fundus* present before the park was created (the tree has been identified through the cells recovered from one of its branches).

However, when the new villa was built toward the middle of the 1st century BC, the architect commissioned to design it focused above all on creating a sumptuous building, rather than on the production of wine and oil. There is no doubt that he was a highly skilled architect, and this is evident from just a quick glance at the clear geometry of the original layout: a compact rectangle ended in the east with the line of rooms (41-43-44-45) and was crossed in the middle by the transept, also rectangular, of rooms (5-20-21) This geometric layout permitted additional refined subdivisions inside. Thus, we have the extension of the transept that em-

phasized the power of the grand Tuscan *atrium*, and the interior layout of the two sections on the sides of the central transept, corresponded respectively to two quarters, one for the *dominus* and one for the *familia* of servants. There was a porticoed garden (32) inside the second portion and a new north-south line crossed the main room (15) of the first one.

The design was evidently modified by later work, but without altering its main lines. As a result, based on the symmetry of the servants' quarters we can arrive at a fairly accurate reconstruction of the dimensions of the aristocratic quarters, part of which have yet to be explored. Unfortunately, the front of the villa is missing as it was cut through by the Sarno canal, but the morphological height difference and the presence of a cryptoporticus under the portico (24) allows us to assume that the entrance from the coast road used the connection of a *basis villae*, which must have offered the opportunity to flaunt a magnificent architectural façade looking out to sea.

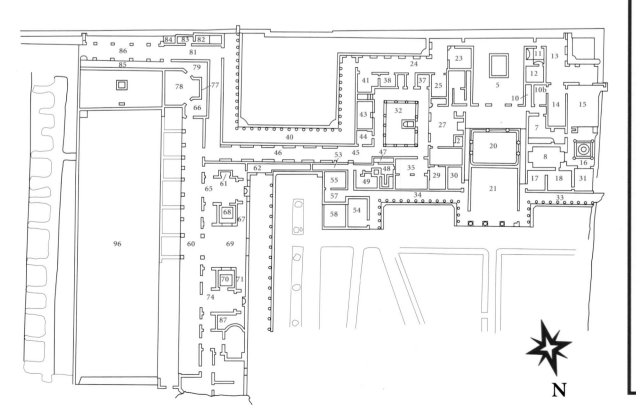

N

ATRIUM (room 5)	PERISTYLE (room 32)
GARDEN (20)	PERISTYLE (room 40)
OECUS (room 15)	HALLWAY (46)
TRICLINIUM (room 14)	OECUS (room 69)
KITCHEN (room 7)	POOL
PORTICOES (room 13)	OECUS (room 21)
CUBICULUM (room 11)	COLONNADES (33-34)

Villa A is oriented as in the plan (the viewer looking down from the north, with the east on the left). The garden, originally planted with oleanders, plane trees, boxwood, myrtle and laurel, extends toward the bottom. The forepart (right), with two columns in the front, marks the older triclinium. It is followed by an internal garden and the atrium, with a compluvium in the middle of the roof. To the left, the rectangular overhang covers the internal garden of the service quarters.

384-385

Frescoes in the Second Style – marked by powerful perspective and meticulous proportions – decorate the triclinium *of Poppaea's Villa, embellished by the geometric motifs of a polychrome mosaic. On the plaster in the more damaged areas toward the ceiling, restoration work has filled in the outlines of the architectural elements that were lost.*

385

The taste for precious trompe l'oeil *distinctive of the Triumphant Second Style, evident in the* atrium, *is expressed in this detail in a sumptuous false door framed by columns and topped by two* imagines clipeatae. *This composition makes it possible to date the decoration to a period just before the first half of the 1st century BC.*

The west wing, only part of which has been excavated, was thus the owner's living area, with a central hall (15), a *triclinium* (14), several *cubicula* and *diaetae* (11, 12) decorated with murals painted in the Second Style. In the northern part of this section, a thermal complex was subsequently installed, built around a small tetrastyle portico (16) with a kitchen-*praefurnium* (7), a *caldarium* (8), a *tepidarium* and other thermal rooms (31, 17) decorated in the Third and Fourth Styles.

The east wing was used mainly for service facilities. Laid out around a central portico (32) with an interior garden dominated by a large tree, probably a chestnut (given that some carbonized nuts were found here), it featured a large room with a lararium (27), many storerooms (35, 44, 43), and cells for the slaves on the upper floor. The service functions were housed mainly in the internal rooms, which were decorated in the final period with plain yellow and blue stripes. The rooms facing the exterior (23, 37, 38, 41, 30, 29), which were decorated with mosaic floors and more refined paintings (in the Second, Third and Fourth Styles), were part of the owner's living quarters and were used to take walks or for relaxing. The arrangement of the small bathroom quarters, with a small *caldarium* (49) and a latrine (47, 48), is particularly interesting.

The north and south porticoes (13, 24, 33, 34) were decorated with paintings in the Fourth Style and it is not clear if they were built during the first phase. However, based on the corner position of rooms 11, 12 and 23, it is likely that at least the two arms of the south portico (13, 24) date from the initial construction.

What is certain is that in the first phase, the east boundary of the villa was aligned with the east walls of rooms 49-44, as a wall with this alignment was found under the floor of room 45. The *pars rustica*, in rooms 82-83-84 (and perhaps also 81) with a *torcularium* (a grape press), was separate from the main building but annexed to it. The dominant architectural theme again appears to be the one of the *atrium*, drawn from the model of the traditional city palace. Thus, this was a way of transferring the function that this room fulfilled in an urban setting – the exhibition of social prestige – to a vacation home.

During the Augustan or Julio-Claudian period, the villa underwent extensive updating and decorative renovation, although certainly in different stages. In fact, the initial work in the east area of the north garden may have been done in this period, with the construction of the brick colonnade (62) that has no architectural relationship to the subsequent area of the swimming pool (*natatio*), as the two floor levels do not match.

Even in this early phase, the portico may have been connected to the older portion of the villa by hallway 62 (and perhaps a transept behind it occupying the area of the subsequent gallery 46). If this is indeed the case, the work seems to have been done in order to add a new colonnade to the garden, upstream from the ancient portion of the villa. In this case, it could conceivably have been repeated on the west and north sides of the north garden. This may also account for the work to renovate the two long sides – north and south – of the older part of the villa. We know in particular that the northern one (33-21-34) was restructured with a magnificent example of a two-armed portico and a central pedimented building, whose design seems to have conditioned the entire plan of the garden.

THE NORTH GARDEN

I t is well known that in these leisure villas, which may have been modeled after the Baian villas, the most distinctive element was the portico-garden combination. This provided long rows of colonnades used for civilized strolls in a scenic area and, in any event, was surrounded by greenery, with quiet corners in which to pause and relax (*diaetae*).

The garden, in turn, was so important that the term *horti* was ultimately used to refer to the aristocratic villa. The *topiarii*, specialized slaves who were much in demand, were responsible for its décor and artistic forms. Between the geometric layout of the paths, they would skillfully alternate cultivated trees, Mediterranean "brush" and pergolas. Around the garden, there were also full-fledged statues here and there, cut from shrubbery and particularly boxwood. This was known as *opus topiarium*, and its invention was attributed to the knight Caius Matius, who lived toward the end of the 1st century BC (Pliny, *Natural History,* XII, 13). The architectural integration between the building structure and the vegetation appears to have been accomplished perfectly in the north garden of the villa of Oplontis. Facing the countryside and the slopes of Mount Vesuvius, this garden offered a view that was certainly inferior to the seascape that could be enjoyed from the south side, but the architect attempted to use art to make up for this natural deficit. Perhaps he was already aware of what Seneca was to observe shortly thereafter (*De tranquillitate*, 2.13): that the secret of *luxuria* lay in varying the scenery, in this case sea and mountain. Thus, his plans called for extending the longitudinal line of the middle transept (*atrium* 5 – hall 21) into the garden with a broad path that would continue this line, creating a view that, from the minute one entered the building, could be enjoyed

through the huge windows in the courtyard walls (20) and through the large central intercolumniation of the propylon (outer monumental entrance) of hall 21. He also added walls to this broad path by lining it with bushes, perhaps so that they could be cut into artistic figures. Converging at the northern end of this path were two wider paths – it has been possible to excavate only the eastern one – that were also edged with shrubbery. Following a diagonal line, they extended symmetrically from the ends of the two arms of the portico, almost beckoning people to continue their shady stroll under the colonnade by taking a walk in the garden. There must certainly have been a dominant element where the three paths converged, probably a columned aedicule as seen in the paintings of the Second Style. In any case, there must also have been a fountain, given that a gutter running toward that point was discovered next to the modern steps that now lead to the excavation. We cannot dismiss the possibility that this fountain originally held the little fountain statue of the "Boy strangling a goose," found in one of the storerooms. The east end of the garden was marked off by a row of five large trees, probably hundred-year-old plane trees (or perhaps poplars, in this case about 60-70 years old). These trees separated the two side-by-side paths running parallel in front of the portico (62) and intersecting with the continuation of the east-west path along the north portico (33-34) of the villa. It has been estimated that the trees were planted between 20 BC and AD 10, and this appears to confirm that portico 62a was built in the Augustan/Julio-Claudian period.Set in the two triangular areas delimited by the diagonal paths – and easily visible from the central path – were four marble fountain-statues (two on each side) of Centaurs and Centau-

In the naturalistic decoration of the internal small gardens associated to the triclinium *on the* natatio, *a marble basin set amidst the fronds of a garden offers birds a cool pause. Enormous care was lavished by the most skilfull* topiarii *on designing gardens, which offered the cultured and wealthy guests of the villas an opportunity to enjoy sophisticated leisure.*

*Sculptures are among the noteworthy elements furnishing Poppaea's Villa. On the
left, two rampant centauresses were part of two fountains set in the north garden.
On the right, a group done in a Hellenistic style, from the edge of the pool,
portrays a hermaphrodite trying to elude a satyr's attentions (Torre Annunziata,
Depository of Poppaea's Villa).*

resses. In AD 79, these statuettes were in the storeroom with the "Boy strangling a goose," in the nearby ambulacrum (33) of the portico. However, the fact that their bases were found in the garden proves their original placement. At the same time, for cultured guests (with an early penchant for structuralism) who noticed the contrasting attributes that the mythical beings held in their hands they must have evoked the dialectical relationship between the civilized and the wild. The woodland animals and the mythical creatures (Satyrs, Sileni, Nymphs, Maenads, Fauns, Pan, etc.) that, according to ancient belief, lived in the forests, were among the most popular themes in the decorations of ancient gardens, as demonstrated by the dozens of statuettes found in the gardens of Pompeii. However, they certainly must have created a completely different effect here, set in a true park with the mountain in the background. The diagonal paths were also embellished with sculptures, herms placed on small brick pillars set in shrubs (probably oleanders), and a

dense thicket that was probably nearly a hundred years old by AD 79 marked the beginning of the path. Three deities, namely Aphrodite and Dionysus (as child and adult), and two humans were portrayed here, and these subjects may have inspired the viewer to make comparisons and draw flattering parallels among the figures (five or even more). Likewise, the dating of the portraits – the woman is coiffed like Antonia the Younger, a style that was fashionable during the Tiberian period – confirms the chronology that has been identified for this layout of the garden. The gardens inside the older part of the villa are equally interesting. While smaller in size, they were just as important in terms of their relationship with the architecture. The garden (20) was just beyond the *atrium* and a flowerbed with potted plants was created around the gushing fountain in the small tetrastyle portico (16) of the bath area of the owner's quarters. There was also a small garden (58) in the northeast corner of the original portion of the villa, behind the *diaeta* (54).

AN EXTRAORDINARY POOL
THE LAST PHASE

The third phase in the villa's architectural development involved its incredible extension, culminating in a constructed area (at least what has been unearthed so far) that – not including the pergolas, swimming pool, gardens and so on – covered about 39,288 square feet (about 425 feet long and 360 feet wide). This previous villa extension was virtually doubled with the addition, east of the original building, of magnificent quarters overlooking a large pool (*natatio*), which must be understood as nothing short of a real swimming pool and was also mentioned by Pliny the Younger (*Letters*, 5, 25) with regard to his Tuscan villa. This large pool (96) was about 200 feet long and 55 feet wide. These dimensions are quite exceptional, as the pool is barely shorter than the one at the Villa of the Papyruses (219 feet) but is much wider (the latter one was 23.4 feet wide). Originally, it was probably also longer. Subsequently, problems tied to the stability of the portico columns (60) made it necessary to narrow the pool and build buttresses to reinforce the foundation of the colonnade. On the west side of the pool, we can easily pick out the design of a single, large architectural complex that was devoted exclusively to entertainment and relaxation. The northern part, set between the two parallel north-south porticoes (60 and 62a), was laid out around the large hall (69) that was almost an exact duplicate of the *triclinium* (21) of the older portion of the villa. However, it was designed more grandly, with a marble floor in *opus sectile*. The room was set on the median transverse line of the *natatio*: in the portico (60) across from it, this position was exalted by the expanded intercolumniation of the marble colonnade and taller columns, which must certainly have sustained a pedimented façade. The twin rooms with apses (65 and 74), both of which were probably used for banquets, were conceived as symmetrical pendants of hall 69. What is even more extraordinary is the fact that there were four small interior gardens (68, 70, 61, 87) set between the two rooms to offer guests a continuous series of sur-

prising views (several scholars theorize that these rooms were guests quarters, or *hospitalia*). Equally striking is the functional device of the service passageways (67, 71) as a continuation of hallways 53 and 62, which were shrewdly dissimulated so that the servants' movements would not mar even the visual beauty of the scene.

We must also note that this layout, with the south arm of the complex of the west wing (*triclinia* 33, 29 and 25, intermediate rooms 31, 2, 27), is absolutely identical to the layout of the pavilion of the Domus Aurea on Colle Oppio. The Oplontis complex seems to predate the Roman one (recently attributed to a variant executed under Nero). If this theory is confirmed, we can state that the

plans of imperial architects Severus and Celerus were inspired by the Phlegrean villas, truly unique examples in terms of decorative and architectural inventions that were thus exported to Rome. This is even more probable if one accepts our theory that Villa A at Oplontis was part of the Campanian property owned by the *Poppaei* (the family also had prestigious houses in Pompeii), handed down from Quintus Poppaeus Asiaticus (consul in AD 9) to his daughter Poppaea Sabina and then to his granddaughter by the same name, who was Nero's second wife (from AD 62 to 65). Considered in this light, we cannot dismiss the idea that Nero and his entourage came to Oplontis when he went to Pompeii and offered a gold oil lamp and emerald

Delicate naturalistic images with a gazelle, a bird and plant scrolls are delineated against a diaphanous white background in this close-up of the decorations of portico 60. The evanescent décor of this area reflects the Fourth Style.

(beryl) earrings at the temple of Venus, protectress of the *gens* Julia, nor can we discard the possibility that Severus and Celerus thus had the chance to borrow ideas from this luxurious residence.

The southern part of the quarter, at the southwest corner of the *natatio*, is laid out at the end of the portico (60) based on an architectural model similar to the one used in rooms 54, 57 and 58. Here, however, the form seems to be updated and enriched in the sophisticated setup of room 78, with windows looking out over the pool and statues in the garden. Unfortunately, the excavation work has yet reached the end of this east quarter on the south side, where the short end of the *natatio* is accompanied by an *ambulatio* with a pergola held up by masonry pillars (86). Likewise, the work has not reached the north or east sides, where the garden continues past the pool to the area that is still unexplored, making it difficult to get an accurate idea of the entire complex and its rapport with the previous villa.

Based on decorative, pictorial and architectural comparisons – for example, with a room in the Centenary House in Pompeii – the quarter containing the *natatio* is datable at AD 50-79. In any case, all of it appears to predate the earthquake of AD 62, which seriously damaged the porticoes, both 62 (which was completely destroyed) and 60, whose columns and marble capitals were found set aside in the *triclinium* (21), waiting to be restored.

Like the north garden, the area around the pool was also elegantly decorated. Less pompous than the famous peristyle and pool at the Villa of the Papyruses, which was decorated with statues of rulers, philosophers, gods and small woodland animals, the garden east of the large *natatio* of Oplontis was laid out with a tree-lined path, almost like a dyohekatonpedon (two hundred feet) racetrack with a series of statues, as commonly done in the Greek gymnasia: two herms of Lysippus' Hercules of Sicyon, two statues of Nike (Victory) evoking Phidias' Olympic ones, an Amazon and an Ephebe. There were also portraits,

a neo-Attic krater with Pyrrhic dancers (which may originally have spouted water into the pool), and a group with a Satyr lying in wait for a Hermaphrodite, a subject found in numerous Pompeian paintings.

The botanical organization is equally interesting. Behind each statue there was a tree, with larger trees (probably plane trees or cypresses) at the two ends of the path. Furthermore, behind the four central statues (which unfortunately have never been found) that guests could see from the large hall (69) overlooking the pool, there were two oleanders, whose presence has been confirmed by the remains of cells from a branch, and perhaps two lemon trees. This row of trees and statues in itself created architectural movement, almost acting as a "natural" portico that was a counterpoint to the real colonnade on the other side of the pool. The effect was that of an outdoor gallery whose extraordinary sight, against the backdrop of the Lattari mountains, could be admired fully by guests at the villa as they strolled around the pool. We must also bear in mind that the examination of this garden has yet to be completed and that the finding of a child's portrait, on one side, and of two new bases and transverse paths at the eastern edge of the excavation site would infer a rather different layout.

The topiary arrangement of the southeast garden (59) is more modest but nonetheless quite interesting. In the garden, the colonnade was accompanied by a double row of trees that were planted directly in front of the columns and were still in their pots from the nursery, many of which have been found. Unfortunately, it is impossible to determine what kinds of plants they were, but the idea of using greenery to create what was essentially a second colonnade next to the first one, perhaps even resting against each other, is intriguing, especially if we consider the effect created by climbing plants.

If we look at the general layout of the villa, we can easily notice the seeming oddity desired by the architect, who set the new quarter for the *natatio* in a north-south direction, rather than the east-west one

393 left

In this close-up of the decoration of the large hall (referred to as room 15), a luxuriant plant composition act as a backdrop for a torch set on a boulder, for a delightfully random touch.

already used in the older villa, which was a sunnier and more panoramic orientation that opened toward the coast. This was probably due to the fact that there were other villas to the east, leaving no room to build anything of the size that had been planned. Whatever the reason, the outcome was not a harmonious one, with two structures set crosswise to each other. To solve the problem of connecting the new quarter with the extant portion, the architect reinforced the transept formed by the previous hallway (62) by adding a new gallery (46) and a portico facing south (40). Although this was a somewhat contrived solution, it was certainly a functional one and it also gave the villa a splendid portico (40) with a scenic view of the bay. It is interesting to draw a comparison with the Villa of the Papyruses in Herculaneum and the one of San Marco in Stabia, which also show the incoherent connection between the

natationes and the older portions, confirming the owners' new passion for pools and the difficulties involved in installing them. The duration of the work at a villa (whose owner certainly must have had ample financial resources) is an aspect that backs the hypothesis, proposed recently on several occasions, that there was an earthquake – unmentioned by the sources – between AD 62 and 79. On the other hand, a possible explanation for the slow pace of the restoration work is offered by the theory that, if the villa did indeed belong to Poppaea, it became part of the imperial treasury. The lack of interest shown by Vespasian and Titus in maintaining the Campanian villas, particularly if they were somehow tied to Nero, has now been proven by the virtual abandonment of the Pausilypon (a luxurious, landscaped imperial villa), near Naples, following the Neronian period and the eruption of AD 79.

PAINTINGS AND MOSAICS

Pictorial decoration has always played an extremely important role in defining the villa as an aristocratic building. It is no accident that the three main examples of large-scale figured friezes, known as megalographies, have been documented in residences of this kind: at the Villa of Fannius Synistor at Boscoreale, at the Villa of the Mysteries in Pompeii, and one found only recently in a quarry in Terzigno. These paintings were preserved by the last owners as relics, alluding to their full mastery of the Greek culture. A similar meaning can also be attributed to the presence of less exclusive Hellenistic elements, such as the friezes of weapons decorating the Villa of the Mysteries or the trophies of Macedonian shields and the *imagines clipeatae* (circular portrait bust) in the *atri-*

um of this villa. The seaside residence of Poppaea Sabina presents such extraordinary pictorial decoration – the work of the same shop that decorated the Villa of Fannius Synistor – that it is now considered the leading pictorial complex of the Second Style extant today. Without delving into every detail, we can briefly note the marvelous composition of the *atrium* that, on the two opposite long walls, repeated the sumptuous colonnaded prospect of a Hellenistic palace with two orders (there are still fragments of the upper Ionic order, which have yet to be positioned) and three doors, two painted ones and a real one corresponding to the passageway to portico 13. The decorative apparatus is extremely rich: the areas over the doors are painted with landscapes, there are door leaves decorated with bosses and winged Victories, *imagines clipeatae*, incense burners and a torch, all represented in the finest detail with a rich range of precious, warm colors. To contrast this array of color, the mosaic floor was done against a white ground, with polychromy reserved only for the meander created in perspective around the *impluvium*. Even the turns of the hallways leading from the *atrium* to the south porticoes were embellished with decorations on the same level, with garlands (to the east) and a suggestive monochrome landscape section reminiscent of Egypt (to the west). Equally magnificent, and intended to impress guests, was the decoration of the large hall (15) in the middle of the master's quarters, with a view of a sanctuary dedicated to Apollo and composed of a Corinthian propylon. Through it, the viewer could follow the depth of space, skillfully colored, of the interior two-order portico. In the center, against the background of a copse of trees aglitter with gemstones and gilt bronze, there

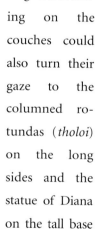

is a Delphic tripod set on a tall cylindrical base. Here again, the complex geometric composition is varied and embellished by the detailing of magnificent peacocks sitting on the pedestal, theater masks, the craniums of antelopes hanging on the walls, the almost metallic volutes (spirals and scrolls) of the acanthus leaves of the capitals, and the torch set under the tripod. The floor, updated to match the style of the era, is equally precious, done in mosaic on a white ground decorated with inserts in polychrome pebbles and marble. The Second Style flaunts all its decorative potential in the paintings of the *triclinium* (14), which are miraculously almost complete. The pictorial space of the walls and the mosaic work of the floor mark

the functions of the room. The anteroom (*procoeton*), between the threshold and a white maze-like band in black and white, is decorated with orthostats with motifs creating exotic yellow monochrome landscapes. This is followed by the actual *triclinium*, introduced by two pillars imagined as supports for the vaulted coffered ceiling (in stucco, now lost). The *triclinium* area is marked on the floor by a carpet of multicolored diamonds that is off-center in relation to the back of the room, in order to set the *triclinium* couches against the wall. The painter matched the spatial variation by using the area of the sumptuous banquets for views of sanctuaries, with extravagant *propylaea* (triumphal entrances) and columns in exotic marbles with sculpted or gilt bronze rooks, wrapped in scrolls with precious stones as also found in the excavations of Roman *horti*. The guests reclining on the couches could also turn their gaze to the columned rotundas (*tholoi*) on the long sides and the statue of Diana on the tall base along the back wall or delight in the sophisticated elegance of the hanging *clipei* (shields) decorated with divine images. Or they could enjoy the bronze griffins on the pillars of the portals, a bird hopping on the *podium* and the lively offerings to the gods (true still lifes), such as the marvelous basket of figs, the glass cup with fruit, the bow and arrow, and the storied *acerra* for incense. Competing with all this decorative exuberance was the small alcove-shaped "biclinium" (11) in the corner of the peristyle. Here, the artist painted two views of a sanctuary with columns on a *podium*, broken pediments, aedicules, statues of gods and walls clad in colored marble. The preservation of part of the ceiling is astonishing, with painted caissons and a number of realistic details, like the garland hanging from the twisted screw. Unfortunately, the lunettes are quite deteriorated. The floor was white with a black border and bands for the alcoves done with a checkerboard motif and overlapping triangles. The decoration of the symmetrical room (23) in the east quarter, on the opposite side of the *atrium*, is extremely elegant. As in the previous room, here again the views done in the Second Style seem to be marked off by niches and closed partitions, leaving only the upper parts to reveal the series of colonnades behind them and patches of blue sky. The focus of the decoration thus shifts to gleaming surfaces with warm colors skillfully scaled from the outside toward the center, going from yellow to carmine to vermilion. Even without statues of the gods, the sanctuary theme can be noted through the offerings: the wicker basket full of fruit and covered with sheer silky fabric, the torch decorated with ears of wheat, the cake on a platter, the glass cups brimming with pomegranates and quinces. And there are exquisite details like birds, bronze hydrias (three-handled water jugs) that are cleverly varied in position, pheasants with multicolored plumage, theater masks, phallic menis-cuses, a charming azure landscape, and rubies in the eyes of the Ionic volutes. In the Augustan and Julio-Claudian periods, the pictorial decoration was more low-key than before. In this period, the rooms that had had to be restructured to meet the owners' changing needs were simply repainted in the Third or early Fourth Style. Due perhaps to these limited aspirations, the proprietors did not hire a top-level workshop, though there were several in Pompeii, and settled instead for average painters. The out-

come was mainly a type of decoration marked by large fields of color (10b, 18, 17, 30) and few decorative motifs. There are two exceptions, one of which is the *caldarium* (8), in the Third Style with sections redone in the Fourth Style. Here there are two figured paintings in the middle area (Hercules in the Garden of the Hesperides, a sacred landscape with a votive column and a holy tree), and still lifes and a landscape in the upper register and on the ceiling. The other exception, the work of a superior workshop, is the somber decoration of room 25 with fantastic aedicules, delicately illuminated in the upper register. The mosaic work of this phase is also simple, mainly with black-and-white carpets. The extensive restructuring work of the Neronian era, which doubled the area of the villa by adding the new quarter for the *natatio*, naturally required extensive painting, done in the Fourth Style in vogue by this time. Once again, mainly local painters – albeit good ones – were hired. However, their assignment did not include the execution of figured paintings. They did only figurines and decorations that were part of the standard repertory. The only notable exception was the long portico (60), done with a white background and decorated with scrolls populated by small animals and tiny, exquisite landscapes. Equally exceptional in terms of the sheer size of the work – the quality is quite good but not extraordinary – is the decoration of the internal gardens of the quarter, with large red windows opening to reveal a backdrop of yellowish shrubs, populated with birds and decorated with images of the sculptural ornaments typically used in gardens. As a way of extending the "true" nature of flowers and real plants with the illusion of art, the same theme of the paint-

ed garden was continued on the walls of the garden (20) in the older portion of the villa, almost as if the elegance of the pool quarters was being heralded from the *atrium*. Likewise, small plants and birds were painted on the other side of a fence, along the white base of the outside wall of the *diaeta* (78) and of the hallway (85). One explanation for the relatively modest pictorial apparatus compared to the magnificent architecture of this phase may be that, as a place of subtle cultural allusions, the villa had increasingly become a place where opulence was flaunted. Thus, the owner found it preferable to display affluence in the main hall leading to the pool (69) by installing a luxurious floor and having the base of the walls done in *opus sectile*, rather than using paintings. Moreover, the recent discovery of a nearly exact parallel in the hall done during the Neronian period next to the *Odeion* of the imperial villa of *Pausilypon* in Naples is yet another argument in favor of the theory that this complex closely parallels the work of the architects from Nero's court. Exotic wood must have been considered at least as refined as marble. Thus, the walls of hall 78, also paved in *opus sectile*, were not done in painted plaster or marble, but using extraordinary wood paneling (preserved in casts) reproducing marble ashlar work.

THE RESIDENTS AND FURNISHINGS

I n AD 79, this villa at Oplontis was in the process of being restored, probably to repair the damage caused by the earthquake of AD 62, and perhaps also by a more recent one that was a harbinger of the eruption. Its owners had moved elsewhere, taking part of the most precious furnishings with them and, most likely, storing the remainder in a safe place. Several sculptures had been removed from the interior rooms and the garden, and were placed under the porticoes or in safe storerooms (the colonnade of portico 60 was disassembled and part of it was being stored in hall 21). The excavation work has also uncovered traces of a work site, for example the young apprentice of a *marmorarius* who was trying his hand at sculpting a statuette of Fortune that was found here, barely started, as well as a freshly dug trench in the floor of room 55. In this trench there was a clay bust of a goddess done in an older style, together with an offering of pine nuts in a vase: could this have been a sacrifice to Proserpine to ward off the peril of the eruption?

In addition to the workers, the members of the servant *familia* must also have been there. The *vilicus*, whose room was probably *cubiculus* 44, was on hand, as were the slaves responsible for maintaining the vast complex and gardens (gardening tools have been found). The graffiti found on the walls, mainly in Greek, demonstrate that there was no lack of educated slaves, probably from the East, who were trained to perform the functions required at a vacation residence. Thus, one of the graffiti (perhaps written by the *vilicus*) contains a prayer for the cult of Cybele, another one is a plea to remember someone named Beryllos, and yet another is an imprecation ("Shame on you"). Another one lists the name of a certain Procopiana. Other graffiti on the walls or tableware include names in Latin: *Draconus* and *Secundus*. A significant inscription is painted on the neck of an amphora, addressed to "…*cundo Poppaeae*" (…to Secundus or Iucundus, slave of Poppaea). This is probably the strongest argument for attributing the ownership of the villa to the *gens Poppaea*.

Since the owners were not present, it is not surprising that the villa's most precious furnishings were not found, such as bronze wares and candelabras. There were only a few glass vases and a some pieces of terracotta dinnerware, most of which were broken. As a faint echo of the magnificent banquets that must have been held here, there were several wine amphorae (from around the Mediterranean) and hundreds of clay oil lamps used to illuminate these large halls: some of them are enormous, and a particularly well-made one portrays Hercules and Omphale.

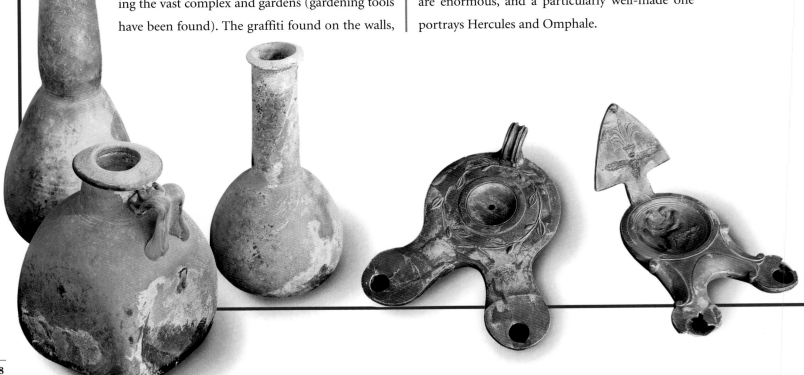

VILLA B

The excavation of this complex, by no means complete, is of enormous interest because it demonstrates the typological variety of the buildings in the settlement of Oplontis. It was constructed between the end of the 2nd century BC and the Sullan period, using Nucerian tufa and *opus incertum*. It was laid out like a large two-story portico surrounded by numbered storerooms. It does not seem to have any of the features of the country villas, although it has sometimes been identified as such. Because of its type and the findings unearthed there, it can easily be recognized as a commercial arrangement: a private *horreum* (granary) similar to those found in all Roman trade centers from Puteoli to Ostia. It faced north and was located along a street paved in large stones, beyond which another building, perhaps of the same type, has been noted. If we consider the fact that another road was identified in the Bourbon excavations east of Villa A, this would confirm the presence of a semi-urban setup in this area.

With its roadside position and perhaps its proximity to a wharf – or even to the port of Pompeii – in the year AD 79 this complex unquestionably offered its spaces and services to a *negotiator vinarius*, as evidenced not only by a painted inscription but also by heaps of amphorae that held Cretan and local wine. In addition, there were stockpiles of farm products: hay (for the donkeys pulling the carts carrying goods), hazelnuts, walnuts and a large quantity of green pomegranates, left to dry on straw mats. The dried skins would yield tannin, a valued substance needed to prepare leather using the Arab procedure for morocco leather. The wine merchant's work involved preparations in the courtyard for coating the amphorae with pitch. Indeed, the splendid wooden strongbox, clad in iron and decorated with elegant molded bronze appliqués, and complete with a secret lock, must have belonged to the owner of the *horreum*, as we know that, by law, he had to keep an *arca* at his customers' disposal. According to the damascened silver inscription on the front of the strongbox, it was the work of the Greek artisans *Pythonymos*, *Pytheas* and *Nikokrates*.

A bronze seal found with other furnishings in the apartment, adjacent to a small bathing area on the upper floors with a view of the sea, has led to the theory that the complex was owned by a certain Lucius Crassius Tertius, who may have been related to the Crassii of Herculaneum. The leading member of the family, Ti. Crassius Tertius, was duumvir in AD 61-62. The wooden box, which ended up on the ground floor when the top floor collapsed, may have belonged to one of the women in his family. It held gold and silver jewelry (rings, earrings, a bracelet) and a stash of about 200 coins (a gold one, 170 silver ones and 20 bronze ones), as well as ointment jars and women's beauty accouterments.

But the most dramatic discovery – in a room on the ground floor of the south side – was a group of about 40 people who tried to flee but perished during the eruption. They had their most valuable possessions with them: coins and jewelry they hoped to use to start a new life.

398

In addition to priceless findings like sculptures, the furnishings found in the villa include "minor" objects, such as glass phials and flasks, as well as fascinating oil lamps with one or two spouts. Given their notable size and exquisite workmanship, the latter fit in perfectly with the villa's sumptuous décor (Torre Annunziata, Depository of Poppaea's Villa).

MOUNT VESUVIUS AND THE ERUPTION

Antonio Varone

Vesuvius, long a distinctive feature in the landscape of the Sarno river valley, is continental Europe's most important volcano and probably its most famous. However, in ancient times it was not associated with the concept of death and destruction that has distinguished it among modern cultures following the terrible catastrophe of AD 79.

Ancient scholars had no knowledge of its volcanic nature, as testified by the Greek geographer Strabo (*Geography*, V 4, 8 = C 247). During the Augustan period, Strabo demonstrated that he fully understood its physical features, describing it in great detail. He even emphasized the sudden change in its appearance near the cone: after the vineyards on the lower slopes and the dense forests along its sides, the terrain abruptly becomes barren, with a uniform grayish mass that bears sinister witness to its ancient effusions. It is not by chance that, in another passage of his work (I 2, 18 = C 26), he compared it to Pyriphlegethon, the eternal river of fire.

Long before Strabo, Vitruvius (*On Architecture*, II 6, 1) also reported the belief, mentioned a few years earlier by Diodorus Siculus (*Library of History*, IV 21, 5), that fire smoldered beneath Vesuvius and had been spewed onto nearby fields in ancient times. Both Strabo and Vitruvius also drew comparisons between Vesuvius and Etna.

At that time, the mountain was probably quite different from the one we know today, given that the great cone, which rises to a height of 3891 feet, seems to have been formed by the eruption that destroyed the city at its feet during the 1st century AD. Consequently, Strabo's description must instead refer to Mount Somma (3714 ft), an older crater, now separated from Mount Vesuvius by what is known as the "Valley of Hell" (although many scholars find this attribution dubious).

Nonetheless, the science of the era was limited to libraries and to the wisdom of a handful of learned men, and it was far removed from the day-to-day knowledge of the general population. Despite men like Strabo, it seems that the people of Pompeii never sensed the danger of the mountain looming over them, or in any event they never demonstrated any great concern about it. Even Pliny the Younger candidly confessed in his first letter to Tacitus about the eruption (*Letters*, VI 16) that it was unclear which mountain had spewed the cloud shaped like a pine tree, and that he did not learn until later that it was Mount Vesuvius.

We must also note that even now, twenty centuries later and with far different certainties about the destruction that these eruptions can wreak in the life of man, the local residents do not seem to show any difference in their attitude toward Vesuvius; they continue to build and develop their city at the foot of the mountain, and even on its slopes. There are indubitably good reasons for this, but all we need to consider is that, while the Pompeians may not have been totally unaware of the risk involved in being so close to Mount Vesuvius, they certainly underestimated it and even may have dismissed it from their minds completely.

Based on the accounts that have been handed down to us, to local residents Mount Vesuvius resembled a protective deity, a *genius loci* that offered abundant game and timber and, above all, the renowned *vinus Vesuvinus*. In the famous painting from the Centenary House, in which the mountain is depicted with rows of vines decorating its ledges, it looks like the natural pendant of the god Bacchus, transformed into a bunch of grapes. The irrevocable pact the Pompeians thought they had sealed with the mountain is also reflected by the fact that *Vesbius*, the name given to Vesuvius before the rise of the language of Rome, was the identifying group name given to public slaves of the colony when they were freed. While this evokes the bond between Pompeii and the mountain dominating it, we cannot discard the idea that it marked an implicit plea for protection, as it was customary for the ancients to entreat deified natural entities to safeguard them.

One thing is certain, however: the catastrophe befell the Pompeians virtually without warning. There were numerous earthquakes on the days preceding the disaster, and current knowledge has interpreted them as warning signs. These quakes were comparable to the terrible one of AD 62 (recounted by the philosopher Seneca) and to other ones that occurred in later years, which recent studies have attributed to the manifestations that precede an eruption.

As serious as the consequences of these quakes may have been, however, the Pompeians do not seem to have connected them with the activity of the volcano. Archaeological research shows that they promptly repaired the damages, including the ones caused by the quakes that had occurred not long before. In short, there was nothing that gave them an inkling of the impending catastrophe.

We moderns are well aware of the drama of what was about to take place, not only because of the findings (some of which are extraordinarily brutal) but also because of the detailed chronicles of those moments, in the words set down by an eyewitness. This was Pliny the Younger, in two letters he wrote to Tacitus at the historian's urging (*Letters*, VI 16 and VI 20).

Pliny the Younger, who was eighteen at the time, had accompanied his uncle, the famous naturalist Pliny the Elder, who was at Misenum in command of the Tyrrhenian fleet stationed there. Thus, at about 1 o'-clock on the afternoon of August 24 of AD 79, he was there to witness the sudden formation of a cloud shaped like a pine tree, produced by the material hurled violently from the mouth of the volcano nearly 20 miles into the air. At that height, having spent the ballistic force of its skyward thrust, this material puffed out into the atmosphere before falling to earth, borne by the wind and forming the odd shape resembling the foliage of the Mediterranean umbrella pine. While at Misenum it was still unclear exactly what was happening, a

messenger arrived, sent by their friend Rectina, the wife of Caesius Bassus. The woman, who lived in a villa built at the foot of Mount Vesuvius, begged the young man's uncle to come save her, as the only escape left to her was by sea. The young man thus witnessed the heroic deed of the admiral who, ever the scholar, had initially considered going to sea in a light ship to observe the phenomenon from a closer vantage point. Nevertheless, when he received the woman's urgent plea, he had the heaviest ships (quadriremes) outfitted so they could also rescue other people in the area.

Pliny the Younger, who stayed in Misenum with his mother, recounts that the admiral, at the helm of the fleet, resolutely headed into the danger that others wanted to flee, heedless of the cinders that – still hot – fell on the ships as they drew closer to the area that had been struck. He tried to reach Herculaneum, but the shallows that had just formed prevented the ships from approaching the coastline, as the boulders that had rolled violently down the mountain were blocking the shore. Consequently, he decided that instead of turning back, he would take advantage of the wind to head to the house of his friend Pomponianus in Stabiae, on the opposite side of the gulf.

Pliny continues his account based on the reports given to him by someone who had accompanied his uncle. He cites the composure shown by Pliny the Elder as he faced the situation, comforting his friend Pomponianus and the man's family, and

downplaying the scope of the events taking place before their eyes. At nightfall, they glimpsed enormous tongues of fire leaping from Mount Vesuvius, but the admiral attributed them to the fact that the houses of the local farmers were burning. He then fell into a deep sleep, from which he was quickly awakened as the rain of *lapilli*, heavier and heavier, started to block the entrance to his room. Violent earthquakes continued to rock the house from its very foundations and as a result, all its residents decided to go outside, using pillows to protect their heads. Dawn did not light the sky as usual, for the pall of cinders floating in the air was impenetrable, and the admiral went down to the shore, noting that it still was impossible to set sail because the sea was so rough. Feeling weak, he stretched out on the beach, lying down on a sheet, and thirstily drank some water. But then the penetrating smell of sulfur, heralding the approaching flames, roused him and forced him to his feet. As the others fled, he managed to stand up with the help of two slaves, only to drop dead instantly. In his nephew's opinion, his death was caused by the cinder-laden air that had clogged his air passages and blocked his throat, which Pliny the Younger notes was weak and often inflamed. In fact, when the admiral's body was found the next day he looked as if he had simply fallen asleep.

Meanwhile, from the house in Misenum Pliny the Younger watched the events unfold from a different viewpoint. On the afternoon of that same day, August 24, after

his uncle's departure he tended to his usual tasks before having supper and going to bed. It was only during the night that the gravity of the danger around them also dawned on those who were miles away, when a series of violent earthquakes forced them to go outside. And yet in the narrow courtyard that separated the house from the beach, he continued to study and a family friend who had come from Spain to meet the boy's uncle chided him harshly about his carefree attitude, then turning to reprimand his mother for being reluctant to seek shelter. It was only with the feeble glimmer of dawn that they decided to leave town, pressed by the insistent quakes and followed by a crowd doing exactly the same thing and urging them to flee. They stopped on the road and became the astonished observers of remarkable phenomena: carts halted on level ground rolled back as if they were going uphill, despite the fact that stones had been wedged under their wheels, and the sea had withdrawn, increasing the expanse of the shore, which was covered with countless beached fish. Above all, however, a threatening black cloud, rent by snaking flashes of fire that were longer than lightning and burst into glowing flames, was moving down toward the sea and was stretching out in the direction of Capri.

Ash was already falling over Misenum, although it wasn't dense yet. However, those who were fleeing were followed closely by a thick haze that resembled a torrent flooding the land, heralding darkness that was far gloomier than the blackness of closed, lightless rooms. Suddenly, a faint glow could be seen once again, like a new fire that was approaching. Fortunately, it stopped but the ash continued to fall heavily in the utter darkness. It was only when the haze thinned, vanishing like rising fog, that sunlight – livid – could be seen again over a landscape that had been turned completely gray by a thick blanket of ash, burying everything like snow.

Up to this point, we have the account of Pliny the Younger, which is accurate and trustworthy, offering precise points of reference in terms of the chronology and dynamics of the events. The two letters take the observations of a person who was in the middle of these events as they unfolded and combine them with comments of an outside observer. These viewpoints have been compared against the results of archaeological research, making it possible to clarify with great accuracy the entire eruption in its different phases and their effects on the people and their surroundings.

We must immediately clarify that the eruption process affected the various locations in very different ways as it developed. Herculaneum, in particular, met a completely different fate than Pompeii, due to the way it was buried. Moreover, if what Pliny the Elder said is true – that he was unable to land there (after 5 pm) because the flow of volcanic mud had altered the shoreline – this means that Herculaneum succumbed to its destiny many hours before Pompeii was destroyed.

Nevertheless, Pompeii is the city we will examine in greater detail, comparing the data from the latest archaeological digs with what can be gleaned from accounts written by Pliny the Younger, in order to sketch out the timing and scope of the events that occurred between August 24 and 25 of AD 79.

First of all, we must repeat that the theory set forth by several 19th-century scholars and taken up again recently – that the eruption occurred in November and not in August – must be rejected definitively. This theory has been based on a tradition from a passage from Pliny's account, which philologists have not hesitated to define as inferior, and on the testimony of Dio Cassius (appearing in an epitome of world history compiled by Johannes Zonaras, a 12th-century Byzantine writer).

At that time, August 8 was considered the first day of autumn and the most authoritative codices of Pliny's writings unanimously indicate the wording *nonum Kal. Septembres* with reference to the sources. However, it must also be noted that Pliny the Elder left Misenum with his quadriremes at about 2 pm and arrived at Stabiae just after sunset following his unsuccessful attempt to reach Herculaneum. This would have been impossible at the end of November, when the days are already quite short, as night would have fallen long before he arrived at Stabiae. Moreover, his nephew relates a very important detail: that morning, the admiral had stretched out in the sun and then bathed in cold water, a

The death of Pliny the Elder was one of the most popular themes of the 18th and 19th centuries, in relation to the pictorial representation of the eruption of AD 79. This one, dated 1813, is by Pierre-Henri de Valenciennes (Toulouse, Musée des Augustins).

summertime habit (*Letters,* III 5, 10-11). It is common sense that a man getting on in years and also in poor health would not have done something like that at the end of November.

Nevertheless, the most substantial proof confirming the accuracy of the account handed down through best codexes of Pliny's writings comes from the archaeological evidence. First of all, the numerous pits from fleshy fruit found during the digs indicate that it was summer. Likewise, studies of the burned grasses and the pollen found under the layer of *lapilli,* performed on various findings from the area around Mount Vesuvius, have constantly demonstrated the presence of the varieties typical of the hottest season of the year.

The scholars who are inclined to date the eruption in November point to the fact that pomegranates, walnuts and olives were found, also noting that the grape harvest was underway. The latter findings actually detract from the theory, as "early harvesting" is still practiced in the region even now. Thus, it is difficult to imagine the harvest at the end of November. In terms of the data on the various plant species, we must cite the phenomenon of the "precession of the equinoxes," which now – two thousand years later – has changed the maturation period of certain fruits. As a result, from a climatic standpoint, August 24 of AD 79 corresponds to September 18 in our own era. Therefore, we can easily understand that before this date it would have been possible to enjoy walnuts, which were eaten

fresh in that era, and that the pomegranate trees were already laden with fruit. The ones found in the excavations around Mount Vesuvius, in particular, reveal peduncles bent back on themselves, a practice adopted in ancient times to prevent complete ripening and make it possible to preserve the fruit in straw in order to prepare medicinal extracts. The few olive pits that have been found induce us to think that they were preserved using the method practiced at the time.

The fact that traces of wool garments were found on the bodies of several victims is of little importance. Wool was a commonly used fabric and those who had decided to flee during the night or at dawn may easily have thought of protecting themselves against the cold in such doubtful circumstances. Therefore, there is nothing to disprove dating the event in August, while there are many insurmountable difficulties for dating it later in the year.

From Pliny's eyewitness account, we know that the paroxysmal emission of material from the volcano's mouth took place at about 1 o'clock in the afternoon. Several hours before, however, there certainly must have been signs that something irrevocable was happening. In addition to probable tremors and muffled rumbling, the initial effusive phenomena characteristic of what is referred to as the "opening phase" of the eruption may also have started. If the messenger Rectina sent with her desperate plea for help reached Misenum shortly after 1 pm, we must assume that when he left the

area of Herculaneum, probably about three hours before, the situation there must already have appeared irremediably bleak. At the House of the Working Painters, which is currently being excavated, on the morning of August 24 the painters were able to work for several hours – without any apparent difficulty – in the large room, which was being redecorated following damage from the recent quakes. More to the point, enormous areas of the walls had already been covered with several layers of fresh plaster, arriving at the last, thin layer that would then be painted. In the same room, the painter who was to create the central frame of the walls (*pictor imaginarius*) had had time to sketch out his *sinopia,* outlined with yellow ocher on the wet plaster, and had started to paint the ground color of the composition in the upper section. In other Pompeian houses, pots placed on the fire, containing food to be cooked, have been found. It is evident that, at least in the early hours of the day, which began at 6 am for the Romans, nothing portended imminent catastrophe.

At a certain point, perhaps between nine and ten in the morning, the painters' work was suddenly interrupted. Their tools, including two valuable bronze compasses and a little bronze pot, plus a set of cups with pigments, were abandoned there. In the middle of the picture the painter was doing on the wall, a large shapeless mass of very fine lime points to the effect of a violent earthquake. It is likely that the lime, placed in a container that the painter held

in his hand in order to keep the wall moist as he perfected his sketch of the composition, was suddenly splashed across the painting when the artist, indubitably standing on scaffolding or a tall stool, suddenly lost his balance. Spilled when the painter instinctively reached out to catch himself, the lime adhered to the wall, where it has remained for almost two millennia.

At about 1 pm, the plug blocking the flow of magma up through the volcano's cone exploded, releasing an enormous mass of volcanic material – gas, ash, chunks of rock and, above all, *lapilli* – for an estimated total volume of more than half a cubic mile. This material was progressively and continuously launched upward at a speed of hundreds of feet per second, reaching a height of 65,000 to nearly 100,000 feet. In the air, it expanded as it was carried by the stratospheric northwesterly winds, which distributed the fall of the *lapilli* by size, so that the finest and lightest ones traveled dozens of miles before they fell to earth, after depleting the kinetic energy that had thrust them upward. This must have been the "pine tree" described by Pliny and this is the phase that is now referred to as "Plinian." Within a very short time, perhaps as little as two hours, this "white" pumice fell on Pompeii, accumulating to a thickness of 50-55 inches. When volcanic material spewed from the crater at the rate of thousands of cubic yards per second, it was driven by new material with the same chemical and physical characteristics. It can occur, however, that the materi-

al varies and this was the case here: the column collapsed temporarily as it could no longer sustain itself, and the erupted material fell to the lowlands, hurtling down the sides of the volcano at very high speed and generating a pyroclastic flow. In all likelihood, one or more of these flows – documented in the soil stratigraphy in the various areas and in the archaeological excavations closest to Vesuvius – completely swallowed up Herculaneum, presumably at about 3 pm.

These flows did not reach Pompeii. Because of the altered composition of the volcanic material, the city was struck by larger and heavier *lapilli*, depositing another layer that was about three feet deep and darker in color ("gray pumice").

The elderly admiral must have reached Pomponianus at Stabiae between about 7 and 8 pm, taking advantage of the twilight after sunset. It seems that the paroxysmal phase of pumice fallout had not yet taken its toll on Stabiae: this is the only explanation for the men's cordial greeting on the beach, the request for a bath and the (feigned) cheer at supper. On the other hand, Pliny the Younger notes that danger was not at hand there, although it was visibly increasing.

Although *lapilli* are extremely light (approximately 0.3 ounces per cubic inch) and, like a hailstorm, are not heavy enough to kill a person despite their enormous falling speed, they are not weightless. A buildup of just several inches can collapse a roof. And if we add the fact that the quakes

must have created notable static problems in the buildings, we can understand that a number of people were killed in this phase. In fact, many skeletons of victims who died during this phase were found in the *lapilli* layer. Even if they were not killed directly by the eruption, for example after being hit by "volcanic bombs" – entire "stones" hurled by Mount Vesuvius together with the *lapilli* – they perished due to related causes, such as heart attacks or, above all, the collapsing roofs under which they had sought shelter. This is what happened to a matron discovered on March 4, 1831 in the *tablinum* of the House of the Faun, crushed under the roof that had collapsed on her. Her jewelry and stash of money, which she evidently hoped to save in her escape if only the gods had allowed it, were found nearby.

After the pumice fallout phase, Pompeii had a respite of several hours in terms of visible phenomena, a fact that is confirmed by careful interpretation of the stratigraphy of the volcanic deposits. In fact, pisolites have been found over the layer of gray pumice, amidst the ash that settled through it to a depth of several layers. Pisolites, small balls formed by the aggregation of moist ash, indicate the onset of a new phase in the dynamics of the volcano, the "phreatomagmatic" one. In this phase, the magma interacts with the deep water table, a phase that ushers in a forceful and terrible new outbreak of the volcanic activity.

During this "transition" phase" (between the "Plinian" phase and the subse-

quent "flow" phase), the drop-off in volcanic activity, which is manifested stratigraphically solely by the sedimentation of ash, was accompanied by intense seismic activity that was clearly felt in both Stabiae and Misenum, as Pliny the Younger described, with a focus estimated at a depth of just 3.1 miles and a magnitude of close to 5. These earthquakes represent the response of the volcanic structure as a whole to the imbalance generated by the emission of the enormous mass of material during the Plinian phase and the ensuing rush of water from the deep water table into the volcanic conduit. At this point, fissures opened up along the slopes of the volcano, spewing flames and spurting incandescent material. This is the fire that could be seen burning on the mountainside from as far away as Stabiae and that, in an attempt to instill courage in his companions and perhaps even within himself, Pliny the Elder tried to pass off as fires burning the houses along the slopes.

It is difficult to imagine what must have gone through the minds of the Pompeians during those unspeakable hours: phenomena that had never been seen before were taking place, and no one could envisage their duration or their scope. When these events first started, people may have thought they were simply experiencing an earthquake. In the House of the Working Painters, for example, the men left their tools behind when they fled suddenly, and yet doors were intentionally closed to keep others from entering and to prevent the

horses in the barn from running away. The skeleton of one of these animals was found with its head raised, as it was leaning on the door that was inevitably shut. Moreover, the skeletons of many fugitives were found with the remains of boxes or bags in which they had gathered up jewelry, money and valuables, just as some of the skeletons were found covered with as much jewelry as the people could wear. For example, the woman from the entrance to the House of the Dioscuri, along Via di Mercurio, was holding a canvas handbag containing *crotalia*, rings, gemstones, a perfume-holder and coins. Likewise, next to four skeletons found on May 19, 1817 in the House of Pansa, there were five gold bracelets, a long gold chain, a pair of earrings and two rings with gems. It is evident that, despite the agitation of the moment, people had enough time to salvage goods that were easy to carry. This means that many of them did not attempt to flee immediately and sought shelter inside their homes, or that after dashing out instinctively, they then had time to retrace their steps to collect their valuables.

It must also be said, however, that it could not have been easy to move about under the hailstorm of *lapilli*, with collapsed buildings blocking the streets. Above all, the city was in utter darkness, as the cloud rising from Mount Vesuvius had completely blocked out the sun. Those who did not flee at the very first inkling of danger, trying to get as far south as possible and heading toward Nuceria (and there was

enough time!), but instead wasted time lingering probably never got another chance to escape, or if they later decided to do so, by this time it was too late.

We can assume that, after the *lapilli* stopped raining down and the new day dawned, a faint glimmer must have illuminated the faltering steps of those who had remained, allowing them to leave the city and set out in the opposite direction of Mount Vesuvius.

Instead, it was precisely at dawn that the most terrifying phase of the eruption was to begin for Pompeii. Caused by the collapse of the magma chamber, this was the relentless phase of the flows also known as surge clouds or *nuées ardentes* ("glowing clouds"). These dense currents of gas, ash and solid products hurtled down the sides of the volcano like a liquid avalanche. The recent stratigraphic studies done during the excavations of *insula* IX 12 in Pompeii have counted six in a row, over a length of more than 100 feet. They accumulated over the layer of *lapilli* when the eruption began again with its greatest power, killing men, women and other living beings, and completely destroying the city.

The first surge to reach Pompeii that morning does not seem to have caused irreparable damage. It left a deposit a little over one inch thick, containing wisps of straw and plant matter that had not burnt, meaning that the temperature must not have been very high. In fact, the two subsequent surges brought death and destruction, respectively.

They must have come very close together. It is easy to understand that the surges were that terrible black cloud, accompanied by flashes of lightning and tongues of fire, that Pliny the Younger observed at seven o'clock in the morning as it reached the ground, going down over the sea and concealing Capri, then covering Misenum with ash. At Stabiae, the advent of the surges was far more noticeable, as the arrival of flames was announced by the penetrating odor of sulfur.

Naturally, as the ash fell and built up it left sediment that, measured today, is many inches deep. However, as it hurtled down at incredible speed, mixed with gases that caught fire, it must have looked like a swollen river rising to a height of several hundred feet, with the heavier products moving along the ground. This ashen river easily crossed over the city walls, already lower due to the buildup of *lapilli*, and spread through the open pathways of the streets going in the same direction as the flow, or essentially north-south. The walls of the houses along the streets then channeled the bottom of the flow, helping it gain even more speed.

The skeletons of those trying to escape were found in the sediment left by this new flow. Quite often, they were in large groups, as in an area outside Villa B in Oplontis, in the small room at the southeast corner of what are known as the Gladiatorial Barracks (the *porticus post scaenam* of the theater area), and in Diomedes' Villa. It isn't difficult to imagine that, when it became

clear that there was about to be another, violent resumption of the eruption, many of those who were already fleeing decided to seek shelter. Based on their experience over the last few hours, they probably expected another heavy shower of volcanic matter, whereas the glowing cloud that enveloped them cut off any possible escape. The ash – in the form of an ultrafine powder mixed with gas – quickly entered their pulmonary cells, blocking their lungs and suffocating them. In Diomedes' Villa, the cloud took one man by surprise as he clutched a key on his way to the garden gate, trying to find an escape route for himself and the twenty other inhabitants of the house, who were huddled in the cryptoporticus. Another dropped to the ground in the *insula occidentalis*, falling on his back on the stairs where, even today, his cast is dramatically visible in the House of Fabius Rufus. A woman in the hallway of this house breathed her last as she clutched her baby to her chest, in a vain and desperate attempt to protect him. In the House of Paquius Proculus, on Via dell'Abbondanza, the carcass of a little dog was discovered in the corner of a cubicle, beneath the remains of a bed: the terrified dog probably hid in what it thought was the safest nook. At the House of Vesonius Primus, another dog, tied to a chain, was overcome as it vainly tried to break away and was found curled up in agony. In the House of the Cryptoporticus, two people clutched each other in the moment of death: due to the consumption of their bodies, the excavators found

the skull of one embedded in the abdomen of the other. There are countless remains of the inhabitants who were overtaken by the cloud in the southern part of Pompeii as they tried to flee the city. This is what happened, for example, in what is known as the Garden of the Fugitives, and bodies were also found recently in the area referred to as "San Paolino." These sad discoveries are marked by the unsettling presence of the skeletons of children, some of whom quite young, giving us a desperate glimpse of the catastrophe and the sense of man's impotence against the forces of nature.

In the alley west of *insula* IX 12, two skeletons were found a few years ago in the very thin layer of ash, proof of the surge that killed the inhabitants. One of them in particular, stretched out perpendicular to the flow that killed him, documents with tragic brutality the overwhelming power of the next flow, the one that struck the city buildings with enormous momentum. Uncovered during the most recent excavations, he was found lying on his right side, and thus with most of his body jutting from the layer of vitric ash in which he died, face up. His skull was pocked by all the blows it received, and although his left arm and leg were completely missing, his left foot was still resting gruesomely against the alley wall. The flow that then covered him, and evidently mutilated him once he was already dead, left a layer that was over three feet thick. Found in this layer were fragments of tiles, beams and other sharp objects that the flow picked up and carried

with it as it poured through the streets.

The body of this poor victim was conceivably mutilated by these sharp objects. The broken tiles in particular, transported at high speed, could have caused the disfiguration visible on the body, as their sharp edges would have had the devastating effect of a scimitar. It is even possible to establish the speed of this flow, which was much larger than the one that had killed the people in the city. Entering from the north into this alley and channeled by it, the force of the flow bent a wall that was set slightly at an angle with respect to its path. However, the upper part of the flow cleanly broke and shoved forward another wall – set at an angle to the first one – that was on the southern side of the house and thus at a right angle to the direction of movement. This fury traveled at a speed of forty to fifty miles an hour.

These terrible flows were followed by others that were also extremely powerful. They moved more and more easily over the city, now filled with the volcanic material that had accumulated to a height of over thirteen feet. This layer held collapsed roofs, the uppermost parts of the walls that collapsed, the bodies of the inhabitants who did not manage to escape – those who had already died lying on the *lapilli*, others swallowed up by the ash, overtaken by the flow of vitric ash as they desperately attempted to flee, and still others who were asphyxiated as they futilely sought shelter in the nooks and crannies of their homes. The ash covered the bodies of these unfor-

tunates like a glove, perfectly capturing their form and features. As it settled, it gradually became conglomerated and solidified, while on the inside the flesh slowly decomposed, leaving a space where the body had once been. When archaeologists come across these hollows today, they use the method perfected by Giuseppe Fiorelli in the mid-19th century. Liquid plaster is poured into them and once it sets, it creates a perfect copy of the shape of the bodies, like a die mold. Thus, once the ash is removed we can even see the people's garments and facial features, just as they were when they drew their last breath.

Pliny's account gives us no further information, and as a result we are unable to determine exactly when these new flows hit Pompeii, in other words if they occurred one after the other or several hours apart. What we do know, based on additional research (shop n. 7, also in *insula* IX 12), is that other undulatory earthquakes struck the entire area after the *nuées ardentes*. But none of the slaves, painters, priests, matrons or shopkeepers who had wandered through the streets of Pompeii just one day earlier could feel them. The lively Roman colony, tragically, had already become part of history.

If anyone had ventured to the site of Pompeii on the morning of August 26, all he or she would have seen was the tip of one of the taller buildings or a jutting segment of some wall: ghosts in a boundless expanse of livid, ashen gray, stretching as far as the eye could see.

THE VICTIMS OF THE ERUPTION
Ernesto De Carolis

The study includes all the reports of excavations conducted in Pompeii and its immediate surroundings from 1748 to our own day and age. The bodies that were found have been divided into two separate groups based on information listed in the excavation reports. Their position and finding in the stratigraphic-temporal sequence of the volcanic material was reconstructed whenever possible.

Group I: victims found in the pumice that accumulated to an average depth of about 8.5-9.2 feet. This group totals 394 bodies, of which 200 found singly and 194 in groups.

Group II: victims found in the pall of ash deposited by surges (*nuées ardentes*) S4 and S5, and buried by S6. This marks the final phase of the eruption, between 7:30 and 8:00 am on August 25, depositing a layer about 4.5 feet thick over the pumice. This group includes individuals found on the ancient flooring, inside the layer of ash that invaded the rooms of buildings that were not reached by the pumice stones. There are 655 bodies in this group, of whom 152 found individually and 503 in groups, including 166 on the floors of the rooms.

Total victims: 1047

Karl Pavlovic Bryullov's painting, imbued with the tragic air typical of the late Romantic period, portrays the last day of life in Pompeii as an apocalyptic vision (St. Petersburg, Russian State Museum).

HISTORICAL — CHRONOLOGICAL OUTLINE

BRONZE AGE

Hut settlements were established near the Sarnus River. Agriculture, hunting and fishing were practiced, and clay containers were produced. In the 15th century BC, north of the river, a community dubbed "The Venice of Protohistory" developed at Poggiomarino-Langola, built on islands separated by canals.

13TH –12TH CENTURY BC

Mycenaean ceramics entered Italy. Sailors from the coasts of Anatolia (modern-day Turkey) reached Italy.

IRON AGE
(2000 – 1000 BC)

Findings from the necropolises show the widespread presence of settlements and cultivated crops in the Sarnus valley. At Poggiomarino, stone and metal were crafted for personal use as well as trade.

SECOND HALF OF THE 9TH –
FIRST HALF OF THE 8TH CENTURY BC

Spread of the Villanovan culture in central and northern Italy (these populations cremated their dead and buried the ashes).

9TH – 8TH CENTURY BC

Formation of the Etruscan population in Tuscany, Romagna, and Campania (Capua, Pontecagnano).

8TH CENTURY BC

Start of Greek colonization. By tradition, 753 BC marks the year Rome was founded. Greeks from the island of Euboea, who had already settled on the island of Pithecusa (Ischia), and the Cumans found the *polis* of Cuma on terra firma in 750. From here, they brought the Greek alphabet to Latium and Etruria. Trade and contact between inhabitants of the Sarnus plains and the Greek colonists. Findings dating from the 9th to the 7th century BC discovered at these necropolises, which were part of the material culture of trench burials (the dead were buried in graves), include Greek-made personal items and ceramic vases.

7TH CENTURY BC

Spread of art with Oriental motifs around the Mediterranean.

LATE 7TH – MID-4TH CENTURY BC

Rome: period of Etruscan kings and major public works (Cloaca Maxima, Circus Maxiumus). Construction of the first walls under Servius Tullius. The Roman Forum was paved. The Etruscans expanded extensively in Campania, maintaining the stronghold of Capua on the Volturnus River, where the ships of Vulci and Cerveteri arrived. The inhabitants of Poggiomarino-Langola start to move toward the mouth of the river. The population knew of the spur of lava extending into the sea, where Pompeii would later be built, but there are no definite traces of stable settlements.

6TH CENTURY BC

The cities of Magna Graecia and Sicily flourished. Various indigenous groups established Pompeii as a true urban center, settling on the rise overlooking the natural port. The first defensive walls were constructed using blocks of soft lava (*pappamonte*), enclosing an area of about 40 acres. Findings of Etruscan Bucchero ware and Greek black-figure vases indicate that these populations were in contact with the more advanced cultures nearby.

540 – 509 BC

Etruscan thalassocracy. Tarquin the Proud ruled Rome. The port city of Dicearchia – Roman Puteoli (modern-day Pozzuoli) – was founded in Campania in 531 BC by populations from Samos.

510 BC

Sybaris destroyed.

5TH CENTURY BC – 480 BC

In the Battle of Himera, Gelon, the tyrant of Syracuse, and Theron, the tyrant of Akragas (Agrigento), defeat the Carthaginians, who had dominated sea trade.

474 BC

The Etruscan fleet defeated by the Syracusans near Cuma.

475 – 450 BC

The maritime empire of Athens was formed. The Greeks in Campania reinforced their influence. Neapolis (Naples) founded by the Cumans.

LATE 5TH – EARLY 4TH CENTURY BC

The Samnites, Oscan speakers from the inland mountain areas, expanded into Campania. Cuma was occupied. The "Samnite period" began in Pompeii. The city walls were reinforced.

The new aristocracy built homes in the northwest part of the city.

415 BC

The Athenian expedition against Syracuse failed.

4TH – 3RD CENTURY BC

375 BC. The Syracusans conquered the city of Kroton.

367 BC

With the Licinian-Sextian laws passed in Rome, the plebeian class gained access to the consulship.

348 – 346 BC

Second treaty between Rome and Carthage. Archidamus, king of Sparta, aided the Tarentines against the Lucanians.

343 – 341 BC

Rome's first war against the Samnites. The army in Campania revolted.

340 – 338 BC

The Latins and Campanians joined forces against Rome.

326 BC

Neapolis became a "federated city" with Rome.

325 BC

Second Samnite War. The Romans were defeated at the Caudine Forks.

323 BC

Alexander the Great died in Babylonia.

303 BC

Peace between the Samnites and the Romans. Treaty between Rome and Tarentum.

295 BC

Roman victory at Sentinum over the Etruscans, Italics and Gauls.

280 – 272 BC

The Romans fought Pyrrhus, king of Epirus and the ally of Tarentum and other southern Greek cities. The Romans were defeated at Heraclea and Asculum Satrianum. Roman victory at Maleventum, which was renamed Beneventum. Tarentum surrendered to Rome.

264 BC

Wars between the Romans and the Carthaginians, led by Hannibal.

222 BC

Rome conquered Mediolanum (modern-day Milan).

218 – 202 BC

Second Punic War: 218-202 BC. Gaul rebelled against Rome. Neapolis and Velia became *socii navales* of Rome. Most of Campania sided with Hannibal. The Romans intervened and punished Capua and Nola, putting an end to freedom and control over trade. Pompeii did not seem to have been affected.

202 BC

Led by Publius Cornelius Scipio, the Romans defeated the Carthaginians at Zama.

3RD – 2ND CENTURY BC

The Roman conquest of the Mediterranean favored traffic by Pompeian traders. Hellenistic culture spread to Pompeii, and the houses were decorated with Greek and Alexandrian subjects.

194 BC

A Roman colony was established at Puteoli, the Italic terminal port for extensive sea trade.

183 BC

Death of Hannibal and Scipio Africanus.

149-146 BC

Third Punic War. The Romans destroyed Carthage. Greece became a Roman province named Achaia. The Temple of Jupiter was built in Rome, the first to be made of marble.

1ST CENTURY BC – 89 BC

The Social War broke out. Roman's allies *(socii)* rebelled in order to obtain Roman citizenship. Pompeii joined the other Campanian cities in the protest; Nuceria (modern-day Nocera) sided with the Romans. The dictator Lucius Cornelius Sulla destroyed Stabiae (modern-day Stabia) and attacked Pompeii.

80 BC

After quelling the last insurrections, Lucius Cornelius Sulla turned Pompeii into a colony to house his veterans. The city became *Colonia Cornelia Veneria Pompeianorum*. The *Deductor* was the nephew of the dictator Publius Cornelius.

1ST CENTURY BC – 1ST CENTURY AD

New populations from central-southern Italy arrived in Pompeii. The Amphitheater was built.

60 BC

First triumvirate of Julius Caesar, Pompey and Crassus.

52 BC

Julius Caesar completed the conquest of Gaul.

MARCH 15, 44 BC

Julius Caesar assassinated in Rome.

43 BC

Triumvirate of Octavian, Mark Antony and Marcus Lepidus. Cicero assassinated.

42 BC

Battle of Philippi against the conspirators who murdered Caesar. Death of Brutus and Cassius. Caesar deified as *divus Julius*.

31 BC

Octavian defeated Cleopatra and Mark Antony in the naval Battle of Actium. Rome conquered Egypt.

29 BC – AD 14

Octavian, the heir of Julius Caesar, became *Augustus* and *Princeps* of the Romans. In Pompeii, old public and private buildings were restored, the Forum was clad with marble, and the public aqueduct and the Palaestra were built. Rome was led by a sequence of emperors: Tiberius (AD 14-37), Caligula (AD 37-41), Claudius (AD 41-54).

AD 54

Nero, Claudius' adopted son, becomes *imperator* of the Romans.

AD 59

A brawl broke at the Amphitheater in Pompeii between the Pompeians and the Nucerians. Shows were banned for ten years.

AD 62

Nero married his second wife, Poppaea Sabina, to whom Villa A at Oplontis has been attributed. In Pompeii, the lavish House of Menander and the House of the Golden Cupids belonged to the *gens Poppaea*, members of the ruling class. Pompeii damaged by a massive earthquake.

AD 64

Nero visited to Pompeii, bearing gifts for the Temple of Venus: a gold oil lamp and earrings made of pearls and emeralds (beryls) for the sacred image of the goddess. Graffiti found at the House of Julius Polybius, on Via dell'Abbondanza, praised the opulence of these gifts. Great Fire of Rome. New urban layout for the city. Monetary reform.

AD 65

The ban on shows at the Pompeian Amphitheater was revoked.

AD 66

Palestine revolted.

AD 67

St. Paul was beheaded in Rome. It is thought that St. Peter was crucified in the same year (according to some historians, he was crucified after the great fire).

AD 68-69

Death of Nero. Civil War. "Year of the Four Emperors": Galba, Otho, Vitellius and Vespasian; the last established the Flavian Dynasty (AD 69-96).

AD 69-79

Reign of Vespasian. The Temples of the Public Lares and of Vespasian were built in Pompeii.

AD 70

Led by Titus (Vespasian's son), the Romans conquered Jerusalem.

AUGUST 24, AD 79

Start of the eruption that buried Pompeii, Herculaneum, Stabiae and Oplontis for centuries. Death of Pliny the Elder. Titus became emperor, only one month before Vesuvius erupted.

GLOSSARY

Aedicule Small sacred building or shrine.

Aediles Public administrators; in Pompeii they were in charge of maintaining public order, repairing roads and buildings, and supervising food supplies.

Ala (plural alae) The small side room opening onto the *atrium*.

Alabastron A small alabaster container used for ointments and balsams.

Apodyterium The dressing room at the Baths.

Apse An area with a semicircular or polygonal layout at the end or on the sides of a room.

Arca *Safe or coffer.*

Armilla Bracelet.

Atrium The large area in the Roman *domus* located beyond the entrance.

Augustales Guild of freedmen devoted to the cult of the emperor.

Basilica A public building used as a hall of justice and for meetings.

Bisellium Chair of honor large enough to seat two people but occupied by only one; used during ceremonies and performances.

Caldarium The room in the Baths used for hot baths.

Capitolium The main temple in a Roman city, devoted to Jupiter and housing the simulacra of the cult of the "Capitoline Triad": Jupiter, Juno and Minerva.

Cardo Road with a north-south orientation.

Cartibulum The prized table kept in the *atrium*.

Caupona Inn or tavern.

Cerussa Ceruse, or whitish make-up.

Coena The main meal of the day, eaten late in the afternoon.

Collegium Guild or corporation.

Compitalia Feast celebrated at the *compita*.

Compitum (plural compita) Crossroads.

Cubiculum (plural cubicula) Small chamber, bedroom.

Decumanus Road with an east-west orientation.

Dieta Garden pavilion or room.

Duoviri iure dicundo The top two political positions in Pompeii and the other colonies, elected every five years.

Emblema The central picture in a mosaic floor.

Epigraph An inscription carved in stone or other material.

Euripus A water channel in Pompeian gardens, intended to evoke a waterway.

Exedra A room used for receiving guests and for conversation; generally semicircular.

Fornix The open space of an arch (or portal).

Forum The main square of a Roman city, with religious, administrative and commercial buildings.

Freedman A slave who has acquired freedom. In Pompeii, many families of freedmen, or "libertines", were part of the wealthiest class of society.

Frons scenae The architectural frontal of the Theater stage.

Fullonica Laundry.

Garum Sauce made of fish marinated in salt.

Gemmarius A gemstone cutter.

Genius The vital force, of divine origin, present in people, different places and the State. Personification of the prince and emperor.

Gens (plural gentes) Stock, set of families linked by common origins, name and traditions.

Graffiti Wall inscriptions scratched on surfaces.

Herm A post surmounted by the sculpture of a human head and part of a bust.

Hortus (plural horti) Garden (also to indicate the city villa).

Insula A set of multistory houses with rented apartments, marked off by roads.

Labrum Bathtub.

Laconicum Furnace, sweatroom.

Lararium Altar, or shrine, for the household cult of the Lares.

Lares Household gods connected with the worship of ancestors.

Macellum Market.

Mausoleum A large funerary building.

Mensa Table to hold cutlery in the *triclinium* and used for serving food.

Natatio Swimming pool.

Necropolis The cemetery outside the residential area (from the Greek meaning "city of the dead").

Nymphaeum An ornamental room, which could vary in size, connected with water and decorated with statues, fountains and mosaics.

Oecus A living room.

Opus sectile Structure made of inlaid colored marble to create various motifs: geometric, floral or figured (generally used only for flooring).

Ordo Decurionum The municipal senate, composed of the decuriones, former magistrates who were elected annually.

Oscillum (plural oscilla) Disk (made of terracotta or other material) hung between the columns of porticoes. Its swinging movement would ward off the evil eye.

Otium The opposite of *negotium* (time devoted to work and business): the period for rest and amusement, particularly intellectual.

Pars rustica The rustic and service area of the villa.

Pater familias The father of the family and the master of the house.

Penates Family deities whose images would follow the owners of a house wherever they went.

Pergula Balcony, loft or room built in the upper part of a room.

Peristyle The internal courtyard of the Roman house, surrounded by a columned portico.

Pictor imaginarius The painter specializing in painting walls with pictures portraying figures.

Pistrinum Bakery.

Praedium (plural praedia) Estate, property. The *Praedia* of Julia Felix in Pompeii are famous.

Psyche (plural Psychai) Female cupids.

Regio (plural Regiones) Quarter composed of several blocks.

Sanctuary Sacred area that included one or more temples, porticoes and buildings used as places of worship (in Pompeii, the sanctuary of Isis).

Taberna Shop.

Tablinum A room in Roman and Italic houses, aligned with the entrance, where clients were received.

Tepidarium A room at the Baths for lukewarm baths.

Thermopolium A public shop that mainly sold hot beverages.

Topiarius The slave who was an expert in *ars topiaria*, or in designing and decorating gardens.

Triclinium A dining room with three couches (*klinai*) set in the Greek-style horseshoe arrangement.

Viridarium Garden.

Volumen The book of the Romans: a handwritten scroll of papyrus.

GENERAL BIBLIOGRAPHY

ABBREVIATIONS

AttiAcPontan = Atti Accademia Pontaniana.

BdA = Bollettino d'Arte.

CIL = Corpus Inscriptionum Latinarum.

ILS = Inscriptiones Latinae Selectae.

JRA = Journal of Roman Archaeology.

MAAR = Memoirs of the American Academy in Rome.

MededRome = Mededelingen van het Nederlands Institut te Rome.

MEFRA = Mélanges d'Archéologie et d'Histoire de l'Ecole Française de Rome. Antiquité.

RivStPomp = Rivista di Studi Pompeiani.

RM = Mitteilungen des Deutschen Archäologischen Instituts, Römische Abteilung.

The bibliographic references on Pompeii are virtually endless. To facilitate consultation of this bibliography, we have decided to list exhibition catalogs and the most important guidebooks separately, whereas the basic texts and most recent contributions have been listed in chronological order, according to the different chapters of this book (M.R.P.).

EXHIBITION CATALOGS

Pompeii. Picta Fragmenta, Turin 1977. Various authors

Domus – Viridaria – Horti Picti, Naples 1992. Various authors

Riscoprire Pompei / Rediscovering Pompeii, Rome 1993. L. Franchi dell'Orto, A. Varone (eds.)

Pompei. Abitare sotto il Vesuvio, Ferrara 1996. M. Borriello, A. d'Ambrosio, S. De Caro, P. G. Guzzo (eds.)

Romana Pictura. La pittura romana dalle origini all'età bizantina, Venice 1998. A. Donati (ed.)

Sotto i lapilli, Milan 1998. J. Berry (ed.)

Homo Faber. Natura, scienza e tecnica nell'antica Pompei, Naples 1999. A. Ciarallo, E. De Carolis (eds.)

Storie da un'eruzione. Pompei, Ercolano, Oplontis, Naples 2003. A. d'Ambrosio, P. G. Guzzo, M. Mastroroberto (eds.)

GUIDEBOOKS

E. La Rocca, M. and A. De Vos, *Guida Archeologica di Pompeii*, Milan 1981.

P. G. Guzzo, A. d'Ambrosio, *Pompei*, Naples 1998.

S. C. Nappo, *Guida alla città sepolta*, Vercelli 1998.

Eva Cantarella, Luciana Jacobelli, *Un giorno a Pompei*, Naples 1999.

C. Malandrino, *Piccola guida della villa romana di Oplontis*, Torre Annunziata 1976.

M. and A. de Vos, *Pompei, Ercolano, Stabia*, Bari 1982.

L. Fergola, M. Pagano, *Oplontis. Le splendide ville romane di Torre Annunziata. Itinerario archeologico ragionato*, Torre del Greco 1998.

HISTORY OF THE EXCAVATIONS

G. Fiorelli, *Pompeianarum Antiquitatis Historia* 1-3, Naples 1860-1864.

G. Fiorelli, *Gli scavi di Pompei dal 1861 al 1872. Relazione al Ministro della Istruzione Pubblica*, Naples 1873.

A. Maiuri, "Gli scavi di Pompei dal 1879 al 1948," in *Pompeiana. Raccolta di studi per il secondo centenario degli scavi di Pompei*, Naples 1950, pp. 20-42.

V. Spinazzola, *Pompei alla luce degli scavi nuovi di via dell'Abbondanza (anni 1910-1925)*, S. Aurigemma (ed.), Rome 1953.

F. Zevi, *La storia degli scavi e della documentazione* in *Pompei 1748-1980. I tempi della documentazione*, Rome 1981, pp. 11-21.

C. Grell, *Herculanum et Pompéi dans les récits des voyageurs français du XVIIe siècle*, Naples 1982.

Corpus Topographicum Pompeianun, V, Rome 1981.

C. Parslow, *Rediscovering Antiquity: Karl Weber and the Excavations of Herculaneum, Pompeii and Stabile*, Cambridge 1995.

M Pagano, *I diari di scavo di Pompei, Ercolano e Stabiae di Francesco e Pietro La Vega (1764-1810). Raccolta e studio di documenti inediti*, Rome 1997.

L. Garcia y Garcia, *Nova bibliotheca pompeiana*, Rome 1998.

S. De Caro, P. G. Guzzo (eds.), "A Giuseppe Fiorelli nel centenario della morte," *Atti del Convegno* (Naples 1997), Naples 1999.

E. M. Moormann, "Una città mummificata: qualche aspetto della fortuna di Pompei nella letteratura europea ed americana," in *Pompei. Scienza e società, Atti del Convegno internazionale per il 250° anniversario degli scavi di Pompei* (Naples 1998), P. G. Guzzo (ed.), Pompeii-Milan 2001, pp. 9-17.

C. Parslow, "The Open-Air Excavations at Pompeii in the Eighteenth Century: New Methods, New problems," in *Pompei. Scienza e società*, ibid., pp. 19-27.

S. Adamo Muscettola, "Problemi di tutela a Pompei: il fallimento del progetto di esproprio murattiano," in *Pompei. Scienza e società*, ibid., pp. 29-49.

F. Delpino, "Vittorio Spinazzola. Tra Napoli e Pompei, fra scandali e scavi," in *Pompei. Scienza e società*, ibid., pp. 51-61.

F. Seiler, "Karl Lehmann-Hertleben e la 'nuova' ricerca su Pompei," in *Pompei. Scienza e società*, ibid., pp. 63-71.

F. Zevi, "Aspetti dell'archeologia pompeiana nel Novecento: gli scavi del Maturi a Pompei," in *Pompei. Scienza e società*, ibid., pp. 73-79.

The history of Pompeii

H. Hescebach, *Die städtebauliche Entwicklung des antiken Pompeji*, Heidelberg 1970.

P. Castrén, *Ordo Populusque Pompeianus. Polity and Society in Roman Pompeii*, Rome 1975.

F. Zevi, *Urbanistica di Pompei*, in *La regione sotterrata dal Vesuvio. Studi e prospettive. Atti Convegno Internazionale* (Naples 1979), Naples 1982, pp. 353-365.

S. De Caro, "Nuove indagini sulle fortificazioni di Pompei," in *Annali dell'Istituto Universitario Orientale. Archeologia e Storia Antica*, 7, 1985, pp. 75-114.

C. Chiaromonte Trere, *Nuovi contributi sulle fortificazioni pompeiane*, Milan 1986.

S. De Caro, "Saggi nell'area del tempio di Apollo a Pompei," in *Annali dell'Istituto Universitario Orientale. Archeologia e Storia Antica*, suppl. 3, 1986.

A. d'Ambrosio, S. De Caro, "Un contributo all'urbanistica e all'architettura di Pompei in età ellenistica. I saggi nella casa VII, 4, 62," in *Annali dell'Istituto Universitario Orientale. Archeologia e Storia Antica*, 11, 1989, pp. 173-215.

M. Bonghi Jovino, *L' insula 5 della Regio VI dalle origini al 79 d.*

C., Rome 1990.

F. Carocci, E. De Albentiis, M. Gargiulo, F. Pesando, *Le insulae 3 e 4 della regio VI di Pompei*, Rome 1990.

F. Zevi (ed.), *Pompei I-II*, Naples 1991-1992.

P. Zanker, *Pompei: società, immagini urbane e forme di abitare*, Turin 1993.

S. De Caro, "Lo sviluppo urbanistico di Pompei," in *Atti e Memorie della Società Magna Grecia Series*, 1, 1992, pp. 67-90.

R. Laurence, *Roman Pompeii. Space and Society*, London 1994.

A. Wallace-Hadrill, *Houses and Society in Pompeii and Herculaneum*, London 1994.

H. Heschebach, L. Heschebach, *Pompeji vom 7. Jahrhundert v. Chr. Bis 79 n. Chr.*, Cologne-Weimar 1995.

L. Jacobelli, T. Froehlich (eds.), "Archäologie und Seismologie. La regione vesuviana dal 62 al 79 d. C. Problemi archeologici e sismologici" in *Atti Colloquio Boscoreale 1993*, Munich 1995.

A. Oettel, *Fundkontexte römischer Vesuvvillen im Gebiet um Pompeji. Die Grabungen von 1894 bis 1908*, Mainz 1996.

A. Wallace-Hadrill, R. Laurence (eds.), "Domestic Space in the Roman World: Pompeii and Beyond," *JRA*, suppl. 22, 1997.

F. Pesando, *Domus: edilizia privata e società pompeiana fra III e I secolo a. C.*, Rome 1997.

A. Carandini, P. Carafa, M. T. D'Alessio, "Nuovi progetti, nuove domande, nuovi metodi" in *Pompei. Scienza e società, Atti…, op. cit.*, pp. 127-129.

A. Wallace-Hadrill, "Towards a history of pre-Roman Pompeii: excavations beneath the house of Amarathus (I). 11-12)," in *Papers of the British School at Rome*, 67, 1999, pp. 37-144.

J. De Waele, *Il tempio dorico del Foro Triangolare di Pompei*, Rome 2001.

Religious life

Various authors, *Alla ricerca di Iside. Analisi, studi e restauri dell'Iseo pompeiano nel Museo di Naples*, Rome 1992.

J. A. K. E. De Waele (ed.), *Il tempio dorico del Foro Triangolare di Pompei*, Rome 2001.

S. Adamo Muscettola, *Osservazioni sulla composizione dei larari con statuette in bronzo di Pompei ed Ercolano*, in *Toreutik und figurliche Bronzen römischer Zeit*, Convention Proceedings (Berlin, May 13-17, 1980), Berlin 1984, pp. 9-32.

G. K. Boyce, "Corpus of the Lararia of Pompeii," in *MAAR* 14, 1937.

S. De Caro, *Saggi nell'area del tempio di Apollo a Pompei. Scavi stratigrafici di A. Maiuri nel 1931-32 e 1942-43*, Naples 1986.

S. De Caro, "La lucerna d'oro di Pompei: un dono di Nerone a Venere Pompeiana," in *I culti della Campania antica, Atti del convegno internazionale di studi in ricordo di Nazarena Valenza Mele*, (Naples, May 15-17, 1995), Rome 1998, pp. 239-244.

Th. Frölich, *Lararien und Fassadenbilder in dem Vesuvstädten. Untersuchungen zur "volkstümlichen" pompejanischen Malerei*, Mainz am Rheim 1991.

M. Torelli, *Il culto imperiale a Pompei*, in *I culti della Campania antica, Atti del convegno internazionale di studi in ricordo…, op. cit.*, Rome 1998, pp. 245-270.

V. Tran Tam Tinh, *Essai sur le culte d'Isis à Pompeii*, Paris 1964.

Public life

W.O. Moeller, "The riot of A.D. 59 at Pompeii," in *Historia*,19, 1970, pp. 84-95.

W. Beare, *The Roman Stage*, London 1950.

B. Gentili, *Lo spettacolo nel mondo antico*, Bari 1976.

P. Castrén, "L'amministrazione municipale," in F. Zevi (ed.), *Pompei 79*, Naples 1979, pp. 45-55.

J. L. Franklin, *Pompeii: The Electoral Programmata. Campaigns and Politics, A.D. 71-79*, Rome 1980.

G. Ville, *La gladiature en Occident des origines à la mort de Domitien*, Paris 1982.

W. Jongman, *The Economy and Society of Pompeii*, Amsterdam 1988.

H. Mouritsen, *Elections, Magistrates and Municipal Elite. Studies in Pompeian Epigraphy*, Rome 1988.

S. Adamo Muscettola, "La trasformazione della città tra Silla e Augusto," in F. Zevi (ed.), *Pompei I, cit.*, Naples 1991, pp. 77-114.

M. Lenoir (ed.), *Les Thermes romains*, Rome 1991.

E. Lo Cascio, "La società pompeiana dalla città sannitica all'età romana," in *Pompei I, op. cit.*, Naples 1991.

S. De Caro, "La città di età imperiale," in *Pompei II, op. cit.*, Naples 1992, pp. 11-38.

F. Yegül, *Baths and Bathing in Classical Antiquity*, Cambridge Ma. 1992.

F. Dupont, *Le théâtre latin*, Parism 1968.

R. Biundo, "I *rogatores* nei programmata elettorali pompeiani," in *Cahiers du Centre Gustave Glotz*, 7, 1996, pp. 179-188.

E. Lo Cascio, "Pompei dalla città sannitica alla colonia sillana: le vicende istituzionali," in M. Cèbeillac-Gervasoni (ed.), *Les élites municipales de l'Italie péninsulaire des Gracques à Néron*, Naples-Rome 1996, pp. 111-123.

N. Savarese (ed.), *Teatri romani: gli spettacoli nell'antica Roma*, Bologna 1996.

W. J. Slater (ed.), *Roman Theater and Society: E. T. Salmon Papers*, Ann Arbor 1996.

Ö. Wikander, "Senators and Equites VI. Caius Sergius Orata and the invention of the hypocaust," in *Opuscula Romana*, 20, 1996, pp. 177-82.

J. Delaine (ed.), "Roman Baths and Bathing," Portsmouth (Rhode Island), 1999 (*JRA* Suppl., Ser. 37).

G.G. Fagan, *Bathing in Public in the Roman World*, Ann Arbor 1999.

K. Hopkins, *A World full of Gods. Pagans, Jews and Christians in the Roman Empire*, London 1999.

R. Biundo, "Struttura della classe dirigente a Pompei e mobilità sociale. I rapporti con il centro," in M. Cébeillac-Gervasoni (ed.), *Les élites municipales de l'Italie péninsulaire de la mort de César a la mort de Domitien. Classes sociales dirigeantes e pouvoir central*, Rome 2000, pp. 33-69.

Commercial life

E. Magaldi, "Il commercio ambulante a Pompei, in *AttiAcPontan* 60, 1930, pp. 61-88.

L. Breglia, "Circolazione monetale ed aspetti di vita economica a Pompei," in *Pompeiana*, Naples 1950, pp. 41-59.

E. Lepore, "Orientamenti per la storia sociale di Pompei," in *Pompeiana*, Naples 1950, pp. 144-166.

D. Mustilli, "Botteghe di scultori, marmorari, bronzieri e caelatores in Pompei," in *Pompeiana*, Naples 1950, pp. 206-229.

S. Bolin, *State and currency in the Roman Empire to 300 A.D.*, Stockholm 1958.

A. Tchernia, "Amphores et marques d'amphores de Betique à Pompéi et à Stabies," in *MEFRA LXXIV*, 1964, pp. 419-449.

W. Moeller, "The Building of Eumachia: a reconsideration," in *AJA*, 76, 1972, pp. 323-327.

J. Andreau, "Remarques sur la societé pompeiénne (à propos des tablettes de L.Caecilius Iucundus)," in *DdA*, 7,1973, p.213 ff.

W. Moeller, "Infectores and offectores at Pompeii," in *Latomus*, 32, 1973, p. 368 ff.

N. Nabers, "The architectural variations of the Macellum," in *OpRom*, 9, 1973, pp. 173-176.

J. Andreau, *Les affaires de Monsieur Jucundus*, Rome 1974.

D. J. Mayeske, *Bakeries, Bakers and Bread at Pompeii*, Ann Arbor 1974.

E. Pozzi Paolini, "Circolazione monetale a Pompei," in *Neue Forschungen in Pompeii*, Recklinghausen 1975, pp. 299-307.

W. Moeller, *The Wool Trade of ancient Pompeii*, Leiden 1976.

E. Lo Cascio, "La riforma monetaria di Nerone: l'evidenza dei ripostigli," in *MEFRA*, 92, 1980, p. 452 ff.

J. Kolendo, "Les occupations agricoles des habitants de Pompéi," in *Acta Pompeiana*, Wroclaw 1984, p. 53 ff.

C. Scotti, "Anfore," in M. Borghi Jovino(ed.), *Ricerche a Pompei. L'insula 5 della Regio VI dalle origini al 79 d.C.*, Rome 1984, pp. 270-317.

J. Kolendo, "Le attività agricole degli abitanti di Pompei e gli attrezzi agricoli ritrovati all'interno della città," in *Opus. Rivista internazionale per la storia economica e sociale dell'antichità*, 4, 1985, pp. 111-124.

R. Angelone, *L'officina coactilaria di M. Vecilio Verecundo a Pompei*, Naples 1986.

V. Gassner, *Die Kaufläden in Pompeji*, Vienna 1986.

G. F. La Torre, "La struttura insediativa di Pompei: l'avvio di una indagine computerizzata per la conoscenza della realtà economica e sociale di una città campana della prima età imperiale," in *Pompei. L'informatica al servizio di una città antica*, Rome 1988, pp. 73-102.

D. J. Mayeske, "A Pompeian bakery on the via dell'Abbondanza," in *Studia Pompeiana et Classica in Honor of Wilhelmina F. Jashemski*, I, La Rochelle-New York 1988, pp. 149-158.

A. Varone, "La struttura insediativa di Pompei…," *op. cit.*, Rome 1988, pp. 25-48.

W. Jongman, *The economy and society of Pompeii*, Amsterdam 1991.

A. Ciarallo, "La regione vesuviana al 79 d.C.," in *Il territorio vesuviano nel 79 d.C. Dallo scavo archeologico alla ricostruzione ambientale*, Pompeii 1992, pp. 9-13.

A. Varone, "Paesaggio e colture agrarie di Pompei nei documenti storici, archeologici ed epigrafici," in *Il territorio vesuviano nel 79 d.C. Dallo scavo archeologico alla ricostruzione ambientale*, Pompeii 1992, pp. 14-21.

R. Duncan Jones, *Money and Government in the Roman Empire*, Cambridge, 1994, pp. 196–197.

R. Etienne, F. Mayet, "Le garum a Pompéi. Production et commerce," in *REA*, 100, 1998, pp. 199-215.

M. Mastroroberto, "Pompei e la riva destra del Sarno," in A. De Simone and S. C. Nappo(eds.), *Mitis Sarni Opes*, Naples 2000, pp. 25-30.

M. Taliercio Mensitieri, "Ritrovamenti monetali a Pompei: problemi di metodo e di ricerca," in *Ritrovamenti monetali: problemi e metodi*, Padua 2000.

PRIVATE LIFE

G. Fiorelli, *Pompeianarum Antiquitatum Historia*, I, Naples 1860; II, Naples 1862; III, Naples 1864.

A. Mau, "Scavi di Pompei. Sepolcri della via Nucerina," in *RM*, 3, 1888, pp. 120 – 149.

H. Diehl, *Pompejanische Wandinschriften und Verwandtes*, Berlin 1930.

A. Maiuri, *La Villa dei Misteri*, Rome 1931.

L. Borrelli, *Le tombe di Pompei a schola semicircolare*, Naples 1937.

S. Augusti, "Sulla tecnica della pittura pompeiana," in *BdA*, 36, 1950, pp. 189-90.

W. Lepik-Kopaczynska, "Colores floridi et austeri," in *Atti del VII Convegno Internazionale di Archeologia Classica*, I, Rome 1961, pp. 135-44.

K. Schefold, "Die Wahl der Farbe in der antiken Kunst," in *Palette*, 13, 1963, pp. 3-19.

W. Krenkel, *Pompejanische Inschriften*, Leipzig 1963.

S. Augusti, *I colori pompeiani*, Rome 1967.

P. Mora, "Proposta sulla tecnica della pittura murale romana," in *BistCentRestauro*, 1967, pp. 63-84.

A. Mallwitz, *Olympia und seine Bauten*, Munich 1972.

P. Zanker, "Grabreliefs römischer Freigelassener," in *JdI*, 90, 1975, pp. 267-315.

S. De Caro, "Scavi nell'area fuori porta Nola a Pompei," in *Cronache Pompeiane*, V, 1979, pp. 61-79.

A. Pellegrino, "Considerazioni sulle tombe a schola di Pompei," in *Pompei 79*, supplement to *Antiqua*, 15, Oct-Dec 1979, p. 110 ff.

H. Solin, "Le iscrizioni parietali," in F. Zevi (ed.), *Pompei 79*, op. cit., Naples 1979, pp. 278-288.

A. Barbet, C. Allag, "Techniques de preparation des parois dans la peinture murale romaine," in *MEFRA*, 84, 1972, pp. 935-1069.

R. Bianchi Bandinelli, *La pittura antica*, Rome 1980.

A. Baldi, *Iscrizioni pompeiane*, Cava de' Tirreni 1982.

M. Frizot, "L'analyse des pigments des peintures murales antiques. Etata de la question et question et bibliographie," in *Revue d'Archéométrie*, 6, 1982, pp. 47-59.

A. Varone, "Note di archeologia sarnese. I cippi funerari a stilizzazione antropomorfa," in *Apollo*, VI, 1985, pp. 195-260.

A. d'Ambrosio, S. De Caro, "La necropoli di Porta Nocera. Campagna di scavo 1983," in *Römische Gräberstrassen* (Kolloquium Monaco 1985), Munich 1987, pp. 199-228.

M. Ranieri Panetta, "Fragranze antiche - Il trucco e le acconciature," in *Afrodite allo specchio*, Taranto 1987.

P. Virgili, *Vita e costumi dei Romani antichi: acconciature e maquillage*, Rome 1989.

Various authors, *La pittura di Pompei*, Milan 1991.

L. Canali, G. Cavallo, *Graffiti latini. Scrivere sui muri a Roma antica*, Milan 1991.

J. R. Clarke, *The houses of Roman Italy 100 B.C. – A.D. 250. Ritual, space and decoration*, Berkeley 1991.

R. Ling, *Roman Painting*, Cambridge 1991.

P. Cinti, "L'intervento di restauro," in *Alla ricerca di Iside*, op. cit., Rome 1992, pp. 115-122.

A. Dosi, F. Schnell, *Vita e costumi dei Romani antichi: le abitudini alimentari dei Romani*, Rome 1992.

Ph. Moreau, *Sur les murs de Pompéi*, Paris 1993.

Wallace-Hadrill, *House and society in Pompeii and Herculaneum*, Princeton 1994.

L. Jacobelli, *Le pitture erotiche delle Terme Suburbane di Pompei*, Rome 1995.

D. Scagliarini Corlaita, "Pittori e botteghe, status quaestionis," in

MededRome, 54, 1995, pp. 291-298.

A. Varone, "L'organizzazione del lavoro in una bottegai decoratori: le evidenze dal recente scavo pompeiano lungo via dell'Abbondanza," in *MededRome*, 54, 1995, pp. 12-136.

A. d'Ambrosio, E. De Carolis, *I monili dall'area vesuviana*, Rome 1997.

E. Cantarella, *Pompei. I volti dell'amore*, Milan 1998.

A. Lagi, in *Pompei oltre la vita. Nuove testimonianze dalle necropoli*, Naples 1998, pp. 61-83.

G. Sauron, *La grande fresque de las Villa des Mysteres a Pompei*, Paris 1998.

M. Ranieri Panetta, *Nerone. Il principe rosso*, Milan 1999.

F. Senatore, "Necropoli e società nell'antica Pompei: considerazioni su un sepolcro di poveri," in *Pompei, il Vesuvio e la Penisola Sorrentina*, Rome 1999, pp. 91-121.

A. Ciarallo, *Verde Pompeiano*, Rome 2000.

S. De Caro (ed.), *Il gabinetto segreto*, Naples 2000.

E. De Carolis, *Dei ed eroi nella pittura pompeiana*, Rome 2000.

E. De Carolis, *Ercolano e Pompei, arredi e oggetti di antiche dimore vesuviane*, Portici 2000.

P. G. Guzzo, V. Scarano Ussani, *Veneris Figurae*, Naples 2000.

Maiuri, *La casa pompeiana* (A. M. Ragozzino, ed.), Naples 2000.

Varone, *L'erotismo a Pompei*, Rome 2000.

D'Ambrosio, *La bellezza femminile a Pompei*, Rome 2001.

A. Ciarallo, "Colture e habitat del territorio vesuviano nel 79 d.C.," in *RivStPomp*, 12-13, 2001-2002.

A. Ciarallo, "Testimonianze di domesticazione di alcune specie vegetali in area vesuviana" in *Atti dei Convegni di Studio sulla Magna Grecia*, XLII, Taranto 2002.

G. Castagnetti, J. Renn (eds.), *Studies on nature, technology and science at the time of Pompeii*, Rome 2002.

L. García y García, L. Jacobelli (eds.), *Museo Segreto*, Pompeii 2002.

A. Varone, *Erotica Pompeiana. Love Inscriptions on the Walls of Pompeii*, Rome 2002.

M.G. Pancani, M. Seracini, S. Vannucci, "Materiali, tecniche e stati di conservazione," in *Alla ricerca di Iside…*, op. cit., Rome 1992, pp. 123-132.

A. Ciarallo, *Il giardino pompeiano: le piante, l'orto, i segreti della cucina*, Naples 2003.

THE ERUPTION

H. Sigurdsson et al., "The Eruption of Vesuvius in A.D. 79," in *National Geographic Research*, I, 1985, pp. 332-387.

M. Gigante, *Le lettere di Plinio il Giovane sull'eruzione vesuviana dell'anno 79*, Naples 1989.

Ibid, *Il fungo sul Vesuvio secondo Plinio il Giovane*, Rome 1989.

E. Renna, *Vesuvius mons*, Naples 1992.

G. Guadagno, "Il viaggio di Plinio il Vecchio verso la morte," in *RivStPomp*, VI, 1993-4, pp. 63-76.

A. Varone, "Più terremoti a Pompei? I nuovi dati degli scavi di via dell'Abbondanza," in *Archäologie und Seismologie*, Munich 1995, pp. 29-35.

A. Varone, A. Marturano, "L'eruzione vesuviana del 24 agosto del 79 d.C. attraverso le lettere di Plinio il Giovane e le nuove evidenze archeologiche," in *RivStPomp*, VIII, 1997, pp. 57-72.

A. Ciarallo, E. De Carolis, "La data dell'eruzione," in *RivStPomp*, IX 1998, pp. 59-69.

E. De Carolis, G. Patricelli, A. Ciarallo, "Rinvenimenti di corpi umani nell'area urbana di Pompei," in *RivStPomp*, IX, 1998, pp. 75-123.

C. Dal Maso, A. Marturano, A. Varone, "Pompei,il racconto dell'eruzione," in *Le Scienze*, July 1999, pp. 58-65.

OPLONTIS

The discovery and history of the excavations

R. Liberatore, "Delle nuove ed antiche terme in Torre Annunciata," in *Annali Civili del Regno di Napoli*, XII, 1834 (republished - M. Elefante, ed.), Torre Annunziata 1998, pp. 95-109.

M. Ruggiero, *Storia degli scavi di antichità nelle province di Terraferma dell'antico Regno di Napoli dal 1743 al 1876*, Naples 1888, p. 100 ff.

A. Maiuri, "Note di topografia pompeiana," in *Rendiconti dell'Accademia di Archeologia, Lettere e Belle Arti di Napoli*, 34, 1959, pp. 81-88.

G. Alessio, "Oplontis," in *Studi Etruschi*, 33, 1965.

G. Maggi, "Oplonti, quartiere suburbano di Pompei?," in *Antiqua*, II, 5 Rome 1977.

C. Knight, "William Robinson ufficiale dei marines britannici "scopritore" di Oplontis," in *Cronache Pompeiane*, V, 1979, pp. 156-173.

C. Malandrino, *Oplontis*, Naples 1980.

M. Prosperi, A. Irlando, *Le prospettive di valorizzazione degli Scavi di Oplonti alla luce delle recenti scoperte*, Torre Annunziata 1984.

M. Pagano, "Planimetrie borboniche della villa A e di quella di C. Siculius," in *RivStPomp*, V, 1991-1992, pp. 219-221.

Villa A or Poppaea's Villa

A. de Franciscis, in *Fasti Archeologici*, 18-19, 1963-64, n. 7420.

A. de Franciscis, "La villa romana di Oplontis," in *La Parola del Passato*, 153, 1973, p. 454 ff.

S. De Caro, "Le lucerne dell'officina LVC," in *Rendiconti dell'Accademia di Archeologia, Lettere e Belle Arti di Napoli*, XLIX 1974, pp. 107-134, Tables I-XXIV.

A. de Franciscis, "La villa romana di Oplontis," in *Neue Forschungen in Pompeji*, Recklinghausen 1975, p. 9 ff.

S. De Caro, "Le sculture della villa di Poppea ad Oplontis," in *Cronache Pompeiane*, II, 1976, pp. 184-225.

A. de Franciscis, "Beryllos e la villa "di Poppea" ad Oplontis," in *Studies in Classical Art and Archaeology. A Tribute to P. H. von Blanckenhagen*, Locust Valley (NY), 1979, pp. 231-233.

W.J. Jashemski, *The gardens of Pompeii, Herculaneum and the villas destroyed by Vesuvius*, New York 1979, pp. 289-314; Volume II, pp. 293-301.

P. Zanker, "Die Villa als Vorbild des späten pompejanischen Wohngeschmacks," in *Jahrbuch des Deutsches Archäologisches Institut*, 94, 1979, p. 460 ff.

J.H. D'Arms, "Ville rustiche e ville di 'otium'," in F. Zevi (ed.), op. cit., p. 65 ff.

A de Franciscis, "La dama di Oplonti," in *Eikones, Festschrift für H. Jucker, Antike Kunst*, suppl. 12, Berne 1980, pp. 111-117.

A. Allroggen-Bedel, "Die Wanddekorationen der Villen am Golf von Neapel," in *La regione sotterata dal Vesuvio. Studi e prospettive, Atti del Convegno internazionale Napoli-Pompei-Ercolano-Stabia* (November 11-15, 1979), Naples 1982, p. 519 ff.

B. Andreae, "I pavoni della villa di Oplontis," in ibid, pp. 531-536.

A. de Franciscis, *Oplontis*, in ibid., pp. 74-83.

A. Lagi, S. De Caro, "Torre Annunziata, Oplontis. Villa A o Villa dei Poppaei," in *Pompeii, Herculaneum, Stabiae*, 1, 1983, pp. 364-375.

Cinque, F. Russo, "La linea di costa del 79 d.C. fra Oplonti e Stabiae nel quadro dell'evoluzione olocenica della piana del Sarno (Campania)," in *Bollettino Società Geologia Italiana*, 105, 1986, p. 111 ff.

W. Johannowski et al. *Le ville romane dell'età imperiale*, Naples 1986, pp. 60-69.

J.R. Clarke, "The early third style at Oplontis," in *RM*, 94, 1987, pp. 267-294.

S. De Caro, *The Sculptures of the villa of Poppaea at Oplontis: A Preliminary Report*, in

E.B. MacDougall (ed.), *Ancient Roman Gardens, II*. Dumbarton Oaks Colloquium on the History of Landscape Architecture, Dumbarton Oaks Research Library and Collection, Washington 1987, pp. 79-133.

W.J. Jashemski, "Recently excavated Gardens and Cultivated Land of the Villas of Boscoreale and Oplontis," in *Ancient Roman Gardens*, Dumbarton Oaks, op. cit., pp. 31-75.

H. Mielsch, *Die römische Villa. Architektur und Lebensform*, Munich 1987, pp. 50-51, 197-198.

A. Carandini, "La villa romana e la produzione schiavistica," in A. Momigliano and A. Schiavone (eds.), *Storia di Roma*, IV, Turin 1989, p. 187.

S. De Caro, "Un graffito da

Oplontis ed altre testimonianze del culto della Magna Mater nella villa romana di Oplontis," in *Studia Pompeiana et Classica in honor...*, op. cit., pp. 89-96.

S. De Caro, "Schede di catalogo di pitture della villa A," in *Catalogue raisonné of the Pompeian Painting*, I-II, Tokyo 1990.

P. G.P. Meyboom, E. M. Moorman, "Appunti sul padiglione della Domus Aurea neroniana sul colle Oppio," in *Bollettino d'Archeologia*, 16-18, 1992, pp. 142-144.

M. S. Pisapia, "I pavimenti di II stile della villa A di Oplontis," in *Atti del IV Colloquio dell'Associazione italiana per lo studio e la conservazione del Mosaico*, Ravenna 1997, pp. 555-564.

M. S. Pisapia, "I pavimenti di III e IV stile della villa A di Oplontis," in *Atti del V Colloquio dell'Associazione italiana per lo studio e la conservazione del Mosaico*, Rome 1997.

Villa B and other villas

M. Ricciardi, G. G. Aprile, "Preliminary data on the floristic components of some carbonized plant remains found in the archaeological area of Oplontis near Naples," in *Annali della Facoltà di Scienze Agrarie dell'Università di Napoli*, s. IV, vol. XII.2, 1978, pp. 204-212.

C. Malandrino, op. cit., pp. 83-87.

A. Lagi, S. De Caro, "Notiziario. Villa B di Oplontis," in *Pompeii, Herculaneum, Stabiae*, 1, 1983, pp. 369-375.

A. d'Ambrosio, *Gli ori di Oplontis. Gioielli romani dal suburbio pompeiano*, Naples 1987.

E. De Carolis, "Due lucerne di bronzo provenienti da Oplontis," in *RivStPomp*, I 1987, pp. 81-84.

M. Elefante, "Testimonianze epigrafiche relative alla gens Crassia," in *RivStPomp*, II 1988, pp. 99-102.

L. Fergola, "Un capitello ionico-italico da Torre Annunziata," in *RivStPomp*, II 1988, pp. 49-56.

M. Ricciardi, G.G. Aprile, "Identification of some carbonized plant remains from the archaeological area of Oplontis," in *Studia Pompeiana et Classica in honor...*, op. cit., pp. 317-330.

INDEX

PHOTO CREDITS

All photographs are by Araldo De Luca/Archivio White Star except the following:

page 6 Araldo De Luca

page 22 Ecole Nationale des Beaux Arts

pages 23 and 29 Archivio White Star

pages 24-25 Archivio Scala

page 25 Fototeca Storica Nazionale Ando Gilardi

pages 28-29 Archivio White Star

pages 30 and 31 Giovanni Dagli Orti

pages 32-33 Ecole Nationale des Beaux Arts

pages 34-35 Ecole Nationale des Beaux Arts

page 36 Roger Viollet/Archivio Alinari

pages 36-37 Mary Evans Picture Library

page 38 Roger Viollet/Archivio Alinari

page 39 top Mary Evans Picture Library

page 39 bottom Roger Viollet/Archivio Alinari

pages 40-41 Archivio White Star

pages 46-47 AKG Images

pages 48-49 Angelo Colombo/Archivio White Star and Elisabetta Ferrero/Archivio White Star

pages 50-51 Antonio Attini/Archivio White Star

pages 58-59 Antonio Attini/Archivio White Star

page 61 Erich Lessing/Contrasto

page 62 Giulio Veggi/Archivio White Star

pages 62-63 Antonio Attini/Archivio White Star

pages 64-65 Antonio Attini/Archivio White Star

page 65 Anne Conway/Archivio White Star

page 74 Antonio Attini/Archivio White Star

page 81 Antonio Attini/Archivio White Star

page 88 Antonio Attini/Archivio White Star

pages 88-89 Antonio Attini/Archivio White Star

page 94 Antonio Attini/Archivio White Star

pages 94-95 Antonio Attini/Archivio White Star

page 98 Antonio Attini/Archivio White Star

page 100 Antonio Attini/Archivio White Star

page 104 Archivio White Star

page 105 Archivio White Star

pages 112 Giulio Veggi/Archivio White Star

page 123 Araldo De Luca

page 128 The Bridgeman Art Library/Archivio Alinari

page 142 top and bottom Giulio Veggi/Archivio White Star

pages 142-143 Antonio Attini/Archivio White Star

page 153 Giulio Veggi/Archivio White Star

page 154 top Erich Lessing/Contrasto

page 155 Erich Lessing/Contrasto

page 157 Giulio Veggi/Archivio White Star

page 161 Antonio Attini/Archivio White Star

pages 162-163 Giulio Veggi/Archivio White Star

page 177 Erich Lessing/Contrasto

pages 218-219 The Bridgeman Art Library/Archivio Alinari

page 229 Vanni Archives/Corbis/Contrasto

page 232 Erich Lessing/Contrasto

page 234 Giulio Veggi/Archivio White Star

page 235 Giulio Veggi/Archivio White Star

page 237 Giulio Veggi/Archivio White Star

pages 248-249 Antonio Attini/Archivio White Star

page 264 Antonio Attini/Archivio White Star

page 313 Antonio Attini/Archivio White Star

pages 314-315 Antonio Attini/Archivio White Star

pages 360-361 Erich Lessing/Contrasto

page 375 Osterreichische Nationalbibliothek, Vienna

pages 376 and 377 Archaeological Superintendency of Pompeii, with the authorization of the Ministry of Culture

pages 378 and 379 Archivio Scala

page 382 Angelo Colombo/Archivio White Star

pages 382-383 Antonio Attini/Archivio White Star

page 388 and 389 Diego Motto, Milano

page 390 top and bottom Mimmo Jodice/Corbis/Contrasto

pages 394-395 Antonio Attini/Archivio White Star

page 398 Diego Motto, Milano

page 402 AKG Images

page 407 The State Russian Museum/Corbis/Contrasto

ACKNOWLEDGMENTS

THE PUBLISHER IS ESPECIALLY GRATEFUL TO

THE ARCHAEOLOGICAL SUPERINTENDENCE OF POMPEII; THE ARCHAEOLOGICAL SUPERINTENDENCE OF THE PROVINCES OF NAPLES AND CASERTA; DR. MARIAROSA BORRIELLO, DIRECTOR OF THE NATIONAL ARCHAEOLOGICAL MUSEUM OF NAPLES; VINCENZA CHIANESE; ANNA D'AMORE; DR. LORENZO FERGOLA, ADMINISTRATIVE DIRECTOR OF THE EXCAVATIONS AT OPLONTIS; PROF. GIOVANNI LOMBARDI, ADMINISTRATIVE DIRECTOR OF THE ARCHAEOLOGICAL SUPERINTENDENCE OF POMPEII; DR. ALESSANDRA MORELLI; VINCENZO LA MURA, HEAD OF SECURITY, AND HIS STAFF.

THE PUBLISHER WOULD ALSO LIKE TO THANK ARALDO DE LUCA'S PHOTO ASSISTANTS, ALESSANDRO COCCONI, FILIPPO TAGLIATI AND GUIDO PARADISI.

416

With five other mosaics, these four mosaic panels in the Fourth Style decorated the floor of the enormous oecus known as the Hall of the Elephants, located in the masters' quarters of the House of the Lararium of Achilles.

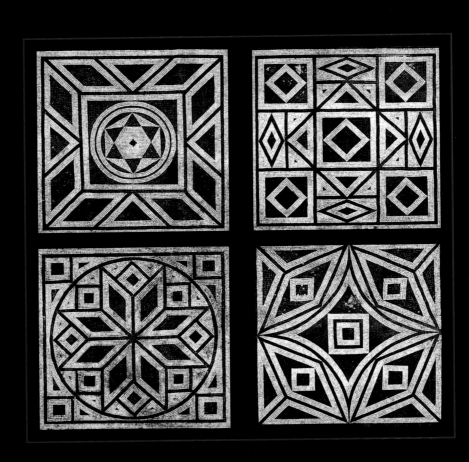